Praise for Ann Packer's

THE DIVE

FROM

CLAUSEN'S PIER

One of the Best Books of the Year
Entertainment Weekly
Newsday
San Francisco Chronicle
San Jose Mercury News

~

*Winner of the 2002 Great Lakes Book Award
and the 2003 Kate Chopin Award*

"Beguiling. . . . An unsettling page-turner. . . . Packer . . . can seemingly get anyone—a lover, a new roommate, a best friend's mother, possibly even the dead—to open their mouths and say things that instantly define them. . . . *The Dive from Clausen's Pier* gains much of its energy from Packer's instinctive sense of the way people talk under the pressure of calamity, love, or ruptured friendship—and especially under the pressure of all three. . . . Packer's quick gift for capturing a character's voice infuses the novel with a generous cast of memorable friends. . . . A humane novel." —*The New York Times Book Review*

"Engrossing. . . . Packer [has] a naturalist's vigilance for detail, so that her characters seem observed rather than invented, and capable of mistakes that the author may never have intended. The result is genuine suspense." —*The New Yorker*

"[Ms. Packer] plays the slower rhythms of Madison against the Broadway boogie-woogie of Manhattan to great effect."

—The Economist

"A winning debut novel."

—Vogue

"Packer writes straightforward prose that carries a good deal of emotional weight. . . . Calls to mind . . . Sue Miller's *The Good Mother*. . . . Will appeal to fans of Jane Hamilton's *A Map of the World* or Jacquelyn Mitchard's *The Deep End of the Ocean*. . . . Full of sorrow and exceedingly real."

—The Boston Globe

"Ambitious. . . . Both a colorful chronicle of life in Wisconsin and New York City . . . and a serious, moving meditation on the nature of love and of loyalty."

—Glamour

"One of those small miracles that reinforce our faith in fiction. It does what the best novels so often do, making the largest things visible by its perfect rendering of life on the smaller scale. It is witty, tragic, and touching, and beguiling from its first page."

—Scott Turow

"Impressive. . . . Packer skillfully distills broad themes into small, personal moments. . . . A thoughtful and satisfying examination of duty and personal integrity."

—Time Out New York

"Remarkably assured, utterly winning. . . . Packer's characters scramble up from these pages as terrifically physical beings, so well does she describe them." —*The Miami Herald*

"Absorbing. . . . The suspense of the book's last pages is intense and moving." —*The Plain Dealer*

"Rich with characters and restrained in its language, Packer's novel is, first and foremost, a great story." —*Minneapolis Star Tribune*

"Ann Packer's first novel has all the weight of reality, tooled with a jeweler's precision. *The Dive from Clausen's Pier* is a poignant and painstakingly rendered account of a woman in flight from catastrophe, in search of herself." —Madison Smartt Bell

"Fresh, contemporary, and fast-paced. . . . A powerful and compelling read." —*The Baltimore Sun*

"Packer knows just where she wants to take us . . . [and] the journey is worth taking." —*Milwaukee Journal Sentinel*

"Multilayered. . . . Absolutely credible and quite surprising." —*The Seattle Times*

"A book I couldn't let go for days after finishing. . . . This book will make you think, so read it and pass it on to a friend." —*Winston-Salem Journal*

ANN PACKER

~

THE DIVE

FROM

CLAUSEN'S PIER

Ann Packer is a past recipient of a James Michener
award and a National Endowment for the Arts fel-
lowship. Her work has appeared in *The New Yorker,*
Ploughshares, and other magazines, as well as in
Prize Stories 1992: The O. Henry Awards. The author
of *Mendocino and Other Stories,* she lives in north-
ern California.

ALSO BY ANN PACKER

Mendocino and Other Stories

THE DIVE

FROM

CLAUSEN'S PIER

~

THE DIVE

FROM

CLAUSEN'S PIER

~

ANN PACKER

VINTAGE CONTEMPORARIES

VINTAGE BOOKS

A Division of Random House, Inc.

New York

FIRST VINTAGE CONTEMPORARIES EDITION, APRIL 2003

Copyright © 2002 by Ann Packer

All rights reserved under International and Pan-American Copyright
Conventions. Published in the United States by Vintage Books,
a division of Random House, Inc., New York, and simultaneously
in Canada by Random House of Canada Limited, Toronto. Originally
published in hardcover in the United States by Alfred A. Knopf,
a division of Random House, Inc., New York, in 2002.

Vintage is a registered trademark and Vintage Contemporaries and
colophon are trademarks of Random House, Inc.

The Library of Congress has cataloged the Knopf edition as follows:
Packer, Ann, 1959–
The dive from Clausen's pier : a novel / by Ann Packer.
p.   cm.
ISBN 0-375-41282-4 (cloth)
1. Young women—Fiction.   2. Accident victims—Fiction.
3. Wisconsin—Fiction.   I. Title.
PS3616.A33 D58 2002
813'.54—dc21   2001042522

Vintage ISBN: 0-375-72713-2

www.vintagebooks.com

Printed in the United States of America
10 9 8 7 6 5

To Jon

ACKNOWLEDGMENTS

For support during the writing of this book, I would like to thank the National Endowment for the Arts, and Literary Arts, Inc. I am grateful to Dr. Edward James for his lucid explanations of medical matters; for additional technical help, my thanks go to Kerstin Hilton, Dr. Mark Krasnow, Dr. Nancy Marks, Patty Schmidt, RN, and Dr. Patti Yanklowitz.

I am very grateful to my agent, Geri Thoma, and my editor, Jordan Pavlin, for being so kind and encouraging and insightful.

Many family members and friends read the manuscript at various stages, and I am indebted to them all. Special gratitude goes to the following, who carefully considered draft after draft: Hallie Aaron, Jane Aaron, Amy Bokser, Scott Davidson, Ruth Goldstone, Jon James, Veronica Kornberg, Laurie Mason, Tony Pierce, Heidi Wohlwend, and Diana Young. Thank you.

THE DIVE

FROM

CLAUSEN'S PIER

~

MIKE ALWAYS TEASED me about my memory, about how I could go back years and years to what people were wearing on a given occasion, right down to their jewelry or shoes. He'd laugh and ask what the weather had been, or who'd had a light beer and who a regular one, and I could almost always tell him. That was how I resurrected the past: people in their outfits, or who sat next to whom, and from there on to what we talked about, what we were like at a certain time.

Every Memorial Day we spent the afternoon at Clausen's Reservoir, about sixty miles north of Madison. It was only a mile or so across, but it was ringed by tall old maples, and it was far enough away so that going there seemed like an event. Mike came for me at a little after noon that year, the year everything changed, and once we'd loaded my stuff into his car and gotten onto the interstate, he accelerated to seventy-two, his opinion of the perfect speed if you factored in gas mileage, highway patrol risk, and safety. My mind was on the long untangling I felt was coming our way, and I stared out the window at dairy farm after dairy farm, their big, well-kept barns angled toward the highway. "Think it'll be hot?" he said after a while, and I didn't look at him, I just shrugged. A little later he said, "I wonder who'll get there first," and this time I just reached onto the floor for my purse and got out some Chap Stick. We were in a cold, dark place, we both knew it, but once I'd done my lips I handed him the tube, and he did his and with one hand twisted the balm back down before he handed it back. We'd been together for eight and a half years, we had all the little familiarities down. It was almost as if we were married, although we weren't, just engaged.

The parking lot was only half full, and we found a spot in the shade. From behind my seat I unloaded a grocery bag of chips and hamburger buns while he opened the hatch. He wore long madras shorts and a pine green polo shirt, and as I watched his movements, the quick, effortless way he lifted the beer-laden cooler, I thought about how that easy strength of his had thrilled me once, and how it didn't anymore.

"Hey!"

I looked up and there were Rooster and Stu, striding down the rocky hill that divided the parking lot from the beach.

"Hey to you," Mike called back. He cast me a watchful glance, and I put on a smile.

Coming into the shade, Rooster pulled off his sunglasses and wiped his arm across his forehead. The sun had gotten to him already: his freckled cheeks were pink, his nose a shade or two darker. "It's perfect," he said. "Warm, a little breeze, and we got the pier no problem."

"Great," Mike said. He looked over at me, then turned back and said it again: "Great."

"Anything else?" Stu asked.

Mike reached into the car and tossed him a Frisbee.

"Ah, the all-important Frisbee no one will throw."

"I figured maybe you'd surprise us this year."

Mike locked the car, and we headed for the hill. It was dusty already—it had been a dry spring—and patches of scruffy grass brushed against my ankles as I climbed. At the top I paused to look down: at Jamie, waving from the pier; at the sweep of dazzling blue behind her.

I started toward the beach. On the pier Bill and Christine sat side by side, apparently together again: their hips and thighs touching, Bill's hand resting loosely on Christine's knee. Following Mike across the sand, I wanted nothing more than to sit like that with him, until I remembered that was what I *didn't* want. This mood I was in: I had to remind myself of its rules sometimes.

Rooster had already started the fire, and soon Jamie and Christine and I were unwrapping the raw burgers and laying them out on a paper plate. Jamie was right beside me, and in a quiet voice she said, "What's up?"

I shrugged. "Nothing."

She looked at me carefully.

"Really, nothing."

After we ate, I took a second beer from the cooler and sat at the end of the pier. The can was icy, almost painful to hold, but I held it anyway, my feet just skimming the water, which I noticed was lower than usual. Wasn't it supposed to come up to my knees? I thought so, but I didn't think so very strongly, and I know I didn't say so.

Behind me Rooster's boom box played one of his compilation tapes, and I could hear everyone talking, the rise and fall of their voices, the little silences before someone thought of something else funny to say. Jamie said, "No, Long Island Iced Teas," and the next thing I knew Mike was standing over me, casting a shadow onto me and the water. He prodded me once with his big toe and announced, "I'm going swimming."

"Mikey!" Rooster hooted.

I could feel everyone looking at me: Rooster, Stu, Bill, Christine— even Jamie. Looking and thinking, *Come on, Carrie, give the guy a break.*

I turned and looked at his strong, hairy legs, then up at his face, which was dark against the bright sun. He'd stripped to his swimming trunks, and as he stood there waiting for me to say something, Rooster came over to stand beside him. "Getting a little spare tire there, buddy?" Rooster said, and he cuffed Mike lightly.

Mike grinned. "Makes two of us, huh? Maybe we should start a diet club, the Spare Tire Spartans. What do you say?"

They all laughed—the Spartans had been our high school mascot. That we were a year out of college and still making Spartans jokes seemed to me to be a symptom of whatever it was we all had, whatever disease it was that had us doing the exact same things we'd always done, and with the exact same people.

"I think I'll wait till after the holidays," Rooster said.

"The holidays are six months away."

"Exactly."

Now Mike looked at me. "So, what do you think?" he said. "Should I dive?"

"Why don't you just jump?" Later, I clung to that as evidence that I'd tried to stop him, but in fact I was just being contrary.

"Dive," Rooster said. "Definitely dive."

I glanced at Jamie, and she smiled at me. "Hey, girl," she said, and she scooted toward me with her hand extended low in front of her, palm side up. I reached over and held my palm on hers for a moment.

"Mayer," Stu said, "you lout."

Mike took off his baseball cap and held it out for me to take.

"What about your sunglasses?" I said.

He dropped the cap onto the pier. "They're coming," he said. "On a joy ride." He looked at Rooster and Stu and Bill with an endearing expression of amusement and challenge on his face, and for an intense moment then, watching him with his friends, I longed to feel again what I no longer felt: that he was just what I wanted. "You guys are wimps," he said. "I'll think of you when I hit that cool, refreshing water."

Everyone laughed again: it was Memorial Day, the water was freezing.

Then somewhere on the reservoir a motorboat started up, and we were still for a moment as we looked across the water to see if we could see it. I remember the sound so clearly, the sound of the boat and also the feel of the icy-cold beer can in my hand. I wish I'd done something to stop him then—jumped up and said I'd marry him that day, or burst into tears, or held on tight to his leg. Anything. But of course I didn't. I was already looking away, when from across the water there came the sound of the outboard revving higher. And then Mike dove.

PART ONE

~

INTENSIVE

CARE

1

~

WHEN SOMETHING TERRIBLE happens to someone else, people often use the word "unbearable." Living through a child's death, a spouse's, enduring some other kind of permanent loss—it's unbearable, it's too awful to be borne, and the person or people to whom it's happened take on a kind of horrible glow in your mind, because they are in fact bearing it, or trying to: doing the thing that it's impossible to do. The glow can be blinding at first—it can be all you see—and although it diminishes as years pass it never goes out entirely, so that late some night when you are wandering the back pathways of your mind you may stop at the sudden sight of someone up ahead, signaling even now with a faint but terrible light.

Mike's accident happened to Mike, not to me, but for a long time afterward I felt some of that glow, felt I was giving it off, so that even doing the most innocuous errand, filling my car with gas or buying toothpaste, I thought everyone around me must see I was in the middle of a crisis.

Yet I didn't cry. The first days at the hospital were full of crying—Mike's parents crying, his brother and sister, and Rooster, maybe Rooster most of all—but I was dry-eyed. My mother and Jamie told me it was because I was numb, and I guess that was part of it, numb and terrified: when I looked at him it was as if years had unwound, and I'd just met him, and I couldn't stand not knowing what was going to happen. But there was something else, too: everyone was treating me so carefully and solicitously that I felt breakable, and yet I wasn't broken. Mike was broken, and I wasn't broken. He was separate from me, and that was shocking.

He was in a coma. Thanks to the combination of drought and a newly banked-up shoreline, the water in Clausen's Reservoir had been three feet lower than usual. If he woke up, it would be to learn that he'd broken his neck.

But he didn't wake up. Days went by, and then it was a week, ten days, and he was still unconscious, lying in Intensive Care in a tiny room crowded with machines, more than I ever would have imagined. He was in traction, his shaven head held by tongs attached to weights, and because he had to be turned onto his stomach every few hours to avoid bedsores, his bed was a two-part contraption that allowed for this: a pair of giant ironing-board-shaped things that could sandwich him and flip him. Visiting hours were three p.m. to eight p.m., ten minutes per hour, two people at a time, but it seemed we'd no sooner get in to see him than the nurses would ask us to leave. It was as if, merely body now, he belonged to them.

Near the nursing station there was a small lounge, and that's where we mostly were, talking or not talking, looking at each other or not looking. There would be five of us, or ten, or twenty: a core group of family and close friends, plus Mike's co-workers stopping by after the bank had closed, the Mayers' neighbors checking in, my mother arriving with bags of sandwiches. There was a rack of ancient magazines by the door, and we offered them to each other now and then, just for something to do. I couldn't read, but whenever the single, warped issue of *Vogue* came my way I flipped through it, pausing each time at an article about a clothing designer in London. I'm not sure I ever noticed her name, but I can still remember the clothes: a fitted, moss green velvet jacket; a silver dress with long, belled sleeves; a wide, loose sweater in deep purple mohair. I was getting through the evenings by sewing, a pair of cotton shorts or a summer dress every two or three days, and those exotic images from London kept appearing in my mind as I bent over my sewing machine, reminding me at once of the hospital and the world.

The two-week mark came, and when I woke that morning I thought of something one of the doctors had said early on, that each week he was unconscious the prognosis got worse. ("Unresponsive" was the word they used, and whenever I heard it I thought of myself in the car on the way to Clausen's Reservoir, not answering his questions.) Two weeks was only one day more than thirteen days, but I felt we'd turned a corner that shouldn't have been turned, and I couldn't get myself out of bed.

I lay on my side. The bedsheets were gritty and soft with use; I hadn't changed them since the accident. I reached for my quilt, lying in a tangle down past my feet. I'd made it myself one summer during high school, a patchwork of four-inch squares in no particular order, though I'd limited myself to blues and purples and the overall effect was nice. I'd read somewhere that quiltmakers "signed" their work with a little deviation, so in one corner I'd used a square cut from an old shirt of Mike's, white with a black windowpane check. I found that square now and arranged the quilt so it was near my face.

He had to wake up. He had to. I couldn't stand to think of what a bitch I'd been at Clausen's Reservoir—what a bitch all spring. It was like a horrible equation: my bitchiness plus his fear of losing me equaled *Mike in a coma*. I knew as clearly as I knew anything that I'd driven him to dive, to impress me. I squeezed my eyes shut and tried to remember when everything between us had been fine. February? January? Christmas? Maybe not even Christmas: he'd given me plain pearl earrings that were very pretty and exactly what I would have wanted just a year earlier, but I found them stodgy and obvious, and I felt dead inside—not because of the earrings but because of my disappointment in them. "Do you like them?" he said uneasily. "I *love* them," I lied.

It was June now. I had the day off work, and at last I got up and made coffee, then started laying out the pattern for an off-white linen jacket I'd been planning to make, first ironing the crumpled tissue and then moving the pieces around on the length of fabric until I was satisfied. I pinned them and cut them out with my Fiskars, then went back and did the notches, snip by snip. I chalked the pattern marks

onto the fabric, and by late morning I was sitting at my Bernina winding a bobbin, entranced by the fast whir of it, by the knowledge that
for hours now I'd be at the machine, my foot on the pedal.

I'd been sewing for eleven years, since my first home ec class in
junior high, when I'd made an A-line skirt and fallen in love. It was
the inexorability of it that appealed to me, how a length of fabric
became a group of cut-out pieces that gradually took on the shape of
a garment. I loved everything about it, even the little snipped threads
to be gathered and thrown away, the smell of an overheated iron, the
scatter of pins at the end of the day. I loved how I got better and better, closer and closer with each thing I made to achieving just what I'd
hoped.

When the phone rang at eight-thirty that evening I'd taken a few
breaks for iced cranberry juice, but mostly I'd sat there sewing, and
the sound woke me from the work. Surprised by how dark it had gotten, I pushed away from the table and turned on a light, blinking
at the jacket parts that lay everywhere, the slips of pattern and the
pinked-off edges of seams. I was starving, my back and shoulders
knotted and aching.

It was Mrs. Mayer. She asked how I was, told me she'd heard it
might rain, and then cleared her throat and said she'd appreciate it if
I'd stop by the next day.

THE MORNING SUN slanted down the sidewalk, aiming my
shadow in the direction of Lake Mendota. My car was already hot
to the touch, and I unlocked it and rolled down the windows, then
strolled to the end of the block and stood looking across Gorham
Street at the water, still almost colorless under the early sky. Mike
loved Lake Mendota, the way the city hugged its curves. He liked to
pull people into debating the relative merits of it and Lake Monona,
Madison's other big lake: he'd reel off a list of ways that Mendota was
superior, as if it were a team he supported.

Mendota and Monona. "Sounds like bad names for twins," a girl
from New York had said to me once, and I'd never been able to forget
it. I laughed, but I was a little offended: she spoke so smugly, flipping
her brown hair over her shoulder and raising her chin. I hardly knew

her—she was in my freshman American history class at the U—but thinking about her five years later, I remembered this: that she'd owned a jacket I'd coveted, pearl-snapped and collarless like something made of cotton fleece, but fashioned from smooth black napa leather, soft as skin.

Across the street two guys sauntered by. They both wore sunglasses with tiny mirrored lenses—one guy's tinted blue, the other's green. "No fucking way," I heard one of them say.

I went back to my car. It had a baked vinyl smell, and the seat scorched my legs. I always took the same route to the Mayers', an easy six- to eight-minute drive up Gorham to University and then up the hill, but today I headed away from Gorham instead. I crossed the isthmus that divided the lakes, and when I got close to Lake Monona I drove up and down the streets parallel to it, braking occasionally to look at some of my favorite houses: Victorians painted colors you didn't see in other neighborhoods, fuchsia and teal and deep purple. At a little lakeside park I got out and walked down to the water, where a cloud of gnats swarmed over the grassy green edge. Both lakes could lift my spirits—silvery blue when the sun was low, or vast and frosty in winter—but today they seemed flat and ordinary.

Unable to put it off any longer, I returned to my car. At the hospital I'd felt Mrs. Mayer watching me and watching me, waiting for me to break down; when the familiar shape of Mike's house came into view a little later, she was watching again, standing at the living room window with the curtain held aside, as if she'd heard I was on my way but didn't believe it.

I got out of my car. The house was big and white, a perfectly symmetrical colonial with black-shuttered windows and an iron eagle on the black front door. I hadn't been over since the accident, but the yard was as tidy as ever, the lawn so well trimmed I couldn't help thinking of something Mike liked to say, that his father came outside every morning and greeted each blade of grass by name. I thought of Mr. Mayer mowing, the smell of grass everywhere while he tried not to wonder if Mike would survive, and my stomach tilted with panic.

Mrs. Mayer opened the door. "Hi," she said with a smile. "I'm glad you're here."

I tried to smile back. At the hospital it had been hard to look at her wrecked face, but this was almost worse: she was pale and drained, as if she'd finally run out of tears.

"Let's go into the kitchen, shall we, dear?"

I followed her through the large, old rooms: past couches where Mike and I had sat together, tables where I'd casually piled my schoolbooks. It was my house, too, in a way.

The air-conditioning was blowing hard, and when we got to the kitchen Mrs. Mayer said she'd make tea. I sat at the big oak table while she filled her kettle and got tea bags from a glass jar painted with hearts.

"Mr. Mayer can't get comfortable this summer," she said. "I try to keep the house cool, but every evening he comes in and complains it's stifling. It's colder than the hospital, don't you think?" She pulled her sweater close, a bouclé cardigan she was wearing over a flowered shirtwaist dress, its "self-belt" knotted in the front. It was the kind of ageless, styleless dress she always wore, the very kind of thing I'd first liked about her, that she was happy to look like a mom.

"It is chilly," I said.

The kettle whistled and she poured from it, then brought our cups to the table. "Let me get you your lemon." She crossed to the refrigerator and took one out, then cut it into wedges. She spread them on a flowered saucer and set them before me. "Would you like a bun? We've been given so much food I don't know what to do with it all."

"Actually, I'm OK."

She pulled out the chair opposite me and sat down. She ran her hand over her hair, and I noticed that her perm had grown out, and gray roots were visible along the part line. She blew on her tea and cleared her throat. "Are you going today?"

I picked up my cup. I thought about trying to explain about yesterday—about the two-week marker, about how our reaching that point had scared me—but I knew she was aware of it, too; and scared, too; and that she'd gone anyway. I blew on my tea and took a sip, the lemon in it tart and satisfying.

"Having visitors means a lot to him."

I met her glance and then looked away. Nothing meant anything to him, that was the problem, the tragedy—that and the fact that his spinal cord had suffered an injury that could leave him paralyzed for life, quadriplegic. Thinking that way, though, that my visiting would mean nothing, made me feel churlish, a dweller on the bad side.

"Carrie?"

She was staring at me, her still-young face lined with concern. *Of course I'll go,* I wanted to say. I wanted to take my thumbs and run them over her forehead and cheeks. When I spoke, though, I sounded distant, even to myself. I said, "I have to work, but I'll go afterward."

She nodded, then reached across the table and took hold of my left hand. She touched the tiny diamond on my ring finger. "Michael was so happy the day he bought this, it was like something he'd made at school, he was so proud. Julie made a remark, about how it wasn't that big or something, and his face just fell. He got that hangdog look on his face and he said to me, 'Mom, do you think Carrie'll like it?' " She let go of my hand. " 'Do you think Carrie'll like it?' He loves you very much, dear."

I looked away from her. "I know."

We drank our tea silently. After a while I told her I wanted to go up to his room, and I climbed the stairs and turned down the hall, going past framed photographs of all three Mayer kids, school pictures mixed in with casual shots, two or three of Mike in hockey gear, his helmet off so you could see his wide grin.

At his door I hesitated, then went in. There was a musty, unused smell, and I wondered, with the air-conditioning going so strong, if his windows had been opened at all since the accident. I crossed to the bed and sat down, running my fingers up and down the ribbed blue bedspread. On his bedside table there was a picture of me from high school graduation, and I picked it up and looked at it. It was a familiar picture, but the girl in it seemed only tenuously connected to who I was now. Her hair was up in a way I never wore my hair any-more, and she wore more eyeliner than I'd had on in ages, but mostly she looked sure of herself, sure she'd stay on Mike's bedside table for years and years and be happy about it.

Mike had never left home, and his room bore traces of all the dif-ferent stages of him I'd known: trophies next to textbooks next to the briefcase he'd begun carrying the year before, when he started working. He had a job in new accounts at a bank near the Capitol, and as I looked around I thought of how he'd been talking lately of finally moving out, saying that since he was making good money he should get an apartment, teach himself domestic life so he wouldn't sabotage our marriage. Three or four times he'd said it, and I'd never responded. It killed me to think of it now: Mike trolling for something—just *Good idea* or *No, better keep saving your money*— and how I gave him nothing. Not even a wedding date: I deflected that question, too. *Later,* I kept thinking. *Next year, the year after.* Or I tried not to think about it at all.

I set the picture back on the bedside table, on the precise spot where it always stood. Then I lifted Mike's pillow to my face and breathed in his smell, a mixture of Dial and Right Guard and a clothes-and-body smell that was simply him.

I WORKED AT the university library, where I'd had a work-study job while I was a student; when I graduated they offered me thirty-five hours a week, and so I stayed on. I could take or leave the job, but I liked being on campus: walking to the Union on breaks, heading up State Street to window-shop. My job was in the rare books room, where the only staff member close to my age was a graduate student named Viktor, from Poland. He was at the desk when I arrived, and I could tell right away he was in a good mood.

"Carrie, Carrie, come here." He motioned me over with a boister-ous wave of his arm. Although he was sitting and I was standing, he seemed to loom over me: he was without doubt the biggest person I'd ever known, six-six with broad, beefy shoulders and a thick slab of a torso. When I first told him about Mike's accident, he grabbed me and hugged me so hard I nearly lost my breath.

Today he said, "This morning I am telling Ania that we must be more social. In Slavic studies we have parties, but they are too Slavic. You can come for dinner when?"

I glanced around. Viktor's library voice conceded nothing to the place, and several people stared at us from the long tables where they sat working, apparently waiting to hear if I'd accept. Dinner at Vik-tor's. This was a first, and I wondered how much it had to do with

Mike's being in the hospital, and whether or not, given that Mike was in the hospital, I should go. I was about to make an excuse when a door at the back of the room opened, and the neat, prim head of our boss, Miss Grafton, poked out.

"Oops," I said quietly, but Viktor put on a big smile and waved genially at her, and after a moment her head withdrew and she closed the door.

"She loves me," he said matter-of-factly, his voice only a little lower now. "I am tall, strong, good-looking. She sees me and thinks of the agony of her dry, sexless life, but she is happy for a moment because I remind her of when it wasn't so."

"Viktor," I said.

"You don't think this is true?"

"It's just you're so modest."

He ran a hand over his bristly jaw. "I am shaving every two days now for my new look." He took my hand and made me feel his chin. "Yes, I think you like it."

I laughed. Mike loved my Viktor stories, and I thought of how funny he'd think this one was, then remembered I couldn't tell him. A feeling of something heavy moved through me, like sand falling through water. I looked away.

"Let's say a week from Saturday," he said. "We are cooking Tex-Mex. Ania is a fabulous cook, you know."

"I don't know, I—"

"Not 'I don't know,' " he said. "Yes. Yes!"

"OK, yes."

He smiled triumphantly, deep lines appearing in his stubbly cheeks. He was twenty-eight but looked older.

I moved away, ready to get to work, and he called my name.

"Viktor," I said, turning back wearily. "Miss Grafton's going to—"

"You have to relax a little, Carrie." He lifted both hands and shook his head mournfully. "We talk and we do our work, and it is not a problem."

I rolled my eyes.

"Anyway, I am just giving you a message."

He handed me a piece of paper, and I walked a few paces away and slipped between a pair of tall bookcases. In his big, blocky capitals it said, JAMIE. 10:30. CAN TAKE LUNCH ANYTIME BETWEEN 12 AND 3 IF YOU CALL BY 11:45. PLEASE CALL. SAYS HI. Sighing, I folded the note and put it in my pocket. Jamie worked in a copy shop three blocks away, and we sometimes met for lunch if our hours were right. The past few months I'd mostly been telling her they weren't, that I'd been given a late lunch or none at all, but recently, since the accident, she'd been pushing it, leaving messages like this one, calling at work just to say "Hi, are you OK?" I knew she was worried about me, and I felt grateful for that, or if not grateful, at least touched. I looked at my watch: 11:35. At the very least I should call to say no, but it would be so much easier not to call, to pretend I hadn't gotten the message in time. I touched my pocket and felt the note in there, the faint outline of it. Then I went and found a cart of books to shelve. Since the accident I could get away with more, which scared me.

THE HOSPITAL WAS like a city, with distinct neighborhoods and commercial areas, and corridors inside like long, long streets. When I arrived that evening I sat in one of the lobbies for a few minutes, trying to get myself ready to go up. A farm family stood conferring near me, the men in poly-blend short-sleeved shirts that showed their brown arms and their creased, dark red necks. Across the way, a very old woman in a wheelchair had been left by herself near a drinking fountain, a crocheted shawl over her hospital-issue gown. Mike and I had passed through this very lobby a couple years ago, when his grandfather was dying of lung cancer: his uncle Dick was too jumpy to sit for a meal, so we were searching for a box of Whoppers for him, the one thing he felt like eating. We finally found them in a gift shop just down the hall, and Mike opened them on the way back so we could each have one. Sitting there two years later, I could almost conjure up the taste of the malt on my tongue, how it burned a little next to the sweet, artificial chocolate.

I wondered: Would he look any different after a day away? Would it be any easier to see how he did look, beached on that strange bed? I hoped he'd be on his back. Seeing him on his stomach, his face framed by a cushioned oval and directed at the floor, was the hardest thing.

I happened to glance at the revolving doors just then, and there was Rooster, coming in, still in his suit. I stood up immediately. He was like Mrs. Mayer, full of hope, and I knew he'd disapprove of my just sitting there, of anything that smelled of pessimism. He put in his hours at the hospital as if they could accumulate to some good, to Mike's recovery.

He didn't see me, and I watched as he caught a glimpse of himself in a mirror and paused to make an adjustment to his tie. I couldn't help smiling: it was still funny to see him in a suit, maybe because he took the image so seriously himself. "The customers want you to look better than they do," he told me once. "It's a psychological thing." For a year he'd been working on the sales floor of a Honda dealership down on the Beltline. He referred to cars as units now, even to those of us who could remember when he'd thought of them as wheels.

I crossed the lobby and met him near the information desk. He looked at me oddly for just a moment after we'd said hi, and I wondered if he knew about my absence the day before, if Mrs. Mayer had told him.

We rode the elevator up to Intensive Care, where it was always quiet and a little dim. Several nurses sat inside the central work-station, speaking in low voices or going over charts. Surrounding them were the patient rooms, a circle of cubicles with open doors flanked by big plate-glass windows, so the nurses could see inside no matter where in the unit they happened to be. I could hear the even beeps of heart monitors, the deep whooshing sounds of ventilators. Opposite Mike's room a cubicle sat empty, and I tried to remember who'd occupied it two days earlier. An old lady, I thought. Had she stabilized and moved on? Or died and been moved out?

Rooster stopped to talk to one of the nurses, and I stopped with him. She was twenty-nine or thirty, blond, beautiful in an icy, Nordic way. Impossible, in other words, which was just his type. I stood behind him, smiling a little whenever she looked my way. The nurses knew who each of us was. Rooster was the best friend. I was the fiancée. They'd all made a point of asking to see my ring.

Mike *was* on his back, and I relaxed a little at the sight of him. It wasn't any harder to see than it had been two days ago, a completely familiar body now ministered to by machines. The only thing covering him was a small cloth draped over his crotch, and the rest of him looked pale and doughy.

"Hi, Mike," Rooster said. "It's me, bud. I'm here with Carrie." He looked at me and waited, then lifted his chin a bit to urge me to speak. The nurses and doctors had encouraged us to talk to Mike, but it made me feel uncomfortable, as if I were speaking into a tape recorder. I stayed silent.

"It's June 14th," Rooster continued after a moment. "Seven-twenty p.m. I came straight from work to see you, bud." He took a piece of paper from his pocket. "Sold a Civic to a guy with a doozer of a name today. OK. This guy's a dentist, right? Moler. Dr. Richard Moler. I said to myself, That's one for the collection. That's one I gotta remember to tell Mikey."

For as long as I'd known them, Mike and Rooster had had a theory about names. Larry Speakes, the former White House spokesman. A chiropractor in the phonebook, Dr. Clinch. Driving through Menominee on their way back from a camping trip one summer, they saw a plaque on a building: Dr. Bonebrake, Orthopedist. Coincidence? Absolutely not, was their attitude. Their favorite was Rooster's freshman advisor at Madison Area Technical College, Mr. Tittman, who Rooster was willing to swear wore a bra.

Rooster folded up the piece of paper and put it back in his pocket. "You never know," he said with a shrug.

I took a few steps closer. With Rooster out of my vision, it was possible to imagine Mike and I were alone. I didn't want to speak out loud, but that didn't mean I couldn't talk to him. I looked at his face, at the shallow cleft of his chin and at his thin, pale lips. I covered his hand with mine and told him not to worry. *I'm here,* I told him. *I'm here, I'm here.*

AT THE ELEVATORS we ran into Mike's family, making their nightly trip back in to tell him goodnight. Mrs. Mayer was plainly relieved to see me, and even Mr. Mayer looked at me for an extra

moment and nodded, as if tucking away for future analysis the knowledge that I was here now but hadn't been last night.

Rooster said he had to go, but I felt I should stay. I headed back
to the lounge with them and waited while two by two they visited
Mike's room. Then the five of us were all in the lounge together,
and although there was no reason to stay, none of us made a move
to leave. It was nearly eight, the end of a long day, and the smell of
burned coffee drifted from the back corner of the room. I knew just
what I'd see if I went over there: dirty coffeemaker surrounded by
spilled grounds, empty blue and pink sweetener envelopes lying everywhere, carton of milk souring nearby.

"Have you seen the doctors today?"

I looked up and found Julie watching me. She was nineteen and
just home from her first year of college; she wore a long print skirt
and dangling silver earrings, and she smelled faintly of patchouli. I
shook my head.

"I mean it, Mom," she said. "We can't just sit around on our asses
and expect them to keep us completely up-to-date. We have to be
active participants."

Mrs. Mayer cast me a sad smile.

"Jesus," Julie cried, and she got up and ran from the lounge.

"Oh, dear," Mrs. Mayer said.

"I'll go," Mr. Mayer said, but he didn't move.

I glanced at John Junior. He was sixteen and heartbreaking, with
wavy brown hair and gray eyes—Mike's hair and eyes—and the exact
body Mike had had six years earlier, muscular but still narrow-
waisted. I saw John and his friends at the Union sometimes, asking
people with IDs to buy them beer at the Rat.

"How are you, John?" I said now.

"Fine." His voice was husky—I thought he was trying not to cry.

"How's the job?"

"OK. Stop by sometime, I'll scoop you a free one."

"Maybe I will."

The weekend before the accident he'd been hired at an ice cream
parlor on State Street. I was at the Mayers' when he came in with the
news, and quick as anything Mike said, "Perfect, bring me home a
pint of butter pecan every night or I'll have your ass." Without miss-

ing a beat John said, "If you eat a pint of butter pecan every night *no one*'ll have *your* ass," and Mike loved that—he told everyone about it for days afterward.

I looked at Mr. Mayer: at his tanned, balding head, at his hazel eyes filmy behind thick glasses. He'd left his coat and tie at home, but he still wore his pressed white shirt, his navy trousers, and his shiny black lace-ups. The orange couch he sat on was too low for him, and as he shifted, swinging his knees from left to right and bringing his arms closer to his body, I was suddenly certain he was about to make a pronouncement.

I stood up. He'd become ministerial in his speech since the accident, one day delivering sermons about hope and patience and the next lecturing us on the spinal cord and its function. I liked him, but I couldn't listen—it made me too jittery.

"I guess I better go," I said.

The three of them said goodbye, and I felt them watch me as I left the lounge. I wondered how long they'd sit there before they went home.

At the elevators I found Julie, her arms crossed over her chest: her cheeks were flushed, her eyes brimming with tears. She pushed her hair away from her face. "I don't want to hear it, Carrie, OK?"

I was taken aback. "I wasn't going to say anything."

"My mother's an idiot. I can't believe I never figured that out until I was nineteen."

"Better late than never."

She half smiled but then quickly shook her head, as if she didn't want to be derailed. "Do you know what she was doing when I got home this afternoon? Ironing *tablecloths*. Do you know when the last time we used a tablecloth was? Christmas! Do you know when the next time will be? Thanksgiving!"

"She has to do something," I said.

"Then why doesn't she do something about Mike?" Julie cried. Then she burst into tears. "Because there's nothing to do," she sobbed. "There's nothing to do."

I put my arms around her and pulled her close. Why hadn't I cried? Why couldn't I? I felt stony. I ran a hand down her hair and felt her shoulder blades, how bony and angular they were.

She palmed her face, wiped her hand on her skirt, then looked up at me. "Why couldn't it have been Rooster?" she whispered fiercely.

As if it had to have been someone: I'd thought the same horrible thing. "I don't know," I said to her. "I really don't."

ROOSTER WAS STILL in the lobby when I got there, standing near the exit, talking to the same blond nurse. Her hair was down now, a sweep of pale waves, and she carried a shoulder bag. After a moment he looked up and saw me, then motioned for me to join them.

"Have you guys actually met?" he said. "Carrie, this is Joan. She's from Oconomowoc, believe it or not."

I nodded: his parents were both from Oconomowoc; it was where he went for holidays.

"You know who Carrie is."

Joan smiled at me. She was taller than I'd realized, nearly six feet, with clear, fair skin and extraordinary pale blue eyes. "I'm sure sorry about Mike," she said.

"Thanks."

"It's way too soon to give up hope, though."

"Exactly," Rooster said.

Joan headed for the exit, and I watched Rooster watching her, his eyes on her even once she was out the door and heading into the parking lot. "Nice," he said at last.

"Nice what?" I was used to his ways. Nice legs. Nice ass.

"Just nice."

He put his hand on my shoulder, and after a moment we started toward the door together. It was muggy and hot outside, the sky a glaring white. Heat blew toward us from the parking lot, thick and exhaust-tinged.

"Let's go for a drink."

I glanced up and found him watching me closely, face flushed, red hair damp at the hairline. I looked away. "I don't really feel like it."

He stopped walking and put his hands on his hips. "Come on, Carrie, be a friend for once, OK? One beer, I promise. We'll go somewhere quiet."

"For once? Why did you say for once?" My eyes burned a little, and I thought it would be incredible if this were what finally made me cry.

"I didn't mean it like that."

"How did you mean it?"

He rolled his eyes. An impatient look came over his face, and he stared out at the sea of cars baking in the late sun. Finally he looked back at me. "I didn't mean it at all, OK?"

I sighed. Rooster always got his way eventually, through sheer force of will. I could go on resisting, but what was the point? "All right," I said, "one beer."

We drove separately, then met up in front of the University Bookstore. While we were standing there trying to decide where to go, we ran into Stu, who talked us into the Union terrace. Rooster stood in line for beer while Stu and I got a table. Lake Mendota was a rippled silver, like a vast piece of silk spread out but not yet smoothed. I remembered the morning, how both lakes had disappointed me, and I decided they'd been tainted: by my failure to visit Mike the day before.

"Earth to Carrie," Stu said.

Rooster had arrived with the beer. I reached for my mug and took a sip. "Sorry."

Stu leaned forward. "How are you doing?"

I lifted my hand off the table and rocked it back and forth.

"And the Mayers?"

"Lousy," Rooster said. "Like all of us." He glanced at me, and I had a fleeting moment of thinking he was accusing me of something.

"It's John I'm worried about," I said. "John and Mister."

Rooster frowned. "I don't think Julie's that hot, either. And Mrs. Mayer told my mom she hasn't slept more than an hour at a time since it happened."

"I just meant John seems especially vulnerable."

"Johnny's tough," Rooster said. "Like Mikey."

I thought of Mike on the pier, completely hyped up to dive into water he knew would be freezing. "Tough," I said. "That turned out to be a good quality."

Rooster and Stu stared at me in shock. A tiny breeze blew in from the lake, and a paper napkin lifted from our table, flipped over once, and settled again. I felt odd, the skin on my upper cheeks tingling a little. *Take it back,* I thought, but I couldn't. I looked at my hands, aware of Rooster's glare on me.

"I can't believe you," he said, and he set his mug on the table with a loud thud. He scraped his chair back and stood up. "I'm out of here," he said to Stu. "I don't need this shit right now, I'll see you later."

I looked up in time to watch him walk away, and I thought there was something sad about the way he looked from the back, his suit coat straining a little across the shoulders. I turned back to Stu. "Sorry. I don't know what's wrong with me."

"You don't?"

"Well, I do." I drank some beer and wished I were home sewing, not sitting on the Union terrace. It was packed, and I thought of similar evenings there in early fall or late spring, when classes had just begun or ended. Evenings with Mike, and a restlessness that we were where we were, that nothing surprising could happen. Sometimes Jamie would be with us, and I'd feel her excitement, feel her looking around, thinking, *Maybe him, maybe him.*

Stu was staring at the lake, his hands wrapped around his beer. He had small hands, and they looked almost childish against the thick, faceted mug.

"What are you thinking?" I said.

He looked over at me, something troubled in his blue-green eyes.

"Stu."

He smiled uneasily. "I was thinking about that word 'tough,' actually. About me and Mike and Rooster walking to Picnic Point on the ice that time."

I stared at him. "What are you talking about?"

He narrowed his eyes. "Mike never told you?"

"Told me what?"

He looked away. I felt a little sorry for him, sitting there in his oxford shirt, his haircut. He'd just finished a grueling first year of law school.

"Stu," I said.

"Do you want some popcorn?"

"*Stu.*"

He shook his head and sighed. "OK, this was freshman year and I—"

"Freshman year of high school?"

"God, no—college." He snorted. "Who remembers high school?"

I did. Sometimes I thought remembering high school was my biggest problem. Those first sweet kisses, the sinking feeling I later learned to call desire. Mike at his best, before I made the list of things I loved about him, in case I forgot.

Stu took a sip of beer. "It was freshman year of college, I was at Marquette. It was Christmas vacation and I was so psyched to see those guys I left Milwaukee maybe five minutes after my last final, although that of course is classified information. Anyway, I drove home and called Rooster, he called Mike, and the three of us came down here. Mike was like, 'I'm here all the time now, let's go somewhere else,' but it was snowing, it was cold, there was nowhere really to go. I was thinking, *I wanted to get home for this?* Then Rooster goes, 'Let's walk out to Picnic Point.' It was fifteen degrees out, but all of a sudden all three of us were trooping outside like it was the best idea we ever heard of. We went down to the lake and it'd been a warm fall, it was hardly frozen, but Rooster started walking out on the ice. I said to Mike, 'I thought he meant go *around.*' Mike goes, 'Be tough.' Tough is one thing and dead is another, right? I said, 'Fuck no, you guys'll kill yourselves.' Mike gives me this look like, *Well, let's hope not, but if we do, we do,* and he goes out on the ice. So what was I going to do? I followed right after them. We walked the whole way there and back without saying a word, and it was the next day that that kid fell through the ice up in Sawyer County, remember? He was in the water for like half an hour while his friend ran for help, and—"

"Stop, I remember, I remember." It had been a little boy, maybe eight: by the time they got back to him it was too late; he was still alive but he died on the way to the hospital. I'd seen photographs of him, but it was his friend's face I recalled now: they showed him on TV one night, and I could still picture his scared little eyes, how you could see in them the question of whether or not he should have stayed and tried to pull the boy out himself.

"I thought Mike would have told you that," Stu said.

I shook my head. I looked out at Lake Mendota, the last sailboats heading in. Picnic Point was across the way, a little peninsula pointing into the water. Four or five times a year Mike and I biked or drove to the parking lot nearest the trailhead and then made the trek out to the end. In winter we bundled up in down jackets and Sorels; in summer we took a picnic and spent the afternoon. It was at Picnic Point that I first felt his finger inside me; and a few weeks later, in the same secluded clearing, we lost our virginity together, on a beach towel I still had. We were sixteen then. We thought we'd waited long enough.

I turned back to Stu. "Would you have dived? At Clausen's Reservoir? If he'd come right up and said, 'Come on, Stu, it's great.' Would you've?"

"Sure," Stu said. "Why not?"

2

~

I MET MIKE A few weeks before Christmas the winter I was fourteen, and it's probably true that if I hadn't met him I would have met someone else, and my story would have run in an entirely different direction. Mike's, too, of course. Away from Clausen's Reservoir. Away from the dive.

Jamie and I were Christmas shopping that afternoon, ninth graders in twin fuzzy hats to ward off the chill, mine purple and hers red. Because I already had my mother's challis scarf bought and wrapped and had only Jamie left on my list, I spent the afternoon standing by while she bought things for her family and dropped big, obvious hints about what I could get her. Gold-plated hoop earrings. A light blue angora sweater. We were best friends, we were allowed to ask each other for the moon.

Late in the day, we wandered into the rink where our school's hockey games were played and took seats on the bleachers. Freshman hockey didn't appeal to us much, but there was always the chance that we'd run into someone interesting while we were there: there was always that chance in everything we did, which is why it's not really an exaggeration to say that as I sat there in my Icelandic sweater I felt as if I were waiting for my life to start.

And there was Mike. In the box across the ice from us, his helmet off: big and young and beautiful. I nudged Jamie. "Number twenty-four," I said. "By the gate, next to number seven."

"Seven's in my math class," she said. "Back row, kind of loud. Twenty-four is good."

For a moment I had the strangest feeling—like a clear, soundproof bubble had suddenly surrounded me, the world still there on the other side but beyond reach. Then everything was normal again.

"Yeah, he is," I said. "Isn't he?"

I don't remember a thing about the game, but once it was over I talked Jamie into waiting around outside the locker room, where there was a bulletin board studded with colorful notices we could pretend to be reading. Finally, out of the corner of my eye, I saw the math class guy come out, and I whispered to Jamie to go say hi.

That was Rooster. Mike was right behind him.

Jamie and Rooster talked about the game for a few minutes, and then together the four of us walked out into the frosty Madison dusk, ending up at a diner on Regent Street that was famous for its hot chocolate. Jamie and I sat on one side of the booth, Mike and Rooster on the other. Our orders came, topped with fluted hills of Reddi-wip.

Rooster talked. Jamie and I were "you ladies." "Where do you ladies live?" he said. "Would you ladies like to go to a movie sometime with me and my mute friend here? Don't mind him, he's just what we call shy." I stole a look at Mike and found him blushing endearingly.

At school the following week the four of us met in the lunchroom and ate together. I thought Mike's mother's sandwiches were a clue about her, him, the whole Mayer family: a perfect ruffle of lettuce frilling the edges of the bread, mustard on the meat and mayonnaise on the cheese. I lived alone with my mother, and I was enchanted. I wanted to see where he lived even more than I wanted him to kiss me, but it all happened at once, on Christmas Eve, thanks to a piece of mistletoe he told me later he'd gotten his mother to hang. Julie was ten then, John Junior seven: they made me think of a TV show, the kind where the younger siblings are pesky but adorable. Rooster and

Jamie were there, too, helping trim the Mayers' tree, still pretending to flirt for the sake of Mike and me and where we were going, where we were afraid to go.

The mistletoe hung in the doorway to the kitchen. I smelled the dissolved end of his Certs. "I knew it," he said when we'd parted. "Knew what?" But he wouldn't tell me.

My mother and I had been alone for over ten years by then, living the quiet, still life of a girl and a woman left long before by a man. Life at the Mayers' was the exact opposite, and I never really looked back. All through high school I went home from school with Mike, stayed for dinner several times a week, hung out there on weekends. When they rented a cabin on Lake Superior each summer, I went too. Their big white house was always full and noisy, with kids, friends, dogs, skates, coats. Music from a couple different stereos, a TV on, someone yelling "Where are my shoes?" Mrs. Mayer bought ten bags of groceries a week. She treated me so warmly it was as if she'd picked me out herself, a gift for Mike like the little gifts she was always giving me—a bar of lavender soap, a picture of Mike as a five-year-old in cowboy boots, a little ceramic vase painted with tulips.

We spent time at my house, too, but things were different there, *we* were different: by the time we were juniors in high school we were in my bed two or three afternoons a week, my mother safely at work. She knew, too: before I left for school each morning she'd tell me exactly when she'd get home that day, factoring in any errands she might be planning for the way home, and when she got back she always made a lot of unnecessary noise coming up the stairs, in case we hadn't heard her pull into the driveway. Sometimes, once we'd emerged from my room, some lie about homework on our lips, she would invite Mike to stay for dinner, and I'd feel torn: his staying meant more time with him, which I always craved, but the dinners had our house's quietness to them, its stillness, and I knew it made him uncomfortable, being the only male.

I have three memories of my father, exactly three, which is fitting given that was the number of years he was in my life. I used to try to come up with others, but it was futile, an exercise that led to "remembering" things I hadn't witnessed, stories my mother had told me, scenes I'd seen captured in photographs that had since disappeared.

When I was eight or nine I excitedly told my mother that I'd suddenly remembered sitting on my father's shoulders eating a black cherry ice cream cone near a lifeguard stand on a big beach. She frowned and considered, considered and frowned, and then understanding swept across her face and she told me no, that hadn't been my father, that had been later, when I was nearly five: her cousin Brian had invited us to spend a week with his family on the New Jersey shore, and it was Brian's shoulders I'd sat on, although I was right about the black cherry ice cream, she remembered that herself.

Memory is strange—part movie, part dream. You can never know if what you remember is the essential thing or something else entirely, a grace note. Of my father, here's what I have: it's late at night, and from a darkened hallway I see a man in a plaid bathrobe yelling at my mother, who's standing before him in a long, pink nightgown, her hands clasped in front of her chest. I watch for a long time, but they don't see me, and though the man is yelling, the memory is soundless. Next I'm at a frost-edged window while the same man hammers fence posts into the frozen ground, each strike ringing out to the snowy world beyond our yard, to the high, frozen branches of black trees and to the endless sky. "To keep out that goddamned bitch hound," he says later, or maybe earlier, but not to me, although no one else is around. Finally, very early one morning, he's raising the shade in my bedroom, a manila panel that he snaps up with a thread-wrapped ring, letting pale light flood in. He's dressed in a suit, come in to say goodbye. On my bed, down past my feet, he leaves—"of all things," my mother will say again and again—a monogrammed pencil sharpener from his desk, as a souvenir.

And that's it, that's all I remember. What I don't know is nearly infinite: his smell, the tenor of his voice, whether or not he ever touched me. A whole book of things, an entire encyclopedia—a volume that I tried and tried to fill at the Mayers'.

I don't have the pencil sharpener anymore. When I was in fourth grade, six years after his departure, I took it to school one morning and at recess snuck out the back gate and heaved it into the Dumpster behind the cafeteria.

·   ·   ·

MIKE DIDN'T WAKE up. Fifteen days, sixteen, seventeen. Late one night, unable to sleep, I left my apartment and crossed Gorham Street to sit in James Madison Park, a grassy stretch alongside Lake Mendota. Already the summer was a contender for the hottest on record, and though it was after midnight I could still feel the air on my skin, an unpleasant thing that pressed against my bare arms and legs, filled my hair and made it heavy. A nearly full moon had risen, and the light from it glinted across the surface of the water. I picked out Picnic Point opposite, a darkness between lake and sky. I thought of Stu's story, of him and Mike and Rooster walking across the ice, and I thought: good for Mike that he didn't tell me.

I took off my shoes and started walking, letting the damp grass prick at the bottoms of my feet. At the base of a tree something round caught my eye and I stooped to look at it. A tennis ball. I picked it up. It was rough, as if it had been in and out of a dog's mouth so often that the fuzziness had rubbed away. It had split open along one seam, and when I tossed it into the air it fell back into my palm with a hollow, off-balance *thock*.

I remembered a summer when Mike and I had played tennis almost every day; by August our games had taken on an anti-competitive feeling, with points and sets observed more for form's sake than because we really cared. Playing became a form of conversation, a kind of physical talking. I suggested this to him one day, and he laughed it off at first, said, "Yeah, we're saying 'Take that,' 'Take that.' " But a few days later he brought it up again, and I had a feeling he'd been mulling it over. "I know what you meant," he said, and then, "You're a thoughtful person," and I knew he was interested in understanding just who I was.

I didn't want to think about it now. I carried the ruined tennis ball down to the water and threw it in, then headed home. The first-floor apartment was dark and silent, so I tiptoed across the porch and made my way up to my place as quietly as I could.

Mike was a few miles away, sleeping. The doctors had said it was wrong to think of it that way—he wasn't *sleeping*—but I let myself anyway: I pictured him lying on his back with his eyes closed. I blocked out the tongs on his head, the tubes, the sound of the ventilator. I undressed and got into bed, and once I was lying down I thought of his face in sleep, his face beside me in sleep, just there on the other pillow.

I closed my eyes and waited. I might rest my hand on his chest, nestle closer—let the darkness take me, too. Or if it was morning I might kiss his shoulder. He might awaken but pretend to sleep longer. Then speak suddenly from complete alertness. "I've been thinking hard about something, and I've decided that I really ought to tell you about it."

"What?"

He turns toward me, his eyes open now, soft gray fringed faintly by pale lashes. He looks into my eyes. "I've been thinking really seriously about waffles."

And we both laugh, the day begun.

I opened my eyes into the dark of my bedroom. Lying there alone, I let myself think again, reluctantly, of that afternoon on the tennis court with him, four or five years ago. "You're a thoughtful person." We were done playing—done with that day's physical conversation. We stood at the fence zipping our cases onto our rackets. It was ninety-five degrees out, and we left the court and sat on the grass under a shade tree. He unscrewed the top from the bottle of water he'd brought, then handed it to me. The ice had melted but the water was still cold. I drank deeply, then gave it back. Grinning, he splashed some onto his forehead before having a drink himself. He recapped the bottle and set it aside, then used the back of his arm to wipe his wet hair from his eyes. He reached for my hand and traced a line down my forefinger. "This is talking, too," he said.

I smiled up at him. "What would the words be?"

He hesitated. "The usual three. That I'm always saying whether I'm saying them or not, because I'm always thinking them." He looked away for a second, and when he looked back again his eyes were a little teary. "Always," he said.

A feeling of pleasure, almost physical, flowed through me, and I reached for his hand. I moved my thigh against his and thought of how different our two legs were, mine smooth and small, his covered with hair and thick, strong. How different and how complementary.

He pulled his hand free and drew me close. "I'm still sweating like crazy here," he said after a while.

"Me, too."

He chuckled. "My mom would say, 'Horses sweat, men perspire, and ladies glow.' "

"OK, I'm glowing."

"No, it's OK, you can sweat. We don't want to have—what do they call it?"

"A double standard?"

"No double standards," he said. "We're a single standard couple."

"Sounds settled."

"It is."

We sat close, our dampness combining. "The thing is," he said, "I actually kind of like to sweat. That's what's great about hockey, you can sweat all you want but the rink's so cold you never feel too gross. But even sweating on a totally hot day is pretty nice. Your body, like, working." He nudged me. "I'm speaking for myself here, aren't I? I'll bet you're wishing you could step into a cool shower right this minute, right?"

It was true, but not entirely: I also wanted to be there with him.

"I'm sitting here talking about the joy of sweat, and you're all, *Gosh, I guess I can stand it for one more minute if it means so much to him.*"

We exchanged an amused smile. He eased his arm off me and got to his feet, then held out his hand.

"What?" I said. "I'm good for a while longer."

He shook his head. "Let's go."

"Really?"

"Yeah, in the spirit of 'Always leave a party at its peak.' "

"Who's that, Dear Abby?"

"My aunt Peg."

"Same difference," we said in unison. His aunt Peg had advice for every occasion: one Easter she'd even pulled me aside and told me she didn't want to butt in, but she was afraid I might not know how good an idea it was to make your man *work* a bit for your affections. "Keep him on his toes," she whispered. "Word to the wise." We had a good laugh about that later, Mike and I, and for a while afterward he'd walk on tiptoes every time he saw her, though she never caught on.

I took his hand and let him pull me to my feet. "But isn't the party us?" I said.

"We'll take it with us," he said. "That's the idea, right?"

"Right," I said, and we walked to our bicycles with our hands linked, swinging them between us, happy. This was what I loved, this certainty, this plan. It was what I'd always loved, how we'd somehow found this thing together, *made* this thing together: a party that would go on and on. Though it wasn't so much a party that would go on and on as something else that would, something not temporal but spatial, like a huge house. I'd thought this before, that what we'd done was build ourselves a house so big there were rooms we hadn't even discovered yet, rooms we could still find and inhabit together. I saw an enormous house on a cliff, beautiful in every light. And as I lay in my dark bedroom so many years later—and Mike lay not asleep but comatose across town, with a machine doing his breathing for him, doing his body's work—I felt I was in a place where that grand old house, invisible for so long now, was suddenly in plain view again. His love. My love. The words to talk about it, the *desire* to. It could open up again, it could all open up. A tearful feeling approached me, moving quickly, and I tensed up, but it was no use—it was coming, getting closer every moment: huge, invincible. I was going to be swept up. Yet just as I was making myself ready for it—longing, even, for the relief of being overtaken—the feeling ebbed back, and then the house was gone, too, and I was simply in my bed again, alone, somewhere between anxious and numb.

3

~

THE NEXT DAY was Saturday, and after my shower I made my way up to the Farmers' Market. The huge square surrounding the high-domed State Capitol was lined with vendors' stalls, and there were pickup trucks everywhere, their beds still full of lettuces, beans, basil, eggplants, zucchinis—of crates of clover honey and flats of marigolds. I walked and looked. The same farmers came summer after summer, and I saw kids who'd hung back last year making change while their parents worked behind them, unloading vegetables or resting for a minute under the shade of a big vinyl umbrella. I passed a smoked trout stand, a stand selling nothing but deep green broccoli. Then I came to a stand of sour cherries, carton upon carton jammed together on a folding table, and I stopped in my tracks.

Mike loved cherry pie, but it was Rooster who had a thing about it—the pinnacle of pie, he always said. Sour cherries had a short season, but at least once a summer a vanload from Michigan showed up at the Farmers' Market, and I bought enough for a couple pies. A small group of us would skip dinner that night and gather for dessert on my second-story porch instead, sweet vanilla ice cream turning the cooked cherries the exact pink of bubble gum. "Perfect," Rooster would sigh, and for a while the only sound would be of forks scraping plates.

Then last summer: "Make three," Rooster said. "Or four. Couldn't you freeze one?" Mike and I had run into him at Coffee Connection, and he'd come up to the Farmers' Market with us and spotted the cherry stand right off. I said I'd make an extra for him to take home, and I bought a huge number of cherries, quarts of them, then headed for my apartment while he and Mike went to help Mike's father with some painting. When they showed up a few hours later I was still pitting—slicing open cherry after cherry and pulling the stone out with the tip of my finger, my hands crimson—and Rooster: Rooster was horrified. It had somehow never occurred to him that removing the pits was work. He couldn't believe how long it had taken. "I had no idea," he kept saying, and that evening, eating slabs of pie with me and Mike and Jamie, he kept pausing to thank me. I was touched, and completely unprepared for what happened next: about a month later he came over by himself one evening and handed me a little paper bag, a sheepish grin on his face as he said, "I got you a present. Well, us. For next year." And inside the bag was a small metal thing that looked a little like a nutcracker: a cherry pitter he'd ordered from a catalog. "Don't thank me," he said. "Thank *you*."

Now it was next year. A line had formed already, at least half a dozen people waiting to buy cherries. I looked at the fruit, round and red and gleaming in the sun, and I wondered: Would Rooster happen by today and wonder if I'd seen them, too? Would he think of the unused cherry pitter in my kitchen drawer? Would he wonder if I'd ever use it now? I'd seen him at the hospital yesterday, both of us awkward after the evening on the terrace with Stu, and for a moment I thought of joining the line and buying just enough for one small pie.

I continued around the plaza, stopping for some lettuce, then went home for my car and drove to my mother's. She came to the door in her weekend uniform: a chambray shirt tucked into khakis, lace-up moccasins on her feet. Behind her the house was shadowy, the living room with its north-facing windows, the narrow staircase up to the second floor. "Honey," she said. "Hi, I didn't expect you."

I'd stopped at a bakery, and I held up the bag. "I brought muffins. But if you've already eaten . . ."

"No, not really."

I knew she had: her reading glasses hung from a chain around her neck, a sure sign that she'd already finished breakfast and started on her weekend paperwork. It had been five years since I'd lived there, but after the accident I'd spent several nights, so I even knew what she'd had for breakfast: bran flakes with skim milk, and coffee made three-quarters decaf. In the pantry there'd been half a dozen identical boxes of cereal, several bags of pasta, a stack of canned tuna at least a foot high. She was a creature of habit.

She took a step backward, opening the door wider. *It's your house, too,* she always said, but I couldn't help knocking, couldn't help feeling it wasn't. I stepped in and followed her to the kitchen. I'd seen her at the hospital a few days ago, but she'd had her hair cut since then and it looked bristly from the back, spiked with more gray than I'd have thought. She worked long hours as a therapist at Student Health; on weekends she holed up in a little room off her bedroom and translated jotted-down notes into fuller accounts of each session.

From the kitchen table I watched as she filled her coffeemaker with cold water, then opened the freezer and reached for the coffee bag that contained her special mix.

"Mom, I need the real thing this morning."

She smiled over her shoulder. "OK, but it'll be on your conscience if I end up with the shakes all day." She got a different bag and started the coffee, then sat opposite me. I pushed the muffins toward her. "These look sinful," she said. "What kind are they?"

"Carrot. But don't worry, I got the ones that were only half butter."

"Well, in that case . . ."

I broke off a piece of mine and put it in my mouth, the crunchy top edge that Mike loved. In my apartment there was often a little white bag containing two or three muffin carcasses, just the bottoms in their pleated paper skins.

"No news?" she said.

I shook my head. No news, no hope, nothing.

She reached across the table and patted my hand.

I looked away, and my glance fell on the curtains over the sink, made of tired, off-white muslin. I said, "I have to tell you something."

A furrow appeared on the bridge of her nose, and she looked at me quizzically. I was sure she thought it was something to do with Mike.

"You need new curtains," I said. "In here, in the upstairs bathroom, and in your office. Have you looked at your curtains lately? They're dingy."

Her face relaxed into a smile, but I could see she didn't have a clue where I was headed. "And?" she said.

"And I was thinking I'd make new ones for you. If you're not too busy we could go get fabric right now."

She lifted her coffee and took a sip, then set the cup down deliberately. "That's a nice offer," she said, "but don't you think you've got enough on your mind already?"

I didn't want to think about what I had on my mind, and I looked away. In my peripheral vision I saw her lift her cup for another sip, then set it down again.

"New curtains would be nice," she said.

I turned back. "Really?"

"I accept."

We finished our muffins and coffee and measured the windows, then got into her car and drove out to one of the big fabric houses on the far side of town. It was a place I hadn't been with her since I'd gotten my driver's license, and seeing it through someone else's eyes made me overly aware of the unpleasant aspects: the bright lights, the vastness, the smell of sizing. There were aisles and aisles of fabric, bolts and bolts of it: cottons and rayons and wools, shiny acetates for lining. Near the entrance a display of Fourth of July fabrics occupied a prominent position, with over a dozen different combinations of stars and stripes. I'd never understood seasonal fabrics, the urge to make yourself a shirt strewn with candy corn for Halloween, a set of leprechaun-print napkins for a St. Patrick's Day party. When I made something I thought of longevity, how the hours I put into it would yield me an exponential number of wearing hours. Never mind the question of taste.

We made our way to the back wall, where the home-furnishing fabrics hung on giant rolls. Right away she picked a stripe for her office and a tiny flower print for the upstairs bathroom, but she was less sure about the kitchen. "Maybe this one with the fruit," she said. "Do you like it?"

"Sure."

"I went by the Mayers' last night," she added casually.

I'd been fingering a flowered chintz, but now I let it go. I felt stricken, hating the idea of her discussing me with Mrs. Mayer. "You did?"

"I took them a casserole."

I smiled. "Did you try to pass it off as homemade?"

"Very funny—it was." She was watching me, her head tilted slightly. It seemed she was trying to decide whether or not to tell me something.

"What?" I said.

"I think she's concerned about you. That you're writing him off, although she didn't put it that way."

I thought of Mrs. Mayer's pale face, the watchful way she'd looked at me over tea the other morning. I tried to focus on the fabrics. For a moment sewing seemed like the saddest of enterprises, a world of hope embodied in the clean rolls of fabric, when all you'd really get would be a new slipcover, a new throw pillow for your same old bed.

"Are you?" my mother said carefully, and I wondered what she was thinking, if somewhere deep inside she was hoping I was. Not writing him off, maybe, but thinking of some kind of ending. I'd never thought she wholly approved of him—of my settling with anyone so early. She never said anything, but I saw it in her reticence on the subject, in the way she was always so nice to him, as if she were waiting him out. I figured if she did disapprove the reason was her own wrecked marriage: not that she wouldn't want me to succeed where she'd failed, but that she'd fear her failure had planted the seeds for mine and would want to protect me from that.

I hadn't said a word to her about the rocky state of things that had existed between me and Mike before the accident. I hadn't said a word to anyone.

"No," I said, looking back at her. "I'm not."

"I didn't think so." She reached to touch a blue-and-white harlequin print. "I told her to worry about her own feelings and let you worry about yours."

"Mom!"

"Oh, not in so many words, silly. I was a good PTA mom, don't worry."

A "PTA mom" was code for the exact kind of mother my mother wasn't. A PTA mom baked chocolate cupcakes and iced them with orange frosting for the class's Halloween party. My mother sent me to school with a giant can of Hawaiian Punch.

"So what kind of casserole was it?"

"Chicken and mushroom. You know, cooking is kind of fun, I'd forgotten."

"Is this the beginning of a new trend? The Working Woman Who Still Has Time for Her Home?"

"Oh, I doubt it. Anyway, you're making the curtains, not me."

I shrugged: I'd finished the linen jacket the night before and I needed another project, simple as that. "True," I said, "but they're not for my home."

"You're not going to move back in with me one of these days? Don't break my heart."

"I don't know what I'm going to do."

She looked serious all at once. "That's all right, you know. It really is."

"I know."

She tilted her head, a concerned look on her face. "Do you have plans for the afternoon?"

"Lunch with Jamie. Then the hospital."

She nodded slowly. She hesitated for a moment, then put her arms around me and pulled me close.

JAMIE STILL LIVED in Miffland, the student ghetto near campus, and to get there from my mother's I had to drive right by the corner I'd always thought of as the breakdown corner. Not once but twice my Toyota had died right outside Hank's Shoe Repair, and both times Mike had come and fiddled with it to get it running again—the second time in his suit, because he was already working at the bank by then. It was my first time driving by since the accident, and I gripped the wheel until I was well into the next block.

Miffland was full of large, wood-frame houses rented nearly to ruin, with scrabbly front yards and overgrown lilacs everywhere. It was a neighborhood where certain houses maintained reputations for decades and more: the dopers' house on the corner of Mifflin and Broom, someone might say in passing, and although the dopers you knew who'd lived there were long gone, six more just like them had taken up residence and were carrying the torch.

I found Jamie sitting on her sloping front porch in a flowered bikini top and cutoffs, her dark blond hair pinned high off her neck. Five or six guys lounged on the second-story porch of the place next door, a house famous for the bright yellow color someone had painted it long ago, faded now to a dirty ocher and peeling so badly you could see the light blue underneath. The guys were on aluminum lounge chairs, sitting in front of a pair of giant speakers that had been set face-out on the sills of someone's bedroom windows. Gangsta rap blasted from them: "something something bitch," I heard as I made my way up Jamie's walk.

"Nice neighbors," I said as I sat down next to her. "When are you going to move?"

She laughed. "They're not bad. They'll be sophomores next year and they just escaped from the dorms. They keep coming over and asking to borrow, you know, sponges. I don't think they're very likely to use them."

I glanced up at the guys. "Probably not."

She set her glass down and looked at me. "So?"

I shrugged. "Nothing new."

"Are you OK?"

I shrugged again.

She picked up her glass and took a long sip. "See the one in the yellow T-shirt?"

I looked up at the guys: the one in the yellow T-shirt was looking down at us. "Yeah."

"He seems pretty cool."

"Cool?" I said. "Don't you mean hunky?"

"What is he, a candy bar?" She smiled. "Just a little smarter than the average nineteen-year-old was all I meant."

"Liar."

"Oh, leave me alone. Go get us some food, why don't you? And I'll have another of these." She handed me her glass, and I headed for the front door.

Inside, the living room was dark and musty. Jamie's roommate lay on a tired gold velvet couch, still in her nightgown, the phone at her side and the receiver pressed to her ear. As I passed by she looked up but didn't acknowledge me. Her fiancé was in Los Angeles, in business school, and they talked every Wednesday night and every Saturday morning. On the first of each month he FTDed her a dozen red roses.

In the refrigerator I found a container of potato salad and a bowl of tuna, and I put them on an old bamboo tray, then added a box of crackers. I refilled Jamie's glass with iced tea and got myself some.

"They're having a party tonight," she announced when I got back outside.

"Who?"

"Those *guys*." She gestured with her head at the neighbors. "They just called down and told me." She forked tuna onto a cracker. "What do you think? It might be good for you."

I smiled. "Not that you have any desire to go yourself."

"Carrie."

I looked at her. We'd been friends for eighteen years—best friends, we used to say, until it was too obvious to mention. I knew she wanted to go to the party, but only if I'd go, too.

"What's his name?" I said.

"I think it's Drew."

"You *think*."

"What I think is that it would be good for you to get out."

"As long as it's just for me," I said with a smile.

"I'm serious." She shifted her chair so her back was to the guys. "No more teasing, OK?"

I shrugged. "OK." I looked up at the guys again. Yellow T-shirt sat with his legs splayed, a beer can in hand, moving a little self-consciously to the beat of the music. I felt as if I knew, or could guess, everything about him.

"He's nineteen," she said—more, I thought, to herself than to me.

"Well, maybe we should fix him up with Julie Mayer. She's nineteen, too."

She shook her head. "No way. Julie probably wants some guy with black boots and a goatee. Sensitive but moody. An artist, or maybe some guy in a band. A beautiful face and long, thin fingers."

"Who doesn't? Where is this person?"

"I don't. God, what a pain. And neither do you, Carrie—do you?"

I didn't answer.

"Do you?" she said again.

"It sounds a lot better than what I've got—a vegetable." I turned away and buried my face in my hands. How could I have said such a thing? How could I have *thought* it? After a moment I felt Jamie touch my shoulder.

"You didn't say that."

I looked up at her. "But I did."

She turned away sharply, and I felt a flash of rage at her. I wanted to prod her, make her call me on what I'd said, but when she looked back it was gone, she'd completely erased it.

"Care?" she said gently. "Do you want me to go to the hospital with you this afternoon? I could just wait in the lounge if you want to see him alone, and then afterward I'd be there if you felt like talking."

I shook my head. "I don't think so."

"You can call me anytime, you know," she said, frowning a little. "In the middle of the night or whenever."

"I know."

We sat in silence. I was just thinking of making an excuse to leave when she spoke again: "Was Roommate Dearest still on the phone?"

"Glued to it."

"Oh, honey," she said in a syrupy voice. "Roses. How—how original."

"You're just jealous."

"Uh uh, Todd's boring. I just hope she never figures that out."

"Not as boring as talking about him."

She shrugged.

"For that matter, why do we always have to talk about guys? *That*'s boring. I mean, here we are, we're smart, we must have something more we can talk about. Politics or books or the weather or something."

"How about men," she joked, but she looked hurt.

"Men are just guys with bad haircuts."

We both smiled, and there was my opportunity to leave. I set my glass on the tray and stood up. "I've got to get going," I said. "Thanks for lunch."

"Will you go tonight?"

I sighed. Sometimes, standing with Jamie at some party, or even just following her into a bar, I felt years too old for what I was doing, like a chaperone who'd rather be home in bed reading.

"I'm working till ten," she said. "Meet me here at ten-thirty and we'll do tequila shots first."

"I'll pass on the shots," I said. "But I'll come." I stood up and held out my hand, and after a moment she covered my palm with her own. I headed for my car. I was parked facing the wrong way, and when I pulled into her driveway to turn around, I saw that she'd already repositioned her chair so she could be seen by the guy in the yellow T-shirt.

THE HOSPITAL WAS crowded. Saturday afternoon, and people milled around, big multigenerational groups of them standing in clumps outside the gift shop, lining up at the florist's to buy stiff arrangements of carnations and baby's breath. I wandered past the cafeteria and looked in. GET WELL SOON read a Mylar balloon tied to a chair at an empty table. A heavy smell of gravy came from the kitchen. In one of the lobbies I sat on a tweedy couch and ended up staying for half an hour, thinking every minute that *now* I'd go. I counted five little boys with casts on their arms before I finally stood up.

On Mike's floor the blond nurse named Joan stood talking to Mr. and Mrs. Mayer. They were at the other end of the corridor from the elevator, standing in front of a glass-encased fire extinguisher. I started to duck down a hallway, but Mrs. Mayer looked up and saw me. "Carrie," she called, "the most wonderful news! Joan thinks Michael is going to wake up soon!"

"Actually . . ." Joan began, but Mrs. Mayer ignored her. She'd been wringing her sweater as if it were a wet towel, and now she tucked it under one arm, came and took hold of my elbow, and started walking me toward Mike's room.

"Joan's worked with a lot of head injuries," she said, "dozens of head injuries, and she's seen people with the exact same thing as Mike who just woke up one day and were—well, practically fine."

"I don't know," I said. "His neck—"

But she wasn't listening. "It all comes down to you and me, Carrie, because women are stronger. Do you understand? It takes *strength* to have hope." Abruptly she stopped walking and stared into my eyes. "Being hopeless is easy, Carrie. And you know who it hurts? Mike, that's who!" She shook her finger at me. "It hurts Mike! You don't believe me, but it's true."

Mr. Mayer came up and took her hand. "It's OK, Jan," he said. "It's OK." He looked at me, and an agreement of some kind passed between us, that soothing her was all that mattered right now. He said, "It's all right, Carrie. We're going out to Sears now before they close. We'll leave you to visit with Mike by yourself."

Mrs. Mayer looked hard at me while Mr. Mayer took her sweater and shook it, then draped it over her shoulders. Watching them walk away, I thought I'd never seen her so disturbed.

Joan came up and gave me an apologetic look. "My fault," she said. "I mentioned a boy we had in here last year who—"

"Don't worry about it," I said.

Mike's room was cold. His room was cold, his hands were cold, his feet were cold. Like on winter nights when he'd stay over: when he came back to bed from a middle-of-the-night trip to the bathroom, he'd hold his feet away from me, his knees, his frozen hands. But if I got up he'd let me touch him with my cold toes, he'd hold my feet between his legs to warm them. "So cold," he'd say, and he'd pull me close until I felt him all along the length of my body.

I stood at the foot of his bed. Next to the wall there was a slice of space a couple of feet wide, wide enough for a sleeping bag, and for a moment I imagined myself moving in, just a nightgown and a tooth-brush and some sad bribe for the nurses. We had never even gotten to live together, never even gotten to try it. Why had the prospect deflated? Why had I begun to cool?

I looked at him. I wanted to see everything there was to see, his arms slack at his sides, his closed eyes. One tube ran into his nose to feed him while another entered a bandage on his throat and brought him air. Two more went into his forearms, and under the cloth draped over his middle he was hooked to a catheter. Filling him and emptying him. They even shaved him, although not every day, and looking closer I saw that it had been three or four days: his beard was coming in striped by a surprising blond. Eight and a half years and I had never wondered how he would look with a beard, never wanted him to look any different at all. I had never really wanted him to be different. It was only myself who was wrong, who had changed somehow, *become* wrong—for him. For us.

4

~

STATE STREET WAS the center of Madison, a half-mile run of shops and restaurants that connected the university to the State Capitol. Closed to all traffic but buses, it was Madison's boulevard, its town square—the place you'd go when you didn't know where else to go. On Wednesday, done with work at five, I trudged past shop window after shop window, hungry for clothes, CDs, shoes, books—for things that I wanted to buy more than have. The sidewalks were crowded with UW students and high school kids, skateboarders flying by. I passed the street guitarist who played bad James Taylor, then the one who played bad Bob Dylan. I was in a funk, struggling over whether or not to call Jamie: Saturday night I'd backed out of going to the party at her neighbors' house, and we'd fought on the phone, a sullen exchange of resentments until, in a troubled voice, she said, "What's *with* you?" a question that I knew pertained not just to the present moment but to months and months.

I could have been honest with her. I could have said: *I don't know. Something. Help me.* But I didn't. Instead I asked her how she could even *wonder* such a thing, and we both hung up furious. That we still hadn't talked four days later was just about unheard of in our friendship, and as I walked I felt gloomy with guilt, certain I should call but equally certain I wouldn't. I didn't *want* to: didn't want to hear whether she'd gone to the party anyway; didn't want to hear about whatever had or hadn't happened with Drew, which would be exactly like something that had or hadn't happened with half a dozen other guys from her recent past.

After a while I came to Fabrications. It was the only boutiquey fabric store in town and it had prices to match, but I loved it, loved going in to wander among the Liberty cottons, to stand in awe before the wall of silks in the back. It was a quiet store, rarely populated by more than one other customer. I'd never bought more than a spool of thread.

From the sidewalk I looked in the window. There was a sleeveless blue dress hanging there, beautifully simple, with a square neckline and a nipped-in waist. The envelope for the pattern had been pinned to one shoulder, a Vogue pattern I'd used once. Through the window I couldn't really tell what the fabric was like, so I went inside and reached over the display ledge for a touch: it felt like silky tissue paper.

I turned around. The store was empty, not even a salesperson in sight, just bolt after bolt of gorgeous fabric. I breathed in deeply. Places like House of Fabrics and the Sewing Center smelled harsh from all the sizing, all the man-made fibers, but in Fabrications the only smell came from a bowl of potpourri on the counter at the cash register, its contents changed with the seasons. I crossed the store and looked into the bowl. Today it held dried peach pits, sprigs of rosemary, and slivers of a fragrant, spicy wood.

From the back room someone coughed, and I left the counter and approached the silks, columns of them on swinging arms. I found the blue of the dress and reached for the tag: thirty dollars a yard. At that price all I could make was a sash.

Yet I didn't turn away. The silks were exquisite: shiny satins and shimmering jacquards; colors clearer than cotton could ever be, subtler than wool. A pale gray shadow stripe suggested a coat dress with a notched collar; a brilliant black and red and gold print some kind of fluid pantsuit with a black camisole underneath. Who knew where you'd wear such a thing, it would be enough just to get the fabric home and touch it, work with it, be surrounded by it for a while.

Reluctantly I turned and left the store, the question of what to do next filling me with anxiety. Then I thought of Mike's brother, scooping ice cream a block farther up the street, and although I had no idea whether he'd be working or not, I headed that way.

It was six o'clock on a weeknight, but the place was jammed—people spoiling their dinners, or maybe having them. John was alone behind the counter, dressed in a blue-and-white striped shirt and a little paper hat, and he smiled when he saw me come in. I took my place at the end of the line and watched him work, admiring how calm he was despite the racket, the voices of all the people ahead of me bouncing off the black-and-white tile floor.

The crowd thinned out and finally it was my turn. "Dinner rush?" I said.

John laughed. "I guess. Personally, the idea of ice cream makes me want to puke."

"Nice."

Behind me there was a couple in navy blue business suits, the woman wearing a little scarf that made her look like a flight attendant. I said they could go ahead, and they moved forward and ordered: a single chocolate chip milkshake that John made in a big metal cup, the sound deafening while the ice cream churned. The store smelled of sugar cones, sweet and waffley. He poured the shake into a paper cup, and they paid and left.

Now we were alone, and John blushed a little, looking at me.

"Do I get a free one?"

"Sure."

"What do you recommend?"

"Bubblegum's popular." He pointed at the container: lots of pink bleeding around the gumballs. Next to it was something called Hawaiian Blue, which certainly was.

"Let's concentrate on the brown family," I said. "How about Toffee Crunch, how's that?"

He dipped a tiny plastic spoon into the ice cream and offered it to me.

I tasted it. "Sold."

"You mean given."

"Right."

He scooped the ice cream onto a cone and handed it over the counter. I licked it and looked at him. "How are things at home?" I said after a while.

He blushed again. "OK."

"Going to the hospital tonight?"

He grimaced. "I have to work too late." He put the scoop back in the water. "Are you?"

I shook my head. It wasn't something I'd decided against, but all at once I knew it was true: I wasn't going to go, I couldn't bear to go, and I felt terrified by the knowledge. What if I felt this way again tomorrow? And on and on?

John was waiting for me to say something.

"I just can't get myself to," I told him. "Do you know what I mean? I know I should. I *know* I should. But I just can't." I took a bite of ice cream, and suddenly tears massed in my eyes and then covered my cheeks, making the ice cream in my mouth feel painfully cold. John passed me a napkin across the counter and I handed him my cone, then dried my face and blew my nose. Here they were at last, my first tears since the accident, and it was shocking how little I felt: just the tiniest easing.

The door opened and a group of teenagers entered the store: boys in gigantic jeans cut off below the knee; girls in various examples of what I thought of as bra-strap dressing, tops and dresses that revealed the shoulder straps of black or light blue lingerie. "Eating on the job," one of the boys said to John, and I recognized him as one of John's friends.

"What's up," John said. He was blushing again.

"Ohhh," said another of the boys.

"Shut up." John handed me my cone and busied himself wiping down the counters.

The girls leaned against the ice cream case, ostensibly talking to each other but looking me over all the same. It was dispiriting to know I could pass for sixteen. I took a napkin from the dispenser and wrapped it around my cone. "Bye, John," I said. "Thanks."

When I was at the door he called my name, and I turned back. "I do know what you meant before," he said. "I do."

I waved and left. Walking by the wide glass windows, I saw the teenagers laughing and moving in to needle him. Then I felt the glow of Mike's accident coming back, and I knew that in a moment their faces would fall, that the teasing would dissolve when they learned who I really was.

WHEN I GOT home it was a little after seven, and visiting hours were still on. Mrs. Mayer was probably there, wondering where I was, and when eight o'clock came I started waiting for the phone to ring, for her to say again, in that casual voice, "Could you stop by tomorrow?" But nine came, and then ten, and the phone never rang.

The next day I had no trouble going. I got off work in the middle of the afternoon, and I went right over, spent an hour or so alone in the lounge and even got the full ten minutes for that hour in Mike's room, with no one else wanting part of it. He was on his stomach, and as I stood there looking at his bare back, at the familiar scatter of freckles across his shoulders, I thought I was OK, I thought I'd be able to return and return, without any more moments like I'd had in front of John Junior.

When I got home I fixed myself some iced cranberry juice and got ready to sew. I set up my machine and threaded it; I got out my iron, filled it with distilled water, and plugged it in; I took the fabric for my mother's kitchen curtains and set it in folded stacks on the table. But I couldn't get to work, and the reason was Mike's back.

I kept seeing it. The pale skin and the freckles, the wiry hairs: all as familiar to me as parts of my own body. There was the broadness of his shoulders, the wide, wide span of his upper back. And he had a place a little lower down that was strangely sensitive: the slightest pressure on it made him flinch, but not in pain—more as if he'd been tickled or poked. I thought of that place and wondered if it had been affected neurologically by the accident, and all at once I was brought up short by the fact of what had happened to him.

This is hard to explain. I knew what had happened to him—I was never far from the sight of it, especially compared to his mother, who at times seemed to keep the neck injury in a different compartment of her mind from the head injury, as if all he had to do was regain consciousness and then he'd be all right. But the idea of that place on his back opened up the whole geography of his body to me, and I felt physically bereft all at once, as if my body were only now catching up with my mind and understanding all it had lost. If he woke, how would he bear it? The diminishment, the dependence. How would he stand it? It was almost more daunting to consider that prospect than its opposite, that he wouldn't wake; wouldn't become, as the doctors put it, responsive again. But if he did, what about me? Would I become responsive again, too? Could I?

Early the previous summer, to celebrate graduating from college, we had gone to Chicago for a weekend, excited less because we'd finished school than because we were moving forward, taking a step: Mike's job at the bank would start when we got back, and I had the library until I knew what else I might want to do.

The hotel elevator was lined with smoky mirrors and we rode up looking at our reflections, Mike's arm around my shoulder, mine around his waist, two of my fingers tucked into his change pocket. The car clanked to a stop, and just before we got off Mike took a last glance at the mirror and said, "That guy's got it made." I didn't know it, but he had bought me an engagement ring the day before and carefully tucked it into his suitcase.

A sign pointed us down the hall, and we made our way to our room. The key was on a bulky plastic tag, and Mike fitted it into the lock and turned it until the door swung open. Inside, we saw the foot of the bed, and beyond that a window with filmy white curtains half-drawn across it. We stood there for a moment, and then—simultaneously, both of us acting at once—we turned toward one another, I lifted my arms, and Mike scooped me up and stepped over the threshold.

How does love change? How is it that I remember that day so clearly, Mike's smile as he dumped me on the bed, the little gray box that held the ring, even the peanuts we ate from the tray on top of the TV, never guessing we'd be charged four dollars for them? How is it that I can trace a line through eight years from one happy day to another but can't locate with any accuracy at all what happened to me next? A slow draining away of my feelings for him, a trickle I hardly noticed at first until the level was so low it was all I could notice, until what remained was dark and murky and it seemed that in no time at all I'd be bone-dry. We'd had dim times before, of course, but with quick, bright rescues: college and the notion of adulthood; my apartment and actually *sleeping* together, learning that that was something in itself, ultimately the most prized. In the months before the accident there was no rescue in sight. I couldn't decide if I *wanted* a rescue. On bad days it was as if I were looking through cold glass at the two of us together while with some kind of remote control I operated my body and my voice. On good days I did my best to ignore myself.

But Mike could tell—I knew he could tell. And sitting there in my apartment, unable to start on my mother's curtains, I desperately longed to undo so many things: my turning away from him; his awareness of it; his hurt and his pain; his fruitless efforts to woo me back. More than anything, I wanted to eradicate that final fruitless effort, the idea for which had overtaken him on the pier: that a playful gesture on his part, half foolhardy and half brave, could wake me to the old feelings at last.

5

~

VIKTOR AND ANIA lived on the other side of the isthmus from
me, near Lake Monona, on the second floor of a big pink stucco
house that had been divided into apartments. I parked under a
sycamore and left my windows open against the hot evening. Next
door, an oscillating sprinkler clicked tighter and tighter and then spun
out, throwing water in an arc across a wide lawn. I could smell someone's compost, the green, fertile scent of it.

All week at work Viktor had raved about the meal he and Ania were
going to make for me and the fun we were going to have, but he'd
never mentioned other guests, so I was surprised to see the table set
for six. I felt uneasy, thinking dinner was one thing, a dinner party
something else entirely. How could I be at a dinner party when Mike
was in the hospital? Why wasn't I at the hospital with him? Why
wasn't *I* the injured one, *he* the visitor? A panicky feeling rose in me,
and I fought to quell it. I forced myself to smile at Viktor. "Who else is
coming?"

"Carrie, you can't imagine." He shook his head mournfully. "Downstairs lives Tom, our neighbor, and we asked him to come, too. Now
he has called us one hour ago to say his brother from New York is

arriving tonight with a friend, and would we allow them as well? Of course I had to say yes." He raised his hands dramatically. "Tell me now, how is this called, is it called bold? Very bold?"

"It's pretty bold, all right. Forward, even."

"Forward, yes! You can't imagine Ania, she is quite put out."

"I am not quite put out," Ania called from the kitchen. I heard a thunk, as of an onion being split, and a moment later she came in, brushing furiously at her eyes. She was tall and broad-faced, the perfect match for him. "I am not quite put out and I am not crying—it's onion tears is all. Hello, Carrie. Viktor, you don't give her a drink?"

"I do," he said. "I do give her a drink."

"Give her one then. And she should sit in the rocking chair so she can see the lake out the window."

Tom turned out to be someone I'd seen on campus a number of times. He would have been hard to miss: tall and skinny, with a headful of unruly blond curls. He was in physics, working toward what he called "a degree so terminal few survive it." His brother looked like a toned-down Tom: not quite so tall, hair shading toward brown, someone whom it wouldn't have been hard to miss.

Tom and his brother were trailed by the brother's friend, a small, wiry guy in jeans and a gray T-shirt. His hands in his back pockets, he hung back a little, stayed quiet through the introductions. He was called Kilroy, though I didn't catch if that was his first or last name.

"So you're what, Czech?" he said to Viktor. Ania had returned to the kitchen, and the four guys were all still standing. Perched on the rocking chair, I wished they'd sit.

Viktor's jaw tightened. "I'm Polish," he said. Kilroy raised his eyebrows, and Viktor glanced at me, perplexed, then turned back. "You don't like Polish?"

"I 'like Polish' fine," Kilroy said. "It's just that I saw your name on the mailbox downstairs, so it didn't make sense."

Viktor looked offended. "Why not?"

"Because it would be Viktor with a W, wouldn't it? In Polish?"

Viktor colored slightly. "A linguist."

"Wiktor!" Tom had been studying a picture over the fireplace, but now he turned, grinning. "It suits you, buddy. Think I'll call you Wiktor from now on, what do you say?"

"Now you see why I have the spelling with a V," Viktor said to Kilroy.

I stood up and went into the kitchen for another beer. If I'd wanted to hear a pair of guys needling each other I could have hung out with the people I usually hung out with. The evening stretched ahead of me, pointless and unending. The only thing I felt like doing lately was sewing, and how much could I sew? Already my closet was full of things I didn't really need—things I didn't even really want. I'd spent most of the day on my mother's curtains, cruising down the long seams. What would I make once they were finished?

Ania was grating cheese, and she paused for a moment to look up at me. "The men are sniffing each other?"

"Too bad they can't just each pee in a corner and be done with it."

Back in the living room I found them all still standing, Tom and his brother off to the side looking at a book, Viktor glowering down at Kilroy. When he saw me he muttered something, then went into the kitchen.

I looked at Kilroy. He was about my height, 5'6", with a narrow, sharp-featured face and straggly brown hair.

He smiled. "I like your necklace."

Instinctively I reached up to touch it. "Thanks." It was just a silk cord that I'd strung with some odds and ends: a too-small ring and some old glass beads, plus a tiny seashell Mike had given me once. No one had ever commented on it before except Jamie, who'd said it looked like something someone's little sister might have made in art class.

"Did you make it?" he said.

"That authentic-looking, huh?"

"No, I like it." He shrugged. "It's pretty."

From the kitchen came the sound of Viktor and Ania talking in their own language, and after a moment Kilroy tilted his head in their direction and then raised his eyebrows at me. "Close friend of yours?"

"I just work with him." I felt myself blush a little, denying a stronger connection in order to look good for this guy.

"Where?"

"At the UW library. What do you do? In New York, I mean."

"I shoot pool."

"No, really."

"You don't like pool?" He shook his head. "You don't know what you're missing. Of course, it helps to have the right place to play. On Sixth Avenue right near my apartment there's a bar called McClanahan's with a pool table that's got a tiny little gouge in the felt right near one of the side pockets, and I'm such an accomplished student of that table that I can just about always make the gouge work for me."

He struck me as the kind of person who was always joking, who joked as a way of life, but still I said, "I meant, what do you do for work?"

He shook his head again. "Work is beside the point, as you'll learn someday when you're a little older."

I blushed again. "I'm older than I look." I lifted my beer and took a long swig, which made me look about twelve. "See how well I can drink beer?"

He smiled, but he was watching me closely, and now he said, "You're twenty-three, I'd say, give or take no more than a year. Right?"

I was taken aback. "Excuse me?"

"You're twenty-three, you've lived in Madison all your life. Let's see—you're engaged to marry your high school sweetheart, who couldn't come tonight because he's on a weekend fishing trip with his father." He tilted his head. "How'd I do?"

My heart was speeding wildly, and I didn't know what to say. Mike *could* have been on a weekend fishing trip with his father—it was something the two of them did once or twice a summer.

"Well?" Kilroy said.

"You weren't entirely wrong or entirely right."

He grinned. "I read minds, sideline to pool. So where'd I screw up—you're not from Madison?"

"I am."

"He's your *college* sweetheart?"

"What makes you so sure I'm engaged?"

He pointed at his own ring finger.

"He's both."

"But I was right about everything else?"

Ania came into the room then, a huge steaming pot in her mitted hands, and behind her came Viktor, carrying a bowl of salad. They put the food on the dining table, then turned to face us.

"Almost everything else," I said to Kilroy. "But not quite."

WHAT KILROY SAID haunted me all evening long. I was wearing something fairly bland, pistachio green linen pants and a white T-shirt, and I wondered how much that had guided him, how much the homemade necklace, how much the way I'd downed my beer. But what information could he really have gotten from any of that? How could he have known I was from Madison? Was there a never-left-home look about me? A never-left-home, never-moved-from-boyfriend-to-boyfriend, never-surprised-anyone look? In Viktor and Ania's little bathroom between dinner and dessert, I looked at myself in the medicine cabinet mirror. Dark hair, blue eyes, a longish neck that had embarrassed me once but that was fine now—enviable even, according to Jamie. I looked and looked, but I couldn't figure out what Kilroy had seen.

The next morning I woke with a headache. I'd stuck with beer while everyone else had drunk Viktor's Polish vodka, but I'd stuck with a little too much of it and I felt terrible. I drank a big glass of water before my shower and another after, and then it was time to go to Jamie's.

We'd made up by then, which was a good thing, since she was throwing a going-away brunch for Christine that morning. Christine was moving to Boston for graduate school, and although it seemed wrong for us to gather without Mike, we had to observe the occasion somehow.

Moving to Boston. I envied her.

On my way over I picked up some flowers for Jamie—gerbera daisies, which she loved. I say we'd made up, but actually our answering machines had: she'd called and left a *Just wanted to say hi, talk to you later* kind of message on my machine; then I'd called and said the same kind of thing to her machine; and by the time we actually connected we were able to chat about nothing for ten minutes, just the amount of time we needed to spend on the phone in order to feel that everything was OK, by which point it was.

It was Sunday morning and Miffland was quiet, sleeping off Saturday night. Across the street from Jamie's a shabby brown house had been extravagantly toilet-papered, streamers of it hanging from the peaked roof and festooning the maple tree in the front yard. I climbed the steps up to Jamie's porch and knocked. The yellow house next door reminded me of the party I hadn't gone to, of the guy Jamie'd been interested in.

"Fleurs!" she said when she opened the door. "Carrie, you doll."

"You like them?"

"I love them, obviously. Come on, come in."

She tucked a stray strand of hair behind her ear and then led me through the dining room, where the table was set with cloth napkins and a glass bowl of strawberries in the center. It was just like her to have everything ready, looking nice, and I felt a pang of regret. There'd been a time when I would have arrived early to help.

"It looks great in there, Jamie," I said once we were in the kitchen. "Christine'll be really happy."

"You think? It's not every day someone moves to Boston."

"Thank God, right?"

"At least it's not you."

"Why would I move to Boston?" I'd been standing across the room from her, and now I went over and put my hand on her shoulder. "I'm sorry about last week," I said quietly.

She turned and hugged me. "It's no biggie. Anyway, I'm sorry, too."

I thought of what she'd said, how concerned she'd sounded. She had no reason to be sorry.

"So did you go anyway?"

"To the party?"

"Duh."

A funny smile came over her face, and although I knew exactly where she was going, I had to ask. "And?"

"He passed out on my bed."

"Drew?"

"Approximately thirty seconds after we lay down. I didn't know what to do—I was on the verge of going to get his roommates to drag him home. I ended up sleeping on the couch. I mean, it's one thing sleeping next to someone after you've . . . you know. It's another to sleep next to a drunk you hardly know."

I didn't point out that she wouldn't have known him much better if they had made love. Fucked. Whatever.

"You'll never believe what happened the next morning."

"What?"

"I woke up to the sound of him puking his guts out in the bathroom. The door was open, and when he looked up and saw me standing there he tried to stand up, and he threw his back out!"

We both laughed hard. "That's priceless, Jamie. I can't believe you waited a week to tell me this."

She shrugged. It was I who'd waited a week to ask.

"Come on," she said. "I got stuff for Bloody Marys. Let's have one now, before everyone comes."

"Maybe we should just have Virgin Marys. We don't want to be trashed when they get here."

"Why not?" She crossed the old linoleum and yanked open a sticky plywood cabinet. She took out tomato juice, Tabasco, and Worcestershire sauce, then got a bottle of vodka from the freezer. "I'll make weak ones. They'll be here soon, anyway."

I watched her mix the drinks. She was so easy to win back, it made me feel like a monster. "Hey," I said, "did I ever tell you about the time my mother tried to order a Virgin Mary at brunch at the Edgewater?"

She looked up and smiled. Of course I had, but it was in the tradition of our friendship that stories be told and retold.

"She ordered a Bloody Virgin," I said, and when she broke into laughter I managed a laugh too, grateful, my face muscles only a little tight.

JAMIE HAD A typical Miffland dining room, with a pass-through to the kitchen, a bay window looking into the side yard, and a wall of built-ins, in this case a bank of drawers below a pair of glass-fronted cabinets that had been painted so often they no longer closed all the way. Jamie's parents had contributed an ancient dining room set they'd inherited from Jamie's grandmother, and once everyone arrived we settled into the heavy dark-wood chairs: Jamie at one end, Rooster at the other, and Bill and Christine opposite me and Stu.

"Stu," Rooster said over a third helping of eggs. "You're mine today."

Stu snorted. "You wish."

Jamie and I exchanged a glance. Rooster and Stu had a history of competitive eating that could be funny or irritating, depending on your mood. According to everyone but Rooster, it had started at Mike's ninth-grade birthday celebration, when they'd matched each other slice for slice through one and a half pizzas each. Rooster claimed it had started years earlier, over corn dogs in their grade-school cafeteria.

"I wish?" he said. "You haven't even finished your first piece of coffee cake. I've *got* today, which puts me at a hundred eighty-seven if you count the corn dogs."

"Wrong," Stu said. "A, you don't count the corn dogs, and B, *I've* got a hundred eighty-seven *not* counting today. You're down at a hundred sixty-two, which if you want to look at it logically is really twenty-five nothing, me." He turned to me. "He's always padding his stats and it makes me very angry."

I smiled. I thought of the night before, of Viktor and that guy Kilroy—at least Rooster and Stu liked each other, at least there was that. They ribbed instead of sparred. The one it bugged was Mike: "Those guys aren't nearly as funny as they think they are," he was always saying. He probably would have said it again on Memorial Day, on the way back from Clausen's Reservoir, if he'd driven me home: they'd gone on at some length about how many chips equaled a burger. But he hadn't driven me home: I'd sat in the back seat of Rooster's car holding hands with Jamie, none of us saying a word, and now, sitting in Jamie's dining room almost four weeks later, I realized that it had never occurred to me to wonder who'd gone back for Mike's car. I knew it was safely in the Mayers' garage, the old black 280 Z Mr. Mayer'd handed down to Mike, but I couldn't stop seeing it in the reservoir parking lot, coated with sand and dirt.

"Natural ability will always win over sheer bravado," Rooster said as he reached for more bacon. "Right, Carrie?"

Everyone was looking at me, and I shook the image of Mike's

car away and managed a lame smile. "You're both pretty impressive," I said.

"Which is a fancy word for fat," Bill added. "In case you guys were wondering."

Everyone laughed, and Bill smiled self-consciously and then reached over and put a hand on Christine's shoulder. They'd broken up and gotten back together so many times even they'd lost count, but now that she was leaving he seemed really sad. Spotting them coming up the walk earlier, Jamie had said, "The Beav looks grieved." He was good-looking—dark and lanky with a sexy silver stud in one earlobe—but he had buck teeth.

Rooster pushed back from the table. He stretched his legs to the side and patted his stomach. "The Spare Tire Spartans," he said. "Just like Mike said. I'll go on a diet when he wakes up."

Everyone was silent. From the living room I could hear the ticking of Jamie's cuckoo clock, a ridiculous Tyrolean thing for which she harbored a not-very-secret secret affection. Finally Stu said, "So, Boston, huh? You know they talk funny out there. 'Pack your cah in the Hahvid yad'—like that."

We all looked down for a moment, all of us but Rooster, who in the angry way he was looking at me when I looked up again told me what I already knew, that we were failing Mike by not talking about him.

"More strawberries?" Jamie said.

And Christine said, "I'll be packing my cah in the Tufts yad—until I'm so broke I have to sell it."

There was a little silence, and then Rooster relented. He smiled and said, "Just don't park illegally—they've got The Boot in Boston. Run out of time on your meter and they'll come along and immobilize your rear end."

"Ouch," Jamie said, giving her ass a pat.

"Actually," Stu said, "there's a paramilitary siege going on out there. Snipers on rooftops, tanks rolling down the streets. You'd be much safer right here in Wisconsin, dear, you really would."

"You guys," Christine said. "I'm really going to miss you."

Rooster shook his head. "Nah, you'll have a ball."

Bill winced. "That's what worries me."

It was almost three-thirty, and we'd been sitting for a long time.

Jamie stood up and began to clear, and I stretched my arms over my head and yawned, then rose to help her. Carrying plates away from the table, I thought that with Christine gone, Bill would probably fade from the picture: he was already the most peripheral member of the group—last to join, via his relationship with Christine, but also somewhat retiring, more observer than participant. Whenever I ran into him alone I felt awkward, nothing much to say without the group's chatter to oil my tongue.

"Let's do something," I said to Jamie in the kitchen. "All of us. Go rent sailboards or play volleyball or something."

"Make like a beer commercial? I could get into that."

We started back out to where the others were, but the phone rang just as we reached the doorway. "Go ahead," Jamie said. "I'll be right there. I vote sailboards."

I found them sitting in silence, all looking stupefied except Rooster, who'd gotten a second wind and was busy with the remains of the coffee cake.

"Perk up, guys," I said. "The day is young. What do you say to a little sailboarding?"

"We could," Christine said, and then Jamie was gripping my arm.

"It's for you," she said. "The phone. Mrs. Mayer."

6

~

MIKE HAD WOKEN up, and now I cried freely. I cried when I hung up the phone, I cried when I felt Jamie's arms around me, and I cried as everyone came into the kitchen and hugged me, Rooster tightest of all. After Mike dove, the circles on the reservoir had widened exactly in time with my growing sense that something was terribly wrong. The relief I felt now was explosive, like the sudden surfacing of someone from under water, sprays shooting everywhere.

Rooster drove me to the hospital and I kept crying, leaning against the window and looking out at the quiet day. "It's OK," Mrs. Mayer said when we'd arrived at the Intensive Care lounge and I'd flung myself into her arms—so glad he'd woken, so glad I was glad. "It's OK."

Dr. Spelman came in a little later. He was the neurosurgeon, and his cool detachment had us all cowed, even Mr. Mayer. He stood in the lounge doorway, his name in black script above the breast pocket of his white coat, and he talked about caution, about how much we still didn't know. "We need to watch him very closely," he said.

I sat beside Mrs. Mayer, listening as intently as I could when all I really wanted was to leave them where they were and run to Mike's room. I wanted his eyes on mine, just the sight of his open eyes again, but the Mayers had been in with him for nearly an hour and now we had to wait.

"That's number one," Dr. Spelman said. "Number two is this, and I know it'll sound obvious, but you'd be surprised how hard a thing it is to keep in sight. You've been waiting and worrying for four weeks, and now that he appears to be resuming consciousness, you're understandably thrilled. The last thing *he* knew, he was having fun with his friends. You can't expect him to be happy or relieved or grateful to find himself alive."

"He's waking up to bad news," Mr. Mayer said. "Even though his waking up is good news."

"Well put," the doctor said.

Mrs. Mayer nodded eagerly. "Thank you so much, doctor. We can't tell you how grateful we are."

Dr. Spelman smiled. "Don't thank me," he said. "I didn't have a thing to do with it."

When he was gone Mrs. Mayer took my hand and held it, the fingers of her free hand busy stroking my knuckles. "I had this feeling last night, after we left," she said. "I think even yesterday he was starting to come out of it. Did you notice? I thought he seemed a little lighter."

I shook my head as another sob made its way up through my chest. I felt sick from all the crying, but calmer, too, convinced I'd been under something heavy myself, a spell of numbness, even apathy. Now everything was different. It was over. He was going to make it. I put my face in my hands and wept.

When we were allowed back in, the Mayers told me I could go alone if I wanted, or with Rooster, but I wanted Mrs. Mayer with me.

Mike lay on his back, no change apparent from my previous visit. The ventilator whooshed and sighed, whooshed and sighed. His arms and legs were heavy and pale, and his eyes—his eyes were closed.

"He's sleeping," Mrs. Mayer whispered. "Really sleeping. It's normal."

I nodded.

"We're going to turn the den into a bedroom for him," she said. "Because of the stairs."

I felt new tears stream down my face, and without looking at me she took my hand. "There's the TV already in there, and we'll hook up his stereo, too. Maybe we'll have to build a new bathroom. His dad thinks we should wait and see, but we have to be ready *before* Michael is."

"That's true," I said.

"Mike," she said. "Michael."

At first I thought I was imagining it, but his eyelids fluttered a little and then opened. He looked straight at me, his gray eyes surprisingly clear. Could he see me? See anything? His eyes closed again, and he slept.

FOR THE NEXT several days I went to the hospital whenever I could—before work, after work, sometimes, almost guiltlessly, during work, explaining to Miss Grafton that I'd be right back and then vanishing for an hour. Sometimes he never opened his eyes while I was there, but at others he seemed quite alert, seemed to recognize me, and I began to talk to him—just "Mike, it's me," and "I love you," and "Everything's going to be OK."

The doctors tested him. They searched for sensation and motion, for reflexes, but below the chest it was as if he were dead. "At least the injury happened at the lower part of the cervical spine," one doctor said. "At least he'll be able to breathe on his own."

And it was true. Although I felt there was some faulty logic in being glad about any of it, the word "quadriplegic" encompassed situations that were far worse than Mike's. "Think of it this way," said another doctor. "With an injury at the C5–6 level he's technically a quadriplegic, but he'll function like a paraplegic without hands." I understood what he meant—that Mike would be able to use his shoulders and upper arms, that with mechanical devices strapped to his forearms he'd be able to manipulate things—but I couldn't banish the gruesome image: Mike with his hands chopped off, blood pouring from the stumps.

"You hurt yourself," we told him. "Remember the reservoir? You dove and hit your head." It was terrible to see the anguish on his face, terrible not to know how much he understood. The breathing tube prevented him from speaking, so even once he was more alert he couldn't ask questions. One doctor told him she'd pinch the tube closed for a moment so he could speak around it, but when the time came the noise he made was unintelligible, a whispered note of misery, a cry for help without words.

Finally the Mayers decided he had to hear it all, a full description of the accident and what it had done to him. We agreed that I would wait in the lounge, then go in afterward. Visiting hours hadn't officially started yet, and I had the place to myself. Out in the corridor, nurses in white passed by, orderlies in blue. Finally Dr. Spelman strode past, heading for Mike's room, and I understood that at that moment Mike knew: the Mayers had asked the doctor to let them tell Mike what he'd lost, but they wanted him to explain how Mike might be able to get a little of it back—surgery to fuse his cervical spine, and then months and months of in-hospital rehab.

The idea of Mike lying there *knowing*. My eyes filled, and I stood up and began pacing, fighting hard not to cry again. I'd once read an article that said women could be divided into two groups: those who feared they'd wind up bag ladies, ranting on street corners, and those who feared they'd end up in mental hospitals, crying uncontrollably. Now I knew which group I belonged to.

A little later, Dr. Spelman appeared at the entrance to the lounge. He came in and looked at me uncertainly, then suggested we sit down. "I've just been with Mike," he said. "He's very strong, your boyfriend. We're going to move ahead on the cervical fusion." He paused, and I wondered why he'd come in to talk to me; we'd never spoken privately before, and I was surprised he even knew who I was.

"I'm glad I saw you in here," he continued. "It's premature to think too far ahead, but here you are, so I'll break my own rule. You're the person Mike seems most concerned about, most aware of. The nurses have noticed that he's a lot more alert after your visits than after his parents', say. And just now he seemed to want to know where you were."

"We're engaged," I said.

"Except that everything's changed now, although that can be hard to keep in sight sometimes. I'd counsel you to go very gently these next few months. Rehab is very hard work—a lot of getting better is wanting to."

He stood up and cleared his throat, and I felt my face burning; my fingers were actually shaking. As he walked away I imagined my own outraged voice calling after him. *You don't know a thing about me,* it said. *Not one single thing.*

I stood up and headed for Mike's room. Just outside, I paused for a moment and looked in. Mrs. Mayer stood at the foot of Mike's bed, looking flushed but composed, but Mr. Mayer was weeping—sitting in the one chair, his glasses askew in his lap, his big hands cupped over his eyes. I stepped in and they all looked at me. Immediately Mike began blinking furiously, and I squeezed past Mr. Mayer and stood over him.

I'm sorry, he mouthed. His gray eyes were hard on me, moving over my face, looking and looking for where I was now. Where, given what had happened to him? Where, given the months beforehand?

Forget all of that, I longed to say—but not in front of his parents. And how to retract something I'd never spoken in the first place? Remorse boiled through me, but I couldn't dwell on it now. I stepped forward and touched his forearm, then moved my fingers around to where he had some sensation. I stroked his skin. "Don't worry," I said. "I love you, don't worry." And grateful relief filled his pale face, coloring his cheeks and outlining his dry lips.

THE DAY OF the surgery arrived. From movies and TV I had an image of efficient bustle, all those people in masks and gowns; that fell apart when I heard Mr. Mayer talking about whether they'd go in from the front of Mike's neck or the back. Knives cutting him open, his blood spilling . . . It was unbearable. *Don't touch him,* I wanted to shriek. I knew the anesthetic was a risk in itself, but at least it would calm his terror.

We had one last vigil, this time near the OR. The Mayers, Rooster, and I. Finally, after almost three hours, Dr. Spelman came in and said, "It's over. Everything went smoothly. He's in recovery." And we bowed our heads and wept, each one of us.

Only one person was allowed in and his mother insisted, so it was the next morning before I could see him. He was back in Intensive Care for one last day of observation, and as I made my way down the familiar corridor I realized this could be my last time here. The ring of cubicles, the nurses' central work area, the hushed busyness and gravity surrounding the treatment of serious illness—it was a world I'd never expected to know, let alone so intimately.

I reached Mike's cubicle and stepped in. He lay flat on his back, his head encircled by a steel band that had been attached to his skull with screws; taut struts joined the band to a bulky sheepskin vest he wore. "Oh, my God," I heard myself say.

Mr. and Mrs. Mayer were nowhere to be seen, but Julie and John Junior were there, and they turned at the sound of my voice, exactly as Mike's eyes found me.

"That's the halo," Julie said flatly.

The halo—the device to keep his neck from moving postsurgery. Somehow I'd expected something less medieval-looking: something more like a halo.

"Hi," I said, and as I moved closer to him I felt something falter in me, some kind of courage or resolve. He looked somber, his face full of shadows. "How—" I said. "I—" My mouth was like cotton. "How do you feel?"

He licked his lips. "My head hurts," he said hoarsely.

I nodded, and it was a moment before I realized: he'd spoken. The tube in his throat was gone. The ventilator was off, its hiss extinguished. "You're talking," I said. "You're off the ventilator?"

He didn't answer, and Julie said, "They're weaning him off it, a little at a time."

"You're an angel, Mike," John Junior said. "Get it? The halo?"

Mike remained impassive, and I saw Julie give John a little kick. "My throat hurts," Mike said after a moment. "I'm thirsty."

I looked at Julie. "Can he drink?"

She shrugged.

"I'll go see if you can have something to drink," I said. "I'll be right back, OK?"

He was watching me carefully, his eyes wide and glassy. "Don't."

"I'll go," Julie said quickly, and once she was gone he closed his eyes; when he opened them again, they'd gone dull.

In a few minutes Julie came back, followed by a nurse I'd never really talked to; she had an angry look on her face. "What are you doing?" she demanded, and for a second I wasn't sure whom she was addressing—she was looking straight at Mike. "One of you has to go. Now."

The three of us glanced at each other. Since Mike's awakening, the two-people-at-a-time rule had been relaxed, along with the ten-minutes-per-hour rule. Joan had told us they'd rather Mike had someone with him, even if it meant shooing us out for procedures.

"He hasn't even been out of surgery twenty-four hours," the nurse said. "Let's give him a rest." She went and stood over Mike. "Ten more minutes, then you're back on the vent." She turned back to us. "I'll be back in a minute and one of you better be gone." She stalked out of the room, her white shoes squeaking on the floor.

"Bitch," Julie said.

I turned to Mike and smiled. "I'll come back later, OK? In a few hours?"

"Don't go."

Julie picked up her purse. "We'll go." She adjusted the strap on her shoulder and looked meaningfully at John. "Mom and Dad'll be back soon, Mike, OK?"

John followed after her but then lingered at the door. "Can you have ice cream? I could bring you some later if you felt like it."

I looked at Mike. "Would you like that?" I said, my voice false and bright. "Butter pecan?"

But he didn't respond—he just watched until John had disappeared.

I looked at the screws going into his head, then quickly looked away. It was important to talk to him, but what could I say? He didn't care about ice cream. Or how hot it was outside, or any stupid thing I could think of. *Everything's going to be OK.* It wasn't.

He made a noise in his throat, as if he were trying to clear it but couldn't very well. "Could you kiss me?" he said.

I was stunned.

"I wish you would kiss me," he went on, "Carrie." And it was only then, when he said my name, that the real, long-missing sound of his voice finally reached me, his distinctive, low voice, which had been silent so long. Tears streamed from my eyes. How was it that I hadn't thought about his voice at all, hadn't missed it?

He was waiting, and I wiped the tears away with the sides of my forefingers, then dried my hands on my pants. I lowered my face but then stopped, unsure how to avoid the halo. What would happen if I touched it—would it hurt him? Slowly, carefully, I pressed my mouth to his cheek, then pulled away.

He had pursed his lips and was holding them together. He stared into my eyes until I bent again and pressed my lips to his. I was about to straighten up when I felt his tongue against my mouth, soft and warm and infinitely familiar.

7

~

FOUR DAYS LATER Mike started rehab, and suddenly everything was different, down to the tiniest detail, down to the *wallpaper*—in the rest of the hospital it was covered with yellow and peach flowers, but here there were teal and raspberry streaks, as if cool tones might help soothe the agony of fighting your body. Here the nurses wore pantsuits and were brisk and businesslike, even a bit military. "Let's go," they'd say, and there'd be no time for protest, they'd have you going, whether it was into your wheelchair, onto your other side, or up to eat.

Rehab was exhausting. Evenings, if he had the energy, Mike told us about it: the tilt table he had to lie on to prepare for sitting up; the range of motion exercises they put his limbs through—rotations and flexions and extensions; the rigorous program of weight shifts and more weight shifts to protect his skin from pressure sores; the assisted coughing, where a nurse would press on his chest while he exhaled. It was like a full-time job, and he hadn't even gotten onto the mats yet, hadn't even started occupational. Sometimes he seemed so overwhelmed he couldn't even talk. He'd just lie there while we chatted with each other, his face drawn with fatigue.

I slipped into despair. I couldn't help it: he was never going to walk again. He was going to live life from a wheelchair—*watch* life from a wheelchair. I showed up to visit, but it was hard for me to talk, hard to smile. I did talk, I did smile—but I felt fake. At home afterward, I sat still for hours sometimes. Or I sewed.

The Saturday of Paddle 'n' Portage came, and Jamie arranged for us to meet Rooster and Stu there. I had no desire to go, but I also had no desire not to, so I agreed.

She picked me up at my apartment and we walked over to James Madison Park. Paddle 'n' Portage was a Madison tradition, a yearly canoe-cum-footrace that drew competitors from all over the Midwest, serious athletes and weekend runners, hundreds of people ready to paddle halfway across Lake Mendota and back; then to run *carrying their canoes* up the hill, halfway around the Capitol, and down the other side; and finally to paddle another course on Lake Monona.

Rooster and Stu had staked out a picnic table. The park was beyond crowded, all the contestants plus the observers, bikes tangled against trees, kids running around with bottles of water to offer up once the race was on. Near us, two men stretched on the browning grass, while just beyond them a woman offered an open tin of sunscreen to her partner, who dipped his finger in and smeared neon yellow on his nose. There were dozens of canoes on the small beach.

Jamie planted her hands on her hips and surveyed the crowd. "Check out that one," she said eagerly.

"The blond guy?" Stu said with a smile.

"His *canoe*," she said, giving him a swat. "It's really cool."

A voice over the loudspeaker announced that the first heat was about to go, and Jamie and I climbed onto the picnic table so we could see. A gunshot sounded, and the canoes hit the water, thirty or forty of them, their destination a sailboat anchored off Picnic Point. We watched them moving across the water, but after a while it got hard to see who was winning and soon even to know who was still heading away and who had already turned back.

"Why do I forget binoculars every year?" Stu said.

"Why do I come every year?" Jamie countered. She climbed down and sat on the table, her feet on the bench. After a moment I sat, too, fanning myself against the heat. It was already at least ninety.

"I'm bored," Jamie said. "Let's do something, let's go to Chicago."

"What, now?" I'd been planning to head for the hospital after the race.

Jamie shrugged. "Why not?"

Stu laced his fingers and stretched his arms over his head. "It's not a bad idea," he said. "Three hours in an air-conditioned car sounds good no matter what's on the other end."

Jamie nodded, eager now. "We could hang out at Water Tower for a while and then get pizza or something and drive back."

"Hanging out at Water Tower," Stu said. "That sounds suspiciously like shopping to me." He turned and looked at Rooster. "What do you say? We could check out a movie or something, then meet these guys for pizza after."

Rooster had been watching me closely, standing there with one foot on the picnic bench, his elbow on his knee. Now he straightened up. "I don't think so."

"Why not?" Jamie cried.

"Because of Mike?" he said. "Remember him?" Glaring at me, he said, "I can't believe you were even *thinking* about it."

"I wasn't," I said, but in fact I had been: thinking less about Chicago than about the freeway, farmland racing by while someone else punched the search button on the car radio. What was *wrong* with me?

Jamie bit at the edge of a fingernail. She pressed her lips together, then let them go again. "Maybe we should all do something tonight anyway. Have pizza or whatever. After the hospital. I think we should."

Rooster shook his head.

"Why?"

"I have a date."

"A date?" Stu said. "Call the papers, it's a miracle."

"Shut up," Rooster said, but he was smiling suddenly, his teeth white against the pink of his face.

Jamie leaned forward. "With?"

"Joan," he said.

I looked at Jamie, then Stu. "Nurse Joan?" I said. "From Intensive Care?"

He nodded.

I couldn't believe it. Joan had to be at least thirty, and then there were her looks: that fragile pale skin and her long blond hair and her height. Rooster's usual date was the kind of girl who'd be cast as the loyal best friend in a movie, not exactly pretty but spunky and with a bit of a mouth, which was where things generally went wrong as far as Rooster was concerned. Actually, his usual date was no one.

People around us moved toward the shoreline, yelling and cheering, and Jamie and I climbed back onto the table to see over the crowd. I thought of the bitter look Rooster'd given me about Chicago, and though it terrified me, I had to ask myself: would I have gone with Jamie and Stu if he hadn't been there to stop me?

"Go!" Jamie yelled. "Go!"

"Who are you yelling for?" I asked her.

"No one," she admitted.

The first two guys were out of their canoe and running with it before I'd even seen them stop paddling. They'd inverted the boat so they were holding it over their heads, and they'd taken off, one in front of the other, legs pumping.

"Mike and I were going to do it this year," Rooster said suddenly. "We were going to surprise you guys."

I looked down at him. Sweat dripped down his flushed face, held his light blue polo shirt to him in damp patches.

"What?" he said. "We were. You know Mike—the man with the plan? He made a training schedule for us. He printed up a copy for me, must have been early last fall. We were going to start with running, then do weights. You know how he is, he had the whole thing figured out. We were going to buy a used canoe as soon as the lake thawed."

I hadn't heard a word about it, but it didn't surprise me. Rooster was right: Mike was persistence itself. If he'd decided to do Paddle 'n' Portage, he'd have done everything in his power to prepare himself for it. It wasn't about competition, though he could be fiercely competitive; it was more a way of looking at life. A style of thinking. It was never too soon to plan something, and the more details you could nail down, the better. That weekend we went to Chicago after graduating from the U, he must have figured out options for every hour. "And what kind of candy are you going to get at the late-afternoon movie on Sunday?" I joked on the drive down. "Raisinets, of course," he said with a smile. He didn't mind being teased. It was sort of like how he teased me about my memory, but in reverse. For him, it was all about the future. For me, the past.

"So why didn't you?" Stu said.

Rooster stared at me. "Mike dropped the idea," he said, shrugging as if it were all a mystery to him. Then he shrugged again, and all at once I was afraid: he was *acting* baffled, but something was coming.

"He just dropped it?" Stu said. "Doesn't sound like Mike."

"Well," Rooster said, "I think there was something else on his mind. I think he was actually really *worried* about something."

My face filled with heat. This couldn't be happening. After a moment I got off the table and walked away. Free of the crowd, I stopped and leaned against a tree. The bark felt rough under my thin T-shirt. I looked out at the lake, Picnic Point across the water, the anchored sailboat that marked the turning-around point of the race.

"He's sorry," Jamie said. She'd come to stand in front of me, her fingernail at her mouth again. "He really is, Care. Look at him."

Rooster was sitting at the table now, his forehead resting on his palms.

"Let's *us* do something tonight," she said. "Go to a girl movie and then stop off somewhere for huge, disgusting sundaes. After you visit Mike—what do you say?"

I looked at her: at the strands of hair by her face, at the wrinkle of concern across the bridge of her nose. She wore a flirty, backless sundress, and I felt touched by her, by how clear she was to me—how she wanted to look cute and available, how she wanted to help me.

"Please?" she said.

"I don't think so."

Small lines appeared by the sides of her mouth. "Well, will you come and watch the end of the race with me? Without those guys?"

I reached for her hand and laced my fingers between hers. "I can't," I said. "I really can't. Just go with them, OK? And I'll call you tomorrow?"

She frowned and looked away.

"First thing tomorrow," I said. "I promise."

ONCE THEY'D LEFT, I went back to the picnic table and sat down.
I watched the end of the first heat and then the beginning of the second—watched without watching. The future and the past. I couldn't
think about the former, and the latter was a minefield of old pleasures
and regrets. I remembered the night before the accident, Mike lying
on my couch in old gym shorts while I made dinner. From my tiny
kitchen I could see him perfectly: drinking a beer, scratching his balls
if he felt like it, flipping through a magazine. Flicking the TV on with
the remote. Flicking it off. And what was I doing? Washing lettuce,
peeling a cucumber, checking the baked potatoes, forming hamburger into patties so he could carry them down to the hibachi on the
driveway and grill them. And hating myself because none of it felt
right anymore. For so long I'd thought of him as necessary, ballast
that would keep me safe. Now the ballast was holding me down, holding me *back*—I wanted lightness, freedom. I started crying and he
was off the couch and holding me in a minute, and I hated that, too,
the easiness of it, the false comfort. I couldn't stand how clearly I
could see from one week into the next, and years down the line.

The stragglers of the second heat were coming in and dragging
their canoes out of the water, and I stood up and started walking away.
I thought of Mike planning to enter the race, and all at once I remembered him sitting on the seat of a rowboat at Lake Superior one summer, oars crossed over his tanned legs, and the particular, private
smile he gave me as I came down the dock to join him. I closed my
eyes and I was practically there, at Lake Superior, the sun shining
through leaves to dapple the floor of the boat and Mike's legs. I felt
the boat tip as I climbed in, smelled the warm-water smell, greenish
in the August heat. A bird trilled and then fell silent. Something bothered me, though, and gradually, with great resignation, I understood
what it was. Another memory pressing in, of the night before the accident: he left right after our silent dinner, and in bed later, alone, I
hated him for that, too.

A guy was coming toward me with a cautiously friendly look on his
face, as if he thought he knew me but wasn't sure. He had light brown

hair and wire-frame glasses, and he wore a retro shirt, burgundy and cream nylon in wide vertical stripes. "Carrie? Carrie Bell?"

I nodded, and he gave me a wide smile. "It's Simon Rhodes. From Mrs. Eriksson's French class, in twelfth grade?"

I clapped a hand to my mouth. "I'm so sorry. Simon, you look totally different. You look great," I added, and he laughed before I had time to be embarrassed.

"I look human. I decided to sacrifice my beauteous locks for a more up-to-date look."

At seventeen he'd hidden behind a curtain of hair. He sat a few rows over from me, spent whole class periods doodling in a notebook. Walking by his desk once on my way to conjugate some verbs on the blackboard, I glimpsed a caricature of Mrs. Eriksson that was so cuttingly accurate I could never really look at her in the same way afterward.

"What's up?" I said to him now. "How are you? Do you still live in Madison?"

He shook his head. "New York. I'm visiting the 'rents." He turned and watched a couple of middle-aged men trudge by with a canoe. "What exactly is going on here, anyway?"

I laughed. "Paddle 'n' Portage, don't you remember?"

"Paddle 'n' what?"

"Portage." I said it again, with a French accent: "Por-tahj."

"Ah, por-tahj. As in carry." He laughed a little. "So why aren't you doing it?"

"Huh?"

"Well, you're pretty much destined for it, aren't you? Carrie—as in carry?"

I laughed, but I thought of Mike and Rooster's name collection, then of Rooster at the picnic table with his head in his hands.

"So tell me," he said. "What ever happened to Carrie Bell? *Dis-moi ce que tu fais maintenant.* Are you still in touch with Jamie Fletcher? I seem to recall a certain inseparableness."

"She was just here," I said. "Twenty minutes ago."

"And Mike Mayer? Cutest couple in the senior class?"

I blushed: even then it had made me cringe. The yearbook staff had made us pose for a picture, and it was the only picture of the two of us I didn't like—holding hands and looking moony. Mike thought it made us both look retarded.

"We're engaged," I told Simon.

"When's the happy day?"

I looked at the lake. A last couple paddled their canoe along the shoreline, evidently just for fun. I watched them stroke, the guy in back, a black nylon tank shirt falling from his muscled shoulders.

"Carrie?"

I turned back. "Mike's in the hospital. He was in a diving accident six weeks ago and he broke his neck."

"Oh, my God," Simon said. "I'm so sorry."

"Thanks."

We stood there without saying any more for what seemed like an age. The park was emptying, the last spectators climbing the hill to watch the last competitors row on Lake Monona. Simon toed the grass with his shoe, a snazzy black fisherman's sandal with a tire-tread sole. Finally, I couldn't stand it anymore.

"I should get going."

"Are you on foot?" He hesitated, the look on his face saying he didn't want to intrude. "We could walk together."

"OK," I said, though I didn't know where we'd go, or what we'd say, or why I was agreeing. I thought for a moment and then tipped my head in the direction of Mansion Hill. We started off, walking side by side, both of us silent. At North Pinckney we turned and headed up the hill. The mansions were mostly pretty shabby, huge brick or stucco structures cut into student apartments, but then we turned again and came upon the beautifully maintained one that was Madison's swankiest small hotel—the place where Mike had always said we'd spend our wedding night, then get on a plane the next morning and fly to the Caribbean. Walking past, I thought of how nice it used to feel to hear him talk like that, and then about how he was probably watching the clock from his hospital bed, waiting for me to arrive.

We wound up walking down Langdon, past the Deltas and the Epsilons—Greek row. I couldn't count the number of parties I'd been to there, the number of times I'd stood in one of those frats holding a plastic cup of beer, no way to move because there were so many people so close.

"So where'd you go to college?" I said.

He looked embarrassed. "Yale."

"Excuse me."

"At least I didn't say 'a little school in Connecticut,' as certain of my acquaintances have been known to do."

"At least there's that."

We both smiled, and he tipped his head toward the building we were passing. "You went here?"

"Alas."

"Were you in a sorority?"

"Please—I would've had to have dyed my hair blond and had half my brain cells surgically removed. Actually, Mike rushed, but then at the last minute he pulled out. His dad was really into it, but Mike realized he'd be living with a bunch of guys out of *Animal House* and he decided no way. He lived at home all four years."

"I'm always doing that," Simon said. "Rushing around and then changing my mind about all kinds of guys."

I studied him, his face still and serious. "Are you gay?"

He nodded.

"Are you out?"

"You mean with my parents?" He grinned. "I broke the news last summer, right after graduation. 'Thanks for flying all the way out here, Mom and Dad. Oh, by the way—I'm gay.' Actually it doesn't seem to bother them much. I'm the youngest of six and I think they're just glad to be done paying college tuition. They're very mellow these days. My father says to me this morning, 'Well, Simon, are you enjoying your social life?' Which is about the closest he's ever come to asking any of us if we were getting any."

I smiled. "It sounds like you get along OK with them. Did you ever think of moving back here?"

He stopped walking. "Look at this." He held his arms aloft and twitched them back and forth, shaking his head violently. "That's me shuddering at the thought."

We found a shady table on the Union terrace, and we sat and

talked—through two cups of coffee each, and then sandwiches, and then ice cream cones. I found myself telling him more than I'd told anyone else: about my slow cooling toward Mike before the accident, my horrible numbness afterward, the despair I felt now.

"What are you going to do?" Simon said.

"What do you mean?" I asked, though I knew: Was I going to be strong and good? And devote myself to Mike? Or wasn't I? A feeling of tightness in my chest that it was even a question. Of course it wasn't a question! But it *was.* I thought of Rooster again, all the looks he'd given me: at the hospital, at Jamie's, earlier today. He knew it was a question. I remembered the day the Mayers explained the accident to Mike and I went in afterward. *Don't worry,* I'd told him. What had I promised? The tightness in my chest increased, and I exhaled hard to try to get rid of it.

"I don't know," I told Simon.

He shook his head. "I can't even imagine. You must be in such pain."

I nodded and tears stung at my eyes, but rather than look away he continued to look at me, his face full of compassion. We'd been at the same school for four years, but he was a stranger. So many people I hadn't known, hadn't bothered with. I'd gone through high school never thinking about other possibilities, other choices.

"I hope you won't think this is weird," he said, "but I'm really glad I ran into you today."

"I am, too."

We'd been sitting for hours and it was obviously time to leave. We pushed back from our table and strolled through the Union, then said goodbye out front. I felt open and elevated—more like the person I wanted to be than I'd felt in months.

I watched him cross the street, then called his name.

He turned and smiled, the sun glinting off his glasses.

"I like your shirt!" I yelled.

It was after three, past time for me to go to the hospital. I started toward home. I walked back up Langdon, back down Mansion Hill. James Madison Park looked trampled after the morning's activity.

The sun had moved behind the highest branches of the sycamore outside my living room window, and my apartment was fairly cool. I drank a glass of ice water and then took off my shoes and settled on the couch. My feet were striped with dirt from the straps of my sandals, but I didn't get up to wash them. On the coffee table a thick issue of *Vogue* sat waiting, and after a while I picked it up and opened it. I'd never really read the articles before, except the ones about movie stars, but now I turned to the beginning and decided to read instead of just looking at the pictures. There was an article about two women designing sportswear out of a loft in New York, another about a textile factory in Italy. I could read, take a shower, eat the watermelon I'd bought the day before. Sit outside when my porch fell into shade. The day would go by whether I went to the hospital or not.

8

I HAD DESK DUTY at the library on Monday. It was the most boring part of my job, and I usually had a crossword puzzle to work on when no one was looking, or a magazine tucked into a partly closed drawer. Today it was a magazine. I was reading covertly, and keeping an eye on the closed door behind which Miss Grafton sat, when Rooster came in at a little after twelve-thirty, his suitcoat in a bundle under his arm. He stood just inside the double doors until he saw me at the desk, then he marched over and said, "We have to talk."

I glanced around and put a finger to my lips.

"Don't shush me," he said evenly. "I drove all the way up here, I had to park on the top level of the ramp, I have exactly twenty-six minutes to eat and get back—so please don't shush me."

Everyone in the rare books room was looking at us. "I'm working," I said. "My break's not till three. I'm sorry."

"Ten minutes," he said. "Five—just walk out into the hall with me."

Miss Grafton had opened her door at the first sound of his voice, and now she walked across the room, her heels clicking on the linoleum. "You may go," she said in a low voice. "I'll sit here until you return."

"I'm really sorry," I said. "This'll never happen again."

I got my purse from the staff room and headed for the door, looking back just in time to see Miss Grafton pull open the desk drawer and withdraw my *Harper's Bazaar*—not, alas, one of the periodicals housed on the shelves of the rare books room.

"Great," I said to Rooster when the double doors had swung shut behind us. "There goes my job."

But he didn't respond. Several paces ahead of me, he led the way down to the ground floor and out of the library, not looking back once. Finally he stopped and leaned against the building. We were on a wide, empty plaza, the sun blazing down and reflecting off the concrete. Across the way, a woman sat behind a blanket arrayed with Guatemalan goods, pants and hats and bracelets woven from colorful yarns. There was no one else in sight.

"Listen, Carrie," he began. "We go way back, and we've always got along pretty good, right? I mean, none of this my-best-friend's-girlfriend shit, right?"

I nodded, although I had no idea what he meant.

"So excuse me when I say you have to try harder."

"What are you talking about?"

His eyes widened. "What am I talking about? What am I *talking* about? I'm talking about Mike. Jesus fucking Christ, Carrie." He threw up his hands in disgust. "You're failing here, do you understand that? You're like, *Oh, poor me, my boyfriend's in the hospital but I'm the one suffering.* It's like *you're* the one this is hard on, forget anyone else. His own mother feels like she's gotta act like it's not so bad in case you take it into your head to walk. She does—she told me so."

"No," I said.

"No what?"

"No, I won't excuse you." I turned to leave and he grabbed my arm and held it tightly, his fingers digging into my flesh.

"Carrie, Christ," he said. "This is *Mike.*"

"Don't you think I know that? Let go of me."

He dropped my arm roughly. Then his expression softened. "He needs you to be there for him, Carrie. I don't care what was going on before, you just have to forget all of that and be there for him."

I bowed my head.

"Look, I'm sorry about Saturday. I shouldn't have said what I did, especially in front of Stu and Jamie. I blew it, OK? But—"

"Did he *tell* you about it?" I said.

"Of course! What do you think?"

I was crushed. The idea that it had been real enough for Mike to have told Rooster, real enough so that he'd *had* to—it was too awful. I could just imagine Mike, the slow, halting way he would have begun, avoiding Rooster's eyes. I wondered when he'd first mentioned it, how many times they'd talked about it. "What did he tell you?"

"I don't know, he didn't go into any details—he just let me know you were having troubles."

I stared at him, and all at once I despised him for knowing, for being the good friend to Mike that he was. " 'Be there for him,' " I said. "I hate that expression."

Rooster crossed his arms over his chest. "When was the last time you were at the hospital?"

The answer was Friday: after skipping Saturday, it had been all too what?—easy, maybe, or inevitable—to skip yesterday, too.

"I *know* when," he said. "Why didn't you go yesterday? Why didn't you go Saturday—because *Chicago* sounded like fun?"

"No," I said. "I didn't go to Chicago."

"Then why?"

"Because I didn't feel like it."

His mouth tightened. "You think I felt like it? You think Mrs. Mayer *felt* like seeing her son with his head in a fucking cage? No one feels like it. You go anyway. That's what love means."

"Oh, really," I said. "I thought it meant never having to say you're sorry."

He turned and slammed the edge of his fist against the wall. "I can't get through to you! Not at all! You know, I liked you for about five minutes back in ninth grade, did you know that? I sort of thought maybe it would be me and you, and Mike and Jamie." He laughed. "Hah. You're some cold woman, Carrie Bell. You're ice. Mike's well clear of you, that's what I think. Well clear of you. Just do it, OK? Don't keep him hanging."

I stood against the library and watched him walk away, his red hair bright in the midday sun. *You don't know a thing about me,* I imagined calling after him. Then I remembered wanting to call the very same words at Dr. Spelman's back, and I covered my face with my hands: Rooster *did.*

"Oh, my God," I said out loud. "Oh please, oh please, oh please, oh please, oh please."

I WENT STRAIGHT to the hospital after that, and for the next four days I spoke to no one but Mike and Mrs. Mayer, skipping work without so much as calling in sick. Visiting hours were much looser in rehab, and I just hung out during the day, before Mike's other visitors arrived—hung out, watched his sessions, stayed out of the way when I had to, kept him company when he was back in bed. I brought bags of supplies with me: books and newspapers and magazines, anything I could read aloud from. He liked to hear baseball scores and political stories, but his favorites were movie reviews, and whenever I read a review of a movie that sounded good, he would sigh a little and say he guessed we'd have to wait for the video. *We,* he'd say—hesitantly, hopefully—and I'd nod, thinking it sounded right. Renting movies had always been one of my favorite things to do with him anyway, because of how he got into them, laughing so hard he'd be falling out of his chair, or sniffing loudly enough for me to hear when something was sad, when most guys would have been saying, *Those raw onions from the chili must be bothering me, babe,* or whatever.

When he asked what had happened, why I wasn't at the library, I brushed him off. "I worked this morning," I said, or, "I traded with Viktor," but what had really happened was that Rooster was right, I did have to be there for him. The question was not a question. Mike needed me. *Mike* needed me—so here I was.

At home I let my answering machine do all the work. Jamie called, my mother, Viktor, Miss Grafton—even Rooster once, his voice high and strained as he apologized, begging me to call him. I left the volume up so I could listen, but I never picked up. I was across the room, at the table where I sat sewing and sewing—my refuge after the hospital, my antidote. I made two skirts that week and decided this: that my next project would be something silk, I didn't know what. I had savings, I'd been sewing for eleven years, and it was about time I made something silk.

On Friday night, the unneeded skirts finished, I put away my sewing machine for the first time in over a week. The table seemed vast. I sat down with an old *Elle* and flipped through it, studying the fashions more carefully than usual, thinking that I wanted to learn to design my own patterns, break free of the confines of Simplicity and Butterick, even Vogue. How to do that, though? Invent a silhouette, break it down to parts, put it together again with fabric. I sat there thinking for a while, then I got a pencil and a piece of paper, sat down again, and started to draw a dress.

The phone rang and I heard the machine click on. After the beep, I heard a male voice it took me a moment to recognize as Simon Rhodes's.

"Hi, Carrie," he said. "I'm leaving tomorrow and I was hoping maybe you'd be free for a drink. Uh, this is Simon. Well, if you get home before too late, give me a call." He started to give the number, and I crossed the room and picked up the phone.

"You're there," he said. "Great. Can you go out for a drink?"

I half wanted to, but I didn't feel like running into anyone. I told him about my week, explaining it to him more satisfying than I would have dreamed. We talked for ten or fifteen minutes, and finally I suggested we have the drink at my place so we could keep talking without my having to brave the world again. I gave him the address and hung up, and the phone rang again instantly.

I looked at the machine.

"Carrie, I know you're there. I've been getting a busy signal for the last five minutes, so I know you're there. *What* is going on? *Why* haven't you called me back? I've left like twenty messages on this stupid machine. Pick up."

It was Jamie. I so much didn't want to talk to her at that moment that it felt visceral, like a physical aversion.

"OK, I'm coming over," she said. "I'll be there in ten minutes."

I crossed the room and forced myself to pick up the receiver. "Hi."

"What's going on?" she exclaimed. "Everyone's worried sick about you. I just talked to your mom and she's having a cow—she'll probably pull up outside your house any minute now. Viktor called her tonight and told her you haven't been at work since Monday."

"Well, I haven't," I said. "So what?"

"So what? Are you sick? Is it because of Rooster going to the library on Monday?"

I held the phone away from my ear. Why did everyone know so much about me? I hated the notion that they were talking about me behind my back, figuring me out. "I've just been out of circulation for a few days," I said at last. "Relax."

"Relax! I don't get it. Why haven't you called? And why haven't you gone to work?"

"I didn't feel like it. I wanted to be at the hospital."

She was silent. When she spoke again her voice was quiet, controlled: "Should I come over?"

I felt a wave of disgust. "No, thanks." I heard her sigh and I said, "I'm fine, Jamie, I am. But thanks."

"Are you going to work tomorrow? Viktor said you're still on the schedule."

"I haven't really thought about it."

"Well, what have you been doing in the evenings?"

"Sewing."

"I'm worried about you," she said. "I really am."

I TRIED CALLING my mother after that, but I got her machine, so I went outside and sat on my upstairs porch and waited, watching the night fall fast from the trees. I didn't know who would arrive first, Simon or my mother, and I thought that it didn't really matter. I thought that aside from being there for Mike nothing much mattered, although I was looking forward to buying some silk first thing in the morning. I guessed that meant I wouldn't be going to work.

Down on the street my mother's car pulled up and stopped, and I stood. When she opened the door, the inside light illuminated her narrow figure and the speed with which she was moving, and for a moment I felt hot and tearful, a heavy storm of feeling gathering around me. Then the car door closed, and I moved to the edge of the porch and called hello.

She stopped and looked up. "Honey?"

"Hi."

"Is everything OK? Are you sick?"

"I'm fine."

"I—I heard you hadn't been at work and I was worried."

I put my hands on the porch rail and felt its rough, splintery surface. A streetlight a couple houses down revealed her shape to me, but I wondered if she could see me at all.

"Are you going to come up?" I said, and finally she made her way up the walk and disappeared onto the downstairs porch.

I went inside. I heard her steps on the enclosed stairway, and I picked up my sketch and pencil and shoved them into a drawer.

She was still in her work clothes, a two-piece beige linen dress over brown suede pumps. She blinked at the bright lights and smiled uneasily. "I've called you, a couple of times," she said. "Is your machine working?"

I nodded. "I'm sorry. I was going to call you tonight."

"Why no work, hon? Can you tell me?"

"There's nothing really to tell. I've been at the hospital." I shrugged. "I guess I should've called in sick."

She shifted, and I noticed she was carrying something, a metal box with a handle.

"What's that?"

She turned it around. On the front there was a red cross.

"I'm really sorry," I said. I turned and went into the kitchen so she wouldn't see me struggling not to cry. There was something about being alone with her and on the verge of tears that made me feel desperate. "Do you want something to drink?" I called. She didn't answer, and I filled two glasses with ice and water and went back to the table. She'd set the first-aid kit down, the blank side up.

"I gather you had words with Rooster," she said.

"Actually he had most of the words. Who told you?"

"Jamie."

"It was no big deal."

"Just a big enough deal to make you hide out for a few days?"

"I don't like my job. I don't want to work there anymore." My heart pounded: the idea had come out of nowhere, but once I'd said it I knew it was true.

"Quit," she said.

"I might."

The doorbell rang then, and our heads turned in unison toward the stairway.

"Who's that?" she said. "Are you expecting someone?" There was a touch of something in her voice that I thought just might be hopefulness.

"It's Simon Rhodes," I said. "A friend from high school."

I started down to let him in, but then I saw him through the glass door, a bunch of pale roses in hand, and I felt the heavy storm again, moving in quickly.

"Hey, don't," he said as I opened the door. "Hey, come on. They're just from my mother's garden. Hey, hey."

"My mother's upstairs," I sobbed.

He shrugged, pressing the flowers into my hands. "That's OK," he said. "That's fine. Does she feel like having a drink?"

LATER HE AND I sat outside on my porch sipping vodka and tonics, the only illumination a citronella candle that wasn't doing much to keep the mosquitoes away. I was in a director's chair, while he'd stretched out on the fraying, webbed nylon seat of an aluminum chaise that Mike had dug out of the Mayers' basement for me when I first got my apartment. My mother had left shortly after his arrival, taking her first-aid kit with her.

"So you're going back to New York tomorrow," I said. "What's it like there? In five words or less."

"Huge, filthy, and wonderful. That's four."

"Do you see famous people all over the place?"

"Not at all. And usually if I do I don't recognize them." He took a noisy sip of his drink. "Once I was out for brunch with a friend of mine, and she spent the whole time making these weird faces at me— opening her eyes really wide and tilting her head. I thought she had something wrong with her contact lenses, but afterward she just about killed me because Liza DeSoto had been sitting at the next table and I hadn't recognized her."

"Liza DeSoto of ReCharger?"

"What can I say?" he said. "She looks different with hair."

I laughed; talking to Simon was such fun. "But is it really romantic and glamorous? Do you go out for dinner at amazing restaurants all the time, you and your boyfriend? I mean, when you're together?" On the Union terrace he'd told me an on-again/off-again story to rival Christine and Bill's. His "saga," he'd called it.

"When we're together," he said theatrically, "*everything* is amazing." Then he sort of snorted. "Actually, when we're together having Chinese food around the corner from his apartment and then going to a movie is pretty much our standard. Sorry to disappoint you."

I shook my head: even Chinese food in New York sounded glamorous. I'd read an article about a Chinese restaurant in New York where almost everything they served you was carved to look like something else—a flower, a bird.

"What about you and Mike?" he said. "What was it like when you were together? I mean happily together."

I felt a constriction in my throat: *happily* together, back in the old days. Was Mike waiting for me to revert to the way I'd been in the months leading up to the accident? I couldn't bear to be an additional source of misery.

Simon was looking at me.

"What was it like or what did we do?"

"Either. Both."

I picked up my glass and took a sip. "We hung out. We played tennis, rode bikes, went out drinking. We went to lots of hockey games, saw movies, rented them. Sometimes we took my laundry to his parents' house."

"*Please* tell me you didn't do his laundry."

"I didn't do his laundry," I said, although in fact I'd thrown something of his in with my stuff as often as not. So what?

He seemed to know I was feeling defensive. He smiled gently and said, "And what was it like?"

What I thought of then was a late afternoon—one of dozens?—when it was just dark enough out so the lights had to be on, and my clean laundry was spilled over his bed, and he was at his desk with a book open but was sitting backward in his chair watching me, and I was pulling socks and underwear away from my sheets, each pull a crackle of static, and we weren't talking but were entirely attuned, so that when one of us finally did speak, the other was almost sure to say, *That's just what I was thinking*.

Simon was waiting for an answer. How could I describe it, the lit room with dusk outside, the companionable silence? "I guess we were regular," I said at last.

He laughed, but I didn't feel offended; I had a feeling "regular" was what he wanted, too.

"So what now?" he said after a while. "Are you going to keep hiding out? If I were going to be around longer I'd hide with you."

I smiled. "Thanks." I thought of how I'd decided earlier to buy some silk first thing in the morning, and now I thought about it again: going to Fabrications, looking at each roll, narrowing it down to a few and then one. Deciding on a pattern and then the moment when I'd take the fabric to the cutting table and a salesclerk would put scissors to it. Washing my hands once I was home again and carefully removing the fabric from the bag, then draping it across the table so I could admire it fully. It was all too appealing, it would spoil me—for the next thing I'd sew, the next thing I'd do. I looked at Simon, waiting patiently for my answer. "I guess I'll go back to work," I said.

9

~

IN MADISON, WINTER went on forever, October to May some years, so long it often felt endless—less "winter" than Madison itself, life itself. Spring was a blink of an eye, fall a brief, surprising chill. The hottest summers felt short, no matter how hot, how humid. This one, though . . . July crept by, one scorching day after another. The humidity was unbearable. Leaving the library or the hospital, I thought of the outside air as malevolent. It should have been green, a witch's breath. Or the gray of toxic exhaust.

Jamie called and called. Did I want to have lunch? Breakfast some morning before work? Dinner? I made excuses until finally she phoned just as I was getting ready to go visit Mike one Friday evening, and when she asked if I'd pick her up on my way to the hospital I had to say yes.

She was waiting on her porch. "I'm so glad I caught you," she said as she got into the car, and I nodded, then managed to say what needed saying.

"Me, too."

I pulled away from the curb. Last night Mike had been very quiet, and I wondered how he'd be tonight.

In the seat next to me Jamie sighed, then shifted.

I glanced over at her. "So how's work these days?"

She answered readily, as if she had material prepared: work was bugging her. The cashiers complained about the machine operators and the machine operators complained about the cashiers. Plus there was this new guy who was kind of cute but also kind of weird—he had a habit of standing really close to people when he talked to them.

"You need to give him an anonymous note about personal space," I said. "Or find an article about it and leave him a Xerox in his box."

"Yeah, but then—"

"Then he might not stand so close?"

"Exactly!" she said, and we both chuckled, then fell into silence. I didn't want her to ask me any questions, but we were almost there; I was probably safe. "Cute how?" I said, and she spent the next few minutes describing the new guy, his blue eyes, his good shoulders, this one shirt he sometimes wore that she didn't really like.

At last I pulled into the parking lot, and we walked to the entrance without talking. She'd pulled her hair into a French braid that highlighted the pale strand near her face, a running light through the dark blond twists. As we entered the hospital she gave me a hopeful little smile that broke my heart.

On Mike's floor, the elevator opened on to a wide corridor lined with stainless steel handrails. Just past a cluster of vending machines, we passed a framed poster of an empty wheelchair. As usual, I didn't look at it and then did look at it: a black-and-white photograph lit from above so that a complicated web of shadow fell from the wheelchair onto the glossy wood floor. GET MOVING read the caption.

"That dress," Jamie said. "That's not the one you bought at Luna last winter, is it?"

My dress had started life as a long-sleeved black number that fell nearly to my ankles: cotton and lycra, not really warm enough for a Midwestern winter, but I'd liked the deeply scooped neckline and the close fit. A few evenings ago I'd attacked it, cut the sleeves off to tight-fitting caps and hemmed the whole thing to a couple inches above my knees. In winter I'd worn a long, skinny cranberry cardigan over it, but now all it needed were some hematite beads. "Sort of," I said.

"I thought so," she said. "What'd you do, shorten it?"

"And cut off the sleeves."

"You're such a busy bee," she said, and I looked away.

A few more paces, and we were at Mike's room. Through the doorway I saw Rooster sitting in the chair Mrs. Mayer usually occupied; it was late enough that she'd gone home. Things between me and Rooster had been a little awkward since the day at the library, almost three weeks ago, and I hesitated, but he turned and gave me a friendly wave, and I stepped into the room. Bill was there, too, perched on the dresser, the black soles of his Tevas tapping against a drawer front. I hadn't seen him since Christine's going-away brunch.

"It's a party," Mike said from the bed. He was on his side, propped by pillows, the head of the bed elevated a little. The large form of his body lay inert on top of the blanket. I crossed the room and kissed him, angling my face to avoid the halo.

"How are you?" Jamie asked him.

"Totally wiped out."

I glanced at Rooster. He gave me a half smile, which I took to mean that at least Mike was answering; Rooster'd been present during Mike's silence last night, too.

Jamie nodded, then went to stand in front of the dresser, near Bill. "Miss James," Bill said to her.

"Mr. B."

He grinned. He'd gotten a buzz cut recently, and he had a military look about him—an AWOL look, actually, given the three- or four-day growth of beard on his face.

From the far bed Mike's roommate was looking at me, and I caught his eye and smiled. He was only fourteen but he looked even younger tonight, his straight blond hair falling past his ears. His name was Jeff Walker, a horrible joke of a name for a boy who'd lost the use of both legs in a car accident. Another one for the collection, though who could bear to add it?

Rooster glanced ostentatiously at his watch. "Whoa," he said. "Is it after eight?"

I looked at the wall clock: it was twenty after eight, forty minutes until the official end of visiting hours, though no one would object if we stayed longer.

Rooster stretched elaborately and then stood up. He'd changed from his suit, but not into his usual after-work jeans: he wore a crisp, short-sleeved madras shirt and khakis, and his cheeks gleamed from a recent shave. He looked like a Marshall Field's ad, like a man in a Father's Day lineup: *Just going to spend some quality time with my family today, maybe go out for brunch.*

"Where are you going?" I said.

"Date," he said with a little smile.

"Joan again?" I said facetiously.

He nodded.

"Are you *kidding*?" I couldn't believe it, and I glanced around at everyone, trying to figure out what they knew. "OK, I need a little more information."

He raised his eyebrows and smiled mysteriously, then went to stand by Mike's bed. He touched Mike's arm and said, "I've got to run, but I'll see you tomorrow night, OK?"

"Watch yourself," Mike said. "You're getting serious."

Rooster grinned but didn't respond. "Catch you guys," he said, and he gave us a little wave as he left the room.

I stared at Mike. Could Rooster really have gotten involved with Joan without my knowing it? Could he have gotten involved with Joan at all? "What's up with that?" I said. "Is this a thing? Isn't she about thirty?"

Mike didn't speak.

"Mike."

"I don't know how old she is."

I looked at Bill. "Do you?"

"I've never laid eyes on the woman."

"Well, he might have told you."

" 'Bill?' " Bill said with a grin. " 'Yes, Rooster?' 'The woman I'm seeing tonight is thirty.' 'Thanks for telling me, big guy.' "

Jamie laughed. "Yeah, C," she said. "Better lighten up a little."

I crossed my arms over my chest. I knew I was being ridiculous, but I couldn't help it. I let out a big sigh, then went and sat in Rooster's chair—Mrs. Mayer's chair, my chair now. Lying on his side across the room, Mike could no longer really see me, and after a moment I scooted the chair over so I was more in his line of vision.

The halo made turning his head impossible, and he'd complained about eyestrain, how you never knew how much you turned your neck until you couldn't. I wished I hadn't just been so pushy.

Bill told us about his new job, working for a prof from the biochemistry department. The prof was conducting an experiment on fruit flies, and Bill had to slice wings off the dead ones and look at them under a microscope to check for a certain cell change. Mike listened, but after a while it was clear he needed to sleep. I nodded for Jamie to go out with Bill and wait for me in the hall, and I went and sat on the edge of the bed and stroked his shoulder for a while. An orderly would be in soon to get him ready for the night. "I love you," I said before I left, and he stared at me and then looked away.

Out in the corridor, Jamie stood waiting by herself. We set off. About halfway to the elevator we came to the fire stairs, and on a whim I stopped and pulled open the heavy door, then stepped onto the warm, muggy landing.

"This way?" she said, coming in after me. For a while there was no sound but our heels tapping down the concrete steps. The stairwell was dimly lit, by bulbs encased in steel cages. A wide red stripe on the wall showed the angle of descent.

"I'm sorry," she said suddenly.

I looked back up at her. "For what?"

She'd stopped walking, and I stopped, too. "Telling you to lighten up," she said. "Rooster was being completely annoying."

"He was, wasn't he?" I shook my head. "Why not just say, you know, 'Yeah, I've seen her a few times, she's really nice.' "

Jamie grinned. "More like, 'Yeah, I've seen her a few times and I think I'm going to score tonight.' "

"Poor Rooster."

"He'll manage," she said with a shrug. "He's definitely enjoying the mystery on this one, the little prick." She paused. "Actually, maybe *that*'s the problem."

We both smiled. "What is it with him?" I said. "I mean really."

She shrugged. "Same thing as it is with me—a combination of bad luck and bad breath." She gave me a look: she'd had a one-night stand with some asshole who'd asked her to brush her teeth before they fucked. One thing about Jamie: in the right mood she could laugh at herself.

She took a step down, then stopped again. "Actually, I'm sorry about something else, too." She hesitated. "When we first got here and I said you were a busy bee."

I touched the neckline of my dress, a black U against my untanned skin. Shortening the dress had been nothing, but chopping off the sleeves had been a big gamble. It was just right now: a summer dress freed from too much black stretch cotton. I looked at her. "You weren't making fun of my dress, you were making fun of me."

She blushed. "I know, I wasn't thinking."

"What do you mean?"

She shook her head. "Never mind," she said, and our eyes locked for a moment before we continued on our way.

I WORKED, I visited Mike, and I sewed and sewed: new curtains for my apartment and then a throw for the foot of his bed, a red-and-white checked rectangle that I filled with cotton batting and machine-quilted. I was at House of Fabrics so often one of the saleswomen started calling me honey. My sewing machine was out all the time, sitting at the head of my table; I ate on my couch, bowls of cereal, potato chips, whatever I could pull from a cabinet and consume as is. I drifted through my job, so deep into autopilot Viktor started giving me worried looks, coming over and jostling my elbow if I stood in one place for too long. After my week away Miss Grafton had brushed off my apologies, but now she seemed leery of me, stayed a couple yards away when we had to talk, as if she might catch whatever I had.

During the days Mike wore a sweatsuit, the most comfortable thing for physical therapy, loose and unconstricting and easy to adjust underneath him so creases wouldn't press into his skin, start sores he couldn't feel. The jacket had long sleeves, and I hadn't seen his bare arms in weeks until I arrived later than usual one evening, after everyone was gone and he'd been changed into short-sleeved pajamas, and found that his forearms had thinned and hardened into the subtle curve of pure bone, with nearly the same paleness.

I met his eyes and then looked away. I couldn't help myself: I looked at the floor, the window, at Jeff Walker lying half asleep in his bed, the remote for the ceiling-mounted TV held loosely in his hand. When I looked back Mike was looking right at me—his eyes narrowed, his mouth slack with unhappiness—and for a moment I couldn't speak.

"Hi," I managed at last, and I crossed to the bed and kissed his cheek. "Sorry, I had to work late."

He frowned. "You don't have to come every night."

"I want to, you know that."

"I don't know why."

"I love you? Could that be it?"

"You loved me. Now you just feel sorry for me."

He stared hard, and I felt he'd tossed the remark out to see what it would catch, how persuasively I could deny it. I had a sense that half of him wanted me to fail, so he'd know he was really at the bottom. Yet I felt strongly that it wasn't true, that I did still love him—that since the showdown with Rooster I loved him, if not more, then better than ever, clearly, without the fog of my own wants, the tedium of needing to be loved back, of needing to be *thrilled*. Just love, the pure thing: one heart uncurled toward another. That could be enough, couldn't it?

"That's not true," I said.

"One of these days it will be. You think we're going to have a fun life together? You, me, and my wheelchair?"

"Mike, don't." I put my hand on his shoulder. "Really. Let's just see what happens, OK?"

"It already has happened. It's over."

My legs went cold. "Us?" I said.

"No, me," he said. "Me. Obviously."

"Oh, Mike." I'd been sitting in a chair by his bed, and now I stood and moved closer to him. Against the white sheets his skin looked pearly gray, a faint flush of emotion coloring his face. His pajamas were the old-fashioned kind, the first real pajamas he'd owned in years: red-and-navy striped, with navy piping along the collar and at the cuffs.

I looked away, and the TV caught my eye, hanging in the center of the room. Before dozing off Jeff had chosen an old Western, and I watched while tiny horses moved across tiny plains.

Then a commercial came on, and I felt Mike's attention tune in, too. A couple in bridal clothes came out of a church under a shower of confetti, moving arm in arm. I felt Mike taking it all in, the bride with her radiant face, the groom beaming, the happy people looking on. *I think he was actually really* worried *about something*, Rooster'd said. Oh, yes. I turned back to the bed and looked at him, his face cut into separate pieces by the steel of the halo. If his next words were *Let's get a minister over here and get married tomorrow,* I would say yes.

10

~

INSIDE A NARROW doorway, metal-edged stairs led up to the Stock Pot, a crowded, three-room café that was famous for soup. They served hot chowders and bisques in winter, cool gazpachos in summer. I sat at a table by the window and looked out on to State Street. On the sidewalk in front of the Athlete's Foot, the juggling guy juggled oranges, his arms flying. You saw him all over town, barefoot and bearded: juggling fruit, bowling pins, even squat, multicolored candles. Rumor had it he'd been around for decades, so stoned he hadn't heard the bad news that the sixties were over.

Ania appeared at the table smiling, her broad shoulders pulling at the sleeves of her black T-shirt. She'd called the night before, suggesting lunch, and while I'd been happy to hear from her I was sure Viktor had put her up to it.

"I can't believe how long ago your dinner was," I said once we'd said hello and she'd sat down. "I've been wanting to have you guys over to my place, but—"

She shook her head. "Please, you have been very occupied, there is no need to apologize. Tell me, how does everything go? Viktor is a very poor carrier of information. He tells me your friend is moved to rehabilitation, but not *how things are*."

"Just the facts, ma'am."

"That's right," she said with a smile. "And the facts are where I want to begin, not end." She leaned forward and widened her amber eyes. "Don't you think this is one of the main differences between men and women? Men want the facts"—she pounded the table—"and we want what's between them, the interesting air circulating around them."

"The truth," I said. "I guess that's sort of right." I thought of how, just a couple days ago, Mike had casually mentioned that Rooster was taking Joan sailing the next day. "So they're in a relationship?" I said, and he said yes as if it were the best-known thing in the world, as if he'd never been anything but forthcoming about it.

"Maybe men stick to the facts as a way of controlling us," I said to Ania. "I just thought of this. We'd prefer the truth and they know it, so they withhold themselves from talking things over and analyzing them because it gives them power over us."

She grinned. "You must come to my women's group. What do you say? You're perfect, you're the neofeminist. It's every other Tuesday night, we take turns hosting. You must."

"I don't know," I said uneasily. "I've never really been in any groups."

"This is not a prerequisite," she said. "It's very casual—just eight or ten women talking. You like to talk." She wagged a finger at me. "I know you do."

I studied her: her wide Slavic face, her pale, yellowy cat eyes. She was wearing clunky, heavy-soled sandals, didn't shave her legs. In my floral slip dress and crisscross platforms I felt prissy and excessively got up, like some ridiculous flamboyant bird.

"I'm at the hospital every evening," I said. "I really can't. But thanks."

She shrugged, and I thought I saw something flicker across her brow—perhaps the bit of interest she'd had in me as it faded away.

We had just gotten our lunches when Jamie and her mother came into the café. Though she'd continued calling, we still hadn't gotten together for a meal; now here I was with someone else.

I turned to look out the window and put a hand up to shield my face. Down on the sidewalk the juggling guy was gone, replaced by a pair of sorority girls holding cans of Diet Coke.

Reluctantly, I turned back. Jamie and Mrs. Fletcher were two tables away, and Jamie was waiting to catch my eye. She gave me a forced smile, then turned away.

"A friend of yours?" Ania said.

I nodded.

"She is not having a very good day, I think."

When we were done I took Ania over to the Fletchers' table to say hello. Jamie chewed her salad briskly, as if she were so involved with her lunch that it was too much trouble to show an interest. "My husband is working with Carrie," Ania said by way of explanation, and Jamie nodded offhandedly.

"Viktor. I know."

Mrs. Fletcher gave me an uneasy smile. She seemed older than she had the last time I'd seen her, softer and more wrinkled. There was something fearful in her shy brown eyes. "Can you girls sit?" she said, patting the chair next to her. "I haven't seen you in so long, Carrie."

Ania looked at her watch. "I am having to return to work, so I'll say goodbye." She turned to me. "Please stay if you like. And thank you for meeting me."

I wanted to walk out with her, but Jamie's eyes bored into me. Instead I said goodbye and watched her go, her long braid motionless against her back.

"She seems nice," Mrs. Fletcher said. "So polite."

Jamie rolled her eyes. " 'I am having to return to work.' Who talks like that?"

"She's Polish," I said. "English isn't her first language. Didn't you notice her accent?"

Jamie stabbed a mushroom slice and put it in her mouth. "Whatever."

Mrs. Fletcher looked away. She seemed out of place in the noisy Stock Pot, the only person present over forty as far as I could tell. She wore a short-sleeved white blouse with a notched collar, a tiny enamel butterfly pinned to one lapel. "Polish," she said thoughtfully, reaching for her glass and taking a sip of iced tea. "I wonder if she has a good recipe for goulash."

Jamie put her forehead onto her palm and shook her head.

Mrs. Fletcher's face pinkened slightly, and I wished I'd left when I could have: now it was too late to do anything but sit in the chair she'd offered me. She met my glance and smiled sadly, then put her soft, freckled hand on my arm and gave it a pat. "I've been thinking of you so much, Carrie," she said. "How are you?"

"I'm OK."

"And Mike?"

"He's working hard," I said. "He's hanging in there."

She shook her head sorrowfully. She wore her thin hair in a new style, shorter and with the bangs grown out, a girl's mock-tortoise barrette holding them off her face. "Jamie says you're at the hospital all the time."

I looked at Jamie. She was stirring sugar into her iced tea, her expression unreadable. "Well," I said to Mrs. Fletcher. "You know."

She nodded. "He must be getting so much strength from you."

I sat with them while they finished their lunches, and then we all headed outside together, the sun shining hard on the crowded sidewalk. We made our way around the corner, to where Mrs. Fletcher's big paneled station wagon was parked.

"Don't be such a stranger," she said to me as she unlocked the door. "You come see me without Jamie sometime." She tilted her head and looked at me. "Say, you don't play bridge, do you?"

I glanced at Jamie, who rolled her eyes again. "No, I don't."

"Darn. One of the girls in my bridge group moved to Fond du Lac, and we're having the hardest time replacing her." She smiled and got into her car, then slowly negotiated her way out of the parking space, inching forward and backward until the nose of the wagon was angled way into the middle of the street.

"And such a good driver," Jamie said under her breath.

"Be nice."

We watched as her mother drove away, her brake lights flashing hesitantly as she neared the far corner. Finally she turned, and Jamie let out a big sigh. "Do you think she's *on* something? Does she talk incredibly slowly or is it just me?" She ran the toe of her sandal along a crack in the sidewalk. "One of the *girls*," she went on. "She's forty-seven years old."

I turned and looked her over, the short sleeves of her Cobra Copy T-shirt rolled as high as they'd go, exposing her thin, pale arms. "What's the matter?" I said. "What were you doing having lunch with her, anyway?"

Jamie frowned. "Talking about Lynn. Sul-Lynn, I should say."

Lynn was Jamie's younger sister: she'd graduated from high school in June and was waitressing at a restaurant on the far west side, no plans to go to college.

"What about her?" I said.

"Her general idiocy."

"Jamie."

She'd been standing with her hands on her hips, and now she flung them to the sides. "She's like a thirteen-year-old too dumb to finesse her curfew! Every night Mom stays awake until she hears Lynn on the stairs, and then every morning she calls me to complain the minute Dad leaves the house. Now she wants me to talk to Lynn."

"Are you going to?"

"Fuck, no."

We were standing in front of a short flight of concrete steps that led up to a hat store, and abruptly Jamie sat down on the lowest one. After a moment I sat, too, and gave her shoulder a pat. Across the street, a couple in matching tie-dye came out of a used record store, and we watched as they kissed and then walked slowly toward State Street, their arms wrapped tightly around each other. Next to me, I felt Jamie sizing them up—the girl's long, snarly hair and bare feet, the guy's leather bracelet and dirty-looking, colorful cap. I felt her disdain, and I felt her arrive nonetheless at the fact that the two of them were in love and she wasn't.

"So did *you* call *her*?" she asked.

"Her?" I said, gesturing with my chin at the hippie girl, though I knew she meant Ania.

Jamie pinched her lips together. A golden retriever nosed past us, a red bandana around his neck.

"She called me," I said.

"Oh." She nodded hastily, bringing herself up to speed. "And did you have fun? What'd you talk about?"

"Actually, she invited me to join her women's group."

Jamie's mouth fell open, and a look of delight came over her face. "Her women's group? Are you kidding?"

I shook my head.

"That is so weird." She grinned. "What is this, the seventies?"

"Maybe it's a women's group for the new millennium."

She laughed. "I can just see you, Bell—all these women with hairy pits and Birkenstocks, and you."

"I don't know," I said. "It might be kind of interesting."

"Then why don't you join?" she snapped. She stared unhappily into the street, her shoulders hunched, her fingers twisted together. I held out my palm to her.

"What, you want to hold hands? Maybe you *should* go to that group, they're probably all lesbians."

I pulled my hand back. I should have lied, should have said I'd had a terrible, boring time. Or I should have had the guts to tell her to get over it.

"You know what I wish?" she said suddenly. "I wish this fucking summer was over. I wish everything would go back to normal."

"Everything like what?" I stared into her face, pink along the cheekbones and tight at the mouth. "Like what, Jamie?"

"Like you!"

"I can't," I said after a moment. "You know that."

She stood up and turned away, then didn't move. After a moment I stood, too. A businessman came out of the candy store next door, a small pink bag in his hand. A strong smell of peanuts wafted after him.

There was nothing to do but make our way back to State Street. We walked side by side without talking. I was done with work for the day, and before she headed toward the copy shop to start her shift we managed to say goodbye. I took a few steps in the other direction but then turned to watch her through the crowd, her small head bobbing along, the ponytail she always wore to work bouncing a little with each step. I loved her: for her loyalty, for her sweet good humor, for the way she held her hair off her neck when she was hot; for the streak of sadness in her and for her belief that one true love could wipe it clean. When we were very young we'd gone everywhere together, even to the bathroom, one of us sitting on the edge of the tub while the other peed, but now that we were grown—now that we were grown we were going to have to learn a little separation. My mother had once cautioned me against spending so much time with Jamie—against putting all of my eggs in one basket, she said—and at the time I was furious, enraged. Now I thought that she had *known* something: not about me or Jamie, but about the particular life of a friendship embarked upon in early childhood.

I TURNED AROUND and headed up State Street. The display windows in the storefronts changed fairly often, but today that seemed like a particularly malevolent lie because the stores themselves didn't change. There was the place with the comfortable shoes, there the one with the Badger paraphernalia. Even the clothing stores were predictable, the one with sweaters and baggy pants, the one with short skirts and leather. There were no big surprises on State Street.

But there was Fabrications. I walked right in, no lingering at the window, no wondering if there'd be anything I could afford. It was nice and cool, all that air-conditioning for a shop in which a single saleswoman sat in front of an open drawer of patterns, a clipboard on her knee, no one else in sight.

I went straight to the silks. First to catch my eye was the blue I'd seen on the night when I cried in front of John Junior at the ice cream parlor, which seemed as far away now as a dream. The fabric was the deep sapphire color of a ring my mother kept in her jewelry box but never wore. It caught the light and seemed to shine, and when I unrolled it to feel it again I was reminded of how light and crisp it was, like expensive wrapping paper. It would make a nice suit—the kind of thing called a "little suit" in a fashion magazine, as if you'd have six or seven of them—and I pictured a short, fitted jacket over what I'd once seen called a tulip skirt, rounded over the hips and then close-fitting to the top of the knee. I'd never in my life been anywhere where I could wear such a thing, but maybe that was the point.

Next I turned to the fluid print in black and gold and red that had caught my eye that same night. It was a very silky silk, the kind of thing that would swirl around you when you walked. It struck me as something a model would wear in a perfume ad, for one of those perfumes described as spicy—she'd be sitting on a couch in lounging pajamas made of this fabric, wearing a lot of gold jewelry, a tableful of burning candles at her side. I looked at the tag: forty dollars a yard. I was about to turn back to the blue when a roll of washed silk caught my eye.

The color was beautiful: a warm, pale gold, like honey in sunlight. I let it run over the back of my hand, and I was enthralled by the feel, soft but not slick, like some kind of magical, weightless suede. I liked the way its appeal was quiet, unlike the print's: the satisfaction it gave would be private and subtle, not obvious to everyone. But what would I make with it? I looked up and found the saleswoman watching me.

"Buying or browsing?"

"Maybe both, but I can't decide."

"On the fabric or the pattern?"

"Either."

Smiling, she stood up and set her clipboard on a counter, then came over and took down the three rolls I'd been looking at. She touched the blue. "This shantung is great to work with—have you ever used it before?"

"Actually I've never made anything out of any kind of silk before."

"You're going to get spoiled. The washed silk's great, too, and it'd be a fantastic color on you. Here, let's try something." She picked up the roll of washed silk and led me to a full-length mirror. "Look," she said, unrolling a couple of yards and holding it up in front of me. "Gorgeous with your dark hair."

It *was* gorgeous, a sheet of pale gold, moving with a subtle luster. I lifted my arm until it met the silk, the softest of strokes.

"Can't you just see yourself?" the saleswoman said. "At a summer wedding, with nice cream-colored shoes and a big straw hat with flowers on the brim?"

That sounded about as stylish as *Ladies' Home Journal*, but I didn't want to be impolite. "I don't know," I said. "I guess if we were doing a kind of country casual thing."

"Not if you were the *bride*," she said with a laugh. "Unless it was your second time or something. Are you getting married? We have some beautiful ivory charmeuse."

I shook my head. Without quite meaning to, I felt for my engagement ring and slid the stone around to the inside of my hand.

"I meant if you were going to be a *guest* at a wedding," she said. With her free hand she gathered the fabric together and held it at my waist. "It's great on you."

Looking at the mirror, I imagined a whole dress of it sliding over my head: not some full-skirted thing you'd wear with a straw hat, but a narrow, slinky one that would lie luxuriously against your skin. "It *feels* so good," I said.

"It's sexy stuff," she said with a smile. "I made a nightgown out of it for a friend who was getting married, and she was pregnant before the end of her honeymoon."

A nightgown. A silk nightgown with spaghetti straps, and over it a long, flowing robe with hugely gathered sleeves and a satin ribbon at the neck. I heard my mother's voice asking if I'd get much use out of it, Jamie's saying I could *buy* a nice nightgown, but then I wondered what Mike would say, and in a moment he was standing in front of me, carefully untying the ribbon, pushing the robe from my shoulders, sliding the straps of the gown down until it slid over my hips and fluttered to the floor, and I thought that although he would probably never be able to do that, I should make the gown and robe anyway: an offering to memory, or to the future.

I CARRIED THE fabric back down State Street to my car, all eight and a half yards of it, over two hundred dollars' worth of silk in a paper bag. I drove home and found a parking place in the shade.

It was August now, and the cosmos my downstairs neighbors had planted looked weedy, the withered magenta blooms fading in front of the gray-brown fence. Our landlord had let the grass go this summer, and it was wheat-colored and stubbly, patches of bare earth showing alongside the walkway.

My apartment was still in the sun. I sat on the downstairs porch, on a wicker armchair left behind by a former tenant. I set the bag on the splintery porch floor, then thought better of it and rested it on my lap. Poor Jamie, I thought, caught between her mother and her sister. Well, maybe not caught between them, but only because she refused to be. Caught near them, anyway. Jamie'd always been torn about Lynn, wanting to protect her at the same time that she wanted to give her a good shake and tell her to grow up. Lynn was the youngest of three girls, and she'd had the bad luck to be born not just last but least smart and least pretty. The beauty in the family was Mixie, the middle sister—she was spending the summer in Southern California, living near Venice Beach with some UW friends and working in a T-shirt store. Jamie suspected her of doing a lot of drugs.

The fast clicking of a bicycle suddenly slowed, and I looked up to see Tom, Viktor and Ania's neighbor, swinging his long leg over the back of his bike. He leaned the bike against the front fence and came into the yard. He wore mud-colored cargo shorts and a torn white T-shirt, and his blond hair stood up in a frizzy crown.

"Bet you're surprised to see me here," he said. "Wiktor gave me your address."

Poor Viktor, I thought, even as I was wondering why Tom had wanted my address.

"So what's up?" he said.

"I just had lunch with Ania, actually."

Tom held his palms to the sky. "And then I appear on your doorstep. The world is full of that, don't you find?"

I suppressed a smile. Mike would have called him dippy, but I thought it was a pose.

"So, I've been a real renegade," he said, shrugging off his backpack.

"What do you mean?"

"I have something for you—I've been meaning to come by for weeks."

I couldn't imagine what he was talking about. "You have something for me? What? Why didn't you just give it to Viktor?"

He shook his head. "Strict orders to hand it to you personally." He climbed the porch steps and sat on the top one, unzipping the pack. Inside was a chaos of notebooks and loose papers, and, inexplicably, half a Frisbee.

"Here," he said, pulling the Frisbee out: he made as if to toss it to me, then stuffed it back in. "Just kidding." He rummaged some more and brought out a dog-eared white envelope. He tried to smooth it out, then gave up and handed it to me. "Oh, well. It got a little mangled. Sorry."

I examined the envelope. "What is it?"

"Kilroy wanted me to give it to you. Remember Kilroy? From that night?"

I nodded.

"Well, he wanted me to give it to you. Sorry it took so long, but I've been working like a fucking dog this summer. Or maybe a horse. What animal do people work like again?"

I shook my head impatiently. The envelope was blank, front and back.

"So how about those Sox, huh?"

I looked up at him.

"Just kidding." He pulled his backpack onto his shoulders and went down the steps to where his bicycle leaned. I couldn't help staring: it was the tallest bike I'd ever seen, the frame a good foot taller than the one on my bike, the seat raised eight or ten inches above that.

"They're selling bikes out at Harry's Big and Tall now," he said. "Saved *my* life." He waved, and then he was on the bike again, his long legs pumping.

I leaned back in the wicker chair and slid my finger under the flap of the envelope. Inside was a piece of lined yellow paper. I unfolded it, looked first at the signature, and then started to read. "Sunday, 2 a.m.," it said at the top.

Dear Carrie Bell,

Finally I know the reason for your sad eyes and silence, and I'm selfishly looking for forgiveness. The problem with reading minds is that you can get awfully close and still miss the essential thing. I hope Mike wakes to your vigilance and love soon, and that you'll be well together.

Kilroy

P.S. Try pool.

I thought of that evening, back in June: Ania in the kitchen cooking, Viktor towering over Kilroy in the living room, so offended by his questions that he finally stalked away. Kilroy with his narrow body and sharp face—staring at me, summing me up.

I read minds, sideline to pool. There had been a quietness to him, some kind of smooth, bland covering over a sharp watchfulness. The sense of an engine in there, running all the time. Something else, too, though: he was cocky at the same time that he mocked his own cockiness. *You don't like pool? You don't know what you're missing. On Sixth Avenue right near my apartment there's a bar called McClanahan's with a pool table that's got a tiny little gouge in the felt right near one of the side pockets, and I'm such an accomplished student of that table that I can just about always make the gouge work for me.*

I read the letter a second time, then I put it back in the envelope and put the envelope in my purse. I'd felt his eyes on me all through dinner that night. Studying me, it turned out. Wondering about me.

MIKE WAS QUIET that evening. His high school hockey coach was there when I arrived, and while it was kind of him to visit I was sure his presence had Mike thinking of skating, the long, powerful strokes across the ice that had come so easily to him and brought him such joy. Coach had retired in June, and he talked about how he was moving on to other things, projects around the house, an Airstream he and his wife had bought so they could see the country. He talked fast, laying it on: his message was that Mike could do the same, "refocus"—he actually used that word. I figured coaching was ingrained in him, but still: I wanted him gone.

"All right, pal," he said at last, standing. He had a thatch of gray hair, and he wore a spotless white T-shirt and blue gym shorts over low white socks and brand-new Nikes. His calves were as ropy as his muscular forearms. So many times I'd watched Mike at hockey practice, Coach yelling, *Come on, you guys—you couldn't beat your sisters skating like that.* Mike all padded up, helmet on, stick taped and ready. Hockey players are all but indistinguishable once they're on

the ice, but even without a numbered jersey I knew him, his hips and
the shape of his butt and the way he tucked his head.

He watched Coach from the bed, purplish marks under his eyes,
his atrophied legs bent spastically. "Thanks for coming," he said.

Coach looked at the floor. He hesitated a moment, then went over
and patted the bed, a foot or so away from where Mike's feet were.
"You've always been a fighter," he said. "With this girl's help you're
going to do OK."

He gave Mike a wave and then headed for the door, resting a hand
on my shoulder as he passed but carefully avoiding my eyes.

"That was nice," I said when he was gone.

"Coach?" Mike said. "Yeah."

He closed his eyes, and I pulled a chair close and settled into
it. *With this girl's help.* Mrs. Fletcher drifted into my mind, still a
girl at forty-seven. And Ania, already so surely a woman. She and
Viktor seemed to have passed a milestone my friends and I hadn't
encountered yet, and not just because they were older and married,
either. Maybe it was being away from their home, from their younger
selves—we might work at banks and libraries and car dealerships, but
somehow the trappings of adulthood were merely that for us, merely
trappings: the truth about us seemed to lie in the fact that we were
still closest to the people we'd known since childhood. It would always
be too easy to remember Saturday nights driving up and down Campus Drive six or seven to a car, passing around contraband bottles of
wine and listening to the driver obsess about how important it was not
to spill because his parents would definitely be able to smell it when
they used the car to go to church the next morning.

"What are you thinking about?" Mike said.

He was watching me closely, and I realized I'd zoned out, that he'd
said something a moment earlier that I hadn't even heard. "Coach
calling me a girl."

"Is that so bad? He's known you since you were a girl—he probably
feels fatherly toward you."

"Well, they do say nature abhors a vacuum."

Mike hesitated and then laughed uncertainly: it wasn't like me to
allude to my father, let alone flippantly.

"What about you?" I said. "Do you think of me as a girl or a woman?"

He moved his shoulder. "I think of you as Carrie. Actually, I don't even really think of you as Carrie. I think of you as 'her.' Or I just think of you."

I reached for his arm and ran my palm up and down it, then took his limp hand in mine.

"How do you think of me?" he said.

"You mean as a boy or a man?" I smiled. "A *guy* or a man?"

"I mean *how*."

"As you. Sometimes Mike, but mostly I just sort of have a picture of you and that's thinking of you."

He bit his lip. "Where am I in the picture?"

"Front and center."

"Look at me, Carrie."

I looked into his face, his worried eyes. The frame of the halo cast a faint gray shadow onto his cheek.

"Am I here?" he said. "Am I paralyzed?"

"No," I lied. Then I looked away. "Well, sometimes. I guess sometimes you are."

He closed his eyes for a moment, and when he opened them again he was on the verge of tears. "I'd give anything for this not to have happened."

"I would, too."

Again he closed his eyes, and now tears seeped out, a single trail moving down each cheek. I set his hand down and began stroking his forearm again. I wish I could say I felt selfless then, unaware of myself. That I was thinking only of him, or that I wasn't even thinking. But I was: *This is me doing the right thing. This is me being brave and strong for Mike.*

11

~

THE SILK WAS like nothing I'd ever worked with before, slippery and so fluid it was almost as if it were alive, slithering from my table onto the floor, sliding off the deck of my sewing machine if I was careless when I pulled the needle out, if I didn't have my hands right there to coax it to stay.

I wasn't careless much. I'd never been so cautious, in fact, not even as a beginner—so slow with pinning, so careful with knots at the beginning and end of each seam. And the care felt good, as if the fabric itself were teaching me how to sew all over again, the right way this time.

Cutting out had been terrifying, each stroke of my scissors a pathway to disaster, but once I began sewing I got into a nice, slow rhythm, and I grew to love the way the fabric felt, all the different textures it had: grainy to the tips of my fingers, satiny to the backs of my hands, heavy at the beginning of a seam, light at the very end. I didn't tell anyone what I was doing, and at night, home from the hospital, I often stayed up until one or two in the morning, a sea of light gold around me, coming together piece by piece.

I made the nightgown first. It was basically two bias-cut panels, Ashaped but just barely, joined along the sides. Simple but not easy—in fact, the word "simplicity" had never seemed so loaded, though it was a Butterick pattern. Hand-stitching the rolled edge at the neck took forever, and then the straps nearly finished me off, strips so thin that when it came time to turn them right side out I had to use a turkey skewer. The first time I tried it the skewer poked through the fabric and made a jagged tear, so I started over with a new piece and this time wrapped the tip of the skewer with just the tiniest bit of cotton from a cotton ball, a trick that actually worked, to my surprise.

I was tempted to save the hem until I'd done the robe, but that seemed wrong somehow, a cheat—I should finish the gown and then do the robe, keep to some kind of order. I had a scary moment trying the gown on, thinking it was going to be too tight, but it wasn't: it was tight, but not too tight, tight the way a well-fitting bias-cut garment is always tight, the fabric smooth and close, hugging me just to the tops of my thighs, where it gradually loosened until at the bottom it was wide enough to twirl when I turned. I finished the hem late one night and then hung the gown on a hanger and put it in my closet, where it would be the first thing I saw when I woke the next morning.

DURING THOSE DAYS of sewing I felt distracted a lot. At work I'd suddenly come to myself, a book in hand, a wall of shelves before me, and I'd actually have to shake my head to get myself clear of whatever stage of the sewing I'd been at when I'd stopped the night before. Viktor shot me his usual looks of concern, and I gave him sad smiles, let him think it was all just too hard, having Mike in the hospital—that that was my problem.

Of course, that was my problem. I knew that every minute, sewing or not sewing, with Mike or not. And he got lower and lower, sometimes barely registered my presence, other times spent whole evenings complaining about little things—why no one had brought a new radio, how tired he was of the pictures we'd put on his dresser—because the big things were too big to complain about, just too big.

Part of rehab was psychological, and one evening his parents told me that he was refusing to see his therapist, alone or in the group meetings on Tuesday afternoons. They were worried. They'd even gone to see the therapist, and although he'd told them that Mike's rejection of him was normal, they weren't comforted.

Visiting hours were over, and I was sitting with them in the main lobby, talking. Mr. Mayer seemed especially distressed. He appeared to regard the whole rehab process as something akin to an assembly line: muscle tone, mind tone; physical therapy, occupational therapy, psychotherapy; one step after another leading to wellness, or at least to Mike's going home.

"It's a stumbling block, is how I see it," he said. "He's got to get beyond this so he can move on."

Mrs. Mayer frowned. "Imagine someone coming around and try-ing to get you to talk about your feelings. You wouldn't like it, either."

"I don't need it."

"What makes you so sure Mike does?"

Mr. Mayer shook his head emphatically. "Lord, you'd think he'd just broken his leg, that attitude! It's part of the treatment."

Mrs. Mayer turned to me. "Do you think he's depressed, dear?"

I nodded, and suddenly I remembered a day with him early in the previous spring—a beautiful day, cloudless, almost soft. It was a Saturday, and after a late breakfast we left my apartment and went to James Madison Park, where we gravitated toward the little play-ground there, full of children. We sat side by side on a bench and watched, and I let myself slip into a reverie of separateness, of wel-come solitude, where I was alone in a place I'd never been before and happy about it. I'd been having such dreams for a while and had mas-tered the art of slipping away without so much as a flicker to alert him to my desertion. But this time he seemed to know. He glanced at me once or twice, then put a hand on my knee, removing it when I looked at him. "What?" I said, and he shook his head. He stared at the chil-dren. "I guess I'm kind of depressed," he said at last, and then we sat there without speaking: I sat there without speaking. Later that same day we went to a movie, and sitting in the dark I actually fought the urge to reach for his hand, as if my body still needed to be trained in the new habits of my mind.

Mrs. Mayer was waiting for me to say something. A pair of doctors walked by, and one of them happened to look right at me just then— a kind-looking older man with thick white hair. Feeling his eyes on me, I thought for a moment that he understood what we were going through, and I felt touched, even comforted. Then I realized: we were just another case to him, the periphery of some illness or accident. His understanding was a given, even a barrier. We were alone— alone together and also alone within ourselves, each of the three of us, just as Mike and I had been that day at the park.

AND YET, MIKE was doing well physically—all the rehab people said so. He was sitting up for hours at a time, had even managed twice to wheel himself all the way from his room to the physical therapy hall. A few evenings after my talk with Mr. and Mrs. Mayer, I arrived for my visit and found him not lying on his bed but sitting in his wheelchair, a first for after dinner, a heavy strap holding his torso in place.

"Wow, you're up," I said. "I can't believe it."

He gave me a look.

"What?"

"Isn't it ironic? I'm a *low* quad, and yet I'm *up*."

A week ago he'd reported that he'd heard one of the physical therapy assistants use the phrase "low quad" in reference to another patient with a relatively low cervical-spine injury. The way it irritated him, I was glad he hadn't heard anyone say "good quad," an oxymoron I'd heard back when we were waiting for him to awaken.

I looked around the room. All the Mayers were there: Mr. and Mrs. in chairs opposite the foot of Mike's bed, Julie and John Junior on the floor to the side.

"Hard day?" I said.

"Just the usual."

"You seem tired."

"I am."

Mr. and Mrs. Mayer exchanged a glance, and I moved closer to Mike. "Are there too many people here?" I whispered. "Do you want me to go?"

"If you want."

"What do you want?"

"Nothing I'm going to get, that's for sure."

I edged over to the bed and half sat on the foot of it. Sitting against the wall, Julie looked sallow, as if she'd spent the summer in a cave— dressed all in black, her skin the color of ivory. She was twisting a thick silver ring around her finger, twisting and twisting. The last few times I'd seen her she'd smelled of cigarette smoke, a sudden, dirty smell when I'd gotten close. Next to her John Junior wore cutoff sweatpants and a T-shirt and looked so much the picture of health, his face still slightly flushed from whatever exercise he'd been doing, that I wondered if it wasn't his appearance that was bothering Mike, making him think of all he'd lost.

"I'm practicing," Mike said.

I turned and saw that his face had softened, as if he'd decided to try. I felt a huge sympathy for him, just for the work of being visited. Why should he be cheerful? Why anything? The doctors had asked us to report any oddities in his personality, indications of some lingering effects of the head injury, but how could we call moodiness an after-effect when he could hardly be anything else?

"Practicing?" I said.

"Spending more time in the chair."

"Is that good?"

"It's tiring." He gave me a one-cornered smile. "How screwed up is it to find sitting tiring?"

"Pretty screwed up."

It was almost eight, and the Mayers began glancing at each other. Leaving was harder when you were in a group, the bunch of you walking out the door without him.

Julie and John were quarreling about something, I could tell. They spoke softly, but there was something in how little they were moving their mouths that told me there was a disagreement going on.

Mike seemed to sense it, too. He reached for the wheels of his chair and slowly rotated himself until he could see them. "What are you guys talking about?"

Julie and John exchanged a glance, and a look of warning came over Mrs. Mayer's face. She stood up and planted her hands on her hips, fingers splayed over the fabric of her navy blue wrap skirt.

"Forget it, Mom," Julie said abruptly. "I'm not lying." She stood up and faced Mike, her long brown hair hanging in sheets by her face.

"We're going out for dinner," she said to him, "the four of us, I'm sorry. And John wants to go to that disgusting German Inn, but they have nothing I can eat."

Mike gave John an appraising look. "So?"

"So I like their pork chops," John said, coloring a little. "They have salad."

Julie frowned. "Yeah, an entire head of iceberg with, like, one measly cherry tomato. Yum."

"Knock it off," Mr. Mayer said. He stood, too, and crossed his arms over his chest. "We'll decide in the car."

Mrs. Mayer glanced at me, then turned to Mike. "I'm so sorry, honey," she said, her eyes full of regret. "I know this must make you feel bad."

Mike gave her a disgusted look. "You think I expect you guys to sit around picking your noses when you're not here? I don't care."

She flushed a little. "I just wish you could come."

Mike frowned, but Mr. Mayer actually seemed to consider the idea. He cupped his chin in his hand, stared off into space. "Maybe we should see if you can next time," he said thoughtfully. "In a few weeks or something."

Mrs. Mayer clapped her hands together. "Wouldn't that be wonderful! I wonder if you couldn't get some kind of day pass or something."

Mike rolled his eyes and laughed harshly. "I'm not in jail, Mom, appearances to the contrary. Anyway, I wouldn't want to."

"Why on earth not?" Mrs. Mayer bit her lip. "I should think you'd love a little change of scene."

"When I want a change of scene," he said, "I tell my buddy here to try channel fifteen for a while."

Automatically we all looked at Jeff Walker, who'd been lying there quietly, his father on the far side of his bed, saying something every now and then in a low voice. After a moment, though he'd given no indication that he was listening, Jeff aimed the remote at the TV and a new picture came on.

"Like that," Mike said.

After the Mayers left an orderly came in to transfer him onto his bed. I moved out of the way and watched as she lowered the bed and then unstrapped him from the chair. She stood in front of him with his knees between hers, wrapped her arms around his chest, and slowly raised him till he'd cleared the chair. Then she rotated him around, settled his bottom onto the bed, lowered his upper body onto the mattress, and swiveled his legs up. She was about my size, and I couldn't imagine how she'd done it, how strong she was. What was going to happen once he was home? How were we going to manage even just the physical part of it?

When she left I dragged a chair closer and sat down. I was about to offer him something to drink when a tall, dark-haired man with gold-rimmed glasses and a full beard came in. He stood just inside the doorway, wearing jeans and a shirt and tie. Mike took one look at him and stared off to the side, plainly furious.

"Hey, Mike," the man said. "How's it going? Thought I'd poke my head in before it got too late."

Mike didn't respond. He looked straight ahead, his face reddening.

"Dave King," the man said, coming over and offering me his hand.

"I'm Carrie."

He nodded knowingly, as if he'd heard of me, had half expected to find me here. He was standing in Mike's field of vision now, impossible for Mike to avoid seeing unless he truly looked away, which the halo made difficult.

"Thought we might spend some time together tomorrow," Dave King said. "Say around four?"

Mike pressed his lips together.

"Hey, a simple yes or no wouldn't be too much to ask, would it?"

"How about a simple no, then?"

Dave King shrugged. He watched Mike for another moment and then left the room, nodding at me on his way out.

"Don't you want to know who he was?"

I looked back at Mike. I had a pretty good idea he was the therapist the Mayers had mentioned, but I didn't say so. "Who was he?"

"The head guy. Total dick."

I couldn't help smiling. "How so?"

"He just is. And if you're going to laugh, why don't you just leave?"

"Is that what you want?"

Mike's face went livid and he shouted, "Stop! Asking me! What! I! Want!" He stared at me with his eyes burning, his words bouncing off the hard surfaces of the room and keeping us both absolutely still. Finally the color in his face began to drain away, and he said, quite calmly, "Why do people keep asking me what I want? I want to walk out of here. Christ. I want to walk."

THE MOON WAS just past full, bright in the indigo sky. Leaving through a side door, I made my way to a bench in a little paved V where two wings of the building came together. I'd left Mike composed but so exhausted I knew sleep would come fast. I sat down and breathed in the night smells, settled car exhaust and boxwood and a faint, moist scent of the lake. How could Mike stand having people *at* him all the time? The rehab people but also us, his family, me. It had to be a nightmare—on top of what was really a nightmare. My worry about him slipped into high gear, and I felt stripped by the tension of it, just opened wide.

Worry. It sounds like such an active thing, but it was more as if that picture of him that I'd told him I had—the picture of him that was thinking of him—had fallen to the bottom of an inky well, and through the dark and rippling water I could see glimpses of his distorted face, down so far I couldn't reach it.

The exit door swung open, and I heard pant legs brushing together, then a low cough. ". . . and we can't have *that*," a man's voice said, and a moment later the man himself appeared. It was Dave King, the therapist. I pressed myself into the shadows, but he looked over and stopped, saying, "Whoa, you may be the first person I've ever seen on that bench."

I looked in the direction he'd come from, but there was no one else, no one for him to have been talking to.

"I was having a small conversation with myself," he said. "Just straightening a few things out." He came closer and set his briefcase down, then stretched: a self-conscious stretch that suggested a desire to engage me in a casual-seeming but nonetheless significant conversation. Could he have followed me out of the hospital?

"Nice night," he said.

"Yeah, it's not so hot anymore."

He unzipped the briefcase and took out a small, shiny package. He held it in both hands and pulled, and the faint pop of air that followed told me he'd opened some kind of food.

"Ritz Bits?" he said, offering me the package.

"No, thanks."

"Dave?" he said, and then, "Why, thanks, Dave, don't mind if I do." He shook out a handful and then just chewed for a while, the bag crinkling in his other hand. "You know, I'm glad I ran into you," he said. "How do you think Mike's doing? Actually, do you mind if I sit down? I feel like I'm blocking your moonlight." He pushed the brief-case aside and sat down a few feet away from me.

I didn't know what to say. Would it be a betrayal of Mike to talk to him? I wasn't sure.

"Maybe you'd rather not go into it," he said.

"No, it's OK. He's really sad. Really sad."

He nodded slowly. "Do you know that more by what he's said or what he hasn't said?" He spoke without looking at me, and I thought he was being very careful, as if I were a valuable but easily spoiled resource.

"Hasn't," I said. "Well, both."

"His parents probably told you he's decided he doesn't want to talk to me." He paused. "As if you couldn't have figured that out tonight." He glanced over at me. "Was he much of a talker? Before the accident?"

"Yeah. I mean, he wasn't a motormouth or anything, but he talked." I thought of lying in bed with him after making love, how open and sweet he always was, as if, business over, we could finally chat. Sitting there on the bench, I could almost feel his leg slung over mine, his hand on my stomach, the vibration of his chin on my shoulder.

"I guess he decided I'm a jerk," Dave King said.

I smiled, thinking of the word Mike had actually used.

Dave King gave me a curious look. "What?"

I shook my head.

He reached into the bag again and threw a couple more crackers into his mouth, then leaned down to stuff the bag back into his brief-case as if he were about to take off.

"He said you were a dick," I said. "If you really want to know."

He straightened up and looked at me. "A dick?"

"I'm afraid so."

He was silent for a moment. "Interesting choice of words."

"I guess it's kind of rude," I said, "but I'm sure he didn't mean any-thing by it."

He rocked his head back and forth. "Maybe he did."

My mouth went a little dry. "Like what?"

He leaned back and crossed his legs. "What do you think his con-cerns are right now? He's lying up there, he's got another seven or eight weeks in the halo—what's going through his mind?"

Understanding hit hard, and I looked away.

"I don't mean to embarrass you," he said softly. "You've probably thought all this through yourself, or maybe you went to the library and found out what you needed to know." He hesitated. "I mean, there are books that explain the effects on male sexual function of an injury like Mike's."

I stared at my hands. This was the one thing Mr. Mayer hadn't researched, or if he had, he'd kept his findings to himself. Still, I didn't have much doubt about it. No motion. No sensation. Twice since the accident I'd woken from dreams so aroused that just turning over or moving a leg had made me come. I couldn't bring myself to masturbate, though: it seemed too final, like an acquiescence.

"I'm sorry," he said. "I've made you uncomfortable."

I looked over and saw him watching me with what I could only think of as a gentle look, and to my surprise I found myself sort of liking him. There was something vulnerable about him, and for an instant I flashed onto his home life: a guy living alone in an apartment with lots of spider plants, an aquarium full of tiny, colorful fish. He'd walk over and talk to them as soon as he got home, the room still dark behind him.

How strange: Kilroy had seen me in the same sure way I'd just seen Dave King. Clear and certain, as if he'd known. *I hope Mike wakes to your vigilance and love soon, and that you'll be well together.* His let-

ter was in my dresser, buried in my sock drawer. When I got low on
socks I could see the envelope, white against the wood grain, a signal
of some kind.

"I'd really like to find a way to help Mike," Dave King said. "That's
why I came over when I saw you sitting here. He's got a rough road
ahead of him, and it can help to talk about things." He stayed still for
a moment, then turned toward me and gave me a quick smile. "Well,
I should get going."

He leaned down for his briefcase, and I found I didn't want him to
leave yet. "My mother's a therapist, too," I said. "At the U."

He straightened up without the briefcase. "What's her name?"

"Margaret Bell."

He wrinkled his forehead. "She's been there awhile, right?"

"Twelve years."

He nodded thoughtfully. "Have you considered talking to someone
yourself?"

I was taken aback. "I don't really think I need to."

He lifted one shoulder. "I don't know about need, but it could be
said that you've got a rough road ahead, too."

A rough road, sure, but not so rough—not as rough as Mike's. I
thought of his rage earlier: *Stop! Asking me! What! I! Want!* Yes,
absolutely.

"Well," Dave King said.

"He's not just sad," I said, "he's angry. He's *furious.*"

"Did he say so?"

"He yelled at me tonight. Right after you left." I told him what had
happened. "The thing is, he doesn't yell. Didn't, anyway. He was easygoing. Rooster would get all tense over someone being really late, or
people arguing over what to do, but Mike—" I broke off, embarrassed that I was blabbing.

"But Mike?"

I shook my head. "Sorry, I don't know why I'm going on like this.
You probably don't even know who Rooster is."

"Mike's best friend?"

I was surprised. Had Mike told him about Rooster? How much had
he told him about me? I stared into my lap, wishing I knew what he
knew. Was he here to tell me what Dr. Spelman had told me? *Rehab*

is very hard work—a lot of getting better is wanting to. Don't you think I *know* that? I wanted to cry.

"You were telling me that Mike was different from Rooster," he said. "Less tense over conflict."

I looked over at him. He was sitting there, waiting. Not in a hurry, like Dr. Spelman. I nodded.

"Can you say more?"

I thought for a moment. "He wouldn't stress," I said. "He could roll with things. But he could also handle Rooster being tense—roll with that." I remembered a winter Saturday a few years ago: we were going up to Badger Pass to ski, and Stu showed up without gear—he thought we were renting up there, which we'd decided against to avoid the lines. Rooster got really annoyed at Stu and his mood sort of took over everyone else. Except Mike. When he and I were alone together for a moment, moving through the house to leave, I cast a glance back over my shoulder in Rooster's direction and made a kind of face, and Mike shrugged and said, "He wanted it to go smoothly." Just that: *He wanted it to go smoothly.* And I had a feeling then— which I remembered now, sitting in the moonlight outside the hospital—that the word for Mike was *kind.*

"There's a lot of uncertainty, isn't there?" Dave King said. "About how he'll be."

I nodded.

"For him, too, don't you think? How he'll be, how he'll fit into the picture he had of the future."

"Yes," I said. My voice was so low it was like a whisper, and I said it again, a little louder: "Yes."

He bent over and picked up his briefcase, then sat holding it for a moment. "Listen," he said, "I should get going, but can I tell you one thing? As far as what we were talking about before?"

"Sure."

He scratched his jaw, and a feeling of nervousness came over me about what he would say, what he might say to me after all. Stay the course. *Stay the course!* Why should that make me so uneasy, when I *was?*

"Guys with spinal cord injuries are using vibrators, electricity, even drugs to ejaculate. Which means, among other things, that it wouldn't be impossible for you and Mike to have a child together somewhere down the line."

"Oh, my God!" I exclaimed.

Behind his glasses, his eyes widened. "I'm sorry," he said. "I didn't mean—"

"It's OK," I said. "I just had a very bizarre thought."

He waited expectantly, but I couldn't tell him, I certainly wasn't going to tell *him*—but then I did: "I thought: I can't have a child, I *am* a child." I looked at the ground, embarrassed now. "Pretty stupid, huh?"

"Doesn't sound stupid to me," he said. "If you were a child none of this would be happening."

I looked up again. "What do you mean?"

"If you were a child, you wouldn't have a lover, and he wouldn't be quadriplegic."

A lover. Heat filled my face. I thought of Mike above me in bed, using his knee to sweep my leg aside so he could plunge into me. Then Mike up in his room earlier tonight, being maneuvered into bed by the orderly.

Dave King was watching me. "I see what you mean," I said, but I couldn't look at him now; I looked past him, into the darkness, to the memory of Mike suspended over me. We're in my apartment, in my bed, and he's got his weight on his forearms, placed on each side of me, and he's inside me, arching, his eyes closed tight, his entire being straining forward; and I rise up to the feeling of him.

No. No, I don't rise. I rose.

12

~

SIMON RHODES CALLED me one evening near the end of
August, and we talked for almost three hours, the longest I'd spent
doing anything but sewing in months. "So what's new in the Carrie
Bell saga?" he said. "Wait'll you hear the latest in the Simon Rhodes
saga." He told me about life in New York: about his problems with his
boyfriend; about the big, dilapidated brownstone he shared with a
bunch of Yale friends; about the Park Avenue law firm where he
worked as a proofreader. It had the unlikely name of Biggs, Lepper,
Rush, Creighton and Fenelon, but he said all the proofreaders
referred to it as Big Leper Rush. What he really wanted was to be an
illustrator.

I told him about Mike's sadness, about how difficult it was to
watch. About the rare moments when some piece of his former self
came through: when he joked with Stu or Bill, ribbed Rooster about
Joan. I'd catch his eye, and there'd pass between us a recognition of
the fact that he didn't have any of that available for me right now. "It
sounds hard," Simon said, and I was grateful: I could tell him anything and it would be OK, the words zooming away from Madison,
safely gone just moments after I'd uttered them.

Before we hung up I said I wanted to pay for half the call, but he wouldn't hear of it. "Are you kidding?" he said. "This is the most fun I've had since I played Twister at Nicole Patterson's birthday party in fourth grade."

I laughed, but I knew what he meant. Fun might not be the word, but there was something about talking to him that was deeply satisfying. Just like Twister, he would've said if I'd told him, so I didn't.

Julie was leaving for her sophomore year at Swarthmore, and she called and asked me to come say goodbye, a surprise given that I saw her at the hospital all the time.

I hadn't been over there since my talk with Mrs. Mayer back in June. Their street had some of the tallest, most densely planted trees in town, a row of soaring maples whose topmost leaves were just beginning to fade and curl. I stepped out of my car, and the thick, warm shade they cast achingly reminded me of every end-of-summer I'd had with Mike, of the feeling of things being about to change.

No one else was home, and Julie and I sat in the kitchen drinking diet sodas, talking idly about this and that—how she needed a new backpack; how Dana, her best friend from Madison, had been a pain all summer. The two of them had been inseparable—like me and Jamie, I'd always thought. They were like us still.

"I can tell you this now," Julie said. "Remember at Lake Superior? The time we had the place by Oulten's Cove? It was Dana who spilled the bug juice on your white sweater. She made me promise not to tell you."

"You think I didn't know that?"

We both smiled, and I thought back to that summer, Mike and I sixteen, Julie and Dana twelve. I bunked with them, fell asleep to the sounds of their voices saying the names of the boys they preferred. They thought it was boring that I preferred Mike; they were always asking who I liked second-best.

"Did you guys write letters last year?" I said.

"A few."

"Maybe it'll just peter out this year."

Julie stood and went into the dining room for her purse, a book-sized black velvet bag on a braided cord. She fished around in it until she'd found a pack of cigarettes, then she laid them on the table between us and stared at me. Nothing could have horrified the Mayers more than smoking: both grandfathers had died of lung cancer.

She gave me a defiant smile. "Yes, Carrie, I smoke. I also drink, and when I'm inclined to I fuck."

"Fucking's fun," I said. "At least I think I remember that."

She stared at me until all at once we both broke into laughter. We laughed for a long time, eyes right on each other—loud, convulsive laughter that hurt after a while deep in my stomach.

"Shit," she said. "I can't believe you said that."

"Neither can I."

We sat there looking at one another, surrounded by Mrs. Mayer's familiar kitchen: the bread-and-noodles smell, the matching ceramic canisters, the collection of ornamental plates hanging over the range. I felt giddy and strange, like the laughter might take over again. On the refrigerator, a familiar-looking grid caught my attention, and I stood to go look at it, glad to be moving.

It was John Junior's practice schedule for hockey.

"John's probably going to start this year," Julie said, tapping a cigarette out and lighting it.

"As a junior?"

She nodded, and I knew we were both thinking: *Just like Mike.* He'd been starting varsity right wing two years in a row. When he decided not to go out at the U, everyone tried to get him to change his mind except me. I understood it, how he could be ready for that part of his life to be over.

"You know what I really hate?" Julie said suddenly. "Flying. I'm scared to get on the stupid plane. I wish I could just wake up and be there."

I pictured her beamed from her mother's kitchen to a plush green lawn in front of a centuries-old fieldstone building. On the basis of a single photograph from a pamphlet she'd shown me once, I imagined I knew just what Swarthmore was like: towering trees, emerald playing fields, old, old dormitories, creaking classrooms, dining halls all paneled with dark wood. At the beginning of twelfth grade my guidance counselor had pressed on me an armful of brochures about colleges from Vermont to Virginia, but although I studied them carefully, fascinated by the photographs of students walking across quadrangles or sitting in classrooms taking notes, I never even applied. I cited inadequate funds to the counselor, but the truth was it would have meant leaving Mike.

"Maybe I'll transfer," Julie said.

"Here?"

She inhaled hard on her cigarette. "It's a good school."

"Because you're afraid to fly?"

She gave me a look: not because she was afraid to fly.

"I think he'd be really upset if he thought you were thinking that. Really upset."

"Do you really think so?" she said. "I doubt he'd care. He doesn't care about much these days." She stood up and crossed to the window. She wore a skinny black tank, and her shoulders looked bony, not an ounce of extra flesh on them. As I watched she raised her hand unsteadily and dragged on the cigarette again. Then she turned and looked at me. "Are you still going to get married?"

I felt a gasp catch in my throat, and my face burned. Julie stared at me with her gray eyes wide, eyes so much like Mike's that it was eerie, his eyes in her face. She was the last person I would have expected to ask me. "I don't know," I said. "Do you think I should?"

She blew a plume of smoke into the air above her head. "I don't know," she said. "Do you want to?"

DO YOU WANT to? Do you want to? Do you want to? By the time I got home from the hospital that night the question had permeated the very air around me, and I couldn't even think of sewing, let alone going to bed. I sat and paced and sat, then finally went out onto my porch. I was barefoot, and as I stood there looking into the night I absently brushed the grit from the bottom of one foot onto the opposite calf, then did the same with the other foot, until I became aware of what I was doing and started pacing again.

I knew I could continue, in Rooster's words, to be there for Mike; I knew I could wait out his sadness or at least that part of it that was most acute. I knew I could stand by and applaud as he slowly, slowly learned how to get around in his wheelchair, how to use what little function he could marshal from his hands to eat, to help dress himself, maybe to turn the pages of a book. But what then? Be his care-taker? His cook, nurse, helper, chauffeur, attendant? And his wife, somehow, too? And also myself? Who might that be?

But I didn't want to walk away—I didn't want to *be* someone who could walk away. Not from Mike.

Out at Picnic Point once, lying on a bed of fallen leaves on a warm October day, we talked about dying. About what we'd each do if the other died. "I'd want to die, too," Mike said, and I felt a narrow gap open up between us because I wouldn't want to, couldn't see thinking in those terms at all. I reached for a yellowing leaf and folded it along the center vein, and I imagined myself in a small cottage somewhere, alone, sweeping the steps and waiting to feel ready for the world again.

It was nearly midnight, but I put on some shoes and went down to my car, the urge to move propelling me across the isthmus and around Lake Monona, the big, round darkness of it glinting with reflected bits of the half-moon. I got on the Beltline heading west and drove, past Rooster's Honda place, past the turnoff to Verona, just drove and drove through the darkness, the road disappearing under my headlights again and again, highway signs blinking by, the twin staring eyes of oncoming headlights. I passed the exit for West Towne Mall, the last of the motels out there. I was coming around onto Middleton when I finally got off, and I slowed to wind through cul-de-sac land until I'd reached the strip of big, faceless restaurants that had been our destination so often, on countless nights when we'd been cruising too long and wanted pancakes, or big, wide platters of French fries. I hadn't been that far west in ages, in I didn't know how long—it was like a strange, foreign land where you'd never see any-one on foot, just oceans of parking lot and low-slung buildings. The Red Barn. Jack Sprat's. Five or six of us in a booth, Rooster across the table wisecracking, Jamie tipsy, Mike and I side by side, pressed close, my leg over his and his hand cupping my inner thigh.

I was about to get back on the Beltline and head for home when I glanced across a nearly empty parking lot and saw a woman standing by herself under the front light of the Alley, a ratty cocktail lounge I'd heard about but never been in. There was something familiar about her, something in the way she stood, but I couldn't figure out what.

I pulled into a gas station and swung around so I could go back out the way I'd come. I drove into the Alley parking lot, skirted the few cars that were parked there, and then I saw: it was Lynn Fletcher, Jamie's younger sister. She was standing just in front of the entrance, one leg crossed in front of the other, wearing a short skirt and an over-sized jean jacket. Her hair was big and disheveled, as if she'd just teased it and doused it with hairspray. I stopped in front of her, and she glanced once at my car and then looked away.

Reaching across the seat, I rolled down the passenger-side window and called her name.

She glanced at me again, this time stooping to look through the open window. Her hand flew to her mouth. "Carrie!"

"What are you doing here?"

"Nothing. Waiting for someone."

"Come here," I said, motioning her to the car.

She hesitated, then took a few steps closer to me. She had Jamie's small mouth and wide-set green eyes, but she was shorter than Jamie, a little chubby.

I shifted into park and let the car idle. Through the window, Lynn looked scared.

"Who are you meeting?" I said.

"A friend from work."

The restaurant where she waitressed was nearby, I recalled— Spinelli's. I wondered how she was going to get into the Alley, if she had a fake ID. Or maybe no one would card her, though she looked about sixteen, standing there in her too-short skirt, big silver hoops hanging from her ears.

She took a step closer. "Don't tell, OK?"

"Don't tell who?" I cut the engine and after a moment leaned toward her and opened the door. "Sit with me for a sec, I haven't seen you in ages."

She looked toward the road, then shrugged and got into the car. She was wearing four or five bracelets, and they clinked together as she settled into the seat.

"I mean don't tell Jamie."

"Don't tell her I saw you at all?"

She looked at me hard, a little frown pulling at the corners of her mouth. She wore a streak of iridescent green on each eyelid, mascara thick as paint.

"What are you up to?"

She raised a pudgy hand and tucked a strand of hair behind her ear. "Nothing."

"Lynn."

"I just have a date."

"With a man?"

She gave me a look.

"Who?"

"Just someone I met at work."

Now I was confused—earlier, I'd thought she meant a co-worker. "You mean a customer? Jesus, do you really think that's a good idea?"

"It's fun."

A car pulled up behind me, and she turned and peered through my back window, blinking at the headlights and craning her neck until she turned back, apparently having decided it wasn't the guy she was meeting. In the dark car her profile looked vulnerable, her chin soft and sloping. I wondered what I'd do if the right car drove up, if I'd let her go.

"Do a *lot* of the customers hit on you?"

"Carrie!" She gave me a hurt look. "They're just friendly."

"I'll bet."

She shrugged, tugging a little at her skirt.

"Do you let these guys think you're twenty-one?"

She laughed and I realized that she'd had a drink or two already, that she was in fact on her way to being drunk. I wondered what was in her purse, a big, slouchy hobo she'd dropped between her feet. A pint of something, probably something cheap and sweet, like peach schnapps, Jamie's favorite drunk when she was eighteen.

Lynn turned toward me with a giggle. "Carrie, don't tell, but I sometimes play this little game with them? I let them buy me a couple drinks, then I say I have to get home for my curfew or my parents'll get mad, and they just, like, freak. 'Your parents? How old are you?' I said to this one guy a couple nights ago, 'I'm sixteen'—just to see what he'd do?—and I swear he had a heart attack. 'You're sixteen? I thought you were twenty-two at least. My daughter's sixteen.' Guy gave me a twenty not to tell anyone."

"Lynn!" I stared at her. "Jesus, are you kidding?"

"It's fun."

"It's stupid!"

Her eyes got big. "You're not going to tell Jamie, are you? She'd tell my mother for sure."

I couldn't think of anything Jamie'd be less likely to do, but I didn't say so. "You have to stop. How long's it going to take to go from getting money *not* to do something to getting money to *do* something?"

"Carrie!" She reached for her purse, then put her hand on the door handle. "I'm sure!" She pushed open the door and extended her legs, gleaming faintly in black nylons. She got out of the car but turned around and leaned into the open door. "Promise you won't tell her? Please?"

I sighed.

"Please?"

"OK, I promise. But you promise you'll stop, all right?"

She settled her purse strap on her shoulder and tilted her head at me, her expression earnest all at once. "Don't worry," she said. "I'm a big girl." She lifted one leg and kicked the car door closed, then took a few steps backward until she was under the entrance light again.

I started the car, thinking for some reason of Jamie—of how, within a couple weeks of the first time Mike and I made love, she found a guy from another high school to screw. "I don't see what the big deal is," she said to me afterward. I looked at Lynn, her chubby legs, her overly made-up face. A big girl was right, a big, big *girl*. And I drove away.

13

~

I HAD THE NEXT day off from the library, and when I woke up I decided to sew all day, just sew and sew, music playing loud, no room in my head for questions or thoughts.

I started my coffeemaker and then took what was done of the silk robe from the pillowcase where I'd been keeping it because the usual paper bag seemed too rough. I was about to sit down at the machine when on a whim I slipped the body of the robe on over my T-shirt and boxers. The feel was wonderful, and I turned from side to side so it could sweep against my bare legs, then went into my bedroom for a look in the mirror.

The fabric was extraordinary, so soft and light. And the robe didn't feel the same as the nightgown, with its alluring second-skin sensation; instead, it was voluminous, an embodiment of plenty—a cloak of everything I wanted from the world. I thought I'd wear the two of them together until they were in pieces again, frayed and softer than ever.

Late in the morning, just as I'd finished attaching the first sleeve, there was a knock at my door, followed by Jamie's voice from downstairs calling up to see if I was home. I looked around the room. Why I didn't want Jamie to see what I was making was a question I hadn't posed to myself, but I knew I didn't. In a hurry I set the robe down and started for the stairway, where I could already hear her footsteps.

"Woman." She was about halfway up, and she didn't stop when she saw me. "I was on my way by, so I figured I'd stop in. If I don't get my hair cut today I swear I will die."

"Better get it cut, then." I leaned against the wall in an effort to suggest that we could have our chat on the landing and then she could be on her way.

She wore a short denim jumper over a ribbed white T-shirt, and her legs gleamed as if she'd just shaved and oiled them. She said, "I'm going to, they're having a special at that place near Hilldale." She reached the top step and held out her palm for mine. "Want to come?"

I touched my hair: I hadn't had it cut since the accident, and the ends were dry and splitting. I shook my head. "I'm broke." This was only half a lie, since I was feeling pinched from spending so much on the silk.

She gave me an exasperated look. "Come on, put it on your credit card, it won't kill you."

I never used my credit card as a way of buying more than I could afford; my mother had warned me again and again about how quickly interest would build, how I'd end up paying double or more for everything I bought.

"You're such a responsible citizen," Jamie added, and I flinched: it sounded like an insult, like saying someone was a really good person.

"Sorry," I said. "I can't."

She frowned and crossed her arms over her chest, then let them drop again. "I was going to treat Lynn, but she was still asleep when I called, the little slug."

I thought of Lynn standing in front of the Alley last night, her big, teased hair. It had been almost one when I'd driven away, probably three or later before she'd gotten home.

Jamie turned a little, and just as I was thinking she might actually leave, she flapped her hand at me once and then stepped past me through the doorway into my apartment. "I have *got* to pee," she said, and then she stopped in her tracks.

It was a sight: pieces of silk hanging from chair backs; my table littered with pattern pieces, pin cushions, lengths of ribbon; my sewing machine sitting there with its little lightbulb burning, like a porch light on in the middle of the day.

"*What* is going on here?" Jamie said.

"I've been sewing."

"So I see, but the question is what." She advanced toward the table. "Is this silk?"

"It's a nightgown." My voice sounded dead as stone, and I tried again. "It's kind of a combo nightgown and robe."

"God, Carrie, and you didn't even tell me." She reached for the robe, which I'd left next to the machine.

"Don't!" I hurried past her to pick it up. "I mean, here, I'll show it to you."

She looked at me strangely. "You're afraid I'll wreck it," she said slowly. "In fact, you didn't want me to see it at all. That's why you came out to the stairs."

I looked away from her.

"It's *true?*"

I was holding the robe tightly against my chest, and I forced my arms to relax a little. "No," I said. "It's just—I didn't know how they'd turn out."

She shook her head. "I don't know about you," she said, but she seemed to relent a little, and I forced myself to show her what I'd done so far, the finished gown and then the robe. By the time she asked me to try them on I was feeling resigned, and I carried the pieces into my bedroom, took off what I was wearing, and put the gown and then the robe on, quickly pinning the second sleeve into place.

"Totally amazing," she said from the doorway. "You could go into business and make a ton of money, I'm serious."

"Right," I said, although I was flattered.

"You could. How much did the material cost?"

"You don't want to know."

"A hundred? One fifty?" Her eyes widened. "*Two* hundred?" She came over and felt the robe. "Still, I bet you could charge four hundred for the two pieces. Look at yourself, you look like some incredibly glamorous actress in an old movie."

I turned and looked in the mirror. "Really?"

"Definitely. All you need is a cigarette in an ivory holder."

I held out one leg.

"Well, and the flip-flops have to go. But with those sort of high-heeled backless slippers with fur trim—what are they called?"

"Mules?"

"Mules, exactly. It's so romantic, don't you think?"

"I guess."

"Honeymoon City."

"Ironically enough."

Her eyes met mine in the mirror, and we looked at each other for a long moment. "Well, you never know," she said.

"I do kind of know is the thing."

She turned from the mirror and stared at me. I was shaky with the shock of having said it, and for a while I just stood there, my face hot, my heart thudding. Then I turned around, slipped the robe off, pulled the gown over my head, and got back into my T-shirt and boxers.

"You're breaking *up* with him?"

I folded the gown into neat thirds, then made a single vertical fold in the robe and laid it carefully on my bed. I didn't want to see the horror on her face again, but finally there was nothing else to do, and I reluctantly turned and looked.

She was staring hard, her mouth open. "Oh, my God," she said. "My God, my God. Do you want to talk about it?"

I shook my head.

She crossed the room and stood at the window. All you could see from there was the ramshackle old garage I shared with my downstairs neighbors, but she stood looking for a long time. Finally, her back still to me, she said, "I've been wondering what you were thinking. I mean, I figured you were thinking about it but I didn't know how you were feeling. I didn't know if you would go ahead and—well, get married anyway. I mean, I knew that would be really hard, and things weren't even so great before the accident, but—" All at once she turned to face me, and I saw that she'd been fighting tears. "God, this has been so hard for you!"

"Not as hard as for him."

"Yeah, but that almost makes it harder."

I shrugged, and all at once the compassion on her face was gone, replaced by massive irritation. "Carrie!"

"What?"

"I just have this weird feeling that I don't really know you anymore! Did I do something? Are you mad at me? Are you even in there?"

I turned away. It was a question I understood, because lately what I mainly felt was hollow, as if the feelings I should be having had vanished and left me clanking around inside my own mind looking for them. "I'm sorry," I said in a low voice.

She came over to where I was standing and touched the back of my shoulder, then reached around me and hugged me hard. "Forget it," she said. "*I'm* sorry. I shouldn't have said anything, I just wish I could help." She turned me around and I let her hug me from the front.

"Are you OK?"

I nodded.

"When do you think you'll do it?"

"I don't know."

"But pretty soon, right? I mean, don't you sort of think you should now that you've decided?"

"I guess," I said, although I didn't really feel that I had decided, had chosen. It was more as if I'd been traveling somewhere unknown and I was there now, looking around, trying to get the lay of the land.

"God," she said quietly. "*God.*" She looked me in the eye. "Do you want me to stay for a while? I can get my hair cut tomorrow."

I shook my head. "That's OK. I mean, thanks, but I really just feel like sewing."

Once she was gone, I sat down at the machine again, but I couldn't concentrate, couldn't focus on the pattern, what I was supposed to do next. I grabbed my keys and locked up, then set off down the stairs and out onto the sidewalk. I felt terrible for Jamie—it was like a chain reaction, what had happened: the accident felled Mike, that knocked me loose, *that* hit her . . . Although of course I'd been knocked loose long before the accident, by whatever—my own fickle heart—and she'd been the target almost as much as he had. There'd been times in the months before the accident when it had taken all my strength not to tell her that I didn't *care* what so-and-so said about such-and-such, or who had a cute butt, or anything else. But to think of her worrying it over in her mind, wondering what it was she'd done—I felt awful about that.

As for Mike, I didn't have any idea when to tell him, what to tell him, how . . . There were too many variables. The only thing I was sure of was that afterward I would be a pariah. Look at how shocked she'd been—and that was *Jamie*. There'd be no more Mayers in my life and definitely no more Rooster. And my mother—what would she say? Approve of Mike or not, how could she be anything but disgusted to see me do the thing that had been done to her?

And Mike. What if there was no more Mike in my life? There was that smile he had when he had something up his sleeve: his mouth stretched wide, all but closed. What if I never saw that smile again? What if I never heard him say "wrong" again in that annoying, endearing way he had? What if I never watched him fall asleep over late-night TV again, never saw the way his eyelids drooped lower and lower, his mouth opened slightly, his breathing deepened? There were things I'd seen in him that perhaps no one else had ever seen or noticed—wouldn't those things disappear along with my apprehension of them? Because we were caretakers of each other's habits and expressions, weren't we, witnesses who didn't just see but who gave existence? Our coming apart would erase all those tiny moments and gestures and looks from everywhere but our separate memories, until even there our history would begin to fade.

I'd been heading toward James Madison Park, and now I slowed down and looked around me. I took in the lake, pale blue and rippled in the early fall breeze; and the people setting up for picnics, throwing Frisbees, running with their big, beautiful dogs. What a simple thing, I thought: to run, to walk.

14

~

I KNEW I SHOULD talk to Mike, but for days I stumbled over the word "but." *I hope we'll always be friends, but . . . I wish it didn't have to be this way, but . . . I still love you, but . . .* Night after night I sat with him, held his hand and tried to interest him in something, anything; and all the while I was racked by my own silent voice picking over words, looking for some that would serve.

One evening John Junior came to the hospital with Mrs. Mayer. He seemed nervous. He started telling Mike about the new hockey coach, and almost immediately I felt the familiar sliding away of Mike's attention. "Mom," he interrupted John at one point. "I thought you were bringing the new *Sports Illustrated* tonight." A little later he asked me for a drink of water, moments after that a Kleenex.

John stood up in the middle of a sentence and walked out of the room.

"Where's he going?" Mike said.

I was leaning against the wall, and when he looked at me I shrugged a little. "You were kind of ignoring him—I think maybe he's a little hurt."

"I was not. What—he was talking about Coach Henry or someone, the new hockey coach. I heard him."

"Henderson," I said. "You heard, but maybe you weren't quite listening."

He rolled his eyes. "Well, excuse me. Who's visiting who?"

"Whom." Mrs. Mayer was sitting very straight, her arms crossed over her chest. "Who's visiting *whom.*"

"Gimme a break."

"Son." Mrs. Mayer frowned, uncrossing her arms and then recrossing them. She lifted a hand and touched her hair. "We're all trying awfully hard, but lately it seems no one can do anything right by you. I think you owe your brother an apology. I'm going to go get him, and then I think we'll go home." She stood up.

"You don't have to go." He glanced at me. "I'm sorry."

"I'll get your brother."

She left the room, and I went over to the bed and took his hand. "*I'm* sorry," I said. "I started it."

"No, I am." He was flushed and teary, ready to cry. "I'm an asshole."

"You're not." I drew the curtain between his bed and Jeff's, then sat on the edge of the bed and took his hand again. "You're not at all," I said quietly. "John just misses you. I think he'd probably like some time alone with you, but that never seems to happen."

"Mom," he said.

"Yeah, but me, too."

"You're different." He looked me in the eye, and then quickly looked away. "I don't know, I don't know what's wrong with me, I'm just so bored! Isn't that crazy? As if that were anything like my biggest problem. But I'm so fucking bored sometimes I just want to scream."

"They don't call them patients for nothing."

He smiled. "You know what I was thinking about the other day? Remember that party Jamie had for us, for our five years? At Fabrizio's?"

"We were supposed to meet her for dinner there, and we couldn't figure out why she wanted to go to Fabrizio's."

"Then everyone was in that little room." He closed his eyes and sighed.

"What made you think of that?"

"I don't know."

"Come on, what?"

His eyes met mine. "Well, I always thought we should go there after the next five. I mean not with everyone—just us. But I guess we won't now, will we?" He looked at me evenly.

I hesitated. This was the edge, the opening I'd been looking for, but I couldn't bear to use it. "I don't know," I said. "I really don't."

"It's OK," he said. "You don't have to feel bad."

"We can't have this conversation right now. Your mother and John'll be back any minute."

He licked his lips. "We've had it, haven't we?"

"No. Please."

He gave me a look of piercing quietude. "It's a relief to me, actually," he said. "I was really tired of wondering."

"Mike—"

He moved his arm, pulled it closer to his body, and I stopped talking. He lifted the arm onto his lap, his hand dragging behind.

"Let's not," he said. "OK? Let's just not."

AT HOME, I filled my tub with hot water and took a long bath. It was September now, the first really cool night of the coming fall, and I lay soaking for a long time, waiting to be filled by tears and terrible regret or by relief—whatever it would be. I lay and lay, and waited and waited, but all I could think—all I could feel—was that I was tired. If an era of my life had ended, its passing was remarkable only for the quiet it left behind, the whisper of myself asking myself what there was now.

Then I knew. I dried off and dressed in clean jeans and a sweatshirt, then made a pot of coffee. By the time I sat down at my sewing table it was almost ten, but that didn't faze me. I'd marked the robe's hemline the day before, and now I cut away all but a perfect three inches, then used my machine to put in a line of basting half an inch from the edge. The iron was heating and I turned the seam allowance under and pressed it, then carefully pinned the hem up using my ballpoint pins, pulling on the basting thread wherever I needed to adjust the fullness. I had four yards to sew, but I didn't feel daunted; I took the robe to a chair near a bright light, threaded a needle, and got started. When my neck felt sore I took breaks, lay on the floor for a while or did some stretches, but I was always back at it within a few minutes. I had to rethread my needle several times, and as luck would have it I ran out again just a couple inches shy of the end, but I didn't feel the irritation I usually felt when that happened; I just cut off another foot of thread, poked it through the eye of the needle, knotted the end, and finished my work.

My body ached. I undressed and slipped on the gown, then the robe. In my bedroom mirror I did look glamorous, as Jamie had said, but only from the neck down, because my face was all wrong: too serious, too plain, too young. I knew I could pluck my eyebrows, put on foundation and blush and lipstick, do something to make my eyes look deep-set and mysterious, but I'd still look like what I was—not a child, maybe, but not a woman either. A girl of twenty-three.

It was nearly one in the morning now, and as I took off the robe and then the gown it occurred to me that there might be some danger ahead, that I might end up being a girl all my life, like Mrs. Fletcher. I thought of what Dave King had said, his suggestion that seeing myself as a child had been self-protective, and I made a wish for courage.

I got dressed and went back out to the living room, where I put everything away—the iron and ironing board, the scraps of fabric, the pattern pieces that I'd never gotten around to returning to their envelope. I unplugged the sewing machine, used a little brush to clean out the bobbin housing, wrapped the cord up and tucked it into its container, and put the cover on. I set the machine by the door, then I went into my bedroom and got out the enormous old suitcase my mother had lent me when I moved from the dorms to my apartment. Working quickly, I filled it with clothes, and when I had finished my dresser and closet were nearly empty. Last in were the gown and robe, folded carefully and wrapped in tissue paper. I found a smaller hold-all for my toiletries and a few other odds and ends, and I carried both bags down to my car. I went back up for a last look around, emptied half a gallon of milk into the sink, took out the garbage, and returned for my sewing machine. And then I locked up.

HOW MUCH DO we owe the people we love? How much do we owe them? When I was in high school something people said in praise of their friends was "He'd put his hand in the fire for me." I think Mike may have even said it about Rooster once, and it's just possible Rooster would have: put his hand in the fire for Mike, given up his hand. What I had discovered was that I couldn't give up my life for Mike—that's how I saw it at the time, that's the choice I thought I had to make. And because I couldn't give up everything, I also thought I couldn't give up anything.

There's a kind of tired you can get that has its own energy. I was exhausted when I started the car, my eyes stinging and my back and neck aching, but once I was driving I discovered that I was actually in no real danger of falling asleep.

I took I-90 down past Chicago and saw the sun rise just as I was passing Lake Michigan. It was a clear day, and soon the states were going by as if they were towns built close together by the side of the highway. I thought occasionally of stopping, but I was in the rhythm of it, I was running on French fries and terrible coffee, and I kept going. Finally, somewhere in eastern Pennsylvania, I got off the interstate and found a motel and slept.

By mid-morning I was back on the road. At one gas station I bought a map, and at another I found a Manhattan phone book and located the address of Biggs, Lepper, Rush, Creighton and Fenelon, the helpful nickname perfectly clear in my mind. Then, just as the morning clouds were thinning and the sky was turning blue, I steered my way onto the George Washington Bridge, and there was New York, stretching down the river as far as I could see.

PART TWO

~

A THOUSAND

MILES

~

15

Simon lived on the edge of Chelsea in a decrepit old brown-stone with taped-over windows and a sheet of graffitied plywood covering the front door. The house was owned by a partner at his law firm: the partner had inherited it from an uncle and was renting it to Simon—for the unheard-of sum of five hundred dollars a month—while he tried to decide whether to unload it or sink a bundle into it and live there himself. A block east everything was leafy and well-kept, neat iron fencelets around the bases of ginkgo trees, but this block was borderline, home not just to some other dubious town-houses, but also to a gas station, an auto body shop, and a double-wide empty lot surrounded by chain-link fence. Simon and some Yale friends occupied the four bedrooms, but he found me an empty alcove on the third floor, and together we dragged a spare futon up the steep, creaking stairs.

He kept apologizing about the place, but I liked it—it was so shabby and easygoing. Water stains mapped the ceilings, bits of base-board pulled away from the walls. The walls themselves looked so battered they might have been attacked, scarred with marks and dents and actual holes that blew plaster dust onto the floors. In the bathrooms, leaky faucets wobbled in their sockets, while ancient bathtubs rested on clawed feet, makeshift shower curtains hanging precariously from rigged-up lengths of pipe. "Like showering in a raincoat," Simon said, and it was true.

There was a dark, cavernous living room, but the kitchen was the true center of the house, the place where everyone hung out. Low-ceilinged and poorly lit, it was full of old appliances: a broken washing machine, a broken dishwasher, a rickety electric range with a broken fan, an enormous dinosaur of a microwave, a free-standing lift-top freezer that served as a countertop, and a round-shouldered refrigerator that gave off an erratic, worrisome hum. On an old metal desk that had been shoved against the wall there was a big whiteboard that Simon told me was the most important piece of furniture in the house: the place where messages were recorded.

At least a couple stereos were usually playing, and it was a little like living in a dorm again: people coming and going at all hours, the sound of a door closing waking me just as I'd fallen asleep. Simon's friends were perfectly nice, but they were all so ambitious I felt like a misfit. Simon was a proofreader but wanted to be an illustrator, one friend was a waiter but wanted to be an actor, another worked at a magazine but wanted to be a playwright. Simon referred to what they were doing now as their meanwhile jobs, as if once they'd held them for a while they'd step past them into their lives.

My ambition was to *have* an ambition, until I found Kilroy. Then I did: to stay in New York.

I'd left his note in Madison, but I'd brought our conversation: I'd brought our conversation, and the intent way he'd looked at me across Viktor and Ania's table, and the name of the bar where he hung out, the place with the pool table that had a gouge he could almost always make work for him. McClanahan's. A few days after my arrival, I sat at the kitchen table with the Manhattan white pages and looked up the address.

It was on Avenue of the Americas—Sixth Avenue—which, according to my map, narrowed it down to about sixty blocks. Nonetheless, I headed off to look, still such a newcomer that the traffic unnerved me, the groaning buses, the scream of an ambulance, the flash and honk of a dozen taxis. The density of people on the streets amazed me—the density and the *variety*: I'd always thought Madison was pretty multicultural, but it was clear now how white it really was. I saw faces from olive to deep brown, heard accents I didn't recognize, languages I couldn't begin to identify. I passed restaurants, pharmacies, laundromats, stationers, florists, liquor stores, coffee shops, and then suddenly there it was, McClanahan's, a corner bar next to a dry cleaner's. What did it mean that I'd done this, tracked this place down? I hurried by, telling myself a story I half believed, that I was just exploring the city and could as easily have been somewhere else.

I was back the next day. There were neon beer signs in the windows—Miller and Pabst, good Midwestern beers—but here the windows were covered by iron bars. I went around the block slowly, wondering what I'd do when I got back. The stretch from Seventh to Sixth seemed endless, a dark, narrow passageway of tall gray buildings. Finally I reached McClanahan's again, and someone opened the door just as I arrived, revealing a long, narrow room that was smoke-filled and dimly lit and nearly empty.

On the third day I planted myself out front. People looked at me as they strode by, or didn't: already I understood how the rules of the sidewalk differed from the rules in Madison or even Chicago. Here you could do anything you wanted—growl, rant, scream—and no one would give you more than a passing glance.

The door to McClanahan's was massive, ornamented with tarnished brass studs. I stood there waiting for something to take over, the urge to leave or the urge to go in. Five minutes went by, perhaps ten; I didn't keep track. I stared at the door until, virtually conjured, Kilroy himself came out.

He looked older than I remembered, wearing jeans and a leather jacket, his face narrow and closed. His hair was shaggy, and he sported a two- or three-day growth of beard. He glanced at me and turned the corner, then stopped and turned back. "I know you," he said, and I smiled a little, feeling foolish and pleased and scared.

He pointed at me. "Madison, Wisconsin. Dinner at that Polish couple's house. How's it going?"

"Fine, how are you?"

"I'm fine, Carrie."

I couldn't believe he remembered my name after—what?—three

months, but he just gave me a sly smile and went on. "No, don't tell me, I'm going for broke here. Carrie . . . Bell. There, I got it. Do you remember my name?"

I told him what it was, and he smiled again, this time a sweet, open-mouthed smile that revealed his front teeth, the way one overlapped the edge of the other. He said, "You're a long way from home, Carrie Bell. What brings you to wretched New York?"

"Why is it wretched?"

"Oh, you know—it's wretched, it's wonderful, it's disgusting, it's divine. All at the same time, usually, which is why I love it so." He gave me an ironic look, as if to suggest that in fact he didn't love it so—or that if he did it was for nothing so simple, nothing he'd be so glib about. He gestured at me with his chin. "But you haven't answered my question. Carrie Bell the Evasive. What's a nice Mid-western girl like you doing in big bad Manhattan?"

"What makes you so sure I'm nice?"

"You've got it written all over you. It's right there on your face next to sweet and good."

I thought of what I'd done, run out in the middle of the night on people who counted on me, and I felt shaky suddenly, ready to cry. I hadn't called anyone in Madison, had no idea what was going through my mother's head, Jamie's. Mike's.

"Oops," he said. "I sense a story. Can I buy you a beer? Or do you want to pretend this never happened, we never ran into each other?"

I looked at the door to McClanahan's. It was four-thirty in the afternoon, and I wondered how long he'd been in there. There were three or four tiny blond hairs growing out of his cheek, up near his left eye, and I longed to reach up and stroke them. "Sure," I said to him. "I'll have a beer."

That first day we talked for four hours, or rather I talked: I told him all about the summer, the jerky slip-slide of my feelings, the weeks and weeks of it. And how since leaving I'd been on a speedway, careening from guilt to remorse to relief to exhilaration, with New York standing right outside it all: massive, impassive, just there and there. I even told him about the last night with Mike, his *We've had it, haven't we?* and the way I waved to him from the door as I was leav-ing, a finger waggle, a light, entirely untruthful wiggle of the fingers of my right hand, as if either of us had any idea what we expected next, let alone what would actually happen.

"You flew the coop," Kilroy said. "You had to."

We were sitting on a bench in Washington Square Park by then, the night black and heavy around us, a pair of pigeons bobbing at our feet. We'd stayed at McClanahan's until it had gotten so crowded we couldn't hear each other, then we'd eaten pizza slices standing at the counter of a place open to the din of 8th Street.

"I think it was brave of you," he went on. "It must've been a very hard thing to do." He turned so he was facing me, one knee up on the bench. "Harder than staying."

"Staying felt impossible."

"Yeah, but staying was static. You acted. I admire it."

I was surprised, and for the first time since we'd begun talking I felt self-conscious: in the bar, with voices rushing past us, it had been easier. The park was bright with activity—a gang of kids on skateboards, a knot of teenagers around a tiny ember, a tall man swooping by on Rollerblades—but it was all far away, modulated, no competition for the sudden strangeness that overcame me.

Kilroy grinned. "You can't believe you're talking to me like this when you don't really know me."

"I don't *really* know you?" I said with a laugh. "I don't know you at all."

He lifted one shoulder. "What's knowing someone? You may not know where I grew up or what I do from nine to five every day, but you know what it's like to be with me for several hours. Doesn't that tell you more than information would?"

"I guess," I said, but I was thinking, *Where* did *you grow up? What* do *you do from nine to five each day—drink?*

He looked at me and laughed. "Go ahead."

"OK, easy one first," I said. "Is Kilroy your first or last name?"

"It's neither."

"It's your middle name?"

"My name is Paul Eliot Fraser. There's no Kilroy in there at all, it's just what I'm called."

"Why?"

"Because it's not in there at all."

Score one, Kilroy, I thought. "All right, where *did* you grow up?"

Smirking, he lifted a finger to his lips. "I didn't. Don't tell."

"Paul Eliot Fraser the Evasive," I said, and he gave me a big smile that lasted and lasted—a smile that anointed me.

"New York," he said. "Born and bred. And the thing I do from nine to five is I work for a temp agency. I get hired out to businesses who need a week or two of word processing done because someone's on vacation, or I go answer the phones while someone's sick. I'm the rambling man of office work, I never stay anywhere very long—I put that Dictaphone behind me and saddle up for the subway ride to the copier on the horizon."

I smiled, but I was surprised: I'd figured he was a struggling something or other, like Simon and his friends. Maybe he *was* a struggling something or other and just wasn't saying.

"Happy now?" he said. "Feel you know me a whole lot better?"

I lifted one shoulder. "Do your parents still live in the city?"

"If you could call it that."

"What—they live in one of the other boroughs or something?"

"Living," he said.

Something in his expression warned me not to ask more. He took his keys from his pocket and began fiddling with them, pulling them around the key ring one by one. Uncomfortable, I looked away, at the teenagers behind us. They seemed so veiled: their faces by their hair, their bodies by their dark, shapeless clothes. A bit of light glinted off a nylon jacket, but otherwise they were barely more than silhouettes.

I turned back and found Kilroy studying me. "Are you an alcoholic?" I asked, no idea where I'd gotten the nerve.

"What gives you that idea?"

"You were at that bar in the middle of the afternoon."

"I'm just a guy who likes bars," he said. "And McClanahan's is about as good as it gets these days, though the yuppie hordes are making inroads." He smiled. "Next time we'll have your first lesson."

"My first lesson?"

"Your first pool lesson—I'm sure I remember that you've never shot pool."

"You have quite a memory."

"I've heard that said before."

By whom, I wondered, but he was getting to his feet, so I stood, too, and all at once everyone stood with me—Mike, Jamie, Rooster, even my mother, everyone I'd been talking about. Why did I have such a crowd along when Kilroy was so obviously by himself?

"Shall we?" he said.

We'd entered the park through an opening on the side, but we went out past the arch, at once massive and curiously ghostly against the night sky. It was my first time on lower Fifth Avenue, and I walked with my head tilted back, the skyline jagged with roofs and lit windows. Far ahead, the Empire State Building was limned with white lights.

"Do you like to walk?" he said.

I nodded.

"That's good. New York is a walker's city, that's the only way to get to know it."

We turned onto 14th Street and went past gated storefronts and tiny bodegas crowded with men. Cold fluorescent light spilled onto the sidewalk. In Madison there would have been a stillness to the night, but here even the garbage in the gutter seemed active, jittering in the wind, ready to dart away. A police car with its red and blue lights swirling shrieked past us and turned at the far corner.

"I love sirens," Kilroy said. "The sound of them, especially at night."

I looked at him.

"I do. My bedroom's an especially good listening point for sirens— it's got my only window onto Seventh Avenue. You'll see."

I stopped walking, and he stopped, too, and smiled at me.

"I'll see?" I said. "I'll see your bedroom?"

He shook his head gravely. "Don't be offended by the truth, Carrie. That's an untenable position, don't you think?"

IT WAS, AND it was only a week later that I saw his bedroom, a week later that I stood beside his bed while he unbuttoned the row of tiny buttons down the front of my sweater, methodically, not a touch through the lengthening opening until the whole was undone. But first we walked. Through the teeming East Village; up and down the wide, traffic-clogged avenues; along the grimy, redolent streets of Chinatown. I couldn't get enough of it, of the crowds, the purposeful-ness. In Midtown I stared upward and felt awed, filled with vertigo by the clouds rushing between the skyscrapers. The steps into the sub-way fascinated me, and I asked Kilroy to stop at station after station while I looked down, simultaneously appalled and intrigued by the stench. "Gol-lee," he said, "we don't have these in Wisconsin," but he said it kindly, and I just laughed.

He was a good guide. He pointed out junkies and prostitutes, stockbrokers and undercover cops as if they wore uniforms, as if they held aloft signs only he could see. A good guide but also opinionated: passing restaurants I thought looked interesting, he said, "This is where the hipsters hang out," "This is where the media people eat." Nowhere he'd go, was the implication. We ate in coffee shops, in little dives you'd hardly notice from the outside. He said they were honest.

He lived near McClanahan's, in a blocky, red-brick apartment build-ing on West 18th Street. His apartment was on the sixth floor, three blank-walled rooms I assumed at first he'd just moved into, there was so little in them. He'd been there for years, though, and there wasn't a picture in the place, a single knickknack. He had no more furniture than was absolutely necessary, and each piece was spare, purely func-tional: an unfinished pine bookcase, a futon couch with a plain black cover and no throw pillows, a rectangular wooden table with four folding chairs. There's a kind of spare you see in magazines that's studied and elegant, each thing an *objet*, a strategically placed sculp-tural vase holding an arrangement of perfect white tulips. Kilroy's apartment wasn't like that. It was more as if he were camping there, poised to make a move. When I asked him why the place was so empty, he just laughed.

The bedroom. Box spring on the floor, mattress on the box spring, white sheets on the mattress, white pillows on the sheets. And Kilroy standing in front of me, his fingers just finished with the buttons on my sweater. There'd been a kiss already, or more like four or five, out walking that afternoon, in the elevator, just inside the front door of his apartment. Really one long kiss interrupted by conversation, by the need to keep moving until we were here.

We were here. He kissed me again and then traced a line from my throat to the top of my jeans and back up, to the clasp of my bra. My breasts fell out and he opened his hand to span them, his thumb on one nipple and his little finger on the other, tiny circles and then he stroked down the undercurves.

I tried closing my eyes, but his hands came up to my face, thumbs at my lashes, and I had to look again, had to see that it was he, Kilroy, eyes dark and gray-blue, black-banded, flecked with the color of the sky. His thin lips, the crease at the tip of his nose. His narrow hands and his long fingers, on my shoulders now, pushing the sweater off, the bra straps.

His lips were still cold from outside, late September and windy, like in Madison but also different, a lower, more subversive wind, not your hair but your body, the very center of you. It was touch, touch, slide open, and his tongue on my lower lip, sweeping from side to side.

I had to yank to untuck his shirt, a stiff denim one, one shirttail and then the other, and then the warmth underneath, the hair on his belly and chest, my fingertips plowing through it, raking up and down, around, down into the back of his jeans, tight, all the way down until each hand was full of buttock, my fingers just at the tops of his legs, finding the lines of sweat.

He unbuttoned his own shirt. Tossed it toward the dresser. Held me skin to skin, his hands alive on my back, coming around under my arms, thumbs on my nipples, mouth, mouth, the bed coming up under me, zippers, jeans, and then suddenly the room, the apartment, the world, my face in my hands.

And his hand on my face, his eyes on my eyes, asking: *Are you OK?*

I was. I pulled the sheet aside, the *we're doing this* of it, sweeping the thing out of the way. And I closed my eyes and felt him hard against my leg, the satiny softness of it, against my thigh, pushing to get in, and then it was *this, yes:* familiar and strange, old and new, me and not me.

16

~

I T WAS ALL I wanted to do. Morning and night, at dusk when he'd just gotten home from work, early on a weekend afternoon. I came up behind him and circled his waist with my arms, then slid my hands down the front of his pants. He was at the sink washing dishes when I did this, or he was on his couch and I went straight for his crotch, kneading the front of his jeans until he was so swollen I had to press myself against him, right then.

He kissed me on my lower back, on the sweaty creases under my breasts, in a line from my shin to my inner thigh. "What are you think-ing?" I'd whisper half into sleep, and his index finger would stroke so slowly down my belly that I'd be wet when it got to me, wet and ready for him.

His mouth there. His tongue reading me like Braille, like he didn't want to miss a word. Mike—well, he'd been reluctant. On my birth-day, maybe after we'd fought. For a special occasion, a contribution to an annual fund—*there*'s money in the bank. But not because he wanted to.

Kilroy wanted to. The first time I tensed up, guarded, thinking *Don't*, wanting to say he didn't have to, but one hand stroked my thigh reassuringly while his tongue lazed along, and I let go of the clenched muscles and turned inward, and something that was half scream and half moan came together and started toward my vocal cords, but so slowly the wait itself was worth a scream, a long, rising scream barely heard from over a distant horizon, and then louder, and louder.

It was fierce between us sometimes, his stubbly face abrading mine, times when I just wanted him to *fuck* me. Other times it would go on so long I'd start to hyperventilate, this tingling on my cheeks, my forearms. *What are we doing?* I'd want to know. *Who are you, what is this?* He'd respond by pushing my head downward, my tongue swiping his furry chest until my face was at his erection and I didn't know what to do because I wanted to rub him against my ears and over my eyelids, and I wanted to burrow deeper into his smell, and I wanted him forcing my mouth open wider than it could go—and I wanted it all at once.

Outside his apartment we hardly touched. No holding hands on the street, no legs coming together under restaurant tables. If we were meeting at McClanahan's we met without a kiss, so that it all stayed in the air between us, ignitable but not ignited.

The world was different because of this. The sky was a blue I'd never seen before, hard and cold, with edges that could cut. Smells emanating from restaurants attached themselves to individual ingredients with startling specificity: melted butter, grilling lamb, cumin in tomatoes, cilantro, frying salmon. From the jukebox at McClanahan's I heard the line of a guitar lift itself from the surface of a song and then settle down again. I wondered if this was what the beginning of crazy felt like. And then Kilroy would say something bland and vaguely cynical, and it would reel me back in to where I was steady again.

We were at McClanahan's a lot, drinking beers at a table near the back, or sitting at the bar when the place wasn't so crowded, Kilroy saying, "That guy needs an appointment at a methadone clinic *yesterday*," or "Watch, now she's going to tilt her head sideways so her diamond earring will show"—and she, whoever she was, would do just that.

"You're an observer, aren't you?" I said one evening. "You should be a journalist. Go around with a little tape recorder you'd talk into. Then you could write these reports about, you know, life in the city."

It was noisy, so we were leaning forward to talk. Sitting at the back of the bar near the pool table, curved glasses of pale beer on the table between us. Kilroy ran a finger down the side of his, leaving a trail-mark in the condensation. He shook his head, but with a smile. "See, there it is right there."

"What?"

"The pernicious little idea that who you are should determine something as trivial as what you do for a living."

"As *trivial*?"

He shook his head again. "Life's not like that. It's not that malleable. It's not that neat." He lifted his beer and took a long drink, then wiped the cuff of his sweatshirt across his mouth. "With that theory *you'd* have to be one of those career graduate students, going from Ph.D. to Ph.D."

I laughed. "What's that supposed to mean, I'm a nerd?"

"I was referring to your inquisitiveness."

My face warmed, and I looked away. The night before, I'd gotten going with questions. We were in bed, entwined after sex, and I'd asked about his last girlfriend: who, how long, what happened. And he became—well, not huffy, but cool. Or not even cool so much as absent. It was like he suddenly wasn't there. We were lying so close I could feel his heartbeat, but he himself slipped away. The monosyllabic answers he gave were deflections, offered up by someone else, Kilroy 2, a stand-in.

Now, in McClanahan's, I felt his eyes on me. I was looking to the side. I watched a guy in a blue-and-white striped dress shirt moving around the pool table. He gathered the balls from a low shelf and began arranging them in a plastic triangle. Something about him . . .

"Hey," Kilroy said. "I'm not complaining."

I turned back and stared into his face, his eyes tight on mine. He was, of course, but maybe it didn't matter. Maybe not knowing didn't matter. I said, "Not too grumpily, anyway."

He smiled and lifted his beer again to drink. After a moment he turned and watched the pool table. The guy had lifted off the triangle and was getting ready to break. His opponent stood off to the side, his cue standing upright next to him. He wore a dress shirt, too, but he was smaller, closer to Kilroy's size, while the first guy . . .

He had Mike's shoulders, that was it. The exact span of them, their girth in a dress shirt. He looked nothing like Mike—older, balding, with a long, olive-complected face—but the shoulders . . . My God, my God. I was dizzy suddenly, queasy with remorse.

Kilroy coughed. "I think tonight's the night."

I turned back and found him studying me curiously, eyes narrowed, head tipped slightly to the side. He knew something had happened.

"I don't know what I've been thinking, waiting so long," he went on. Then he smiled. "Well, maybe it's that I haven't been thinking."

I shook my head. "I'm not sure what you're talking about."

"Your first pool lesson, of course." He extended his left hand out in front of him with his forefinger curled, drew his right hand close to his side, and mimed a shot. "What do you say—you up for it? Not to put any pressure on you or anything."

I shrugged. I felt torn, half in the moment and half back in the anguish of seeing Mike's shoulders in another man's shirt. Mike's old shoulders. It was wrong to be having a conversation at this moment, yet the fact that I was here, in this bar, in this city with another man— how much more wrong was that?

Kilroy raised his eyebrows. "Well? Want to give it a try?"

"I guess."

He sat still for another moment, looking at me, then he stood up, fished some change from his pocket, and went over to the table. With the men watching, he set two quarters on the edge of the pool table, then another two right next to them.

"What was that all about?"

He eased back into his chair. "I'll play the winner and then you'll challenge me."

"I'll *challenge* you?"

"Pool has its protocol, just like everything else."

"What if you don't win?"

He grinned. "I'll win. Those guys have hardly played at all since college, when they used to goof around on the table in the rec room of their frat house."

I laughed. "Now you're making assumptions. Maybe they didn't go to college, let alone belong to frats."

"Right," he said with a snort. "They're dressed like that for their jobs selling hotdogs at Nathan's." He shook his head. "They graduated from college within the last five years and now they work on Wall Street or I'm—" He broke into a grin. "Or I do."

"The least likely thing in the world?"

"Pretty close."

We turned sideways in our chairs and watched the men play. The smaller one bent over and sized up a shot, the solid red ball just in front of a corner pocket. An old Propane Cupid song came on the jukebox, and I waited for the part I liked: *Riding a Greyhound to L.A., passed your picture on a billboard. You're not—ready. You're not—ready for me.* What was I distressed about? Mike, yes, but more: over the pool table a bright pendant lamp shone on the deep green felt, and I dreaded standing in its light.

"Hey, not to worry," Kilroy said.

I turned, and he was watching me with the same curious, narrow-eyed look.

"Are you worried?"

I lifted a shoulder.

"You're going to do very well."

"You seem awfully sure."

"I am."

"Why?"

"Because you're one of those fetching small-town girls who's full of surprises."

I couldn't help smiling. "Is that what you think of me?"

"As if I'd tell you."

"Now you have to."

He raised his eyebrows briefly and then looked away, his nose in profile coming to a sharp point. My mouth was dry, and I took a sip of beer. I glanced over at the pool table: the men were almost done, just two balls left.

"It's a city," I said. "Of over a hundred thousand people."

He shook his head. "Doesn't matter, you're still a fetching small-town girl. That milky-skin thing you've got going confirms it." He grinned. "Oh, and lean forward a sec, there's a little straw in your hair." He reached across the table and pretended to pluck something from behind my ear, and the edge of his hand brushed the side of my face, suddenly electric.

The men were done. We looked at each other for a long moment, and then Kilroy got up and went over. I watched as he slid his first two quarters into a little metal drawer on the pool table, pushed it in, then fished the balls into the plastic triangle. He spoke to the tall guy, but it was too noisy for me to hear. It was a noisy, noisy bar in the middle of Manhattan. I was sitting at a table watching my lover play pool.

The game passed quickly, Kilroy moving around knocking ball after ball into pocket after pocket. When they were done he offered the guy his hand, and they shook.

I set my beer down and stood up. Why was I pretending to be interested in playing pool when I'd passed up hundreds of opportunities at home? Actually, I was interested. I was more than interested—I wanted to shoot one ball home after another, I wanted to astonish him.

"Are you going to get a cue?" he said.

"Yes."

I went over to the wall and looked at the cues hanging there, finally choosing one at random. Its heft was unfamiliar: all awkward, unbalanced length, the wide end so much heavier than the narrow. I found a cube of chalk and rubbed it against the tip, then turned back to the table.

"OK," he said, "I'll break, then we'll ignore the rules and you can just try shooting for a while."

He made his way to the far end of the table, drew his cue back, and sent the white ball racing toward the triangle of colored balls, which broke apart with a satisfying *knockknockknock*. The green one slid into a corner pocket, and he looked up and smiled at me. "Go for it."

The yellow stripe was halfway between the white ball and one of the side pockets. I bent over the table. I liked the idea of the little guide Kilroy had made with his forefinger, to slide his cue through. I curled mine and got the cue situated, then practiced drawing it back a few times, aware of Kilroy's eyes on me. At last I took a breath and fired, so off the mark that the white ball twisted back and stopped closer to me than it had started.

"Shit."

He came around the table and stood next to me. "You have an idea what it's supposed to look like, but you're not quite looking *at* it. Here, let's try something."

He moved the yellow stripe out of the way, then stationed the white ball so it had a free path to the far end of the table. "Just work on hitting it, forget about making it hit another ball. Think of the cue as an extension of your arm."

I moved closer to the table and leaned over. I lined the stick up and did the drawing-it-back thing again, but this time I focused on the ball. I poked it with what I was sure was insufficient force, and it rolled away from me and knocked smartly against the opposite edge.

We repeated this several times, and then he started setting up shots for me: angleless shots that should have been easy but weren't.

I was about to shoot when a guy with a goatee came over and set a pair of quarters on the table.

I looked up at Kilroy. "Uh-oh. What's the protocol now?"

He turned to the guy. "You have someone you want to play with?"

The guy shrugged. "Yeah. Whatever."

Kilroy tilted his head toward me. "I'm giving my lady a lesson right now. Give us a little more messing-around time and then the table's all yours."

"OK."

The guy walked away, and Kilroy turned to face me. "Go ahead," he said, but my heart was pounding.

"You called me your lady."

A smile lifted the corners of his mouth, and I felt my mouth twist into a smile, a question, I wasn't sure. *Say* something, I thought at him. Say *something*.

Amusement and pleasure were on his face, but there was something else, too: some kind of surprise or even misgiving. What was it? He didn't want to think about it. Or he didn't want me thinking about it. He looked away, rolled his lips inward, looked back. The noise in the bar seemed much louder now, deafening. Finally he ran the back of his hand across his forehead and shook it once at the floor, as if shaking off sweat.

"So?" I said.

"So shoot," he said with a grin. "The protocol is that now you shoot."

A tingling nervousness collected somewhere near my center. I couldn't shoot but I had to. I bent over the table. He'd placed the ball a foot from the corner pocket, a perfect globe, the embodiment of the color orange. I got behind the cue ball and shot, and the orange rolled smartly into place.

"What did I tell you?" he drawled. "You're a natural."

Later, we walked back to his place. It was chilly, a mist falling so lightly you couldn't really call it rain. We passed shuttered shop windows, iron gates drawn across entire storefronts and padlocked. In a high-ceilinged second-floor apartment across Sixth Avenue, a gooseneck lamp illuminated a table with a broad-leafed plant on it. Behind the table, a picture in an elaborate gilt frame hung by itself on a dark red wall, too far away to be distinct. *I'm giving my lady a lesson right now. My lady. My lady.* A choking feeling in me, to think about it. To think about how he'd reacted. He'd wanted to erase it. Not the fact, I didn't think—just the words. Just my wanting more words, like last night. The fact was fine with him. The fact was where we were headed right now. Walking along, a foot apart. He'd left his leather jacket unzipped, and the bottom edge flapped as he walked. He took long strides, his legs lean and hard under his jeans. His legs were so thin compared to Mike's. His arms, too—compared to how Mike's used to be. Mike had always dwarfed me—he could have contained me as easily as the largest in a set of Russian nesting dolls contains the next one down, with room to rattle. Kilroy and I were nearly the same size. I could wear his sweaters. In bed our bodies lined up piece by piece.

"Why were you so nervous?" he said.

"When?"

"Right before you got your cue."

I thought of how I'd wanted to do well. How I'd wanted to surprise him. McClanahan's was a center of something; it was my ticket to stay. Or maybe pool was. I looked over at him and shrugged.

"Did you have fun?"

"I can see the attraction."

He nodded. "It's a great combination of focus and control, the mental and the physical."

"I guess so," I said, but I was thinking of Mike again, Mike and hockey. Mike all padded up for a game, out there on the ice, the blades of his skates freshly sharpened. Getting checked, he'd go with the slam, absorb it. The mental and the physical. That's what his life was now, but the physical was a burden, not a resource. In my mind I saw him flying across the ice, then saw him seeing himself flying across the ice, from the stationary point of his wheelchair.

17

~

I COULDN'T STAND TO think of him. Lying in his hospital bed, wondering where I'd gone. Each time the door opened, each time the phone rang: *Is that Carrie?* I imagined his face, the bars of the halo framing his hopefulness, and then the dashing of hope when he'd learned who it really was. Not me. Never me. I'd been gone two weeks, three, and he had no idea what had happened to me. No one did.

Finally I called my mother. I was sure she'd be upset, maybe angry, but when she heard my voice she just said "Hi" very evenly, as if we'd spoken only the day before.

"I'm in New York," I said. "Staying with a high school friend. Remember Simon? Who you met that night? I just—I needed a change, I needed to get out of there."

And she said, "I know."

There'd been phone calls, trips to look up at my apartment windows, reports on my last visit with Mike, but she said she'd never been worried, not really: she figured I'd done just about exactly what I'd done.

"How are you doing?" she said. "Do you need any money?"

"I'm OK, thanks." I had some savings at home, about fifteen hundred dollars, though I couldn't quite see running through it just to dally in New York. What was I doing here, anyway? How long was I going to stay? The evening before, walking through the West Village with Kilroy, I'd seen a fortyish couple climbing the front steps of an immaculate brick townhouse—both of them wrapped in expensive coats, their expensive leather shoes faintly gleaming. Watching them had felt like watching something not quite real, a demonstration of some kind: *This is how you go home when you own a piece of the world.* Their lives seemed impossibly distant from mine.

My mother was silent. I imagined she was weighing the wisdom of asking me about my plans, and I braced myself a little. When she spoke, though, she said, "You had such a hard summer," and immediately tears pricked at my eyes and then spilled onto my cheeks. I was in the brownstone kitchen, and I squeezed the phone against my ear and used one hand to steady the paper towel roll while with the other I tore a piece off. I wanted to blow my nose but I didn't want her to hear me. I blotted my face and tried not to sniff.

"How do you feel?" she said.

"I don't even know."

"Oh, honey."

Across the room a Styrofoam take-out container sat open like a giant clamshell. I went over and looked inside: the remains of something in a tan sauce, plus a collapsed orange slice and a limp piece of lettuce.

"Guilty," I said. "I feel guilty. What does it say about me that I'd leave? What kind of person does it make me?"

She didn't reply for a moment, and I felt the long span between us, the miles and miles of wire. At last she spoke. "The kind of person you are."

A rush of laughter escaped me. "What?"

"It makes you the kind of person you are. People have this idea that what they do changes who they are. A married man has an affair and he thinks, Now I've become a bad person. As if something had changed."

"Meaning he already was a bad person?"

"Meaning bad isn't the issue. Meaning you do what you do. Not without consequences for other people, of course, sometimes very grave ones. But it's not very helpful to regard your choices as a series of right or wrong moves. They don't define you as much as you define them."

"You're sounding very mystical," I said. "Are you saying it was my destiny to leave?"

"Not at all—you could just as easily have stayed. But that wouldn't make you a good person any more than leaving makes you a bad one. You're already made, honey. That's what I mean."

"And whose fault is that?" I joked, surprisingly comforted.

"I take credit for everything except your big feet."

We both laughed, and then suddenly I felt conscious of another presence, almost as if someone were listening on the extension. "I wonder what *he'd* say," I said.

"Your father?" my mother said without missing a beat. "What do you think?"

We talked for a while more, and it wasn't until later, until we'd hung up and I'd climbed the stairs to my dusty alcove, that the idea of my father came back to me, together with the words to an old Paul Simon song I'd heard on the radio somewhere in western Pennsylvania. What would my father say? *Jump on a ferry, Carrie. Just set yourself free.* It was almost funny, until it occurred to me that perhaps it had been his voice all along, since my earliest feeling that something between me and Mike was wrong; perhaps it had been his voice all along, saying: *Go. You don't need this. Nothing's making you stay. Just go.*

I sat on the futon and leaned against the wall. I could see the railing along the open stairwell, its two missing posts like gaps in a row of teeth. Halfway down the stairs, one tread had a foot-sized hole that Simon had covered with a plank on which he'd painted a huge, wide-open mouth. I heard the front door open and close, then footsteps moving along the hallway to the kitchen. Please, I thought. Stay downstairs. I wished I had a room of my own, or at least a curtain to pull across the opening of the alcove.

Just go. Just go. I didn't want to be anything like my father. Had he had the possibility of leaving in him from the beginning? Was that how my mother explained it to herself? That was certainly the story told by the few pictures she'd kept: they showed a tall, skinny guy with dark hair and an upturned, ski-jump nose, a guy in the process of realizing he'd made a big mistake. You could see it progress from picture to picture: in their wedding photo he was serious in a suit and tie, clearly the type who wasn't going to smile just because a photographer said to; by the final picture, taken two years later, he was sitting on the back stoop of the house we lived in then, in a close-fitting shirt with a splayed collar, and his eyes were absolutely vacant.

Where was he now? I hadn't given it any thought in years. He was a Midwesterner, born and bred: he'd grown up in a small town in Minnesota, lived for a while with relatives in Iowa after his parents died, then gone to Madison for college. I'd always figured he was somewhere in the Midwest, but what if he'd wound up in New York? What if I happened to pass him on the street one day—would he look familiar? If I had one of those photographs in front of me now, could my mind perform its own computerized aging process on it to learn what he'd come to look like? Would he be gray-haired? Balding, fat, thin? Would he recognize me?

Could you pass a relative on the street and feel nothing?

In high school biology we did a project on genetics—hair and eye color, size, that kind of thing. Mike was in the class, too. We worked on the assignment one afternoon in the Mayers' kitchen, and when it came time to fill in my father's side of the family, all I could do was put my pencil down and sit there. Realizing what was going on, Mike got riled up—pissed off at my father for walking out on me when over a decade later I might need to ask him questions so I could do my homework. *Asshole,* Mike said. He didn't have abandonment in his DNA.

IT WAS A few more days before I called him, and by then word had reached him, as I'd known it would. I could almost see it, word: flying across Madison, burning the phone wires.

"Hey, it's Carrie the city slicker," he said when he heard my voice. "New Yawk."

I pictured him in his hospital bed, the head raised, his face winter pale. I said, "I'm sorry I haven't called. I'm sorry I just disappeared."

"No problem," he said cheerfully. "New York sounds like fun, you must be having a great time."

My throat felt full, and I forced myself to swallow. "It's pretty amazing."

"So you're hanging out with that Simon guy?"

I thought of Kilroy, with whom I'd woken up that morning: who'd woken me up, pressing his erection against my bare thigh, his hand on my side. "Yeah," I said to Mike. "Simon and his housemates."

"Well, just promise you won't get weird, OK?"

"What do you mean, weird?"

"Oh, you know—pretentious, jaded."

"OK," I said with a laugh. "But don't you—I mean, I'm sorry about not saying goodbye or anything."

"It's cool," he said. "Hang on, I've got this new thing for talking on the phone and it's kind of slipping." His voice got fainter for a moment: "Oh, wait wait, thanks—" Then clear again: "Carrie?"

"Yeah?"

"Sorry."

"No problem." I licked my lips. "So what's been going on?"

"I'm on the computer now in occupational. It's pretty cool, really— you'd be surprised what a feeb like me can accomplish."

"Mike."

"OK, a gimp."

There was a crash in the background, then voices, laughter.

"What was that?" I said.

"Rooster decking my bedside lamp."

We talked for a little longer, about nothing—certainly not about how long I'd stay away, nor about what, if anything, we still meant to each other. He sounded so happy—better than he had in ages.

"Well, have fun," he said as we were about to hang up. "Send me a postcard of the Empire State Building, OK? And shit—hockey season starts in a couple weeks. Go see a Rangers game for me, all right? I mean, if you're still there."

We said goodbye. Simon was in his room, but I grabbed a jacket and headed for Kilroy's, hurrying on the darker cross streets. In the vestibule of his building I ran my finger down the row of tiny steel buttons until I found his.

He buzzed me up and met me at the door to his apartment, a book closed around his index finger. He pulled me in and then backed me against the closed door. His face was warm and scratchy. We stood there kissing for a while, and then I pulled away and told him about the call, about how Mike had sounded, as if he'd meant what he'd said in his hospital room the night I left: that he *was* glad he didn't have to wonder about us anymore.

"Do you wish he'd sounded more upset?" Kilroy said. We were in the living room now, standing near his couch—we didn't quite know how to sit together yet. His thumbs were in his belt loops, hands splayed over his front pockets.

"Not more upset," I said, but then I broke off talking.

Kilroy tilted his head to the side. "Tell me."

I breathed in deeply and looked at him, his sharp features and shaggy hair. *Tell me.* They meant something, those words—they meant he wanted to know. He stood there looking at me, a watchful, interested expression on his face.

I didn't know what to say, how to put it when I wasn't quite sure what "it" was. "I hope I don't want him to be upset," I began. "I mean, all summer—" Suddenly tears surged from my eyes. "I didn't want to hurt him," I cried. "But sometimes sitting there with him I felt like I was watching myself sitting there with him. Like: *Look at her, she's doing the right thing.* I felt so *distant.*"

Kilroy nodded thoughtfully.

"And now I've left. And I mean, what does it *mean* to him?"

He rubbed his chin and considered. "You don't want him to be upset," he said, "but you want him to be thinking about it."

That was it. I wanted him to be thinking about it, just as I was thinking about it. But I had this, too: I had talking about it, with someone I'd be in bed with before long. It was too much, the over-lappingness of it all: Mike's feelings and my feelings and Kilroy taking my hand and pulling it toward his mouth.

18

~

SIMON LIVED A busy life. Drinks after work, dinners, movies. If he didn't have plans, he generally stayed late at the law firm, which meant free Chinese delivered to the office and a Dial-a-Cab home when he was tired, not to mention overtime for the extra hours he worked. Proofreading paid surprisingly well, and given his low rent he had a lot of expendable income. It wasn't unusual for him to see a couple of plays in one week, then go to a concert on Friday night and out dancing on Saturday. I was always welcome but I was afraid to spend the money—and I was generally with Kilroy, anyway. One evening, when I hadn't seen Simon in about a week, he sought me out on the third floor and asked me to go to a gallery opening with him. "There'll be free food," he said. "I won't take no for an answer."

"It's not that you want to do something with me," I teased him, "you just want to make sure I don't starve to death."

He shook his head adamantly. "I want to make sure *I* don't starve to death." He reached for my hand. "And I *do* want to do something with you, which hasn't been that easy, you know. You're not exactly around a lot, my dear."

We got ready and then made our way down the street. It was early evening, the colorless sky just graying. We crossed Ninth Avenue and then strolled down a block of neatly kept townhouses until we came abreast of my dirty, unused car. There it sat, parked under a ginkgo tree. I never drove it except to move it from one parking place to another—I was constantly racing out of the brownstone in order to obey the system of rules controlling when you could park where.

"Poor car," I said, giving it a pat as we passed by.

"It does look a little sad."

"I guess I should've taken the train."

Simon shook his head vehemently. "That wouldn't have been nearly so satisfying." He loved the story of my flight. He loved how long it had taken me to let anyone know where I was. "Driving was perfect," he added. "You needed to see Madison in your rearview mirror."

"It was dark."

"Metaphorically speaking." He reached up and scratched the back of his head. "Maybe you should sell it," he said casually—too casually, I thought, as if he'd been waiting for the opportunity.

But I couldn't sell it—no way. It wasn't much of a car, and I certainly didn't need it right now, but I couldn't possibly sell it without telling Mike, and telling Mike I'd sold it would be like telling him I'd decided to have a dog we'd adopted together put to sleep. "It's a good little car," he'd said the day I bought it. "It'll last, or it'll have me to answer to."

Simon was watching me. "Alternate side of the street parking is really a pain when it snows," he said. He smiled gently, and the fact that snow would come—the fact that time would pass and I might still be here and I might not—made me tense with anxiety.

At Eighth Avenue we headed downtown, past overflowing garbage cans and great stacks of flattened cardboard. There were so many restaurants: Italian, Japanese, Italian-Japanese; Scandinavian and Spanish and Tex-Mex. There were places for hearty casseroles, places for delicate salads and barely cooked fish. A delicious smell of grilled meat drifted from an open door, and I turned and saw a neon sign that said BUTCH.

"There's a place on Ninth called Femme," Simon said. And then, with a grin: "Just kidding."

At 19th Street we waited for the light and then crossed. The urgent rumble of a subway train rose through the sidewalk grates, and I realized I was getting used to New York: when I'd first arrived that sound had spooked me.

The gallery was in a storefront on 16th Street. At the door a guy about our age—tall and skinny-pale, with a shaved head—glanced idly but surely at everyone who entered. "An art-world bouncer," Simon whispered as we waited to go in. "Beware his deadly look of contempt."

Inside, a few dozen people milled around under hot track lights, not paying much attention to the pictures. They were photographs, of chairs: kitchen chairs, armchairs, lawn chairs. All in black and white, all composed so the chair was alone in the frame and empty.

We moved along one wall, studied a picture of a bentwood chair with a cane seat, another of a worn-out velvet armchair with a matching ottoman, its nap rubbed away. "These are great, don't you think?" Simon said. "It's like they're waiting for something."

I liked them, too—how they conjured up rooms, whole worlds—but I couldn't help thinking of the rehab poster back in Madison, the wheelchair casting its net of shadow onto the polished wood floor. GET MOVING.

A couple came up behind us and I looked over my shoulder at them. The woman was tiny, with masses of curly dark hair; she wore a wine-colored dress that looked as if it were made of crumpled paper. Her companion was a tall, ponytailed man wearing a black cashmere sweater tucked into voluminously pleated black wool pants.

He said to her, "There's an interesting decontextualization going on, don't you think?" He extended his finger and outlined the shape of the chair. "It's about forms and negative space—she's taken the chairness away from the chair and left it purely object."

Simon dug his elbow into my side, then grabbed me and pulled me across the room. "Don't you love New York?" he said. "You hear the best things." He shrugged off his jacket and glanced around. "How do you take the chairness away from a chair?"

"You must have to do it in stages," I said. "First take the seatness away from the seat and move on from there."

We stood in a pocket of space near the back of the gallery. The lights were so hot I took my jacket off, too. Voices and laughter bounced off the white walls, and scraps of conversation floated by. *A cunning little Kandinsky . . . Sort of a cross between Sarah McLachlan and Philip Glass . . . Do they still go to Fire Island?*

Near us, a large, auburn-haired woman in a multilayered green dress glanced down at her mixed-metal necklace, saw that the pendant had turned upside down, and quickly righted it with a look around to see if anyone was watching. Everyone looked as if they thought they were being looked at—something self-conscious in the set of the shoulders.

Simon ushered me to the bar and we each got a glass of wine. "Did you see the hors d'oeuvres tray before?" he said. "The shrimp looked good."

We leaned against the wall. In the center of the room stood a short woman with a hennaed crew cut, her skin fair and so translucent I could see the vein in her temple, like a light blue twig painted on porcelain.

"The artist," Simon said.

"How do you know?"

"Can't you feel the vibe?"

I watched her smile at a portly man with thick white hair, say something close to someone else's ear, then reach over and touch the sleeve of a wraithlike woman walking past.

"No," I said.

Simon smiled. "Just kidding. I saw a portrait of her in another show. 'Photographers on Photographers.' It was actually kind of funny—in at least half of them you could tell the subjects looked worse in the pictures than they would in real life. Like, *You're my competitor, so I'm going to dogify you.*"

" 'Dogify'?" I said.

"Make doglike. You know, with that kind of here's-the-brutally-honest-photographer-turning-his-unpitying-eye-on-real-life type thing."

"Was she dogified?"

"Completely," Simon said. "Houndified. Muttified. The picture was lit from the top, and you could see her scalp between her hairs, like bare ground where someone planted grass from seed."

I smiled. "That's the Wisconsinian in you talking."

He clapped his hand to his mouth. "I told him to keep quiet tonight."

We went back to the bar for more wine, then happened onto three separate waiters with hors d'oeuvres trays: huge shrimp, little rounds of potato topped with sour cream and caviar, bits of puff pastry covered with crumbled goat cheese. Minutes later we were standing there wiping our mouths, holding toothpicks we didn't know what to do with.

"Five more of each of those," Simon said, "and I'd feel like I'd had dinner."

We moved toward a picture of a canvas director's chair, two of its legs sitting in an inch or so of foamy water, the other two pressing into dark, wet-looking sand. The canvas itself was droopy, the impression of someone's butt and back still there, suggested.

"It's like he just went in for one last swim," Simon said.

"God, I was thinking of something completely different."

He looked at me. "What?"

"That it had been left behind after the summer was over." I shrugged. "You know, abandoned."

He raised his eyebrows. "Art as Rorschach test?"

"I guess so."

Someone tall came and stood behind us—I felt him more than saw him. I was aware of Simon glancing back over his shoulder, then something in the air changed and he was exclaiming, "Oh, Dillon—hi. It's Simon, Kyle's friend. Hi, how are you?"

I turned and saw that his cheeks were pink and that he was looking up at a man with beautiful bone structure and extraordinary silver-blue eyes. This was a man from a movie, from a cologne ad—stunning, a bit bored-looking, with a mouth that wasn't supposed to smile.

He nodded vaguely but didn't speak.

"Aren't you Kyle Donohue's friend?" Simon continued. "I work with him. I'm sorry, I—I think we met." He was blushing deeply now, his fingers playing with the button on his jacket cuff.

The man just stood there. At last he nodded. "That's right."

Simon nodded, too. "So this is Carrie. We were, um, just looking. At the photographs." He waved his hand in the man's direction. "This is Dillon," he said to me.

"Nice to meet you," Dillon said flatly. He looked at Simon. "Do you know Renata?"

Simon shook his head. Renata was the photographer—Renata Banion. Her name was on the wall in pale gray paint.

"I liked her last show better," Dillon said.

"Oh, with the old people?"

Dillon lifted a shoulder. "I thought of them more compositionally. They weren't people so much as forms of shadow and light."

"Oh, that's really interesting," Simon said.

I looked away. What were Mike's words? Pretentious and jaded. What Simon had found comical before he was dishing out himself now. Or lapping up, anyway. And this guy was clearly an asshole. Gorgeous, but an asshole.

"Speaking of shadow and light," Simon went on, "have you seen *Spectacular Creatures*?"

Spectacular Creatures was a movie I'd overheard him and his friends talking about a few evenings ago. It had been the subject of at least three newspaper articles I'd read, a low-budget, independent movie that had won prizes at a bunch of film festivals. Apparently the director had gone to Yale—years ahead of Simon and his friends, but they talked about him with a kind of reverential intimacy.

"Apparently the lighting is really interesting," he said now.

"I saw it last night," Dillon said.

A look of disappointment passed fleetingly over Simon's face. "Oh, how was it?"

Dillon looked at his watch, then glanced around the gallery. At last, as if as an afterthought, he looked at Simon again. "OK. I wouldn't say the *lighting* is really interesting, but the costuming is quite good."

"Huh," Simon said.

"It highlights the absence of sexuality in a pretty interesting way. Actually, the whole thing is very anti-sexual—subtextually, of course."

Simon nodded seriously. "Sort of like his last movie, how drugs took the place of sex."

"Exactly," Dillon said. "In twenty years he'll be the Fellini of abstinence. And Swig Lawlor will be his Marcello Mastroianni."

Simon smiled. "His Marcello Mastroianni *and* his Giuletta Masina."

Dillon laughed, and Simon said, in a rush, "Hey, maybe we should have a drink sometime."

There was an awkward silence. "Maybe," Dillon said doubtfully. "I'm pretty busy." He glanced around the gallery. "I mean, get my number from Kyle if you want and we'll see if we can figure something out." He looked at his watch again and this time feigned surprise. "Oh, I have to get going."

"Bye," Simon said, but Dillon was already moving away, that vague look on his face back again, as if to suggest it wasn't rudeness that kept him from saying goodbye but simply an unavoidable preoccupation with something else.

"Oy," Simon said.

"What's 'oy'?"

He smiled. "God, you're goyische. It's Jewish for 'Jesus Fucking Christ, that was mortifying.' "

"You're not Jewish," I said.

"Honorarily," he said. "Which is all that counts." He smiled. "Benjamin's Jewish." Benjamin was his ex—*permanently* his ex, he'd told me the night I arrived. He took my arm and led me in the opposite direction from the one Dillon had taken. "Did I just make the most gigantic fool of myself? 'Hey, maybe we should have a drink sometime.' Like, 'I'm not sure I've revealed the depths of my uncoolness yet—let's try this.' "

"Simon."

He leaned against the wall and closed his eyes. Nearby, the interesting decontextualization guy had a hand over one ear while he bowed his shoulders against the crowd and tried to talk on a cell phone.

"Totally mortifying," Simon said. "I'm the biggest idiot in the world."

Across the gallery I saw Dillon in the middle of the crowd, bent close to a blond man with deeply tanned skin.

"Do you want to go?"

"We can't," Simon said. "It would look like I was slinking away."

We turned back to the pictures and continued our tour of the gallery, nabbing hors d'oeuvres when we could. Fifteen or twenty minutes later we were at the door. Dillon had vanished, whether into the crowd or from the gallery, I couldn't tell. Glumly, Simon put his jacket back on, and I followed suit. I looked outside and saw that it was true dark now.

"My theory," Simon said, "is that you measure your arrival in New York by when you stop looking at other people and start assuming they're looking at you."

I laughed. He wore a gray sweater over twill pants, a virtual uniform for invisibility. I wasn't much better: black sweater, black pants, silver teardrop earrings—an I-don't-know-what-to-wear outfit. "You could be visible," I said. "You just have to cultivate a more flamboyant look." I grabbed a handful of his plain, zippered black jacket and pulled it stylishly tight.

He shook my hand off. "It's not clothes, it's attitude."

An older woman came in just then, her hair in a perfect gray pageboy, her lips a deep, dark red. She took off her coat and I stared at her velvet dress, slate blue and tied at the side, the hemline angling up in front to reveal a thin, crepey underskirt of the same color. It was gorgeous, set off perfectly by sheer gray-blue stockings and matching thick-heeled, gray-blue suede pumps.

"It's also clothes," I said.

19

LEATHER JACKETS AND stretchy pants. Square-toed boots and fedoras. Skinny knits and clear plastic purses. Fashion was everywhere, and I was entranced. Walking around, I got so involved in looking at other women that I began bumping into people stopped at crosswalks. "Excuse me," I'd say—then I'd check out *their* outfits.

I went to SoHo again and again. That hard blue sky visible between the tops of buildings, cars creeping up and down the narrow streets. I jaywalked between them, the better not to miss a single alluring display window. Everything was presented as if it meant something: a pewter bowl full of pomegranates, a bracelet of frosted amber plastic. "SoHo?" Kilroy said one evening when we were out walking. "It's Disneyland for grown-ups. Turning over your platinum AmEx card as heart-stopping thrill."

I didn't care. I visited one store where everything was chiffon, another where everything was mauve or black: tiny sweaters with velvet ties, long, droopy skirts, tops with bits of inset lace. I imagined Jamie's disdain—so *weird*, she'd say. Well, she wasn't here. I'd been considering calling her, but now I thought I'd wait a while longer. I liked an eight-hundred-dollar pair of wide-leg knit pants with delicate

ruffles at the hem, then a twelve-hundred-dollar silk dress with an
intricately cut neckline and crinkle-pleated sleeves. They weren't weird,
they were unusual—exquisite. I'd been thinking I could stretch my
money thin: sleeping for free in Simon's alcove, eating honest food
with Kilroy—bagels and more bagels, coffee shop sandwiches, the
occasional carton of kung pao prawns. Now I was plagued by doubts.
The very existence of something that cost all I had was weirdly tempting. I had an urge to blow my whole nest egg, literally go for broke.
Then I thought of Mike, one night back in August. *You loved me,* he'd
said. *Now you just feel sorry for me.* He'd been after the same thing,
knowledge of what hitting the bottom would feel like, and I understood that he was there now no matter how he'd sounded on the
phone: the place where nothing could be worse.

One afternoon I found a fabric store just under the wing of
Carnegie Hall. Outside taxis blared and buses hissed, but the store
itself was quiet, an urban version of Fabrications, run by a phalanx
of heavy, besuited salesladies who watched wordlessly from behind
the cutting tables as I strolled around. There were hundreds of bolts
of fabrics, on shelves running to the high ceiling: silk prints and
jacquards, panne velvets with swirls of gold and silver, soft wools so
full of subtle color they conjured places I'd never been, the heathered
Scottish highlands, the emerald-flecked gray of the Irish countryside.
I longed to buy something, just some small thing, and I was feeling
hopeless until I remembered: when I slept at the brownstone instead
of at Kilroy's, a small window in the stairwell let a wide band of light
into my alcove and woke me up. Broke or not, I could spend five dollars to make a curtain, couldn't I? I found an inexpensive off-white
cotton, and with a feeling that I was getting away with something I
bought a single yard.

That evening I set up my sewing machine in the brownstone
kitchen and got to work. Kilroy had come to keep me company, and as
I pinned he ambled around the room looking at things—a days-old
copy of the *Times;* a *New Yorker* missing its cover; the whiteboard,
where someone had written *Greg, Steven Spielberg called you. NOT!*

"Greg's the wannabe actor?" Kilroy said.

I looked up from my work and nodded.

He uncapped the marker and wrote *Steven Spielberg? But is he an*

ARTIST? Then he glanced at me and wiped it off, leaving a blue smear. "Oh, well," he said. "Guess I shouldn't offend the natives."

I hadn't really thought about how it would feel to have him at the brownstone. Simon was the only one he'd met, and when I asked Kilroy afterward what he thought of Simon, he hemmed and hawed and then said he thought Simon was trying to be something he wasn't. "Well, yeah," I said. "He's trying to be an illustrator." But he just shook his head.

Now he wandered over to the range and peered at a spider trapped under the smudged plastic cover of a small analog clock set into the control panel. He tapped at it a couple of times, then paused, then tapped again.

I turned back to the curtain. I was still full from dinner—we'd eaten huge plates of ravioli at a dinerish Italian place in the Village. A restaurant out of a movie: the waiters carried platters all along the lengths of their arms, yelled jokes to each other across the crowded room. I'd wanted to go to Little Italy but Kilroy had said this place was less touristy.

I heard the front door open, and in a moment Simon and Greg came into the kitchen, both dressed as if they'd been out somewhere special, in nice shirts and jackets and even, surprisingly, ties. Simon's was beautiful, a dark teal imprinted with little yellow and green lozenges that shimmered a bit when he moved.

"You're sewing?" he said, loosening the knot in the tie and unbuttoning the top button of his shirt. "What are you, feeling the call of the Midwest?"

"It's the call of the early-morning sun," I said. "Piercing the alcove and waking me up too early. I'm making a curtain for the window in the stairwell."

He smiled. "I guess that would make sense if you ever—" He glanced at Kilroy. "Oh, never mind."

"If she ever what?" Kilroy said.

Simon looked over at him. For an uncomfortable moment I was reminded of the first time I saw Kilroy, at Viktor's house in Madison—that sparring.

"Have you met Kilroy?" I said quickly to Greg, looking back and forth between the two of them.

Greg had been standing near the sink, but now he came forward and offered Kilroy his hand. He looked handsome in his jacket, his wavy black hair nicely set off by the charcoal wool. He was very tall, and Kilroy had to look up for their eyes to meet.

"So Carrie," Simon said. "We were just at this party, I swear, you would've died. This guy Jason, this friend of ours from Yale? His father is the heir to a New England department store fortune, and they have this annual party every October to, I don't know, celebrate their wealth or whatever. Anyway, this is in a Park Avenue duplex, and—"

"They have eight bathrooms," Greg said, and in my peripheral vision I saw Kilroy bridle.

"What does that even mean?" he said. "I could fit eight bathrooms in my apartment and still have room for my La-Z-Boy."

"You don't *have* a La-Z-Boy," I interjected, trying for a light tone, though I was nervous all at once.

He snapped his fingers. "Damn, I better get one." He turned to Simon. "I live in the kind of place where a La-Z-Boy would *add* character."

"What kind of place is that?" Simon said.

"Oh, you know—herringbone parquet floors, wall-to-wall windows that never get washed on the outside, completely featureless interior. Sometimes I think these buildings were built to institutionalize ugliness—God forbid a postwar building should have any character."

"So why do you live there?" Simon asked.

"I like the enforced anonymity."

"That *would* be hard to give up."

Kilroy gave Simon an amused nod, but he crossed his arms over his chest, and some kind of inner turbulence seeped out of him. What was going on? What had happened to his mood? An edgy silence filled the room, and for a long moment no one spoke.

"Well, anyway," Simon said. "Carrie, this party. Perrier Jouet, and I mean cases. Waiters passing little smoked salmon dealies, tiny filo pastries, et cetera. Flowers like you wouldn't believe, I swear there was this one doorway with a lilac *tree* growing in a kind of arch around it—*white* lilacs, in October. And Mr. Kolodny was going around to all of Jason's friends saying, 'Please come visit us in Aspen,' 'Please come visit us on Block Island.' "

"He's in the Forbes Four Hundred," Greg said, and Kilroy gave him a look of disdain.

"You mean he has a lot of money?"

"Well, yeah," Greg said, glancing at me and Simon. "Obviously."

"Like hundreds of thousands?"

"Like millions and millions," Greg exclaimed. "Jason used to get driven up to school in a limousine."

"Really?" Kilroy said. "Was it by chance a *stretch* limousine?"

Greg blushed. After a moment he put his hands in his pockets, then pulled them out again.

"Well," Simon said. "On that note, I think I'll go watch TV." He made a face, a sort of ironically freaked-out face that was meant to say he actually *was* freaked out, and then he left the kitchen.

My face was burning. I bent over the sewing machine and lowered the needle into the fabric. Poor Greg—he'd never been anything but nice to me, and now my boyfriend was making him look like a fool. What was Kilroy's problem? Was it Greg, or the subject of people with money? I'd noticed something like this before. "When you're driving a Range Rover you're *entitled* to double park on West Broadway," he'd scoffed one day; on another, making fun of a huffy man in a store, it was " 'How dare you keep me waiting—can't you tell by my shoes that I could pay your salary ten times over and not even feel it?' " It wasn't only envy, I didn't think—people like this got under his skin, they *bugged* him. Maybe it wasn't envy at all. He lived very frugally, took pride in buying the cheapest beer available, in inconveniencing himself to get to an early-bird matinee when all he'd be saving was two or three bucks, yet there were signs that he had more money than he otherwise seemed to: a cashmere overcoat in his closet, the time he took me to a Japanese restaurant and casually dropped a hundred dollars so I could try sushi. It was as if he were frugal not by need but to make a point, the same point made by the inward frugality that kept his walls empty of pictures, his floors bare. It was a frugality that said: *I don't need anything.*

And I wondered: where did that leave me?

Greg came and stood beside me and looked down at my work. He rested his fingers on the table, and I saw they were shaking slightly. He said, "It's too bad we don't have another room for you."

"I feel pretty lucky to have the alcove."

"Yeah, but it must be frustrating to know Alice is never even *in* her room."

Alice had the room on the other side of the wall from me. I'd only seen her a few times—she spent most of her time at her boyfriend's place in the East Village.

"I guess I'll head upstairs, too," he said. "I didn't get home from the restaurant until after two last night."

Kilroy was standing across the room, staring through a window at the dark backyard. He turned around. "You're a waiter?"

Greg nodded. "Five nights a week."

"Sounds grueling," Kilroy said.

"Actually, it is. The whole idea is that I'm working nights so I can go to acting class during the day, or auditions, but I'm so wiped out I end up sleeping all the time."

Kilroy grinned. "Sounds like a pretty good life."

Greg gave us a little wave as he headed for the door. "Nice to meet you," he said to Kilroy as he left, and Kilroy lifted his chin and smiled.

"You, too."

Alone again with him, I turned back to my sewing. What a strange thing, that little flash of hostility at Greg, and then the attempt to smooth it over. I stitched several inches, and as I worked I felt him move around the table and come to a stop directly behind me. He stood there without speaking while I continued to the end of the seam. I backstitched for a knot and then used the handwheel to raise the needle from the fabric. I pulled the curtain from under the presser foot and began taking out the pins I'd stitched over. All at once, so surprising that I jumped a little, his finger was on the back of my neck. He stroked from my hairline down into the back of my shirt and then did it again. I wanted—I was suddenly desperate—to turn and press my face into his shirt front. The urge was enormous, an electricity activating my muscles, making them want to *move*. Why had Mike never had this effect on me? I'd felt desire for him, but not this intense need, this wish that felt violent at times, to *be against him*.

Kilroy's finger left my neck. He moved back and I heard him pick up the newspaper again. I looked over my shoulder and he glanced up and gave me a benign smile, then went back to reading.

I was working on the channel for the rod a little later when I heard a step and looked up. It was Lane, whose room was on the third floor, too, on the other side of Alice's. I liked her, but I hadn't talked to her much—I had the impression that she was shy. She was one of the smallest adults I'd ever seen, barely five feet tall or ninety pounds, with pale skin and wrists like saplings, and wispy, ash blond hair cropped close to her head. The first time I'd seen her, coming out of the third-floor bathroom in striped pajamas, I'd thought she was a little boy.

"Hi," she said now. "I just got home and I couldn't go upstairs without coming in here first to see what that noise was."

I smiled. "Was a sewing machine the last thing you expected?"

"Pretty close. I was torn between a dental drill and a blender."

"Or maybe just a really big hummingbird," Kilroy said from his spot against the counter, and Lane laughed her high, thin laugh.

I introduced her to Kilroy, and after they'd said hello she turned back to me. "I've never actually seen anyone sew. How do you do it?"

I motioned her over and guided the fabric under the presser foot. "You pretty much just pin and go." With my foot I felt for the pedal, and then I gave a little demonstration, the needle bobbing up and down as I stitched a few inches. "Didn't you have to take sewing in high school home ec?"

She shook her head. "I went to one of those progressive schools where you didn't have to do anything, including attend classes. I don't think they even offered home ec."

Kilroy laughed. "High school as self-actualization?"

"Pretty much. There was this thing called Meeting, where whoever wanted to would gather every morning, and if you felt like it you could talk, about anything."

Kilroy tilted his head. "And this was where?"

"In Connecticut. Seward Hall is the name of the school, but it's not like that, I think the 'Hall' part is to placate the trustees."

A strange look came over Kilroy's face. He said, "Actually, there was a big movement led by the trustees to drop the 'Hall' and rename the school 'Seward Country Center,' and the *students* fought to keep it Seward Hall."

Lane grinned. "Did you go there, too?"

He shook his head but didn't add anything, and Lane glanced at me with a question on her face. "Well, did someone you know?" she asked.

"Someone I knew."

"Who?" she said. "When? It's such a small place, I—"

"This would've been before your time."

He went back to the newspaper, and she bit her lip and gave me another curious look.

I shrugged. I couldn't explain it—this was just Kilroy. Mr. Mysterious. Mr. I-don't-need-anything. But that wasn't right, was it? He needed me, didn't he? Or wanted me, anyway? I thought of his tongue on my earlobe, the delicious agony as he slowly, slowly tickled me with it.

I only had a little more work to do. I stood up and went out to the hall, where a narrow little closet held an ironing board and iron, along with an ancient upright vacuum cleaner Simon had told me he'd bought at a flea market because it fit in so well with the kitchen appliances. I wrestled the ironing board out of the closet just as Lane passed by, heading for the staircase. She stopped for a moment and faced me, then seemed to think better of it and headed off again. "Goodnight," she called over her shoulder.

In the kitchen I stood the ironing board near an outlet, then brought the iron out, plugged it in, and poured a little water into the reservoir.

"You know," Kilroy said, "I think I'll head home."

I was stunned. I was fifteen minutes from finishing, twenty at the most. "I'm almost done," I said.

"Yeah, but I'm really beat. I'm going to take off." He hesitated a moment and then nodded, as if in confirmation. He was looking not at me but past me, so I couldn't tell what this meant for me, whether he wanted me to follow when I was finished, or quit now and go with him, or what. Maybe he was looking past me *so* I couldn't tell.

His jacket was draped over a chair, and he crossed the room and pulled it on. He gave me a smile and a wave, said, "See you," and moved past me to the doorway. I turned and watched as he made his way down the dimly lit hallway, less and less distinct in the growing darkness until he opened the front door and disappeared.

My heart was pounding. I could still feel the place on my neck where he had touched me, all the possibilities that touch had suggested. *Our first fight,* I thought, but it didn't seem cute, it seemed incomprehensible. What had even happened? Not a fight. He'd been angry, but not at me. *I* was angry—at him, for leaving—but more than that I was mystified. Why hadn't he said the name of the person he'd known who went to Lane's school? Why say you knew someone and then refuse to say whom? And what about what had happened with Greg?

Once I was done with my work I put everything away and carried my sewing machine back upstairs. I'd hang the curtain tomorrow, once I'd bought a rod. For now I flopped onto the futon. Near my pillow I'd hung a little cardboard-mounted watercolor of a pear that I'd bought from a sidewalk vendor in SoHo. On the vendor's table it had looked refreshing, a breath of summer, the perfect yellowy green of the pear, but hanging in the alcove it just seemed forlorn—it made the wall look all the dingier. The floor space of the alcove was barely bigger than the futon. I was living in a little beige box. And yet I wasn't—I hadn't slept here in almost a week. I thought of Kilroy's bedroom, his bed, how quickly we had established which side each of us slept on, he on the left and I on the right. It had taken some getting used to, being on the right, because with Mike I'd always slept on the left. When Mike and I lay like spoons with him behind me, it was my right side his arm lay across, my right shoulder he held. For many, many nights of my life, up until five months ago. I remembered what he looked like sleeping, and then what he looked like in the hospital, not-sleeping, unresponsive. I'd never asked him exactly what it had been like to emerge from that. The resumption of consciousness. I'd seen what it had been like, I knew he'd been confused, but what had he thought? What had it meant to recognize himself as not entirely himself—as unable to move? To feel? I'd never simply said *Tell me.* I hadn't wanted to know.

Out on the landing there was a telephone with a long cord, and I pulled it into the alcove. It was almost ten, almost nine in Madison. Mrs. Mayer answered, and then stayed absolutely silent once I'd identified myself. I waited a moment, then another, and finally asked how she was.

"Fine," she said, and then, "*I'm* fine," as if I might have thought she'd been speaking for him, too.

"Can I talk to him?"

There was a lot of rustling, and then he came on, saying, "Hi, Carrie," in a bright voice that made me ache. "How's it going?" he said. "You haven't sent me my postcard."

His postcard, of the Empire State Building. I'd completely forgotten. "God, I'm sorry."

"Whatever. Do it when you can. So what's up?"

I looked down at my ring, the stone dull in the dim light of the alcove. Why was I still wearing it? I couldn't take it off, but I couldn't say *Tell me,* either. What could I say? I said, "I was thinking of you." He was silent, and I added, "I've been thinking of you a lot, wondering how you've been doing."

"Not bad," he said. "Really pretty good. How about you—what have you been up to?"

I hesitated, wanting only to avoid the truth, to avoid Kilroy. "Walking," I said, and then immediately felt sick, ashamed. Walking? Why not just say *Something you can't do?*

"Is it fun?" he said.

I swallowed. "Yeah. It's like every day I discover some new part of the city I've never heard of. The neighborhoods all have these names, like Turtle Bay."

"Turtle Bay," he said. "Sounds like a good place not to go swimming."

"It's not a real bay."

He was silent, and after a moment I added, "I'm sorry, Mike. I just wanted to say I'm really sorry." And then there was more rustling, and his mother came back on.

20

~

I WOKE THE NEXT morning feeling disoriented and leaden, guilt and doom returning to me instantly. Trying to fall asleep, I'd spiraled from Mike to Kilroy to Mike, and right away I was at it again. Mike's voice all metallic with the effort to sound upbeat. Kilroy walking away. Mike unhappier even than he had to be, because of me. Kilroy receding down the hall, always out of reach.

It was dim in the alcove, the flat light of early morning. I reached for my watch and was surprised to find it was after ten. I got up and went to the soon-to-be-covered stairwell window. No wonder I'd slept in: the sky was close and gray.

I rummaged in my messy suitcase for clothes, then went into the bathroom for a shower. Afterward, in the foggy glass of the medicine cabinet, my face looked puffy. I used my towel to rub a spot clear, and my face *was* puffy.

Lane and Alice had made room for some of my stuff on a shelf that held their toiletries, and I reached for my blow dryer and plugged it in. I half dried my hair and then stopped, tired of the effort. I got into my clothes and tried to smooth out my sweater, but gave up. It was hopeless. Every so often I opened my suitcase and tried to get it organized, but it only lasted a few days. Wearing wrinkled clothes was just part of my life.

When I stepped out of the bathroom Lane appeared almost instantly in her doorway, as if she'd been waiting.

"Oh, I'm sorry," I said. "Did you need the bathroom? I was in there forever."

She smiled. "No, I wanted to say *I* was sorry. About last night. I mean—I think I offended Kilroy."

I shook my head vehemently, and she gave me a puzzled look. "I didn't offend him?"

"To tell you the truth," I said, "I don't really know what happened." To my dismay, tears pricked at my eyes, and I looked down. After a moment, I pressed my fingertips against my eyelids and wiped the wetness away. When I looked up again, a furrow had appeared between her pale eyebrows.

"Are you OK?"

I nodded.

"Do you want to come in? And sit down?"

I looked past her into her room. It was the nicest in the house: she'd repaired her walls and painted them a pretty pale green, offset by a glossy dark gray on the moldings. She was never home at this hour, and I wondered if she was sick. Her hair stuck up in places, but she was dressed, in skinny black pants and a gray top that dwarfed her, its neckline so wide it exposed one shoulder.

"Come on," she said, and she moved in and stepped aside for me, then pointed me toward a little pale blue armchair in the corner. She sat on her bed and gave me a warm smile. There was something comfortable about her, or maybe comforting. She always kept her door ajar, called "Good morning" or "Goodnight" to me as I went to or from the bathroom. When the door was closed I knew her girlfriend was staying over.

"Do you—" she began. "I mean, I don't want to pry, but if you want to talk . . ."

I looked into my lap. I thought of the early years of my relationship with Mike, how I'd told Jamie everything. It had been as if things hadn't really happened until I'd described them to her. The two of us on the phone, or lying on the floor in her bedroom . . . I wasn't telling anyone about Kilroy. Simon had asked a few times, but I hadn't felt comfortable.

My lips were dry, and I licked them. "Thanks."

A series of waist-high bookcases lined Lane's walls, and I scanned them. Their tops were covered with framed pictures and all kinds of objects, from seashells to baskets to ceramic bowls full of buttons and marbles. Near me, a blue glass bottle held a single sprig of lavender, and I leaned over and smelled it.

"Amazing how the scent lasts, isn't it?"

I looked over and found her smiling gently. "It is," I said. "Your room is so lovely," I added, and my face warmed a little. "I mean, I'm not sure I've ever called anything lovely before, but it's the right word for this."

She smiled. "Thank you. I'm sorry not to have invited you in before."

"Oh, no, please—I've been this weird neighbor, you didn't know how long I was staying. You still don't. *I* don't."

She shrugged. "What difference does it make? Miss Wolf says plans are for the bourgeois." She smiled. "Of course, at the same time she's asking if I can come at nine instead of nine-thirty the next day because she wants help dealing with the new cleaning lady."

Miss Wolf was her employer, an elderly writer of some previous fame who lived near the Metropolitan Museum in an apartment with views of Central Park. Lane was her paid companion.

"No work today?" I said.

She shook her head. "She's got her niece visiting."

"How'd you get that job, anyway?"

"The old-girl network, lesbian track," she said with a smile. "My favorite professor at Yale was this same niece's best friend's cousin. Miss Wolf is an unequal opportunity employer and I fit the bill perfectly: 'a young, frail sapphist poetess,' to quote her. Her last companion is now the director of a retreat for lesbian artists in upstate New York, so you can see the wide career path ahead of me."

I smiled. "Are you a poetess? A poet?"

Lane's pale face filled with color, and she nodded.

"I didn't know that," I said. I thought of the others, Simon with his illustrating, Greg with acting. I'd been in nearly as many conversations with Lane as I had with Greg, and she'd never mentioned anything but her job.

"It's not something I really talk about," she said.

"I'd love to read something you wrote. If that's not too forward."

She looked down for a moment, her face even redder. "I'm sorry," she said. "This is ridiculous. I'm stupid about this." She wiped her palms on her gray duvet cover, then went over to one of the bookcases and withdrew a slim paperback book, the cover a soft periwinkle blue. "Here," she said, holding it out to me.

Parapraxis and Eurydice, it said on the cover. *Poems by Lane Driscoll.*

"You already have a book?" I said.

"It's just a chapbook."

I took it and turned to the table of contents, which was like a poem itself: "The Blue Door in the Garden," "Where You Stood," "Knowing the Vocabularies of the Body." I flipped a few pages and read at random, conscious that she was watching me. Part of it went:

> Of the you in me:
> *l'uomo vero,*
> the true man.
> The father of memory,
> of all my time.

"Wow," I said. "Did this come out while you were still at Yale?"

"It was printed then," she said, blushing again. "It didn't really come out, it's just a chapbook."

I handed it back to her. "Well, I'm impressed."

She slid it back onto the shelf, where there were eight or ten other copies, their narrow spines carefully aligned. She turned back and smiled at me. "Simon, in typical Simon fashion, ordered a case and sat outside our dining hall trying to sell them—my publicist, he said he was. He had a sign made up. I've never been so mortified."

I smiled. "What was he like then?"

"Like now, but with a little more Wisconsin around the edges." She shrugged. "How about in high school?"

He was quiet in the French class we had together—not unfriendly, but very self-contained. Around school he smiled when he saw me, but to himself, as if he thought me vaguely comical. Which I probably was, joined at the hip to Mike. Out of nowhere I recalled sitting on Mike's lap in the cafeteria one day and seeing Simon in line by himself, nothing on his tray but a container of red Jell-O. He paid and then carried it to an empty table at the far edge of the room. "I didn't know him that well," I said at last. "He was shy, I guess."

"Closeted?"

"Definitely." I looked at her. "Was it hard to be gay at Yale?"

"More hard not to be. We lucked out, timing-wise. It was more like certain people were closet heterosexuals."

I thought of how open Simon was now. How he'd told me he no longer went anywhere where he had to pretend to be straight. If he'd stayed in Madison would he have reached that point? I doubted it.

"I didn't come here expecting anything like this to happen," I said.

"With Kilroy?"

I nodded.

"Because of . . ."

"Mike. I mean, Simon told you, right?"

"I adore him, but he's *not* discreet."

"It's OK," I said. "It's fine." I looked at her for a moment, then turned to a nearby shelf and stroked my finger over the rough surface of a tiny starfish lying there.

She took something off her bedside table and carried it to me in her outstretched palm. "Look at this," she said. "Feel it. It's really soft."

It was a sand dollar. I took it from her and held it in my hand, a pure white disk etched with delicate spears. I touched the surface, so soft I imagined a fine dust would come away on my fingertips.

"I found it on the beach when I was a little girl," she said. "I'm always amazed I haven't lost it."

I handed it back and watched her set it carefully on her table again. I imagined her alone on the beach, alone but not minding it. A little girl in a flowered bathing suit and a big straw hat. Digging in the sand. Knowing she was safe.

LANE HAD ERRANDS to do, so we headed out together, then said goodbye on a street corner. The cloud cover was lifting and separating, revealing ribbons of watery blue. I checked on my car, then headed for a hardware store in the neighborhood. The sidewalks were alive with people, passing me with their gesticulating hands and their focused expressions. Where but in New York could you see a woman in a pink sari walking alongside a man with green hair and a pierced eyebrow, their faces turned toward each other in obvious delight? I liked the juxtapositions of stores: Cool Comix next to Manny's Shoe Repair; Laundromatic next to *Faïence de Provence*. For a while I just looked at people's feet, wondering at the number of foot-miles each block of sidewalk supported each day.

The hardware store had six different kinds of curtain rods. The spring-loaded one I needed was only $3.99, and I carried it around the store with me while I wandered through Tupperware and extension cords and garbage cans. It was its own kind of pleasure to browse among things that were entirely practical, things people *needed*. Down one aisle I found packages of cardboard you could assemble into furniture: bedside tables, file cabinets, sweater chests to slide under your bed. The biggest package contained an entire dresser, a shrink-wrapped stack of cardboard printed with cabbage roses. For twenty bucks I could unpack.

Back at the brownstone, I ripped into the plastic and found the instructions. They were three pages long, all Slot A and Flap B, and within minutes my knuckles were rubbed red, but I wasn't daunted. I pushed and pulled at the cardboard, and an hour later I had a dresser. It fit snugly between the futon and the wall, five drawers that didn't exactly glide open but that *worked*. I dumped the contents of my suitcase onto the futon, a chaos of clothing twisted together. No more. I began folding and arranging, sweaters, shirts, and pants, even dresses and skirts, because I didn't want anything left in the suitcase, not a single sock. Last on the futon were the silk nightgown and robe, still wrapped in tissue but all twisted and crumpled now. The bottom drawer couldn't really open—the dresser was that tightly wedged between the wall and the futon—but I cracked it a few inches, unwrapped the two silk pieces, smoothed them out as well as I could, and arranged them inside by feel. I took the empty suitcase down to the first floor and wrestled it onto the top shelf of the closet with the ironing board and the vacuum cleaner, then I went back upstairs and gave my cardboard dresser a pat. Much better.

Kilroy called at five. He was about to leave the advertising agency where he'd been working all week, and he wondered if I wanted to meet him at McClanahan's, or maybe meet him at his house beforehand so he could get out of his work clothes . . .

I met him at his house. I got there first and waited in the vestibule, wondering what to say about last night, what to think. At last he pulled open the outside door and came in. His hair was tucked behind his ears, his face smoothly shaved. He always came home to change before he did anything else, but I liked how he looked in his work clothes, uncomfortably handsome. Today he wore khaki pants and a blue dress shirt that brought out the pale flecks in his eyes. "Sorry you had to wait," he said. He seemed a bit breathless. He let us into the lobby and went into the mailroom for a moment, then came back out and pressed the button for the elevator. "Phew," he said.

"Tiring day?"

"I've just been hurrying." He tucked his mail under his arm and reached for my hand. He interlocked his fingers with mine, but then the elevator arrived and he let go and we stepped on.

"What'd you do today?" he said.

"Bought a dresser."

He raised his eyebrows.

"Cardboard," I added.

A smile curled his lips. "That's very cutting edge, actually. Frank Gehry has these cardboard chairs that people in the know are very into."

"Do they have cabbage roses on them?"

"That I doubt," he said. "Though I may not be up on the latest developments."

We reached his floor and he held the elevator door as I stepped off. In his apartment he dropped his mail in the kitchen and then went into the bedroom. "Want to go get a beer?" he called.

I made my way down the hall. He was standing there in his blue shirt, his khakis already tossed over a chair back. The last twenty-four hours spun through my mind, the ravioli dinner we'd had in the noisy

Italian restaurant, Kilroy talking to Simon and Greg in the kitchen, then the thing with Lane and her school. Mike's voice on the phone, my night alone, talking to Lane this morning. I didn't, actually, want to go get a beer. I approached him, and as I walked I pulled my sweater over my head and tossed it onto the bed. When I reached him I slipped my fingers into the leg of his jockeys and touched his supple balls, rolling them for a moment between my fingers until I was ready to wrap my fingers around his hardening erection.

"You surprise me," he said in a soft, choked voice.

"Still?"

"Yes."

I put my palm over his mouth and then unbuttoned his shirt and pushed it off his shoulders and onto the floor. I flung my bra away and moved us both to the bed. I tugged his jockeys off and then moved down until he was right there between my breasts, engorged, and I squeezed my breasts together and slid up and down on him, his smooth warmth. I lowered my mouth and licked and sucked for a while, then stopped abruptly. I sat up and yanked my jeans and underwear off as he lay beside me breathing hard. I moved back and got his knee between my legs and my breasts sandwiching him again, and we moved and moved, and then he groaned and flipped me onto my back and pushed into me, and then he pumped and pumped harder and harder, his face hovering over me, his hair brushing my forehead, and then I came, and then he did, and then we lay there damp and panting, a heap of entangled arms and legs, and we didn't talk.

21

~

THAT SUNDAY KILROY decided we should cook. Too much take-out, he told me, was bad for the soul. It was a cold October day, a day he said was crying out for beef stew. We left his apartment and headed downtown, my mind for some reason racing ahead to put us in a store in the Village that I'd wandered into one day. It had been crammed full of the most appealing foods I'd ever seen: beautifully stacked fruits and vegetables, sausages hanging from the ceiling, bins of breads, shelves of exquisite cakes, trays of olives, jars of imported mustards, fresh, clean fish laid out on beds of ice. And the most incredible array of meats. Everything perfect, everything way out of my reach. How much would my share come to? Could I plead no appetite to reduce the amount of meat we bought?

"Balducci's?" Kilroy said when he figured out what I was thinking. "You don't buy stew meat at Balducci's."

"You mean *you* don't."

He shook his head. "I don't buy anything at Balducci's. Well, maybe a piece of imported cheese that would stink to high heaven, on a day I was in a weird mood. But no one would buy stew meat there—the whole point of stew is to take a so-so piece of meat and cook the toughness out of it until it can't be anything but delicious."

We went to the A&P instead. Filled our cart with prepackaged stew meat, carrots, onions, mushrooms, bacon, tomato paste, beef broth, bay leaves, and a loaf of French bread. At the cash register Kilroy waved off the money I took from my wallet.

"My idea, my treat."

"But," I said. "But . . ."

He picked up one bag and pushed the other toward me. "You'll emasculate me if you fight me on this."

"But not if I carry one of the grocery bags?"

He shook his head. "That's actually a notch *down* on my scale."

Back at his apartment we settled into his immaculate kitchen. I chopped carrots and onions on a big wooden cutting board while he browned the meat three or four pieces at a time. It was all very familiar, and after a while I realized why: in high school, Jamie and I had once checked Julia Child out of the library and made a complete French dinner for Mike and Rooster, from *soupe à l'oignon* to *tarte aux pommes*. (It was pathetic, now that I thought about it: Mike had proudly brought a filched bottle of horribly sweet white wine, and at the end Rooster'd asked if there was ice cream for the "pie.") The centerpiece had been a dish nearly identical to the one Kilroy and I were working on, a beef stew with sauteed mushrooms and braised pearl onions. "Hey," I said, "isn't this basically *boeuf Bourguignon*?"

Kilroy looked up from the stew pot. "It would be if we were in France. Here it's just beef stew."

I blushed. "Oh, I see."

He cocked his head. "Come on, don't be like that. I just have a theory that you have to be careful about importing foreign names and pronunciations. Sometimes it's necessary, but other times it smacks of affectation. I used to know this woman who'd say, 'Well, I'm off to *Roma* next week.' 'Would you like some *veecheesoizzz*?' It was tempting to throttle her."

"Who was she?" I asked.

"She was a woman."

"You said that."

He turned back to the stove and tossed some more beef into the pot.

"She sounds like a snooty rich girl," I said. "Was she a friend of yours?"

"What a horrible thought." The meat sizzled and spat, and he concentrated on it, turning it with a long wooden spatula.

"So?"

He turned around. "She was a friend of my mother's, OK? I don't know what I could tell you about her that would make her interesting."

My face burned, and I stared at the pile of chopped vegetables on the cutting board. Here we went.

"Say *boeuf Bourguignon* again," he said, something apologetic in his voice as he changed the subject.

I looked up at him. *"Boeuf Bourguignon."*

He smiled. "I was right, you do have a good accent."

"French for six years. Did you take it, too?"

"I lived there for a while, a long time ago."

I set my knife down and stared. "In France?"

His smile broadened and he nodded.

"I've *always* wanted to go to France," I exclaimed. "I read a book about the House of Dior that made me want to *be* French for a while. How long were you there?"

"About two years."

My mouth fell open. I picked up a piece of carrot and set it down again, my fingers damp.

"No need to be so impressed," he said.

"I'm not impressed, I'm flabbergasted. Did you live in Paris?"

"Paris part of the time, Provence for a while." He shrugged. "I spent a summer in the Dordogne."

"I can't believe this. How old were you?"

"Twenty-seven, twenty-eight."

Suddenly I was confused. "And this was *when*?"

"Ten years ago. More, actually."

I felt my mouth fall open.

"I'm forty," he said. "If that's what you want to know."

Forty. I'd been assuming late twenties, thirty max—at Viktor and Ania's I'd thought he was my age. The idea that he was forty and a temp worker, forty and living in an apartment with no more pieces of furniture than you could count on your fingers, no art on the walls, no *junk*—it bothered me somehow.

"What are you thinking?" he said.

"I don't know."

"Don't you mean you don't want to say?"

I pushed some scraps of carrot peel together, making a little pile. "OK," I said. "I'm wondering why you never told me before."

He raised his eyebrows. "That I lived in France for a while?"

"That you're *forty.*"

"It never came up," he said with a shrug. "What was I supposed to do, fill out an application? 'Age.' 'Places lived.' " He gave me a pointed look: " 'People known.' " He moved closer and put his hand behind my neck, pulling me forward until our foreheads touched. " 'Ability to appreciate a fetching small-town girl who's full of surprises.' " He kissed me and his lips were warm, his stubble scratchy on the skin around my mouth.

"What does it matter, anyway?" he said, moving back toward the stew pot again. "Forty doesn't say what I am, I say what forty is."

"Maybe," I said, but I was reminded of what my mother'd said on the phone, weeks ago, about defining versus being defined by what you did, and thinking of her made me realize: Kilroy was closer to my mother's age than to mine.

I ENTERED A phase of intense listening, in the hope that I could learn more about him. I wanted facts. I saw myself as the perennial graduate student he'd said I should be, but a student of him, a researcher in a carrel, typing notes into a laptop. I'd left one library only to build myself another.

Yet the shelves were bare. Or all they held were real books: what I learned was how much he liked to read. He went through a book every four or five days—huge, heavy books on the geology of the American Southwest, or Russian art and iconography, or the history of fundamentalism in the Middle East. Evenings, he read while I sewed: I went back to the fabric store and bought two different kinds of black microfiber for a couple of pairs of side-zip pants, then took my Bernina to his place so I could work there. Some nights we'd go hours without talking, the only sounds my sewing machine stuttering a quick seam, then his book answering with a flip of a page. Other nights he'd look up after half an hour and say he was thirsty, how about a beer and a game of pool at McClanahan's?

He liked to read. He liked to drink beer. He liked to shoot pool. He liked to make love with me. These were things I knew.

One Saturday afternoon he lay on his couch reading while I hand-sewed the hem of the first pair of pants. At one point I found myself thinking, *I take up a thread from the leg side, then I tunnel about a quarter inch through the hem side,* and I realized I was explaining myself to him, silently narrating the commonplace so that it could take up residence in what he knew of me.

I heard a thump and looked up to see that he'd closed his book and dropped it onto the floor. He shut his eyes and stretched, his arms reaching over his head and his stocking feet arching. Relaxing, he looked at me and said, "Do you hear it?"

"Hear what?"

"The call of a bookstore. Don't you hear that little voice calling, 'Kilroy, Kilroy'?"

"You finished that one?"

He swept his hair from his forehead. "Really we should go to the Strand so I can make some space, but I don't think they'll have what I want."

"What do you mean, make some space?"

He gestured at his bookcase, tall and narrow and so crammed with books that I didn't see how it could hold another volume. "Time to thin it out. They buy used books at the Strand."

"Why not just get another bookcase?" This was something I'd thought before: he certainly had the wall space for one.

He shook his head. "That's strictly forbidden."

"By whom?"

"Myself, of course."

I gave him a look.

"This is my bookcase," he said. "When it's too full, I weed out whatever's lost its glitter for me."

"Why?"

"Because that's what I do, Carrie. Why do you put your pins like that?"

I looked down at my pincushion: somehow or other I'd gotten into the habit of sticking my pins into it in lines. "I'm organized," I said.

"So am I."

"No, you're self-denying."

"Just a form of organization," he said with a smile.

I glanced around his apartment, the afternoon sun slanting in to throw blocks of shadow onto his bare walls. "Is that why you don't have any family pictures around?" I said. "Any art?"

His head shot around. "My God, I forgot the art."

"Be serious," I said. "Wouldn't it be nice to have *one* picture up? One really nice picture that you really, really liked?"

"Think of the pressure," he said with a mild smile. "*One* really nice picture. I'm not man enough for that decision."

He sat up, and I sighed and began putting my things away, frustrated. Recently tired of the little watercolor pear hanging above my futon at the brownstone, I'd taken it down and put in its place a photograph of a house in a field, taken through a deep, wet-looking mist. If Kilroy couldn't settle on one picture, why didn't he do what I did, start his own cycle of choose and replace? Was he already at the other end of that, forty and tired? Ready for some visual silence? I didn't think so. The blankness of his apartment was an avoidance, no less a one than the blankness of his past.

"That's a cool pincushion, actually."

He was standing near me now, and I held out the pincushion for him to see, a little red silk one Mike's mother had bought for me in Chinatown one summer when they all went to San Francisco. It had a ring of tiny stuffed figures on the top of it, arms joined, each a different bright color.

"It's from San Francisco," I said.

"City of mussels marinara."

"What?"

"I've eaten next to nothing else there. Great place, huh?"

"I've never been. Mike's mother bought it for me."

We looked at each other for a moment, then he returned the pin-cushion to me and moved away while I put it into my sewing basket, next to my orange-handled scissors and my heavy pinking shears.

"Were you close to her?" he said.

I hesitated for a moment, oddly sure he hoped for a certain answer, though I didn't know which one. "I was," I said at last. "We were sort of like this incredibly polite mother and daughter. She called me honey, I helped her in her garden sometimes."

"And then?"

"You know."

"Yeah, but you and Mike were already on the outs. What did that do? What was your relationship with her just before the accident?"

Those last months before the accident, the slow thaw of spring . . . I remembered standing with her in front of their house, admiring the first purple crocuses, how she held her hands together at her throat, so pleased. But on another day, a couple weeks into May, I was sitting at their kitchen table while Mike was upstairs getting something, and she came and stood near me and asked, in a low, concerned voice, "Is everything OK?"

"I think she was trying not to see it," I said to Kilroy. "Like every-one else."

WE HEADED DOWNTOWN, toward the dreaded SoHo—there was a bookstore on MacDougal Street that he thought would have what he wanted, a translation of a biography of Galileo. Above us huge, gray-rimmed clouds churned across the sky. I thought of how, having grown up here, he had the city in his blood, how the traffic and people and noises must feel as natural to him as their absence would have felt to me. I didn't think the commotion of New York would ever feel natural to me, not if I lived here for the rest of my life. I hoped it wouldn't, because I liked how aware of it I was, how going outside was always an event, the running of some kind of gauntlet.

In the bookstore we separated, and I wandered back to a display of big, expensive books of fashion photography. I paged through one after another, studying how one designer got from point A to point B, how another's sense of color evolved. If only I had more money, I'd try making something complicated after the pants—maybe a suit. Or I'd try combining two patterns, getting rid of the ugly sleeves on one but keeping the silhouette, changing the front opening of another from a round neck to a V, to see if I could.

Money, money, money. I was running through my savings, ten dollars here, twenty there, thirty. I'd asked my mother to find a month-by-month subletter for my apartment, and she'd gotten a law student who was paying me a hundred dollars a month beyond my rent, but that was fluff in New York, subway fare. My credit card virtually glowed in my wallet, but I didn't want to start down that path—I was still the responsible citizen Jamie'd accused me of being. Selling my car was the obvious move—it was an albatross, a royal pain. But it was my car, the one place in New York where I could go to feel like myself, even just for the ten or fifteen minutes it took to move it every few days.

I set down the book I'd been holding and turned to another. On the cover was a rich black-and-white photograph of a woman standing in front of an old stone building—a church, maybe. She wore a voluminous dark cape with the hood up, and all you could see of her was her beautiful face, secret and closed: long, arched eyebrows and a full-lipped mouth.

There was someone right behind me. I turned and found a woman of forty-five or fifty: carefully made-up, with gold on her earlobes and at her throat. She wore a long, tobacco brown coat over pants and a sweater of the same color—a coat for every outfit, I figured.

She met my glance, then peered at the photograph. "The complacence of extreme beauty," she said with a little sniff.

I laughed. "I was thinking she looked complicated and mysterious."

She shook her head. "That's what they want you to think, but she's like a Matisse odalisque or something, blissed out on self-approval." She stood there for a moment, then turned around and studied the shelves behind me, where a little wooden shingle hanging into the aisle read PHILOSOPHY AND RELIGION.

I turned back to the book, disappointed she hadn't said more. It was another New York moment, like at the photography show with

Simon: a stranger delivering up an inscrutable, glittering sentence—pretentious, maybe, but also unforgettable—and then moving on. Maybe that's what New York would end up being to me, a collection of such moments that would accumulate into a life.

I looked at the photograph again. It struck me now that the most important thing about it was not the woman but the cape, how the dark, smooth expanse of it contrasted with the rough, pale stone, and how the hood, draped over her head, made you think of a bell. A cape wasn't a category of garment I'd ever taken seriously, but now I thought I'd been wrong, and as I admired it—its long, fluid lines; its elegant, cursive hood—I began to reimagine it in a charcoal tweed, with a soft rose lining, cashmere or merino wool. And then suddenly, as clear as an actual voice, I imagined Jamie saying, *Yeah, if you want to look like the French Lieutenant's Woman,* and I felt a hard tug away, all Jamie's hurt pulling me back home. I had to call her, soon.

A little later I found Kilroy in the travel section, an open book in his hands. When he saw me he flipped to a big color photograph of a street lined by towering horse chestnut trees, all abloom. "April in Paris," the caption read.

"Let's go," he said.

"Did you find your Galileo book?"

A slow smile lifted the corners of his mouth, and he tapped the book. "To *France,*" he said. "Let's go to France."

I stared at him, his hair hanging over his forehead, his sharp, pointed nose. There was something serious in his expression, something urgent. "OK," I said, "let's," and he nodded briskly.

"Good, that settles it."

He bought the Galileo book and then we left the store and wandered east. It was late October, and the women I saw reminded me of the colors of hunting season, the browns and tans of the land, the brilliant dark greens of game birds. One older woman wore a paisley shawl over one shoulder, and it lay along her side like a richly colored wing.

I told Kilroy about the woman and the fashion photography book. "She said it like a proclamation: 'The complacence of extreme beauty.' Then she went back to browsing in Philosophy and Religion."

He threw back his head and laughed. "That's perfect. It's probably a known pickup spot, the last place would-be intellectuals try before putting a personals ad in *The New York Review of Books*. Did she have a look of advanced sexual avidity? Why 'the complacence of extreme beauty,' anyway? Why not 'the beauty of extreme complacence'? Or something else entirely—it's a nice syntactical formula, just pick two nouns and an adjective and have fun with it. 'The absence of identifiable intelligence,' for example." He elbowed me. "Come on, your turn."

I shook my head. "I can't think of one."

"The charm of excessive modesty. The perfection of complete innocence."

"Are you making fun of me?"

"Absolutely not, of me. The *bouleversement* of sudden happiness." He gave me a sweet smile and took my hand, which he'd never done before on the street, and I felt strange all at once, as if I had a long-distance crush on him, as if we were circling around each other, wondering what was going to happen.

We hadn't had lunch, and a little later, somewhere on Lafayette, we stopped for soup at a tiny place I wouldn't have noticed if Kilroy hadn't pointed it out, a narrow storefront with high ceilings and ridged-glass pendant lamps hanging over each booth. We sat at the counter and ate clam chowder with oyster crackers while he talked about food marriages: solid old matches like this one, terrible mistakes like bacon in warm potato salad, risky unions like beef cooked in beer, which worked, and pears doused with chocolate sauce, which didn't. Chocolate sauce, he said, should be reserved for vanilla ice cream, and vice versa.

"Then there's carrot-and-raisin salad," he said. "One of the all-time worst things I've ever eaten."

I had a spoonful of soup in my mouth and I had to struggle to swallow it without laughing. I'd eaten dozens of carrot-and-raisin salads, maybe hundreds: it was one of Mrs. Mayer's signature dishes, right up there with beef Stroganoff. Mike had brought a Tupperware container full to the reservoir on Memorial Day, and I could vividly see my spent paper plate sitting on the pier, a crescent of hamburger bun and a wet spot with a few carrot strips clinging to it, beaded with mayo dressing.

"What?" Kilroy said. "Is carrot-and-raisin salad a big favorite out Wisconsin way?"

"Very big. No barbecue is complete without it."

He shook his head. "What an abomination." He reached for his package of oyster crackers and shook a few more onto his soup. "Barbecues, too. Think about it: 'Let's take a piece of animal flesh and set fire to it.' I guess it speaks to early social man, the camaraderie of the campfire, the attempt to shut out the dark world just beyond."

He gave me a grin, and I smiled: he'd spoken in what I thought of as his pseudovoice, the one he used to mimic posers and proclaimers. He was an intellectual, too, but the kind who stands outside the circle, criticizing everyone else. What he really liked was spinning theories, telling me that all New York streets were edgy, regal, or closed; that all taxi drivers were strained or loose. A few nights ago, out for a late walk, he said he'd decided that the pigeons in Washington Square lived according to an intricate social structure that made the given bird you saw at a given time a function not of randomness but of secret order.

"You're a snob," I said now. "An urban snob."

"Ouch. What, did you barbecue a lot?"

"Of course," I said, but that wasn't the whole story: it wasn't that I did but that *we* did. We had. Mike and I. And all at once I was back in Madison, on the night before the accident again, watching from my bedroom while Mike set our hamburgers on the hibachi on the driveway and then leaned against the old garage while they cooked. My eyes were still hot from the cry I'd had, the sobbing that had started in the kitchen while I watched him on the couch, watched him lying there as if it were the one place in the world where he truly belonged. When he heard me he got off the couch and came right in, but after he'd held me for a while I pulled away and took up the plate of raw burgers, passing it to him so that it was between us, the plate, forcing his attention off what had just happened and onto the idea of dinner. He took it and without a word went down the back stairs and out onto the driveway. Watching him from my bedroom window a few minutes later, I sensed something inside me breaking loose, and I felt wild. *Look up,* I thought. *Look up.* And finally he did, looked up and stared right at me: a long, plain look. He stood with his arms at his sides, the spatula in one hand, looking, and just as I thought I couldn't stand it anymore, just as I was about to wave, he switched the spatula to his left hand, raised his right hand to his forehead, and saluted.

Kilroy was beside me, his spoon in midair, looking at me. "What?" he said.

I felt shaky. I let my spoon fall into my soup bowl with a clatter. I put my hands on my face, covering my mouth and nose but leaving my eyes free, leaving them open so that I could see the blackboard on the other side of the counter with its specials, clam chowder, reuben sandwich, turkey and gravy. The waiter, a dark-skinned guy about my age, sitting on a stool reading the *Post*. The coffee machine, not espresso but coffee, with its brown-lipped regular pot and its orange-lipped decaf. The people behind us, reflected in a band of mirror: two black-clad women in their thirties, an older man covered with paint spatters, a young guy with a ponytail talking to a gray-haired woman in a mustard brown suit. Nothing to say New York, to say not-Madison, but that's what it said. Maybe it was the pendant lamps, the double-height pressed-tin ceiling. Maybe it was me.

"It'll be slow," Kilroy said, touching my arm. He lifted his hand and ran it down the back of my head. "It'll take as long as it takes."

22

~

I KNEW KILROY WAS right, that what I needed was time, but I wanted to be done with it, to be wherever I was going. At the same time, I wanted Mike to be where he was going, too, and to be OK with my not being there with him, which I knew was impossible.

Fall was so cold in Madison, wind blowing off the lakes and penetrating everything. I thought of the long, wide windows of the physical therapy room and what Mike must see through them, trees bare of leaves, skeletal against the gray sky. We'd always made a point of going to Picnic Point in October, taking the long walk out through the turning trees. It was almost November now. I thought of him more and more, until thinking of him became not an act but a presence in me, a dull ache in the center of my chest. Yet I didn't call again. What more could I say, beyond *I'm sorry*? I couldn't think of a thing.

It started raining, a thin, cold rain that turned the entire city dreary. Being outside was unpleasant, but so was being inside, trapped, the idea of all the other people in the city feeling pent up, too. I was too restless to read books, so I bought a stack of fashion magazines and read them as carefully as texts I'd been assigned for a class.

One afternoon I sat in my chilly alcove flipping through *Vogue* by the feeble light of my lamp. The sheer spring dresses made me shiver, but I kept paging along. What was it about fashion? Since arriving in New York I'd been nurturing this fascination, this compulsion to look at clothes. It was less about beauty than about transformation. Who would I be in a turquoise paisley slip dress and beaded sandals?

By five it was completely dark out—the early, weighty dark of a November afternoon, a long night still to come. I heard footsteps, and Lane appeared at the top of the stairs carrying a collapsed umbrella that was still dripping. She did a double take when she saw me huddled under Simon's scratchy blanket. "Carrie," she said, "you look like you're freezing."

I shrugged. "Just the hand I'm turning the pages with."

"Come into my room," she said. "Seriously. I'll make us some tea— Miss Wolf had me reading to her all afternoon and my throat could use it."

Her room was warm, pans of water under the radiators so it wouldn't feel so dry. She pointed me to the armchair and plugged in an electric kettle, then held out a tin cracker box full of assorted tea bags. I picked orange pekoe and she took lemon mint for herself, then got cups from a shelf and arranged the tea bags in them. When the kettle whistled she unplugged it and poured the steaming water.

"You know, you can hang out in my room when I'm not here," she said. "It's way too cold out there."

"Thanks."

The tea was fragrant. I sipped mine slowly, then raised the cup to look at the tiny flowers along the edge—little purple blossoms interspersed with dark green leaves. There was a gold line on the cup's fragile handle, another ringing the base.

"It was my grandmother's," Lane said from her bed, where she sat cross-legged on her puffy duvet. She held up her cup, which matched. "I inherited the set when she died."

"You did? Not your mother?" My mother had her mother's china in a cabinet in the dining room. When we used it, for birthdays and holidays, she joked that it was my legacy so we should be careful— wash it by hand, dry it and put it right back again.

"This was my father's mother," Lane said. "He died when I was a child, so I was her only descendant."

I glanced at her bookcase, where the periwinkle blue books were. What was the line from her poem? *The father of memory.*

"I also have her piano," she said. "And no idea what to do with it."

"You don't play?"

"I do a little, but I'm not exactly going to bring it here."

We exchanged a smile. The ground floor of the brownstone was furnished entirely with castoffs—stained old couches, broken tables, chairs that needed recaning. Anything nice was in the bedrooms, held separate.

"Someday you'll have a house to put it in."

"Or an apartment," she said. "Maura and I might get one together."

Maura was her girlfriend—a tall red-haired woman who worked on Wall Street. "Where does she live now?"

"In a studio way up in the East Nineties. It's a pain, but she refused to live here."

"Why?"

"She likes Simon in smaller doses." She got up and crossed the room, then took a photograph from a shelf and held it out to show me. An old lady in a flowered dress sat on a wicker chair in front of a big, wood-frame house, a small child on her lap. Nearby, a couple in matching straw hats held hands. "My grandmother, my parents, and me," she said.

I took the photograph and studied it. The couple were young, thirty or so, the man standing there with his toes pointing slightly to the sides, just as Lane sometimes stood. In the child I could see the Lane I knew: in the pointed chin and the narrow, arched eyebrows. "How old were you when he died?" I asked her.

"Seven."

I gave her the picture back, nodding.

"What?" she said.

"What do you mean?"

"Your expression. Is your father dead, too?"

I wondered what she'd seen. After a moment I said, "He walked out on us. When I was three."

"Oh, I'm sorry."

"It's OK."

She reached for a package and offered it to me, shortbread cookies wedged tightly in plaid cellophane. I wiggled a cookie out, then she took one for herself.

"He just—walked out?" she said, holding her cookie without biting into it.

I took a bite of mine and nodded.

"But you know where he is," she said. "You see him."

I shook my head. "He could live in China for all I know. Or New York."

Twin creases pinched the bridge of her nose, and she went back to her bed and set the cookie next to her tea, then faced me again, a troubled look on her face. "You haven't seen him since you were three? He's alive out there and you don't know where?"

I nodded. "Presumably."

"What about child support?"

"Ever hear of the expression 'deadbeat dad'?"

"God," she said.

"My mother tried to find him for a while, but then it was like, if he didn't want to be with us . . ." I let my voice trail off and stared into my lap. It was strange to be talking about it.

She lifted her tea cup and blew, then set it down again without having any. She said, "I guess we have something in common then—growing up without fathers."

"I guess so." I set my tea on the floor, then stood up and wandered to the window. My reflection stared back at me from the black glass, my hair hanging to my shoulders, a little frizzy from all the rain.

She said, "Do you ever wonder what your life would be like if your father had stayed around? If you'd even recognize it?"

Without turning I nodded. On and off over the years I'd thought that if my father hadn't left, everything would have been different—I might never have even gotten involved with Mike. I remembered my phone conversation with my mother back in September—how afterward I'd felt that my father had somehow caused or at least encouraged my disillusionment back home. Now I took it further, saw his desertion as akin to a physical force that had blown me from my mother's quiet house to the Mayers' noisy one, and then had blown me on again, having taught that loyalty, responsibility, and love were as nothing, valueless, light as soap bubbles and just as easily dissolved. *Jump on a ferry, Carrie. Just set yourself free.*

"What are you thinking?" Lane said.

I turned around. "Something along the lines of how events are so powerful—how they determine so much."

"That's what I always think about people."

"Like your father?"

She smiled a faraway smile. "He was a strange guy. He'd be full of plans one minute—he was going to take me to the circus, we were going to stage our *own* circus—but then he'd go lie on this old couch in our living room, his bare feet up on the arm, his toenails all horned and yellow, and he'd hardly know I was there. He had a brain tumor, see, but I didn't know that until later, and I was six, seven, it's not like the words 'brain tumor' would have had more power than he did." She smiled again. "I think it's him as much as the fact that he died."

"What is?"

She shrugged. "Me."

I considered the man I remembered. The bathrobe man yelling at my mother, the fence-post man out in the snowy yard. There was a feeling I used to get when I thought about him, a dull, lowered feeling that I'd always assumed came from what he'd done, not who he was. Now I wondered what it was like during those three years when he was around, my mother with a small child in the house, this man with his anger and his misery. How many times did she sit spooning applesauce into my mouth while he ranted or lurked, came in or stormed out? My mother with a baby in her arms, then a toddler on her hip, so that she didn't even have the full use of herself to contend with him. She was twenty-one when she married him, twenty-three when I was born—the age I was now.

Lane set her tea to the side and swung onto her stomach, planting her elbows on her duvet and propping her chin on her small fists. Her hands were translucent, the veins pale blue and sinuous, like distantly viewed, meandering rivers. "Miss Wolf is always telling me that the family is the enemy of the artist," she said. "Well, I think the family *is* the artist. Just like the sky is, or all the books you've ever read."

I nodded, but I was thinking all at once of Kilroy's evasions about his family, his past. What was he doing with all those books he read but filling himself, *re*filling himself—pushing further and further away what had been there before?

A FEW DAYS later a small package arrived at the brownstone with the morning mail, a little padded envelope inscribed with my name. The handwriting was faintly familiar, but I couldn't place it. The postmark was Madison.

Inside, all by itself, with no note of explanation, was an unmarked cassette tape, and all at once I knew it had come from Mike, that my name had been written by his mother, who'd been unable to bring herself to put her own name and address on the upper left-hand corner.

The brownstone was empty, and though I was sure it would be OK to use any of the stereos in the house, I didn't feel right not asking first. I took the tape out to my car, which was parked under a bare tree two blocks to the south. The driver's seat was cold through my jeans. The car started easily, then sputtered and died. It smelled damp from all the rain. The engine caught again, and I gave it some gas, then switched the heater on and slid in the tape.

There was a scratchy sound at first, and then Mrs. Mayer's voice, whispering, "OK, you're all set." Then her footsteps, and I saw her hurrying from Mike's bed to the door. Then a faint click—the door closing.

The first thing from Mike was a deep sigh, and I bit my lip, wondering how I would be able to stand it.

"Hi, Carrie, it's October thirtieth. I guess I should say that—if I were writing you a letter I'd write it. I was going to try to write, on the computer in occupational, but I didn't want it to take five years, so . . . Hey, thanks for calling the other day. Are you still walking all over the place? Be careful, you know. I'm sure you don't need me saying be careful, but don't walk alone at night or anything, OK?" There was a long silence. "God, this is weird. Sorry. You know, when you write a letter you can stop and figure out what to say next, but if I stop you just get blank tape. Or maybe you'll hear me breathing.

"Hey, what am I thinking, I have some amazing news. Are you ready for this? Rooster's getting married. To Joan. Can you believe it? No one can, everyone's been going on and on about how they can't believe it, which is really pretty much of an insult to Rooster, if you think about it. I guess he popped the question in Oconomowoc, they'd gone over there one Saturday. Guy's the happiest I've ever seen him. And she's really nice, I don't know how well you got to know her, but she's great. It's going to be in late December, and—well I mean, would you be coming home by Christmas anyway? I know he'll want you to come, I'm sure you'll be hearing from him.

"What else. Hey, I have a new roommate, Jeff went home. This guy's pretty cool. He's like my dad's age, but he doesn't act it. No offense to my dad or anything, but this guy's not so kind of business-manny. He's a fireman, actually. Or he was, I guess he's a quad now. He was in a car accident and injured his spinal cord—higher up than mine, the poor guy. He can't hear me right now, in case you're wondering. His wife brought him a Walkman and he listens to it a lot. Opera. He had her play one of his tapes on my player for me, and it was kind of pretty, really. The music part. The singing's kind of hard to take.

"Rehab's going OK. I might be getting the halo off next week—they'll do X rays, then we'll see. Stu and Bill came by the other night, I hadn't seen either of them for a while. And Jamie was in. She—Well, don't get mad, but I think you should call her. I mean, it's none of my business, but—Oh, never mind. Scratch that. Too bad I can't blank out parts of the tape. The stupid buttons on this machine are impossible to press down, I need to get a gimp one. I guess I could ask Mom to edit it for me when I'm done, but I don't exactly want her listening in—you should've heard me trying to explain why I wanted her out of the room while I talked. I guess I have a sort of juvenile mentality, being so secretive. King says I'm worried about losing my privacy. You know, once I go home and stuff, not that I have any here. So anyway, I've been trying to worry about that for him." Laughter. "That counselor guy, you know, Dave King. I call him King Dave. He's not so bad. He tells me what I should be worrying about and then I worry about it. It's pretty weird, really. Counseling. I keep thinking about your mom. You know how she's kind of quiet and

guarded sometimes, how she'll kind of look at you while you're talking like she's really thinking hard about what you're saying? Well, that
always bugged me. I mean, I can tell you this now. It made me not
want to talk around her. But I've been thinking maybe it's because of
her job, you know? And she can't help it. I don't know. Talking to
King, I got to thinking about those letters we used to write each
other, remember? Kind of goofy things sometimes, and we'd leave
'em in each other's lockers? Did you save mine? Yours are all in my
closet at home, I know exactly where they are, and it really bugs me
that if I ever want to read them again I'll have to have someone get
them down for me. You know? I mean for some reason that's a lot
worse than knowing my dad's going to have to handle my dick for me
every day for the rest of my life. Or his, depending who lasts longer."

There was a silence, and I reached onto the passenger seat for my
purse and got out my wallet, where there was an old picture of him,
his school picture from senior year of high school. He was grinning
his school-picture grin, wearing the blue shirt I'd helped him decide
on. I'd been behind him in line, and I'd watched him perch on the
stool and then stand again so the photographer's assistant could twist
it lower. Before he sat down again he called to me, "Come on, let's
both be in it," and I had a moment of thinking there was no reason on
earth for us to be photographed separately.

"Anyway," he said on the tape, "everything's pretty much the same.
Harvey says we have to make our minds as active as our bodies used
to be. My roommate, did I say his name before? He has his wife reading philosophy to him every night, he says he's going to spend the rest
of his life getting the education he was too much of a fuckoff to get in
college. She was reading him Plato last night. That's Pla-to, not Play-
Doh. Remember Play-Doh? The smell?" A pause. "He had her bring
in a Charles Dickens tape for us to listen to. *A Tale of Two Cities.* You
know, just an hour or so a night—it's like ten hours long or something.
So we're going to start it tomorrow. Kind of different from the days of
Jeff, huh? What?" There was some noise I couldn't identify. "Wait a
sec, wait. I'm talking to Carrie. Yeah. Say something to her, say hi."
More noise. "Hear that, Carrie? That was Harvey saying hi. Hey, say
it again but louder, OK?" There was silence and then a faint new
voice saying, "Hi, Carrie. I'm Mike's roommate. Nice to meetcha."

Then Mike again. "Well, that was Harvey. His tape's over. I guess maybe I'll stop now, too. I told Mom fifteen minutes so she'll be back in a sec to stop the tape. Well, I guess I should keep going till she comes back. Uh, how's the weather? Ha, ha. Hey, what are you doing for Thanksgiving? I might be home by then. Well, who knows. Oop, here's Mom. No, no, I'm done, I'm done, it's OK. Bye, Carrie. Bye."

There was a final click, and then the blank tape whirring in the machine. I reached over and pressed rewind, then rested my forehead against the steering wheel. I felt bright and strange, floodlit around the edges and dark at the very center.

THAT AFTERNOON I was meeting Kilroy at McClanahan's after work. He liked six o'clock there, the bar only half-full. Fewer yuppies.

Out on the sidewalk in front of the brownstone, I buttoned my jacket and headed east. I'd spent the day thinking about Mike's tape, then trying not to think about it. I'd used the upright vacuum cleaner to vacuum the entire ground floor of the house and then the stairs, until suddenly I'd felt like Mrs. Mayer. She was a ferocious housekeeper, and I put the vacuum cleaner away and made myself some tea, then dumped it out because that made me think of her, too. Then I made some more, because damn if Mrs. Mayer was going to keep me from drinking tea.

Walking along the crowded sidewalks to McClanahan's, I thought about Rooster getting married. How could Rooster be getting married? He was Mr. Guy—I couldn't see him giving up all of that, his rat-hole apartment with the couch that smelled like dog, Kraft dinners with a couple hotdogs cut up in them. I couldn't see her wanting that, beautiful, cool Joan: wanting him and the things he was good at, fixing stuff and being the one to drive all night while everyone else slept, and belching the loudest after a beer.

Then there was how they'd met, in the Intensive Care unit while Mike was unconscious. Forget love and fate and all that: I kept coming back to the simple question of how they could build something on the back of Mike's bad luck.

And also to the simple question of how I could.

Kilroy was sitting at the bar when I arrived, wearing his leather jacket over a brown shirt, a half-finished beer in front of him. He looked up and gave me what I thought of as his amused smile, as if he were amused by me, by the fact of us. Mike had always greeted me in a physical way, with a one-armed hug, a kiss to my forehead, a hand snaking around my waist. And a smile that said *I'm glad to see you.*

"What news?" he asked as I climbed onto the stool next to his.

I shrugged.

He gave me a quizzical look, then reached for a pack of matches and fiddled it between his fingers. "No news is good news then, I guess. Beer?"

"Sure."

He waved for the bartender, Joe, a fiftyish man with a perfectly bald head. Joe ambled over and raised his eyebrows.

"Carrie here will have a draft," Kilroy said.

Joe smiled. "I think that can be arranged." He moved to the taps, and I watched while he filled a glass, holding it at an angle while the beer streamed in. At the other end of the bar a man in a suit sat by himself, holding an old-fashioned glass.

Setting the beer in front of me, Joe gave Kilroy a funny look, and I wondered how long Kilroy'd been coming here, whether Joe had seen other women come and go from the spot where I now sat. I took a sip of the beer, cold and grainy with fizz. My arms felt tingly.

"So?" Kilroy said. "Talk to me."

"I got a tape today."

"A tape?"

"From Mike."

He raised his eyebrows, and I said, "Well, he can't write."

"I know that," he said. "I know." He took a sip of his beer, then wiped his fingers on his jeans, the holey 501s he changed into after work every day. "You seem upset."

I shook my head.

"What, then?"

"Sad."

"Got it."

I felt a kind of fury rise through me, and I gripped my beer until the cold hurt.

"What did he say?" Kilroy said.

I stared straight ahead. "Well, for one thing Rooster's getting married. To Joan, the Intensive Care nurse. And he has a new roommate—Mike, I mean. In rehab. He's in rehab, you know—his mother had to press the buttons on the tape recorder for him." I stopped talking and faced Kilroy. I wanted him to feel what I was feeling, the same wildness. Or I wanted him to reach in and soothe it, tame it down. He didn't speak, though, and after a moment I turned back to my beer glass and lifted it for a long swallow. "Why is it," I said, "that you don't want to tell me about any of your old girlfriends? When was the last time you were involved with someone?"

A weary look passed over his face. "Does self-involved count?" He sighed. "Sorry, that's a line from a movie." He scratched his jaw. "I don't have old girlfriends the way you have your old boyfriend, OK?"

"Then how do you have them?"

"I don't." He laid his forefingers side by side on the bar. "You're barking up the wrong tree."

Joe leaned against the bar sink, his arms crossed over his chest, and I thought of what Kilroy had said to me our first evening together—*I'm just a guy who likes bars.* I wondered if over the years he'd laid out his life for Joe, bit by bit, or if liking bars meant laying out precisely nothing. I faced Kilroy again and found him watching me with an odd look on his face, a look on the edge of becoming something else. In a small, crowded voice I said, "Which tree should I bark up?" and when Kilroy looked away I couldn't help it, I had to press harder. "Well? Which tree?"

"Why don't you try not barking?" he snapped. He stared at me with a terrible sneer capsizing his mouth, and finally I got off my stool and slunk away, past the bar, between the empty tables, through the heavy door, and out into the night.

I set off down Sixth Avenue, skirting idlers and saunterers, walking fast. What was wrong with him? What was wrong with me, to have put up with what I'd put up with so far, the secretiveness of him, the fortress? Oh, he was kindness itself, he was compassion, understanding, but it was all coming away from him and there wasn't a single way in.

A block or two before 14th Street I cut east, through dark canyons, past old warehouses and stalled, waiting trucks. I saw a couple pressed against a building, both tall, both wearing black leather jackets. Three guys about my age, walking fast without talking. A skinny black man wearing a Sherlock Holmes hat, standing in a doorway saying, "I'm *waiting* for the *moment,* I'm *waiting* for the *moment.*" A lumpy old woman in a bathrobe, standing under a low roof of scaffolding, a dazed look on her face. And a beautiful girl who climbed out of a taxi and stepped up onto the sidewalk just as I went by, her hair a silk sheet, her pants fashionably short over square-toed boots, her face tranquil but covered with tears.

I thought: If it doesn't work out with Kilroy, I can stay in New York anyway, I can become a New Yorker.

New Yorkers were different. Old or young, crazy or brilliant, plain or gorgeous—they didn't just walk outside, they made a presentation, they presented themselves. They said, *This is who I am, today I'm someone wearing these boots, I'm walking with this look on my face, I'm having this intense and troublesome discussion with this difficult but beloved friend.*

I walked for a long time. I went down Broadway, took in the parade along St. Mark's Place, followed Avenue A until I'd crossed East Houston and entered the narrow old streets of the Lower East Side. The city was lit up, the streetlights, the windows of people's apartments, curtains or blinds open so that looking up you could see the top of a picture, a doorway leading to darkness. I'd forgotten my gloves, and I pulled my arms inside my jacket and walked with my hands tucked in my armpits, my empty sleeves dangling.

I didn't get back to the brownstone until nearly nine. Simon, Greg, Lane, and even Alice were sitting around the kitchen table, drinking red wine and eating from a platter of sliced peasant bread and marinated vegetables, the reds and purples glistening with oil. A quick glance at the whiteboard told me Kilroy hadn't called.

"Pull up a chair," Simon said. "You look like you could use some wine."

I found a chair against the wall and dragged it over to the table, next to Lane. She wore a baggy thermal T-shirt, and her pale face was pink across the nose and cheeks, as if she'd dipped a fine paintbrush into her wine and tinted herself very faintly.

Simon poured wine into a tumbler for me. "So, Carrie," he said. "How abjectly pathetic do you think I am?"

I glanced at the others and saw from their suppressed smiles that they knew where he was going.

"On a scale of one to ten," he went on. "With ten being, you know, the kid in fourth grade who smelled weird and never got invited to any birthday parties, and one being Kevin Spacey."

"Kevin Spacey's not pathetic," Greg exclaimed. "He's totally cool. He's God."

"That's my *point*," Simon said, rolling his eyes. "Jesus."

"Simon," Lane began, but he waved her off.

"This is between me and Carrie. How abjectly pathetic?"

"Three?" I said. "No, two."

He looked at Alice and they both burst into laughter. "You are *way* too nice to live in New York," he said to me. "Greg and Lane probably wouldn't give me more than a five, and Alice—" He tossed her an arch look. "I don't know, doll, what do you think—eight? Or nine?"

She smirked and ran a hand through her short, bleached hair, which she wore in a stylishly disheveled flip, the bangs flopping onto her forehead. "Sweetie," she said. "Gosh. I had you at seven, easy."

He smiled and turned back to me. "It's a question because of what I did today."

"What?"

"I called Dillon." He gave me an ironic smile. "From the gallery, remember?"

I remembered: Dillon of the gorgeous face and the bored conde- scension and the pseudo-intellectual talk. "Wow," I said. "Are you going to meet him for a drink?"

His face went pink, and he started laughing again. Lane frowned a little and looked down at her hands. He laughed harder, his face red- der still.

"Careful," Alice said. "You're about to drool."

He shook his head, but he was laughing silently now, convulsively. He wagged his hand at Alice in a kind of summons.

She took a sip of her wine and looked at me. "Dillon said, and I believe I'm quoting accurately here, 'You know, I'm reorganizing my file cabinets right now, and I just feel really, really overextended.' "

Greg giggled, and I looked at Simon. "Really?"

He nodded dramatically, still laughing noiselessly. "In other words," he managed at last, wiping tears from his eyes, " 'Would you please take your revolting self and cease to exist?' "

Alice shook her head. "I think it's more like 'Would you please go pick up my Prozac refill for me?' I mean, reorganizing his file cabinets?"

"Alice," Greg said with annoyance. "Don't you get it? He's saying he'd *rather* reorganize his file cabinets than go out with Simon."

A look of impatience passed over Alice's face, and she opened her mouth to speak, then seemed to think better of it.

"Thanks for the exegesis, Greg," Simon said.

"You had a bad day," Lane said suddenly. She looked at me for a moment, then turned back to him. "Just, you know—"

"What?" he said. "Shut up about it?"

"No," she said softly. "You know that's not what I mean."

He sighed. "I know." He reached for a piece of bread and dipped it in the olive oil. He took a bite and then set what was left on his plate. "So," he said to Alice. "Where's Frank, anyway? I don't know when you were last here at this hour."

"Having dinner with his asshole cousin," she said. "I came down with a crippling headache at the last minute." She smiled. "Hey, did I tell you guys? He wants me to move in."

"Move in?" Simon said. "You already live there."

"Officially," she said.

Lane studied her. "Are you going to?"

Alice shrugged. "Maybe. His place is so tiny, if nothing else having me and my stuff there all the time would probably make us break up sooner."

Simon and Greg laughed. "You're psycho," Simon said.

"Plus think of the great material," she went on. "I could do a one-act where the whole thing took place on a bed."

She wrote plays, or maybe just wanted to: day after day I went by the open door to her empty room and saw her unused computer sitting on her desk, covered by a Barbie beach towel. I'd mentioned it to Kilroy once, and he'd made some remark about my living in a wannabe house. I remembered what he'd said of Simon—*He's trying to be something he isn't*—and my fury at him intensified. What was so terrible about wanting to be something other than what you were? How could you become anything without having wanted to be that thing first? All at once I was ashamed of having written off Alice's writing. For all I knew she also had a laptop, or wrote longhand, or just *thought* about it a lot! Shut up, I thought at Kilroy, and then something fell in on itself and I felt myself sink into despair. What did it mean that I was yelling at him in my mind? Was I even in his?

"Are you OK?" Lane said, looking at me with concern.

I took a swallow of wine and nodded.

Now everyone was looking at me, Simon with his head tilted to the side, his eyes narrowed behind the lenses of his glasses.

"I guess I'm kind of tired," I said.

"You know," Alice said, "this whole time I've been sitting here thinking how much I like your shirt, but, like, stupidly not saying it. It's really cool."

I was wearing a long-sleeved red T-shirt to which I'd added some embellishments about a year ago, one weekend when I was bored: red-and-gold braid around the neck and down the front, alongside which I'd sewn a brass button every couple of inches. I'd even put a three-inch slash of braid across where each of my hipbones hit, to suggest little pockets. "Thanks," I said.

"It reminds me of my grandmother," she added.

"Alice," Simon exclaimed.

"It's a compliment," she said. "My grandmother has a lot of style." She tucked her hair behind her ear. "Seriously, it's like the jacket of one of her Adolfo suits, but with an ironic spin. It's very postmodern and fin de siècle—Adolfo overtaken by the Gap."

I looked around for someone who thought this was as silly as I did, then realized that the person I wanted to exchange a glance with— the person I was really looking for—was Kilroy.

I stood up and carried my glass to the sink.

"Where are you going?" Simon said.

I turned and saw everyone looking at me, Simon with his face still a little pink from before, Greg dark-haired and kind and half a step behind everyone else, Alice stylish in a polyester blouse and heavy black eyeliner, Lane quiet and watchful. Who were these people? Why was I with them? "Upstairs," I said. "I have to make a phone call."

On the third floor, I flopped onto the futon. I wanted to call him and didn't, wanted him to call me and wanted him to vanish. I looked around the alcove, illuminated by a single ugly lamp, fake brass with a yellowing shade. It was empty of everything, this little space: myself and all my life, which I'd taken to Kilroy's and hung carefully on the walls in the exact places where the pictures weren't.

From the kitchen I could hear a faint murmur of voices, then the rise of laughter. I went out to the landing for the phone and carried it back to the futon. Halfway through dialing, I pressed the disconnect button. I sat there holding the phone on my lap, and then, without really thinking about it, I dialed Jamie in Madison.

When she heard my voice there was a long silence, and then she said, "How are you," in such a way that I couldn't possibly misinterpret it as a question. She laughed a short, cold laugh.

"I'm sorry, Jamie," I said, aware that I was echoing myself, echoing what I'd said to Mike: I'm sorry, sorry, sorry. "I should've called earlier. I should have."

She breathed in deeply, and I heard her let it out again, loud, like a sigh. I knew somehow that she was in her kitchen, the day's dishes neatly arranged in the drainboard by the sink, just a single light on, hanging low over the speckled linoleum table.

"Jamie," I said.

"What."

"Please try to understand. I had to leave."

She was silent for a while, and I imagined how she must look, her light hair framing her face, her clear green eyes. "I understand that," she said at last. "I didn't at first, but now I do. But that was almost *two months* ago. Every day I wonder what it is about me that makes you hate me." She began to cry, and as I listened I felt huge and monstrous and disconnected from her: her tears had exactly no effect on my heart. They filled me with pity, but it was a cold, cerebral pity—it was pity for myself, not for Jamie.

"I don't," I said. "I don't hate you, Jamie. It's just—"

"You called Mike," she sobbed. "You called him twice."

"I know."

I heard her footsteps and then the muffled sound of her blowing her nose.

"Jamie?" I twisted the phone cord tight around my finger and then untwisted it again, my skin indented red like a barber pole.

"What?"

"Can I—can I ask how you are, what you've been doing?"

She blew her nose again. "Well, to give you an example, last Saturday night I played Parcheesi with my parents and Lynn. Oh, and get this—we broke for popcorn after game three."

I had a vivid image of the four of them, Mr. and Mrs. Fletcher on opposite sides of the wobbly card table in their pine-paneled family room, Jamie and Lynn between them. Mrs. Fletcher vague in a blouse and sweater, needing reminding every time it was her turn. Mr. Fletcher barely there, Jamie wishing she weren't. And Lynn— Lynn with too much eye makeup on, glancing at the clock. I thought of her at the Alley in that short, tight skirt, and I wondered how *I* could have been giving *her* advice: I, whose life was a mess. "How is Lynn?" I said after a moment.

"Ridiculous. She and Mom are driving me nuts about each other. She *has* to move out."

"Too bad—if I'd thought of it sooner she could have sublet my place."

There was a silence, and then Jamie said, "You *sublet* your *apartment*?"

I felt a spike of fear. Didn't she know? How could she not know, when everyone in Madison knew everything about everyone else?

"Well?"

"Yeah, I did."

There was a thunk, and then nothing, silence, just the whoosh of all the space between us.

"Jamie." I waited and then I said it again, and again—"Jamie. Jamie? *Jamie*?" Then I understood: she'd set the phone down and walked away. I could picture it, Jamie standing across the kitchen staring at the receiver, enraged and teary. "Jamie!" I shouted, but although I stayed on the line for several more minutes, saying her name over and over again, she never came back.

I hung up and carried the phone back out to the hall. At the little window in the stairwell, I pushed the curtain to the side and peered out. The brownstones behind us were patchily lit: a low window here, a high one there, then dark, dark, and a whole blazing four stories. Someone else might have looked for a message in the pattern of illumination, but I just stood there staring, filled with a sense of myself as occupying the smallest of places in the world.

23

~

KILROY CAME OVER the next morning. I was alone in the house drinking coffee, and when I answered the door I was shocked to see him: standing in the cold, bright light, barely more than a silhouette outside the dark, recessed entryway. He had his hands on his hips, a gruff, irritated look on his face: he was there on sufferance, under his own orders.

"Aren't you going to ask me in?"

"Do you want to come in?"

"Yeah, I do."

In the kitchen I poured him a cup of coffee, then sat down. After a while he sat, too, unshaven, dressed in his jeans and a torn gray sweatshirt and his leather jacket, which he didn't take off. It was ten-twenty; he must have decided not to go to work.

"That Kilroy," he said, taking a sip of his coffee. "What is it with him?"

I understood that he wasn't going to apologize any more directly, and it was all I could do not to laugh.

"What?"

I shook my head.

He lifted his mug and looked at me across the top of it. "So what'd you do last night?"

"You mean after I walked to the Lower East Side and back?"

A faint hint of surprise passed over his face and disappeared. "Yeah."

"I sat around drinking wine with Simon and everyone. Alice said my shirt was very postmodern and fin de siècle—Adolfo overtaken by the Gap."

Kilroy shook his head. "Oh, the frailties of youth."

"What's that supposed to mean?"

"It's like that woman in the bookstore a couple weeks ago. 'The complacence of extreme beauty.' Talking for the sake of how it sounds, not what you really want to say."

"And what do you really want to say?"

He held my glance for a moment, then looked away.

I carried my coffee to the sink and poured it into the right-hand basin, which was jammed with chipped mugs holding the milky remains of my housemates' coffee. Neither of the two basins was bigger than a mixing bowl, and they were both always crowded, no room to wash anything. In the left-hand basin, last night's glasses gave off a winey smell. I moved the mugs over, then centered a rubber stopper on the drain in the right-hand basin, turned on the hot water, and added a squirt of dishwashing liquid.

"What's the shirt?" Kilroy said.

He'd come to stand beside me, his back against the counter, one leg crossed over the other. He sipped from his coffee and stared at me.

"The shirt?"

"The fin de siècle one."

"Don't you mean 'end of century'? What happened to your rule about foreign phrases?"

He smiled and shook his head. "Fin de siècle has to be fin de siècle because it connotes the depravity of eighteen-nineties Paris, the disgust."

I turned the water off and started washing the mugs.

"I was a history major," he added. "At Princeton. Have I ever told you before that I went to Princeton? I graduated magna, not to brag. I had a different roommate each year, but the one thing they had in common was they were all Southerners with drinking problems. There was a lot of throwing up, and I spent my weekends elsewhere. Oh, and many years later I happened to run into one of them at a movie theater, and he said to me, 'Kilroy, you son of a bitch, are you still alive?' " Kilroy stared at me. "What do you think of that?"

My heart pounded. He set his cup on the counter, reached for me, and pulled me close. "You know me *better* than that kind of information," he said very softly, his mouth at my ear. "You may not think so, but you do." He kissed me and I turned my face away, angry and then suddenly wanting to kiss him, and then angry that I wanted to kiss him. I pushed away from him and went and sat at the table.

"I called Jamie last night," I said. "For the first time. She didn't know I'd sublet my apartment. When I mentioned it, she did something weird—instead of hanging up on me she just put the phone down and walked away." I stared at him, no idea why I'd said this rather than something else: *What do you want? What the fuck are you doing in my life?*

"She froze," he said.

"Froze?" I was surprised he'd responded.

He shrugged. "Sure. She couldn't do anything else. She couldn't say anything, she couldn't hang up on you, it was all she could do."

"Why couldn't she hang up on me?"

"Because she loves you," he said. "As do I, though in a somewhat different way."

A light sweat gathered on my forehead and upper lip. "You love me?"

He nodded solemnly. "Of course I love you." His face was bland, his voice matter-of-fact. "Don't you know? I'm head over heels. I'm knocked for a loop."

HE LOVED ME, and it seemed that was all I had been wanting to know, all I'd been needing to hear to take the next step. I asked for a key to his apartment, and I took to being there when he returned from work, flipping through a magazine, drinking a beer, eager for a fuck. *Very* eager for a fuck—the more I had, the more I wanted. Sex was our medium, as enlightening as a long exchange of information.

Because what, really, did I need to know? I could know names and places and dates, or I could know that he liked to have his nipples teased by my tongue, that he read the newspaper from back to front, that there was a place on the outside of his left calf with no hair, as if someone had taken a finger and wiped it away.

My days were full of free time, but this didn't change me so much as it changed time itself: mornings were busy with the walk back to the brownstone, a long shower and the decision over what to wear. I had breakfast at noon, coffee that I made in the empty brownstone kitchen along with, every single day, a soft-boiled egg on buttered toast, the egg yolk hot and runny, salt-enhanced, the white cooked just enough to hold a shape in my mouth. In the afternoons I barely had long enough for the little tasks and projects I assigned myself: move my car, do laundry, take a walk or even a subway ride to a part of the city I had yet to see. For company I had my thoughts, my fascination with how it felt to be loved so cryptically, to let love stand in for so much. After all, love with Mike had been completely different: a fast plunge, the two of us falling together. We were in love with each other, in love with love. We waited for each other outside of classrooms, walked with our sides pressed together, sat as close as we could, his arm around me and his fingertips just inside the waistband of my pants. We talked on the phone for hours every night, fell asleep with pictures of each other under our pillows. We were fourteen, granted, but it was more than that: it was that Mike was wide open, without corners, while Kilroy was a maze I was wandering through, a place full of dead ends that I occasionally stumbled into and then had to find my way out of.

I knew they were there. I knew it was just a matter of time before I encountered one again.

THANKSGIVING MORNING. WRAPPED in a terrycloth bathrobe, Kilroy dumped flour directly onto the kitchen counter and began pinching small cubes of cold butter into it, his hands snapping open and closed like someone showing how someone else did nothing but talk talk talk. We were taking a dessert and a vegetable to the brownstone later that day; though he'd lobbied for turkey sandwiches at his place, I'd argued that Thanksgiving wasn't just about turkey, it was also about a big crowd of people, and eventually he'd given in.

Yawning and still muddled with sleep, I watched from the doorway while he worked. I took a sip of the coffee he'd made before waking me and said, "Some people would use a bowl."

He looked over his shoulder and smiled. "Ah, but they'd be missing out. This is far superior."

"It looks far messier."

"It's the French way," he said. "The French have a genius for mess." With the back of his floury hand he brushed some hair away from his face. "Can you get me some ice water?"

I set my mug on the counter and got a glass. I filled it with ice, added water, and then stirred the cubes around until my finger was cold. Setting the glass down next to him, I said, "How do you know the French way?" I half pictured him in some farmhouse kitchen with a dark-eyed mademoiselle showing him what to do, but I couldn't really believe it.

"I took a class," he said. "In Paris, at the Cordon Bleu. When we go I'll take you by there, it's pretty great."

We exchanged a smile that meant, on his part, *Because we are going, you know;* and on mine, *Yeah, right.* He mentioned France a lot, said, *You'll love Aix* or *Wait'll you see how much better the Metro is than the subway here.*

With his fingers he sprinkled some water onto the flour. He said, "I was thinking we could boil the carrots and sweet potatoes and then do them in a gratin dish with butter and a little Calvados."

"No miniature marshmallows?" I said.

He looked up at me and smiled. "That would be the Wisconsin way?"

"The Mayer way."

"You had Thanksgiving with the Mayers?"

"For the last eight years. It would be like twenty Mayers and Mayer cousins, and my mother and me. But really, it would be twenty-one Mayers and Mayer cousins and my mother, because I was one of them."

Kilroy had worked the flour mixture into a loose dough, and now he washed his hands and wrapped the dough in plastic, then put it in the refrigerator. "We'll give that an hour," he said. "Did your mother mind?"

I thought about it. How before dinner she always stood in the kitchen while Mrs. Mayer and her sister, Aunt Peg, bustled around the stove and oven; how they gave her small tasks like putting out the butter, but more as a favor to her than so she could do one for them. Mike and I would be talking to his cousin Steve, or down in the basement with the younger kids organizing a darts competition, and whenever I passed the kitchen my mother gave me one of those mouth-only smiles. She usually went home right after we ate, left me to get a ride with Mike later. A couple of times she skipped it altogether, accepted another invitation but said to me, *No, go ahead—it's fine.*

"I guess she went along with it," I told Kilroy, and he nodded gravely.

"The famous line of least resistance, a real trap."

"What do you mean?"

"You think, *Well, I'll go along to get along*—and next thing you know you're somewhere you never wanted to be without a ticket back."

"I don't know," I said. "It was just Thanksgiving."

He laughed. "Just Thanksgiving. That may well be an oxymoron."

When the dough was ready, I peeled the apples, removing their green, lemony skins in long spirals. I cut the flesh into crisp, white slices, which I tossed with sugar and cinnamon and then arranged in the pie pan Kilroy had lined with thinly rolled pastry.

A little later, the pie in the oven and the vegetables cooked and arrayed in a casserole, he went to take a shower. I poured myself some more coffee, thinking how much I liked his domesticity, the fact that *he'd* woken *me* to start cooking. I loved watching him in the kitchen, how he never used a cookbook but moved surely from step to step, as if he understood the ingredients so well that he knew just how much of each would yield the right combination of flavors.

I finished my coffee and then set about cleaning, sliding the peels into the garbage, washing the bowls and knives we'd used, wiping down the counters with a sponge that had been sprinkled with vinegar, one of his tricks.

I heard his shower shut off, and a moment later the phone rang. I stared at it. Somehow this was a first, the question of whether or not to answer his phone: it rang that rarely.

It rang a second time, and I crossed the room and picked it up, thinking it could be Simon asking us to stop for something on the way over. "Hello," I said, and there was a long silence before a woman's voice came over the line and said, very tentatively, hello back.

"Is this—" she said. "Do I have—" She started again: "Is Paul there?"

I nearly said she had the wrong number, but then I realized: Paul, his real name. "Just a minute," I said, and I carried the cordless handset into his bedroom, my palm over the mouthpiece, and knocked on the partly closed bathroom door.

He pulled it open with his foot, naked, a smile about to alight on his face. The room was full of steam, the cedary smell of his soap heavy in the damp air. He held a drift of shaving cream in his palm, stiff like beaten egg whites.

"Phone," I said, and I handed it to him and walked away.

I thought of closing the bedroom door on my way out, but I didn't, and then it was too late. I heard his hello, and then a long silence. In the kitchen I turned on the water, then quickly turned it off again. The woman's voice had sounded—there was no other word for it—cultured. Older. Although older than myself or older than Kilroy, I didn't know.

"No," he said, and then there was another silence. "Because I don't," he said, and then, "As a matter of fact I do," and then I turned on the water and let it run until something caught at my peripheral vision and I looked into the bedroom in time to see the handset land with a small bounce in the center of the bed.

Dressed in his usual jeans but also a pressed white shirt, Kilroy came into the kitchen a little later and clamped the handset to the wall unit. He bent and cracked the oven door. "Ten more minutes," he said, and he let the door fall back so hard that through the window I saw the pie jump a little.

"Who was that?" I said.

He licked his lips. "My mother." He stood still for a moment, then picked up the sponge and began wiping the counters I'd already wiped, with sharp, jerky strokes.

"I did that," I said, and he tossed the sponge into the sink from across the room. He looked at me, but in a strange way—at my mouth rather than my eyes, his face too blank. He turned and walked into the bedroom, and I followed, watched him stand for a moment at the window and then kick off his shoes and settle on the bed with a pillow behind him. From his bedside table he took up the book he was reading.

"Are you OK?"

He nodded.

I went and sat on the edge of the bed, down near his feet. He wore black socks, and I cupped his toes, then released them. "What's she doing today? Or they. What are they doing?"

"They," he said from behind his book, "are having a goose, although at this point, they are also probably having a cow."

I waited for him to look up and smile at me, or at the very least receive my smile, but he didn't—he just sat there, one knee crossed over the other, his face obscured by the book.

OUTSIDE IT WAS cold and quiet—businesses closed, few cars on the streets. The sky was thick with dusk, pulling darkness down onto the city. Wrapped in my coat and warmest wool scarf, I held the casserole while Kilroy carried the pie, extended in front of him like a folded flag at a military funeral. For the sixth or seventh time in the last few hours, I went over his part of the phone conversation I'd overheard. *No. Because I don't. As a matter of fact I do.* It was easy to imagine what his mother had said: Do you want to come for dinner? Why not? Do you have plans? What I didn't understand was how curt he'd been, and then how bothered. That was the only word for it:

bothered. Her hello had sounded sophisticated, worldly. Like someone who'd have a friend who said "veecheesoizzz"—or who'd say it
herself. Like someone who'd eat at the restaurants Kilroy disdained,
who'd have the patina of entitlement he abhorred. If he'd been a
trust-fund baby, what had happened? When had he fallen off track?
Or climbed off—I didn't think he did much accidentally.

We turned onto Simon's street and walked past my car, the wind-
shield so filthy I'd have to bring paper towels and Windex the next
time I needed to move it.

At the brownstone, we deposited our food on the kitchen table.
Kilroy got himself a glass of wine and joined Lane and a few others in
the living room while I stayed with Simon, who was standing over a
saucepan at the stove.

"Making gravy?" I said.

"No one else knew how. I told them you had to get the fat out of the
roasting pan, and they were all, like, 'Gross.' " With a wire whisk he
stirred quickly, running the loops all over the bottom of the pan.
"Being from the Midwest has its uses," he added.

"Speaking of which, did you talk to your parents this morning?"

He grinned. "My mother's all business on the major holidays. The
first thing out of her mouth was 'Now don't forget about the rice for
your soup.' I was like, 'Happy Thanksgiving to you, too.' Oh, and it's
snowing there, they got three inches last night."

"Your soup?" I said.

"Turkey soup, babe. Gotta make it. It'll be good, we'll eat it for
weeks. You'll see, or you would if you were ever here." He gave me a
pointed look, then dipped a spoon into the gravy and handed it to me.
"Here, taste this."

From the deep, rising smell I could tell how hot it was, and I blew
on it first. I sipped and it was like drinking pure sin, salty and fat
enough that my lips felt coated. I finished it off and returned the
spoon to the saucepan for some more.

"Double dipping?" he said. "From Carrie Bell? I can hardly believe
my eyes."

"Shut up." I sipped again, then put the spoon into the crowded
sink.

"Did you talk to your mother?" he said.

"Last night." Hearing her voice had made me miss her, then made me realize I'd *been* missing her, without really knowing it.

"How about Mike?" Simon said.

I shook my head. I hadn't talked to him in a month, hadn't written to thank him for the tape, had somehow never even sent him the damned postcard of the Empire State Building. Three inches of snow. I wondered if Mike had gotten home. I imagined Mr. Mayer wheeling him up their shoveled walk to the front door, the lawn iced with white on both sides, but then the image broke down: I had no way to get him up the brick steps.

I headed back to the brownstone living room, which was hardly ever used. They'd worked hard to make it festive: there were tiny white votive candles everywhere, clustered in the dark corners of the room, lined up on the broken mantel. Simon had even begun a mural on one wall, a picture of a real dining room: a table laden with napkins and silverware and glasses of wine. He'd evidently run out of time, though; the entire thing was sketched, but only one edge was painted.

Kilroy was talking to Lane and her girlfriend, Maura, who was tall and broad-shouldered, with thick auburn hair and dark brown eyes, the darkest eyes I'd ever seen on a redhead. She wore a gauzy rust-colored dress and was beautiful in exactly the opposite way Lane was beautiful—tall and strong and colorful versus tiny and delicate and pale. I joined them, and she turned to me and said, "I was just telling Kilroy that he looks incredibly familiar to me."

He raised his glass for a sip of wine. He shrugged and said, "I have one of those faces."

She wrinkled her brow. "What faces?"

"You know, one of those dominant facial types some people have. You have one, too. Carrie and Lane are more recessive."

Lane grinned. "I'm not sure I like the idea of being recessive."

"You should," he said. "It means the more unusual in you has power over the more usual. In your face it's your chin and your eyebrows."

Her pointed chin and her narrow, arched eyebrows. I remembered the photograph she'd shown me, in which her child self sat on her grandmother's lap. Even then her chin and eyebrows had been distinctive.

"Is Kilroy your first or last name?" Maura asked.

"Neither, it's just a nickname."

"What's your real name?"

"Paul Fraser."

"Fraser," she said thoughtfully. "Fraser."

He pressed his elbow into me. "Shall I tell them how I got my nickname?"

"I don't know how you got your nickname."

He gave me a blank look. "You don't?"

I thought of our first evening together, in Washington Square Park:

Is Kilroy your first or last name?

It's neither.

It's your middle name?

My name is Paul Eliot Fraser. There's no Kilroy in there at all, it's just what I'm called.

Why?

Because it's not in there at all.

What was he up to? Lane looked at me curiously, then looked away.

"Well," he said. "I'll tell you too, then. You know that Second World War thing 'Kilroy Was Here'? That American soldiers drew all over the place, with that little face?" He shifted his wine to his left hand and drew something in the air with his right forefinger. "It was this big deal, a kind of graffiti—they drew these little faces and wrote 'Kilroy Was Here' next to them. Well, I was a big Second World War buff in high school, I read everything I could about it, and after a while I started writing 'Kilroy Was Here' on my friends' notebooks and stuff, their lockers, just for the hell of it, Kilroy Was Here, Kilroy Was Here. Before long they started calling me Kilroy, and it stuck."

I drank from my wine and didn't look at any of them. I was embarrassed that he hadn't told me before, that I'd learned the innocuous story of how he got his nickname along with Lane and Maura. There was a pressure behind my ribcage, a breathless feeling. I inhaled deeply and then let it out again. In Madison I'd wanted something different. I'd wanted life to be less predictable, people to be less predictable. Standing next to Kilroy, his hand holding a wineglass just inches from my shoulder, I thought: *Be careful what you wish for.* Then I thought: *No. Be different, too. Be OK with this.*

Leaving the brownstone after dinner a few hours later, Kilroy and I headed west, away from his apartment, without discussing it. We walked without talking, making our way south and farther west until we'd reached the Hudson—big, dark warehouses behind us and in front of us the river, fast-moving and streaked with light. New Jersey was opposite, but it seemed farther than a river's width away, part of some other, lesser world. I thought of the thousand miles I'd crossed, the stretches and stretches of empty land that were quiet and black now. And Madison out there, its little spill of lights glimmering on Thanksgiving night.

He led me to a bench where we sat down, our shoulders touching. In front of us, a spent pier jutted into the water, caved between the pilings as if it were made of cardboard. He arched his neck and looked at the sky. "It might have been good to be an astronomer," he said. "Living in the middle of nowhere in an observatory on a hill."

"Why not be one now?" I said, looking at his profile.

He glanced at me and smiled ironically. "It's too late, I already am who I am."

Who was he? A Princeton graduate. A former Second World War buff. The son of a woman who ate goose. I looked away from him, out at the water and then up at the sky, where, off to the south, a plane descended toward Newark.

"Let's do something," he said. "Let's go to the top of the Empire State Building."

"What, now? Is it even open on Thanksgiving?"

"It should be."

We found a cab and rode uptown, the streets muted; it was strange to think of how many Thanksgiving dinners had been eaten in such close proximity. At 34th and Sixth we got out and walked east, the wind shuttling toward us. We had to ride an escalator downstairs for tickets, then another up to wait in line for the elevators. At the top, I bought a postcard of the building for Mike, angular against a bright blue sky. I felt terrible that it had taken me so long, but every time I'd thought of it I'd been stymied by what I could write, what tone to take. With Kilroy watching I put the card in my purse.

The wind was even fiercer on the viewing platform. I pulled my coat close. High above the city, we tried but failed to find the riverside spot where we'd been half an hour earlier, the Hudson itself a swath of crinkled black taffeta, creased with light. Below us the city multiplied and divided, neighborhoods and blocks and buildings—but within the buildings whole countries, whole worlds. The lights went on and on, and we walked to the north side of the platform and saw Central Park, like an enormous dark lake ringed by spangled forest. Fifth Avenue ran down the side of it, lit up and glowing.

"That's where your parents live, isn't it?" I said. "The Upper East Side?" I hadn't even known I'd thought so until that moment. The Upper East Side—where the rich people lived.

Kilroy nodded. "A-yup."

We continued walking, and he showed me Queens and Brooklyn, both vast and diffuse. Finally, at the south end of the platform, we stopped. The wind was stronger than ever, and I knotted my scarf tighter and tucked my gloved hands under my arms.

Kilroy shoved his hands into his pockets. "What does Maura do?"

I was surprised by the question, so out of the blue. "Maura, Lane's Maura? Investment banking, why?"

He raised a shoulder and let it drop. "Just curious," he said casually, but there was something artificial in the casualness, as if he'd really wanted to know—as if he'd suspected, in fact, and had thought to ask for verification precisely because we were staring down toward Wall Street.

He turned and leaned his back against the barrier, rubbing his bare hands together against the cold. "I was figuring her for a boho wannabe like the rest of them," he said. "A sculptor or something—she has the hands for it."

I stayed silent for a moment. "Why is it so awful to want to be something?"

A flicker of surprise passed over his face. "It's not, unless it's just a way to avoid having to think of yourself as ordinary." He wrapped his arms around his chest and hunched his shoulders against the wind.

"What about you?" I said. "Did you ever want to be something other than what you were?"

"Sure," he said. "I did and I do."

My heartbeat picked up a little. "What?"

He shrugged. "Quiet in my head."

My eyes filled, and I held them open wide. I imagined him on his couch reading, on the sidewalk walking. In McClanahan's shooting pool, a look of sweet concentration on his face. Quiet in his head. He stood just a foot away from me, yet I felt there was a huge gap between us, a gap full of noise: the world's and mine. Here it was, confirmed.

A woman with big blond hair and a red coat walked by us just then, and when she saw my teary eyes she gave me a look of pity. *No,* I wanted to say, *it's not like that*—but I didn't know what it was like, either.

~

24

Eᴀʀʟʏ ɪɴ ᴅᴇᴄᴇᴍʙᴇʀ Rooster called one Sunday when I'd returned to the brownstone to shower and change my clothes. I congratulated him on his engagement and he thanked me, saying, "Bet you thought the day would never come. I sure didn't." His voice was familiar, and yet somehow also unfamiliar—tinged with uncertainty. He seemed unsure how to talk to me, this person whom he'd known forever. This person who'd run away.

"So are you guys busy planning?" I said.

He laughed. "Joan's real organized. Every now and then she'll haul me somewhere to taste cake or whatever, but mostly she's doing it with her mom."

"Mike said late December?"

He hesitated. "Yeah." There was a silence, and I thought he was going to say more. When he spoke again, though, it was to change the subject. "So you're having fun? You like New York?"

"It's amazing." I sounded flat, and I tried again: "It's really great." I was disappointed that he wasn't telling me more about the wedding.

"So what?" he said. "You're living in some tenement or something? For free?"

I explained about the brownstone. "Eventually, the guy who owns the place will either remodel or sell it, but for now it's basically the lowest rent around, and *no* rent for me."

"That's pretty lucky."

"I know." I'd told Simon recently that I felt guilty not helping with the rent, but he'd brushed off my concern. *Yeah, it's a real problem for all of us that your stuff—not even you but your stuff—occupies a tiny bit of floor space that couldn't be used for anything else.*

"Carrie?" Rooster said hesitantly, and now I saw I was waiting for an *invitation* to the wedding—that I wanted one. That was why I'd been disappointed earlier.

"Yeah?"

"I'm mad at you," he said. "I mean, I have to be mad at you, you know? But I also get it. You were under a lot of pressure."

My throat felt full. I remembered the day outside the library, back in July, how he slammed his fist against the wall. And how, visiting Mike right afterward, the two of us could hardly look at each other. "Thanks," I said.

"But I am mad," he said.

"I know."

"The other thing—" he began, but then he broke off talking, and silence fell along the phone line. I had a sudden intimation of how hard this was for him. He'd talked about it with Joan. They'd planned what he would say. "Well," he said, "this is probably selfish or something, but it would mean a lot to me if I thought you were happy for me."

A warm feeling rose through my chest and into my face. I thought of all the years I'd known him, the Rooster who'd scared off dates with flowers and too much enthusiasm, the Rooster who'd shown up at my apartment on the odd Sunday morning to report sheepishly to me and Mike about the girl he'd just left, how she'd been weird waking up: *like she was* mad *at me.* It came over me all at once: Rooster had never had this before. Love. He'd never had it.

"I am," I said. "I'm very happy for you. She's lucky, Rooster. Really. And I always thought she seemed really nice."

"She *is,*" he exclaimed. "She's *really* nice. And she, like, likes me. I mean obviously, but—" He broke off. "Look," he said, "this is awkward, I don't know what your plans are, but Joan and I would really like to have you at our wedding, that's all. That's really what I called to say. It's going to be on December twenty-third, and you're invited."

"Rooster." Tears seeped from my eyes. "Thank you so much. I'll be there, I accept. Thank you."

"Really?" he said. "You'll come?"

"Yes."

There was a brief silence. "Can I tell Mike?"

I hesitated. Tell Mike what? I'd come back to New York afterward— I knew it without having to think about it. I'd come back and get a job. Obviously I wasn't going to just float along like this forever.

"Carrie?"

"You mean tell him that I'll be at your wedding?"

"Yeah."

"Sure," I said. "Go ahead."

"OK, I will."

I'd get a job, and Kilroy and I—would we live together? Maybe it would be better if I had my own place somewhere, tiny, maybe shared. Or maybe he'd ask me to move in with him.

"So," Rooster said, "I'll send you an invitation, but it's going to be at our church at four o'clock."

"Your church?"

"What, you mean because Joan's from Oconomowoc? Normally I guess it's in the bride's hometown, but this way makes it a lot easier for Mike to be there."

"That's really nice," I said.

"There's no way I'd get married without Mike there."

"I know you wouldn't."

He took a breath, then let it out. All that couldn't be said hung there, between us. What he'd do for Mike. What I wouldn't.

"Oh, I almost forgot," he said. "There's going to be a dinner thing at my folks' house the night before, too. I mean, if you want. It's going to be small—just our families and Mike and the Mayers. Oh, and Jamie and Bill." He chuckled a little. "The new item."

"What?"

There was a brief silence. "You don't know?"

"Know what?"

He laughed. "Jamie and Bill are *dating*."

I was stunned. "Since when?"

"A few weeks ago, and you can't imagine what they're like together. It's like, if they were capable of this, how could they have known each other all that time and not gone crazy?"

"Capable of what?"

"Major PDAs. I don't even want to think about what goes on behind closed doors. Jamie's completely manic—I can't believe she hasn't told you."

I couldn't believe she hadn't told him she was never speaking to me again. And her with Bill: I couldn't believe that either. What had she said at the going-away brunch for Christine? *The Beav looks grieved.* I remembered Bill across the table from me, stroking Christine's hair. Christine was up in Boston now, just a day's drive away. Did she know? Did she care?

"I thought you'd know," Rooster said.

"Well, I didn't."

We talked for a little longer, but soon we ran out of things to say. There was only so far we could safely go, or so I felt. I was in the kitchen, and after I hung up I walked over to the door and looked outside. An old picnic table sat in the backyard, not far from where a Weber grill balanced on some crumbling bricks. In the summer Simon and his friends had reportedly run an extension cord out there and made piña coladas in the late evenings, when the sky was just falling to darkness. The idea reminded me of summer nights at home, a group of us eating sour cherry pie on my second-story porch. Mike and I and our attendants, Rooster and Jamie. Who were attending no more. Life had clicked onward. Now it was their turn.

I NEEDED SOMETHING wonderful to wear to the wedding. I had in mind something quietly stunning, something to set me apart as different now, changed. For the next few nights I lay awake late, dreaming up outfits. With Kilroy asleep beside me I imagined a brown stretch-lace T-shirt over a long brown taffeta skirt, a knee-length burgundy satin dress with a matching swing coat. I wanted something dark and rich for a Christmastime wedding. A gold peplum jacket over a paisley brocade skirt, a deep red wrap dress with a plunging V neckline. I'd need shoes and a bag. I'd need about ten thousand dollars.

On Wednesday I put on a pair of the side-zip black pants I'd made and a nice chenille sweater and went to Midtown, where I left the slow-moving crowds of shoppers on Fifth Avenue and entered Bergdorf Goodman. I just wanted to browse. To see what was available.

I'd been in plenty of department stores in my life, in Madison and Chicago, but never one like this, thick-carpeted and deeply quiet, a museum of the expensive. I moved through Accessories and Perfume, circling the hushed and scented ground floor, studying the exquisitely dressed saleswomen. There were few other customers: a pair of tweed-suited dowagers looked at gloves, while a tall blond couple in riding clothes examined a shiny wallet, talking softly in a foreign language.

The escalator rose quietly. Upstairs I wandered around, past clothes hanging like art in carefully lit tableaux. I liked a stretchy gray pant-suit, then a midnight blue beaded sweater with silk embroidery on the cuffs. In another department I found a deep purple top with a wide U neck shown over a two-layered wrap skirt in purple and silver. A gorgeous copper dress hung nearby, sheer taffeta with a slinky brown underslip visible inside.

A knee-length dress of green velvet beckoned me closer. It was a deep forest green that was almost black at certain angles, the velvet silky and deep, lush as a dense woods. The design was fitted and plain, with a round neck and a sculpted shape. A row of small satin buttons ran down the back, the same green as the velvet. There were satin cuffs, too, long and fastened by three more buttons, and hanging from one of these was a price tag that said $3,000.

"Would you like to try it on?" a saleswoman asked, appearing out of nowhere.

I followed her to an enormous dressing room with a chintz arm-chair, an adjustable three-way mirror, and lights dimmed to flatter. I took off my clothes and slid the dress on, the lining cool and silky going over my head. Just as I was wondering how I was going to button it up again, the saleswoman returned and did it for me, smoothing the velvet over my shoulders. When she was gone I looked in the mirror. The dress fit perfectly, the curved seams answering my curves, the sleeves fitted but supple enough for movement, the satin cuffs riding my wrists like silk bracelets. Exquisite.

I managed to unbutton enough of the buttons to get out of it, and then, idly, I turned it inside out and glanced at the lines of the seams.

"Do you need anything?" the saleswoman called, and I righted the dress, then put on my clothes and went out, telling her with a sad smile that it was just too big in the shoulders.

Dark green velvet. That's what I wanted. The pinch of my poverty gave me a suffocated feeling, and I took a deep breath, then slowly let it out again. It was still early December. I had time to find something.

On the ground floor I wandered around again, touching scarves, walking through the just-sprayed mists of hundred-dollar perfumes. In Jewelry I looked at strings of black pearls, at intricate, sculptural earrings. My little diamond seemed frail here, from another time, another world. I wondered if Mike ever thought about it, if he guessed I was still wearing it. I wondered how he felt, knowing he'd see me in a few weeks.

"Carrie?"

I turned and there was Lane, dressed in black velvet overalls and a skinny ribbed T-shirt, her hand supporting the elbow of an elderly woman who was barely taller than she was, despite the beautiful dove gray suede pumps the woman wore, with covered three-inch heels.

"This is Miss Wolf," Lane said. "Miss Wolf, this is Carrie Bell, the new friend I was telling you about."

Miss Wolf took a step toward me and gave me an appraising look. She was probably eighty, her face drooping from the bones, her hair a pale gray puff, but she studied me with a look of fierce concentration, and her dark eyes were clear and focused. "Yes," she said. "The Midwesterner, isn't that so."

I glanced at Lane, surprised she'd mentioned me to Miss Wolf, though it occurred to me that she must always be looking for things to talk about with her, news of the world.

"That's right," Lane said. "Carrie's from Madison, Wisconsin."

Miss Wolf pursed her lips. "There was quite a distinguished English department at the university there many years ago, but I don't suppose it's managed to fend off the theorists better than anywhere else."

She stared at me as if she expected a response. As an American studies major I'd taken a number of English classes, but for some reason what came to mind was a Shakespeare survey Mike took senior year, a course that had earned the nickname "Whores, Wars, and Bores."

"We're just going to tea," she said. "At the Palm Court, of all the silly places. Will you join us?"

We walked out of Bergdorf's into the fading light of late afternoon. Taxis streamed down Fifth Avenue, and a line of black sedans stood in front of the majestic building I knew was the Plaza Hotel. Lane kept her hand on Miss Wolf's elbow as we walked, then stood just behind her with her hands up and ready as Miss Wolf negotiated each of the red-carpeted steps to the lobby.

Inside there were giant flower arrangements, and vast, glittering chandeliers hanging from the distant ceiling. The walls were creamy white marble, shot through with flecks of gold. People stood talking in small groups, important-looking in their suits, their carefully groomed hair.

The Palm Court was in the center of the lobby, dozens of white-draped tables surrounded by towering potted palms. Miss Wolf waved off menus and told the waiter to bring us a full tea.

"There," she said when it arrived. "Will you pour, Lane?" There were pitchers of hot water and cold milk, and the waiter had set a filigreed tea strainer across a small, shallow bowl. The lemon was in paper-thin slices, set on a plate, each piece flat and barely touching its neighbor.

I took the cup Lane offered me and sipped from it.

"Tell me," Miss Wolf said. "How are you holding up?"

I set my cup down and looked at Lane, who gave me a quick, exaggerated frown, as if to apologize.

"I'm OK," I said. "I'm fine."

"And you've been here how long?"

"Almost three months."

Miss Wolf lifted her cup and took a sip. "Smokier than usual," she said. "Not that I mind that." She set the cup down with a clatter. "I'm interested in you," she said to me. "You remind me of myself when I was young. I was from the Main Line, of course—quite different, as you perhaps know—but the story . . ." Her voice trailed off and she closed her eyes. Sitting there like that, in her good wool suit, her powdery old face as creased as a crumpled piece of paper, she struck me as almost unbearably sad, something so forlorn about the traces of haughtiness and grandeur that were still in her.

Lane reached across the table and put her fingertips on Miss Wolf's sleeve.

Miss Wolf opened her eyes.

"I'm not sure Carrie's read your book," Lane said.

Miss Wolf pursed her lips. "I didn't say she had." She reached for a slice of cake from the three-tiered stand the waiter had brought us: some kind of pound cake, a narrow piece lying on its side, sprinkled with powdered sugar. She pulled away the doily it was sitting on and bit in, leaving a few specks of sugar dust on her upper lip.

Lane turned to me. "Miss Wolf's first novel was about a woman who left behind an invalid friend to go to Europe."

My face grew hot, and Lane gave me another look of apology. I shook my head a little, because rather than offended I felt intrigued, and curious about the book.

"That's the *plot,*" Miss Wolf said a little peevishly.

"How's the pound cake?" Lane asked her. "I think I'll try one of these." She reached for a small crustless sandwich, triangular and so thin it was hard to think there could be anything inside. "Cucumber," she said, taking a little bite. "Delicious. Carrie, try one."

"You girls need to *move,*" Miss Wolf said.

Lane set her sandwich down, and we both looked at Miss Wolf, her fingers laced at the edge of the table.

"Lane, this goes for you, too. Listen to an old lady who knows. Go to Europe, go to the Far East, go far enough away so that the telephone will be too expensive, but *go.* The family is the enemy of the artist—of any young person trying to live seriously and meaningfully. You have to go."

I looked at Lane, but she was carefully avoiding my glance, a thoughtful expression on her face as she listened politely to what she'd heard many times before.

"You think I don't mean it," Miss Wolf said.

Lane dabbed at her mouth with a small cloth napkin. "If I went," she said gently, "where would that leave you?"

Miss Wolf flapped her hand. "Dead. Give me a year or two, that's really all I want."

"Miss Wolf," Lane said.

Miss Wolf turned my way, her deep brown eyes boring into me. "You're listening," she said. "I think you're hearing me."

When we were finished the two of them caught a cab, and I headed west on Central Park South, past hansom cabs with their broody, snorting horses, past cars and taxis stalled in traffic. It was cold enough for fur now, and when I had to pass close by a tall woman in a long dark mink, I snuck a hand out and felt it, all cool and silky.

The family is the enemy of the artist. I recalled the day Lane and I drank tea in her bedroom, how she said she disagreed with Miss Wolf, that she thought the family *was* the artist. *Just like the sky is, or all the books you've ever read.* Her book with its periwinkle blue cover—by what process had its contents come into being? She was different from Simon and the others: she never talked about poetry as something to strive for; it seemed more inside her, something to draw out. If I had something like that in me—well, I'd be different, I'd be someone else.

The dress, though. The dark green velvet dress, up there in Bergdorf's. In a way I felt I had a version of that dress in me, somewhere in there, possible. At Sixth Avenue I cut down to 57th Street and made my way to the fabric store I'd found in October.

It was quarter to six, fifteen minutes till closing. An older man watched me from behind the cash register, an apron tied over his white shirt and his wide polyester tie. There were three dark green velvets, one cotton, one rayon, and one silk, and I chose the silk for its perfect piney color. I found a shimmering satin for the cuffs, in just the right green, and I decided to go all out and get China silk rather than acetate for the lining. At five to six I sat down with a Vogue pattern book and within minutes had found almost what I was looking for, a plain, fitted dress with a round neckline. Almost but not quite. I looked up at the man, standing with his arms crossed over his apron, ready to kick me out despite the three fabrics I'd put on the cutting table. Could I depart from the pattern, substitute buttons for the back zipper, find a way to design my own deep cuffs? I stood up and found the Vogue patterns, tracked the numbers until I'd located the right drawer, rolled it open and riffled until I'd found the right pattern number, then my size. I carried the envelope to the cutting table and set it down, then I opened my wallet and reached for my credit card.

25

~

I SEWED. VELVET MAKES dust, and there were fine green fibers all over Kilroy's dining table, a skirting of them on the floor around my chair. I'd never worked with velvet before, and I was slow and careful, the sheer weight of it reminding me that this was serious. And exciting: I had to recruit knowledge from previous projects to figure out the back buttons, experiment with tissue paper and muslin before I could determine the right shape for the cuffs. My solutions worked, but I longed for more certainty, the sureness Kilroy brought to cooking or navigating the subway lines: a sureness born of knowledge and experience.

Christmas filled the city, and Kilroy and I visited the tree at Rockefeller Center, crept in late to a performance of Handel's *Messiah*. When I commented that he seemed to like Christmas, he said no, no, I had it all wrong: it wasn't Christmas he liked but the preparation for it, the intentness of people. For me the two were indistinguishable.

On the evening of December 21st we walked out of a Spanish restaurant in the West Village to find that it was snowing lightly, flakes like tiny petals passing through the illumination of the streetlights. Above the spindly black trees the sky was yellow. We stopped in our tracks, delighted. Our eyelashes caught flakes, our hair. We held our heads back and let the snow come into our mouths, soft and then cold and then wet. We walked slowly northward, watching the city go white. I was flying to Madison the next morning.

Back at his place, he handed me my Christmas present.

"Can I open it now?"

"Of course."

He'd wrapped it in a section of Sunday comics, some kitchen string for ribbon. I pulled the string off and peeled up the tape. Inside there was a framed photograph of a building, or part of a building—the top story and the roof, steeply pitched and gray, and above it a sky alive with clouds. Behind the roof there was a clothesline strung with white underthings: a man's and a woman's mixed together.

"It's Paris," he said, and I looked up at him.

"And you took it."

He wiggled his finger a few inches from the surface of the picture. "I lived over here for a while."

"I love it," I said. "Thank you. Did you frame it yourself?" The frame was beautiful, wood painted the exact gray of the roof.

He shrugged. "I always think the nicest presents are the ones you make yourself."

I suppressed a smile. I'd made him a corduroy shirt, in hours stolen from my dress. I went over to the closet and withdrew the shopping bag in which I'd hidden it. I said, "You can save it for Christmas morning if you want," and we both smiled: after the Thanksgiving Day phone call, I was assuming he'd spend Christmas alone, walking the deserted streets and then sitting in his apartment reading a brand-new book he'd bought for the very purpose. Did he have siblings? Would a whole clan of Frasers spend Christmas Day together, a whole clan minus one? Or would his parents be alone together, having a cow?

"I think I'll go ahead," he said.

The shirt was dark burgundy, a pinwale corduroy that had left its own fine dust all over the place. He pulled the paper off, then opened the box. "Nice," he said, pulling the shirt from the box and shaking it out. "Really soft." He laid it on the table and ran his hand down the front of it. I'd been careful with the nap, and a downward stroke flat-

tened the corduroy, darkened it. At last it dawned on him: he pulled
down the collar to look for a tag.

He looked at me and I nodded. He let his head fall back, and his
neck stretched taut. He said, "I don't know what to say."

" 'Thank you' will do."

"Not really."

He carried the shirt to the window and peered out. We'd left the
lights low and I could just make out his reflection, a ghostly smudge
against the darkness. He stroked the shirt and then turned around.
"See, no one's ever made me anything before, not—not in a really
long time." His voice was wobbly; I could hardly believe it. "This is
incredibly nice." He came back to where I was and with the edge of
his hand pushed my hair away from my face. "You are coming back?"

In twenty-four hours I'd be there, sleeping in my old bed on the
second floor of my mother's house. I'd have ridden in from the airport
with her, down streets I knew I would find wide open and eerily
quiet. I'd have seen Christmas trees framed by living room windows,
colored lights along gable after gable. New York would be a dream by
then, barely trustworthy in the face of so much that was so well
known. What I wanted was for Madison to be the dream—for this
room, this evening to be what lasted.

"Yes," I said. "It'll go fast. You'll see."

ASLEEP THAT NIGHT, my plane ticket ready in my purse, I
dreamed Mike healthy again. I was at the bottom of the stairs to my
Madison apartment, watching him go up backward, on his butt. He
was dressed in khakis and a plaid flannel shirt, and he had the halo on,
but I knew there was nothing wrong with him—that if he'd wanted
to, he could have walked.

Then we were on a hospital gurney together, making love. There
were no sheets on the gurney; we were right on the vinyl. He was
heavy on me, his ass hairy and damp in my palms, and I could hardly
breathe, though I was also incredibly aroused. He thrust into me
again and again.

In the morning the sky was blue, the air outside Kilroy's bedroom
window bright with the recent snowfall. With Kilroy still asleep

beside me, I got out of bed and went to look out. Several inches had accumulated, and the sidewalks were frosted; the wide expanse of Seventh Avenue was shiny wet. Down at the coffee place across the street, a couple pushed out the door, capped cups in their gloved hands, and walked the slow walk of the first snowfall until they were out of sight.

"Hey."

I turned and saw Kilroy lying on his side looking at me, his head propped on his hand.

"It stuck." I came back to the bed and got in next to him, the sheets on my side still warm.

"What stuck?"

"The snow."

He smiled and reached over to touch me. "Too bad you're leaving. We could have gone tromping."

"Isn't that something you do in a field?"

"Urban tromping," he said. "It's a subcategory."

"Where would we have gone?"

He thought for a moment. "Gramercy Park."

I'd spent over three hundred dollars on my plane ticket, another big charge on my credit card. I'd RSVPed to the wedding, for which I'd worked diligently to make a very expensive dress. I was expected at the rehearsal dinner tomorrow night—Rooster's mother had called me herself to echo Rooster's invitation. My own mother had asked me to save at least one evening for a special dinner with her. And I'd sent Mike the Empire State Building postcard with *See you soon* written on the back—I'd sent it to him at home, because he was there now, out of the hospital, ready to start the rest of his life.

But I didn't want to go. I was very clear on that all at once: I didn't want to go.

"Maybe I'll stay," I said.

Kilroy raised his eyebrows. "Do you want to?"

I nodded.

"Then do." He touched my shoulder, stroked it a few times and then moved his hand down my arm. He had the nicest touch, dry and firm. He ran his fingers up and down my forearm, then over my collarbone and down the very center of my chest, between my breasts.

Next was my face. He traced my forehead, my jawline. He took his time, gave attention to every part of me. Mike had been a faster lover, less democratic. My dream rose up in my mind and I tried to bat it down: Mike's big, heavy body on me, pressing me to the gurney. Kilroy's fingers were between my toes, up my shin. My knee and the inside of my thigh. His palm slid up my hip and higher, to my breast. I ran a hand up his leg, to the soft, wiry nest of his balls. I closed my eyes but it didn't matter: Mike was there, too, standing against the door watching us.

I HAD TO call my mother at work, and I got her voice mail, left a message saying there was a change and I'd try again later. Then I phoned the Mayers' house. I was sure I'd get Mrs. Mayer, but John Junior answered, his voice lower than the last time I'd talked to him. Mike? Sure, he was right there.

"It's me," I said, and right away I knew he knew: he stayed silent, let me hear his breathing. "Listen—"

"Don't." There was a pause, and he said, "OK? Let's just—let's talk for a while, can we?" And I nodded, as if he could see me, my heart bent on itself, a mangled thing. I'd brought the phone into the bedroom and closed the door, but I could hear Kilroy in the kitchen, moving around, making coffee.

"How is it to be home?" I said.

He hesitated. "Good. We're still kind of working things out."

"And where are you right now?"

"In the living room."

The living room. Sitting in his wheelchair. Would he stay in one place for a long time, or would he wheel around, antsy? The Mayers' living room was crowded with furniture: couches and tables and the big antique Mrs. Mayer called the whatnot. At Christmastime everything got moved around, crammed even tighter.

"Is there a tree up?" I said.

"An eight-footer."

It had always been Mike's job to string the lights—how hard it must have been to watch while someone else did it. The ornaments in their tissue paper, the mugs of hot cider, the carols on the stereo—the whole process had always been such a reminder, of that first kiss of ours under the mistletoe.

"So why aren't you coming?"

I'd decided that a good, solid excuse was the way to go, but now I balked—an excuse would be for me, not for him, to make me feel a little less unkind. "I just can't yet, Mike," I said. "I don't want to."

"That's what I figured."

"When you heard my voice?"

"No, when Rooster told me you said yes. I didn't tell anyone, but I figured you'd change your mind."

I sighed, and then I sighed again, for having let him hear the first sigh. I said, "Don't hate me, OK?"

"Why not?"

It was a good question, a question for which I had no answer.

"I don't," he said. "But I don't know why I don't, either."

A LITTLE LATER, Kilroy and I went out for a late breakfast. I felt happy and sick. People walked gingerly past the restaurant windows, careful on the snowy sidewalks. Traffic moved at a crawl. When we were done we headed for the brownstone so I could take a shower and change. It was a Saturday, but no one was around—out Christmas shopping, maybe. I felt a pang, remembering we'd opened our presents last night. What would we do on Christmas Day? Go to a movie, maybe. Or cook something Kilroy would know about, something involved and delicious. Or both.

The sky had clouded over again, and as we headed across town snow began blowing off the sidewalks, little gusts of it swirling at our feet. I'd never been to Gramercy Park before, a rectangle of townhouses built around a small locked park. A light snow began to fall, and the houses formed an intimate enclosure for the leafless trees. I might have imagined we were in another century but for the Acuras and Lexuses parked everywhere, many with their trunks open to receive the bounty of a holiday to be spent outside the city.

"Nice, isn't it?" Kilroy said.

I looked at him, wondered for a moment if he was being

sarcastic—because of the fancy cars, the obvious priciness of the houses. But he seemed serious.

"It's beautiful," I said. "You can almost imagine you're in the old days and cars don't exist."

He gave me a wide smile. "That's exactly what I was thinking—exactly." We'd paused in front of a red brick townhouse, and now we started walking again. He said, "I sometimes wish I'd been born in another century, you know? Things would've been harder. Just think of all we have now—think of electricity alone: lights, heaters, refrigerators. Not to mention all the fancy stuff like computers." He looked at me hard. "Imagine if there was no electricity—no way to read at night without a candle. Imagine having to chop firewood and carry it inside, or freeze. Think of the physical exhaustion of achieving even a minimum of comfort."

"You could still live like that," I said. "More or less. If you wanted to."

He shook his head dolefully. "No, it would be an affectation."

We headed up the East Side, stopping when we got to the United Nations to cross the wide, flag-lined plaza and stand looking at the East River, steel gray and rushing under the pale sky. My hair was wet from the new snow, Kilroy's damp at the edges under the wool cap he wore. He put his arm around me and pulled me in. He kissed the side of my face, then burrowed his head close, his frozen nose coming to rest against the side of my neck. Standing there, I imagined the two of us in a snowbound cabin, a fire in the fireplace, windows cold to the touch. Outside, icicles hung from the eaves, while farther away, encircling us, white-topped pine trees soared into the sky, creaking a little in the wind.

WHEN WE GOT home it was early evening. Kilroy defrosted some homemade mushroom barley soup, and we ate it without talking, my feet in his lap under the table. After, he washed the dishes while I took the phone back into the bedroom to call my mother. She picked up on the first ring, then listened silently while I explained that I'd decided to stay, my voice faltering as she failed and failed to speak. I heard Kilroy stacking dishes, and I wished I could be more like him, just say what I had to say and be done with it.

"Well," she said when I was done.

"What?"

" 'What?' " she exclaimed. "You ask me *what*? Do you know how many times Mike's called to find out what time you were arriving today? Three separate times. And it's not easy for him to make a phone call!"

"I know," I said. "I just don't feel ready."

"This isn't about whether or not you're ready," she cried. "Are you heartless? This is about how Mike was waiting for you. This is about *cruelty*."

I began to cry, noisily, my eyes hot and drowning. I pressed the phone to my ear and it got wet, and my palms, and my wrists. My mother never talked to me like this, and I sobbed and sobbed, waiting for her to say something that would take it all back. She was usually so evenhanded. When we were little, Jamie always said she wanted to trade moms, have my calm one instead of her nervous one. Where Mrs. Fletcher worried and scolded, my mother said, *How did that make you feel?* Apparently there was behavior that was too dreadful for such an approach. An image of Mrs. Fletcher came to mind, a table knife in her soft, freckled hand as she spread icing on a cake, her pink lips pursed thoughtfully. For a time *I'd* wished Jamie and I could trade mothers, too, until I met Mike and it was his family I wanted—and his family I got. I imagined my mother in her clean, spare kitchen, the curtains I'd made last summer hanging cheerily over the black windows, and I wondered how she could have let me go. I sobbed again, my shoulders shaking.

"Honey," she said. "I'm sorry."

"No, it's true," I said. "It's true."

"It's a rough time for you," she said. "I know that."

I shook my head again. I didn't want to think about her alone in that kitchen, but I couldn't help it. Maybe she'd cooked something for the two of us to eat. Maybe it was on the counter now, a lasagna she'd been planning to put in a low oven before she headed off for the airport. "Mom," I said. "God. I didn't even think about *Christmas*."

She was silent, and I imagined that she was thinking as I was, of the Christmas tradition we'd shared for as long as I could remember: breakfast by the fire while we opened our presents; the afternoon working together in the kitchen; and then, shortly after dark, the two of us in the dining room with a perfect rare roast beef resting on a silver platter, because we didn't have Christmas dinner with the Mayers.

"Mom," I said again. "I'm so sorry."

"Don't worry about it," she said. She was silent for a moment, and then she said, in a rush, "Oh, listen—that wasn't on my mind before at all. I'll be fine. I've got a big new book I've been wanting to read, I'll just load up on firewood and lounge the day away."

Which meant that because of me she'd spend Christmas in the exact way I'd been envisioning for Kilroy: alone, reading. I could just see her, book in hand while Vivaldi played, and a small, pro forma Christmas tree sat in the corner, strung with tiny white lights.

~

26

N ew york was full of men. Young men with pierced noses, old men with aluminum walkers. Black men, Latino men, Asian men. And middle-aged white men, thousands of middle-aged white men who might have been my father.

Away from Madison, I felt more and more aware of him—of his absence from my life. On the street I studied men I wouldn't have noticed a year earlier, looking not so much for my father as an idea of him: a facial expression, a span of shoulder. I wondered if he had other kids, maybe a string of them left around the country, half siblings joined to me by all we didn't know.

One cold day in early January I made my way up Fifth Avenue to the New York Public Library. The pre-Christmas snowfall had long since melted, but dirty water still filled the gutters, and I had to leap across great lakes of it. The library was warm and smelled of dust and sweat. I knew they'd have every phone book in the country, and I found them on microfiche and spent several seasick hours spinning through the little plastic cards. My father's name was John Bell, and he lived everywhere, of course: in Chicago and Cheyenne; in Seattle,

St. Louis, and Sioux Falls; in Houston, Austin, Arlington, Albuquerque, and Atlanta. Twelve of him lived in Manhattan alone.

I left the microfiche reader and wandered dizzily through the famous library, into the great rooms and down the wide corridors. I was down to my last few hundred dollars. My mother had sent me a check for Christmas, but I could barely hang on for another month or two, especially with credit card payments to worry about. I thought of finding out how to put in an application to work here—I knew libraries, after all—but then I saw a lank-haired woman in her early thirties, standing with a cart of books, her hand resting on their spines while she stopped for a moment to read a notice pinned to a bulletin board, and I looked at her sallow face and thought *No*.

Back at the brownstone I set myself to folding laundry I'd done earlier. Library or not, I should get a job, and soon. I'd even asked Kilroy about temping, but he'd responded with horror, said it was like considering a career in pulling the hairs out of my head one by one. "You do it," I said, and he frowned and shook his head. "Trust me," he responded. "You'd hate it."

Now, folding clothes, I thought instead of working in a store in SoHo. Being one of those women with perfect hair and perfect eyebrows, making sure the garments were spaced evenly on the rods they hung from. I'd get a discount on clothes, spend my lunch breaks walking around looking in the windows of rival stores. The only problem was I didn't have the right stuff to *get* a job like that. The right clothes, though maybe I didn't have "the right stuff," either.

I heard a step, and Simon appeared below me on the staircase, coming up from the second floor in a T-shirt and sweatpants.

"What are you doing home?" I said. It wasn't even four in the afternoon.

"All-nighter at work last night," he said, running a hand through his disheveled hair. "I got home at seven-thirty this morning. Just woke up."

"That sounds horrible."

"Actually, it's not bad. I get double for last night and I still get paid for today even though I don't have to go in."

I shook my head. "You are so lucky."

"High-paying drudgery has its charms."

"Could you get me a job there?"

He hesitated for a moment, then shook his head. "You don't want to work there."

I was holding a pair of socks, and I balled them together and tossed them onto my sock pile. "Everyone's telling me where I *don't* want to work. Where should I work?"

He stepped onto the futon and then settled himself against the wall, sitting cross-legged. "Hmm."

I reached for a T-shirt and folded it. "Yeah, nothing really leaps to mind, does it?"

"You're just about broke?"

I nodded.

"Great city, terrible prices."

"Tell me about it," I said, pulling a pair of jeans from the tangle and shaking them.

"But things are good with the K-man?"

I thought of last night, how Kilroy and I had roasted a chicken and eaten it with our bare hands, pulling the meat from the bones until our fingers and mouths gleamed with grease. When we were done he got up and brought back hot washcloths, then cleaned my fingers for me one by one.

"They are," I said.

"He's kind of an odd duck, but I think that's good in a way."

I smiled. "I'm so glad you approve."

"Hey, I'm your sponsor here—I get an opinion."

"My sponsor? You make me sound like a foreign exchange student."

He studied me for a long moment. "Are you OK?"

I nodded. I'd finished my folding, and now I stood up and began putting things into my cardboard dresser, underwear and socks in the top drawer, shirts and sweaters next. The dresser wasn't holding up very well. I'd thought of trying to find a cheap wood one somewhere, but it hardly seemed worth it, given how depressing the alcove was. That morning, getting ready to go do laundry, I'd wrestled the sheets off the futon, and when it thumped back down clumps of dust darted across the floor like tiny mice.

"You can't use the bottom drawer, can you?"

I turned and looked at him sitting against the wall, a concerned expression on his face. There were times, usually when other people were around, when I forgot how much I liked him. I said, "There's not enough space for it to open."

He pressed his lips together thoughtfully. "I bet you could really use the extra room. There's got to be a way." He sat for another moment, then suddenly got to his feet and headed for the stairs. "Hang on, I'll be right back," he called over his shoulder as he hurried down. I heard his footsteps continue to the first floor, then move in the direction of the kitchen.

I turned back to my clothes. Part of the problem was that the drawers were way too full. I wiggled open the third one and jammed my jeans in, on top of the pants and skirts that were already in there. I should get rid of some of this stuff: there were things I hadn't worn since arriving in New York, things that were just too dowdy. If the people in the stores in SoHo knew I even had this stuff, they'd write me off in an instant.

I thought of the green velvet dress, hanging in Kilroy's front closet so I wouldn't have to crumple it into the dresser. "When are you going to wear it?" he kept asking me, but now that I'd bailed on wearing it to the occasion that had inspired it, I didn't have a clue. It wasn't exactly the right thing for the Cuban-Chinese greasy spoon we'd tried a few nights back.

Simon's footsteps became audible again, and from the second-floor landing he called, "You're going to be so happy." I went out to the top of the stairs, and there he was, halfway up, two stacks of bricks held precariously against his body. He smiled a big smile. "They were in the backyard," he said. "They'll be perfect."

He reached the top of the stairs and carefully squatted, then set the bricks on the floor one by one. There were about a dozen of them, red and crumbling, a bit dirty in places. We brushed them off into the bathroom garbage and then rocked the dresser onto its side and slid three stacks of two underneath it. Simon got his fingers under the other side and lifted, and I wedged the remaining ones in, trying to separate them so the weight would be supported evenly. "You're totally brilliant," I said.

"If I were totally brilliant I would have thought of this the first time I saw your little cardboard wonder."

He went into the bathroom and washed his hands, then came out, squatted in front of the dresser, and pulled open the bottom drawer. "Voilà," he said, but then his expression changed, and he reached in and pulled out my silk nightgown and robe. "Whoa," he said. "What are these?"

My face was warm. "Nothing."

"They don't look like nothing." He took hold of the gown and straightened up, and it dropped open, a tumble of gold. He held it by the spaghetti straps and turned it this way and that, and the long drape of it caught the light. He laid it on the futon and picked up the robe, which he unfolded carefully. "Jeez, Carrie, where'd you get these?"

"I made them."

He stared at me, his eyes wide. "As in sewed them? You better not be fucking with me."

I smiled. "I'm not."

He placed the robe next to the gown and then stood looking at the two pieces, a pool of silk waving a little over the wrinkles in the scratchy green blanket he'd lent me. "Jeez," he said again. "And you don't even wear them with lover-boy."

I stifled a smile. I couldn't imagine showing them to Kilroy, let alone wearing them with him.

"This is the answer, you know," he said.

For a moment I thought he meant the answer to my problems with Kilroy, and my heart pounded. But I didn't have problems with Kilroy: I had Kilroy, who was a bit of a mystery sometimes, but not a problem.

"You don't get it, do you?" Simon said. "You're going to become a famous clothing designer."

I smiled. "Probably by tomorrow."

"Carrie, come on. I've noticed—you're interested in clothes. In fashion. You are. And look at these things: you're obviously talented."

"I can sew."

"So push it," he said with exasperation. "Seriously. Take a class."

"I have no money."

He sighed and then got down on his knees and began folding the robe. He was careful with it, smoothing it as he went. He put it in the drawer, then did the same with the gown. "I'm going to take a shower," he said. "And then you and I are going for a walk."

WHERE WE WENT was Parsons School of Design, and what we got there was their course catalog, the one with continuing studies offerings. We took it to a coffee shop and looked through it together, the course names interesting to me and then thrilling, full of promise: Color and Design, Draping, Patternmaking. Fashion Trends, Design Sketching, Couture Sewing Techniques. Simon sat beside me bristling with pleasure. On a paper napkin he doodled a dress, then wrote "Carrie Bell, Designer" off to the side. "I'm so pleased with myself I can hardly stand it," he said. The classes started in a few weeks, and they were $380 each. Which meant there was only one way I could make it work: by selling my car. It was suddenly that simple—give up the car I never used, and get something I could use. Of course I would sell my car! The fact that Mike had been a kind of guardian of it—that he'd helped me buy it, had packed a roadside emergency kit to keep in the trunk, had rescued me a couple times when it died—this no longer mattered. Or it mattered differently from how it had. Before, it had been a reason to keep the car, a nerve connecting me to a body of old habits. Now it was free, a small foreign body wedged inside me next to the ongoing ache of my failure to go home for Christmas.

I got $2,500, from a thirtyish couple in Patagonia jackets who had a weekend place on Long Island and wanted an extra car to leave out there. I registered for Draping, Patternmaking, and a class called Process, new this spring, that was described as "a general and wide-ranging introduction to fashion." Waiting for the term to start, I pondered my wardrobe, what to wear with what, how to give it verve. The January sales pulled me into store after store, and before long I'd succumbed to a black velvet shirt, then a pair of black ankle boots, and finally a bucket-shaped black leather bookbag with brushed nickel hardware.

It was strange to go back to school. I felt all the excited jitter of school beginnings in Madison, of being a third-grader in a new dress, a high school senior wondering what a new year would mean to me and my boyfriend. My classes were held at Parsons' Midtown campus, just a couple blocks from Times Square, and it was a rush of stimulation to leave the subway and enter the street with its chaos of honking cars and squealing buses, its towering buildings, its giant electronic signs, its hotdog smells and crowds and crowds of people. Once I was in the building the commotion subsided, or didn't so much subside as change, into a commotion of looks: of hair dyed blacker than black; of high, high heels or enormous, bulbous-toed boots; of bold interplays of color and pattern. Downtown was full of this, but it was odd to find such a concentration in the middle of that other New York, the New York of tourists and huge commerce: an enclave of edge.

Draping and Patternmaking introduced skills I saw right away I'd use forever, but it was the Process class I looked forward to. The teacher was a small, plump Italian named Piero Triolino, who wore a different-colored merino-wool mock turtleneck to each class, tucked into black jeans. In his accented English he told us again and again that inspiration was everywhere—in movies, through the viewfinders of microscopes and telescopes, in the daily lives of a hundred foreign cultures. He had us get large, hardbound books with unlined pages, and he told us to record our ideas in them—about color, silhouette, whatever. At first I felt frozen, thinking I *had* no ideas, but then a guy in class showed me several pages of fabric swatches he'd stapled into his book, and suddenly I got it. I taped in slips of paper from Chinese fortune cookies because I liked the grayed pastels; I bought colored pencils and markers and experimented with unexpected combinations, like cherry and pale yellow, or olive green and light blue. Remembering how I'd tried to draw dresses during the summer in Madison, I even tried sketching some ideas for clothes.

A freakishly warm Saturday in February pulled me and Kilroy out onto the street, and before I knew it he was steering us to the Museum of Modern Art, where I'd never been. I wasn't wild for museums, but it was the exact kind of thing Piero was always encouraging us to do, *Go to new places, see with new eyes,* so I was game. I had my sketchbook in my shoulder bag.

At the museum we entered the lobby and checked our coats, then stood in line for tickets. Near us stood a tall, angular girl wearing the shortest kilt I'd ever seen, and I got out my sketchbook and drew her, changing her top from the long, baggy Shetland sweater she wore to a skinny, cropped cardigan that would leave half an inch of midriff exposed. I eliminated her tights in favor of a pair of knee socks on which I scribbled the cables from some Bonnie Doons I remembered from grade school. On her feet I tried for a pair of clogs, but feet were hard. *Sketching* was hard: I wanted to take Design Sketching next, or maybe even Life Drawing.

"So what do you want to see?" Kilroy asked once we'd paid.

"Everything, I guess," I said with a shrug.

He grinned. "You thought I wanted to just traipse through the whole place? Forget it, that's window shopping with a forty-pound pack on your back. The only way to tame a place like this is to pick four things to look at, max, and be out in an hour. No wonder you hate museums."

"I don't hate museums."

"Sure you do," he said with a smile. "They make your feet hurt, and you always end up feeling stupid."

I had to laugh, it was so true.

"When was the last time you were at a museum?"

I looked up at the high ceiling, considering. "A few summers ago, with Jamie. We went to the Art Institute in Chicago. She'd just finished a course in Impressionism, and she was just insufferable. There's this painting there that's all dots—*Sunday Afternoon on the Grande Jatte*? I had to hear all about 'pointillism' for twenty minutes."

"It's a pretty cool painting," Kilroy said.

"You've been to Chicago?"

He nodded.

"It's OK," I said.

I thought of the day with Jamie, a day I hadn't thought of in ages, had perhaps never really thought of. It was the summer before our senior year at the U, and the two of us were in Chicago for the weekend, staying with her aunt. We did the whole Michigan Avenue thing, bought sandals in some shoe store in Water Tower, the same sandals, although she bought white and I bought brown. After the Art Institute we got cups of ice cream from a sidewalk vendor and sat on the steps, side by side, spooning it up. Jamie was coming off a bad crush, and while we were sitting there I happened to look over and see tears on her cheeks. I set my ice cream down, about to put an arm around her shoulder to comfort her, but she shook her head hard. "I'm happy," she said. "I'm crying because I'm happy."

Kilroy was watching me, his eyes searching mine. "Call her," he said, but I shook my head. Calling wasn't the thing. I'd called Mike right after New Year's and had found his voice so low it had seemed he wasn't articulating his words so much as merely releasing them. In not going back at Christmas, I'd done something to Madison and everyone in it: set it on an ice floe and given it a push. What was I going to do now, make a big deal about waving goodbye?

We rode up the escalator and for fifteen minutes sat on a bench in front of a giant, all-black painting. People wandered in front of us, but mostly our view was clear. The painting just seemed black to me: I wasn't about to say I could have painted it myself, but that's pretty much what I was thinking until all at once the edges began to tremble. Nothing had changed, not the light in the room, the noise level, not my mind in any way I could recognize, but when Kilroy nudged me and asked if I was ready to move on, I found it hard to pull my gaze away.

Next we looked at a painting that I thought was enchanting, although I could tell Kilroy didn't think much of it—when I slowed in front of it, he glanced almost longingly toward the doorway to the next room before stopping with me. What I liked were the colors, rose and sky blue and a clear grass green, all against a cream background that played a trick when you studied it and seemed to become foreground before it ebbed away again. In my sketchbook I wrote, *Raspberryish pink but a little grayed, Blue over Lake Mendota mid summer,* and *Green like grass in sun, not kelly, yellower—yellow-green like a pear, but saturated.* I wondered if the words would ever lead me back to these colors. It was too bad I didn't have my colored markers with me.

Kilroy said he had another part of the museum in mind for the last two, and we made our way to a room full of what I recognized as Matisses.

"Now these you like," he said, and when I turned to look at him he was grinning.

"Yeah, don't you?"

"Pick one."

I scanned the room before settling on what seemed to be a view through a window, but from deep enough inside that the window itself was part of the picture. Outside was a little harbor with boats, a couple of houses, nothing really earth-shattering or important but the longer I looked the more I simply liked the picture until I found that I loved it—for the colors, the way the edge of the curtain reminded you of the room, the jaunty scene below, but mostly for the pleasure with which I was certain it had been made.

"I love this."

Kilroy smiled. "It's delicious."

"Why do I have the feeling that's the kiss of death?"

"Not at all—who could not like it? But come when you're done," he added, "and I'll show you another," and he moved into the center of the room to wait for me, as if delicious or not there was nothing more in this particular picture for him to see.

I knew he was saving his favorite for last, and when I saw it I had a sinking recognition that I was going to have to choose between disappointing him and lying.

"OK," he said, "now you know who this is, right?"

"Picasso?"

"There you go. This is my favorite painting in the whole world. If I could paint like this I could go to my urn completely happy."

I looked at him, surprised. "Do you paint?"

He shook his head.

I hesitated. "Did you?"

He grimaced. "No, Carrie, I didn't paint. I didn't write, I didn't compose music—I didn't play the piano or take acting classes or do photography."

"So much you didn't do," I said.

"It hasn't been easy."

We stared at each other in the warm room, people moving around us. I felt moisture gather on my upper lip. "You read everything you could about World War Two," I said after a while.

"That's true," he said. "That I did."

A couple came into the room then, and I watched while the woman bent over to say something to the toddler they were pushing in a spiffy little navy blue stroller. Like his parents he was dressed all in black, with cunning little red-and-black shoes and a black leather baseball hat on his curly head. A tiny black leather jacket was draped over the stroller handle.

"Now that's a stylin' baby," Kilroy said.

I looked over, and his face wore a faint sneer. "What do you mean?"

"Poor kid doesn't stand a chance. They should be arrested for dressing him like that."

"He looks cute."

Kilroy shook his head with disgust. He seemed about to go on in the same vein, but then something shut off and all he said was "Oh, well, it's MOMA on a Saturday, what do you expect?"

He looked at the Picasso again, but I felt distracted, unable to concentrate. What was going on? Something was at stake, but I didn't know what.

"What'd you mean before," I said, "about going to your urn?"

It wasn't quite the question I'd intended, but before I could amend it he turned to me with a smile and said, "It was a figure of speech—when I die I want to be cremated. Don't you?"

"I haven't really given it much thought."

"Must be the age difference," he said with a grin.

I gave him a look. "Do you also know where you want your ashes scattered?"

He thought for a moment. "Maybe on a hillside in France." He nodded. "Yeah, on this hillside in the Var, about half an hour inland from Cannes. The place where I figured out the meaning of life."

"Which is?"

"That it's meaningless, of course. That you can spend your life doing anything you want and in the end it won't matter at all." His tone was light but he was flushed suddenly, and I reached for his arm, then drew my hand back when he didn't look at me.

"So, anyway," he said, "my feeling in response is: look at this pic-ture. Find a picture and just look at it."

I did as he said. I faced the picture and really looked at it, a small, dark portrait of a human face, refracted through a terrifying prism and recomposed with no regard for nature or happiness. Cubism. I found the word inadequate to describe what was going on in the pic-ture, how ominous I found it.

"It's hard to look at," I said, and he nodded.

"Of course. That's what makes it so brilliant. You can look at Matisse all day and not have to think about anything."

I smiled.

"That's nothing against Matisse or you, but don't you see how much more significant this is? How much tougher, how hard? Just wait till Paris—we'll go to the Picasso Museum and it'll all fall into place for you."

"Or it won't," I said.

He shook his head impatiently. "Of course it will, it just takes a while. It *is* hard to look at—but it's also hard-edged, tough, uncom-promising." He paused. "Haven't I ever given you my lecture on soft and hard art before?"

I shook my head.

"Well, then." He adopted a mock-scholarly tone and said, "All art, whether painting, poetry, music, dance, or anything else, can be divided into two groups, hard and soft, and as pleasing as the soft is, the hard is always superior—it might as well be a rule of nature." He paused for a moment, and when he started talking again he'd dropped the posing tone and was speaking faster. "Matisse and Picasso are just two of the most obvious examples. Think about Renoir: totally soft. Monet, Sisley—you could eat them with a spoon. Whereas Vermeer, who puts them to shame, has that incredible rigor. It's the same with music, with sculpture—I happen to love Beethoven, but he's roman-tic, he's soft, and for excruciating perfection you just can't beat Bach, because he's got that *hard edge.*"

He stared at me with his eyes bright, and there was something in him I'd never seen before, maybe delight. Then all at once it disap-peared. He barked out a strange laugh. "God," he snickered. "I'm sorry. Jesus."

"What?"

"Nothing. You just reminded me of someone else. Or of myself with someone else."

My heart pounded. Now that this moment was upon us, I was intensely nervous. "Who?" I asked tremulously. I was sure his answer would open up an encyclopedia of jealousies, because of course he meant a woman. "Who?" I said again, thinking this time, this time he had to answer.

But: "No one," he said. "Forget it. It doesn't matter," and I sighed and turned away, not angry so much as embarrassed. And sad.

"Shall we go now?" he said, and I turned back to find him smiling awkwardly. "It's been an hour," he went on. "Much longer and we'll develop museum foot."

I followed him to the escalator and down to the exit, thinking about the little speech he'd just given—hard art, soft art. It was almost as if I'd witnessed a mystical phenomenon, like someone speaking in tongues. He'd hopped from idea to idea as if he'd been impelled. *You just reminded me of someone else. Or of myself with someone else.*

Outside, the afternoon had grown colder. He buttoned his coat with an absent expression on his face, and as I watched him, the city street fell away and I saw him on that hillside in France—in the Var, whatever that was—a man standing alone on a hillside. I saw him on a low, grassy hill that probably wasn't a French hill at all; in fact, it was a hill outside of Madison, where I'd sometimes gone with Mike for picnics, but never mind that, for what I saw was that as he stood there figuring out the meaning of life, he felt something he hadn't remotely touched on back in the museum.

~

27

THERE WAS A buzz at the brownstone the following week. Alice was moving out—really moving out, giving up her room to go live with her boyfriend in his two-room apartment near Tompkins Square. As Simon pointed out, she was going to be paying more rent to have less space, but that was love for you.

And luck for me, because I could have her room. Her high-ceilinged, twelve-by-fourteen room with two windows and a closet and a *door*. At $125 per month, it would mean adding just $25 to the $100 I got each month from my Madison subletter. It was so real, so thrilling, so *easy*.

"What do you think?" I said to Kilroy. "Should I take it?"

We were in his living room, he lying on the couch reading, I perched on its edge, still wearing the coat I'd put on for the walk over. It wasn't really a question, I was just babbling, but the way he looked at me—something going on with his mouth, a kind of tightening of the upper lip—gave me a rush of fear.

"I mean," I said. "That is—"

He closed the book around his finger and rested it against his stomach. "Why does it matter what I think?"

My heartbeat stumbled, and I looked across the room, to where the uncovered window reflected us back at ourselves. "It doesn't," I said. "I mean it does, but it shouldn't." For some reason I thought of my silk nightgown and robe, hidden in my bottom drawer. I looked back and met his eye. "I don't know, for a while there I was worried that you didn't even think I should be taking my classes at Parsons."

He sighed and looked away, then crossed his arms over his chest, his book still held tight. "Officer Kilroy," he said. "Is that what I am?"

I was taken aback. "No."

"Good," he said. "I don't want to be anyone's cop, least of all yours."

"Why least of all mine?"

"Because that way madness lies."

"Excuse me?"

"It's just an expression," he said. "A quote, as people so ignoramously say." He opened the book and glanced at it, then closed it around his finger again.

"I'm confused," I said.

He shook his head. "Never mind, let's drop it. Take the room, by all means—I think it's a good idea."

I stared at him, his forearms crossed over the book, his blue-jeaned legs bent at the knee. I said, "I don't want to drop it."

He looked away.

"What's going on?" I said. "You're so aloof sometimes. You're like this mass of untouchableness."

He looked back and raised his eyebrows briefly, and the gesture enraged me: he could see this through, was what it meant. Bide his time till I was finished.

"Why do I know next to nothing about your past?" I cried. "Who did I remind you of in the museum?"

"You seem upset," he said blandly.

"Fuck you!" I launched myself from the couch and stormed into the kitchen, where I opened the refrigerator, then slammed it shut once I'd felt the waft of cold. There was an empty beer bottle on the counter, and I could almost feel the smooth glass, the way it would roll across my palm before smashing into the far wall.

He came in after me and then stopped abruptly, his hands jammed in the front pockets of his jeans. After a moment he pulled them out and stuffed them into his back pockets. "I'm sorry," he said. "I know this is hard for you. I'm not all that forthcoming."

"You're not *all that* forthcoming?"

He didn't smile.

"What's the deal with your parents?" I said. "With you and them?"

He shook his head wearily. "I'm not being evasive, it's just—I wouldn't even know how to begin to tell you."

"Just do it."

He exhaled hard, blowing upward so his hair lifted from his forehead for a moment. "One person's 'just do it' is another person's Mount Everest, OK?" He frowned. "Look, it's just—I've always been a very private person, and being in this relationship with you is new to me."

"Why are you in it?" I said sharply. My frustration felt huge, a great flying creature inside me, frantically beating its wings.

"Because you were irresistible," he said. "Were and are."

I sighed.

"It's true."

"Did you never want someone before?"

"Someone or anyone?"

"Either."

"Not really. Sex was sort of a problem, but I found various ways to sublimate."

We both laughed, and I felt a little better: his face lit up when he laughed, in the nicest way. I thought of crossing the room, the solace of his body. The solace and then the silence. We could make love right now, maybe right here in the kitchen, standing against the sink: with each thrust close, closer, and almost merging; and then afterward we'd stay pressed together while our quickened pulses slowed again, and the ebbing back into ourselves began.

He watched me hopefully—it was up to me. I ignored the temptation. "Why don't you have any friends?"

He took a deep breath and let it out again. "Over the years I've had people to talk to and go to movies with and sit next to in bars and restaurants, but for one reason or another I mostly haven't kept up with them."

"You're so casual about it."

He shrugged. "It doesn't matter to me, it's not what I think about."

"What do you think about?"

"Come on."

"What?"

He rolled his eyes. "I think about whether or not to buy the *Daily News.* How to get from here to Chinatown without having to take the L. I think about the skin on the inside of your upper arm and whether or not I like sun-dried tomatoes."

"Why the skin on the inside of my upper arm?"

"Fishing for compliments? Because it's soft and private and I can smell a tiny bit of BO behind your deodorant."

I snorted out a half laugh. "I guess I asked for that."

"You didn't ask for anything. Neither did I. We just—well, here we are, we're together, and I'm glad." He moved toward me and held his hand up, high-five style. After a moment I put my hand against it and he threaded his fingers between mine and held tight until I curled mine down, too. He said, "Are you in any doubt that that's what I want?"

I shook my head. That was the funny thing—the hilarious thing: I was in no doubt at all. He wanted to be with me and I wanted to be with him, despite his secrets and his flares of misanthropy. They were part of the package, but mostly I kept them tucked away in a dark little room in my mind. I gave it a wide berth, sticking instead to the main corridors, where everything was clean and well-lit.

"No, I'm not."

He let go of my hand and went over to the counter. He hoisted himself up so he was sitting by the sink, his heels against the dishwasher. He said, "You wanted to know what I thought about your taking the room. I guess that made me uncomfortable because it sort of raised the question of why you weren't living here."

I felt my face color, and I looked away. Refrigerator, range. The kitchen was so clean. There was nothing out, not a salt shaker, not a mug. It was like a kitchen in a model apartment, all potential. I was disappointed by what he was getting at, yet I didn't really want to live in this place. I wouldn't be able to add so much as a colorful potholder without fearing I'd upset him somehow.

"It's OK," I said, facing him again. "I understand. It's too soon."

He grinned. "My internal body clock is set on glacial time."

I knew what he meant, that he moved with the slowness of glaciers, the incremental progress of ice inching through time and space, but what I thought of was the chill of it, the chill inside him.

THAT WEEKEND I moved into Alice's room. Simon and I dragged the futon together, then carried the dresser between us. Arranged against the walls, my furniture gave the room a desolate feel. Having a bed on the floor had been fine for the alcove, where there wasn't really any floor left, but it was awkward here, a car stalled in a vast desert.

A few minutes after Simon left there was a knock, and I turned to see Lane standing in my doorway, a vase of purple tulips in hand.

"Here's a little housewarming for you."

She handed me the flowers and I thanked her and leaned in to them, let my cheek feel their downy firmness. "You're so nice."

She smiled. "I'm glad you have a real room now."

I hadn't seen her in over a week, but somehow it didn't matter. My friendship with her was different from any friendship I'd ever had before—from my friendship with Jamie. Lane and I were like lines that intersected and then split apart again, without a pattern but with a kind of purpose. Jamie and I were DNA, a double helix. Or had been—we were nothing now, although at odd moments I sometimes got a sense of her out there, as if her half of the helix had grown invisible but was still present, spiraling alongside mine.

I set the tulips on my dresser and turned back to Lane. "They add a lot—it was a little depressing."

She looked around the room. "Alice never got around to painting. That and a rug would probably do a lot."

A new coat of paint. I thought of a pale blue-green for the walls, maybe a dark slate blue for the moldings. I had the exact colors in my pencil set. I said, "I'd love it to feel like your room eventually. Tranquil."

She smiled. "Funny how rooms have moods, isn't it? Like Simon's is boisterous."

I laughed. Simon had a red-and-pink zigzag bedspread, a bookcase he'd painted to look like leopard skin. On the wall was a painting he'd done of three dogs sitting on a couch, all doubled over with laughter.

Rooms having moods reminded me of my Process assignment. In our last class Piero had handed out cards to everyone, each bearing a single word—"Whimsical," "Melancholy," "Reclusive." Mine was "Witty." Next week, we were supposed to bring in a garment that expressed the mood on our card. I told Lane about it now. "So if you can think of a witty garment, just let me know."

"Like a bra that tells jokes?" she said, and then: "Just kidding." She tilted her head toward my dresser. "We could go through your clothes together."

I shook my head. "If my stuff talks at all it says, I don't know, timid, cautious. Definitely not witty."

She narrowed her eyes. "Your stuff or you?"

"Probably both."

She frowned. "I don't know how you can say that."

"Why?"

"You're so brave."

I put my fingers to my sternum. "Me?"

"Think of how you left home."

I looked down at the floor. After a moment I looked up again. "Don't you mean selfish?"

A shocked look came over her face, and she shook her head. "Not at all. My God, is that what you lie awake at night worrying about?"

"No, I lie awake worrying about what I'm doing with Kilroy."

As soon as the words were out, a jittery agitation invaded me. What had I just said? What did it mean? I didn't lie awake at night, I slept, slept next to him the whole night through, woke rested, alert, aware. Buzzing. Worried.

"Shit," I said.

"It's not easy, is it?"

I shook my head. I thought of Simon saying Kilroy was an odd duck, and I wondered if he and Lane had talked about Kilroy. My weird guy. My nut to crack.

Lane said, "Maura and I had a really rocky beginning. Like, we'd sleep together, and then the next day we'd see each other in the din-

ing hall and we'd both think the other person was acting cool and so
we'd act cool, and—well, it was pretty awful for a while there."

"What helped?"

"Time," she said. "And a lot of therapy on my part."

I thought of the summer night when Dave King had found me—
followed me?—outside the hospital. How he'd asked if I'd thought of
talking to someone myself. An image came to mind, of my mother in
her little office with its two chairs set face to face, and I shook my
head to erase it.

"Can I ask you something?" Lane said.

"Sure."

"Do you love him?"

I thought of his face. Of being scratched by his stubble when we
kissed. Of how quick he was, and how funny, and how kind. Of the
way the beginning of his erection felt against me when we were lying
like spoons and he hadn't yet shifted his hips back so it could lift. "I
do," I said.

"Well, then, that's probably what you're doing with him."

We talked a little more, and then she said goodbye and went into
her own room, where I heard her moving around, the floor creaking under her feet and then, after a while, the faint whistling of her
kettle. I opened my closet door and looked at the green velvet dress,
which I'd carried over from Kilroy's earlier. It seemed out of place in
this dusty closet. It expressed a mood I wasn't in.

I crossed my room and sat on the futon. My legs jutted out in a way
that reminded me of the dead witch's legs in *The Wizard of Oz*, sticking out from under the crushing weight of Dorothy's house. I scooted
backward, then lay back so my head was on my pillow. Staring at the
ceiling, I noticed a web of cracks emanating from the light fixture.
The sight reminded me of something, and I stared, trying to figure
out what. Then I realized: it was like roads leading away from a town.
Verona, Oregon, Stoughton, Lake Mills—I was thinking of the roads
out of Madison.

I ARRIVED AT Piero's class early that week, my witty garment
folded into my shoulder bag. Piero came in right on the hour, and

while a few people usually continued chatting until he'd cleared his throat and begun to speak, today everyone stopped abruptly. I figured they all felt as I did, worried about what they'd brought. I wondered if anyone had been given a card that said "Nervous."

"Let's hang up the work, please," he said, and we all stood and began arranging our projects on hangers and then hooking them onto short retractable rods that pulled out from the walls.

"What do you think?" he said. "Hang your word nearby, or no? Perhaps no, then we can try to determine the word from the work itself."

We started at the far side of the room, where a pink-haired girl had hung up a black linen jacket with a high, mandarin collar and a loose, baggy shape.

"What does this say?" Piero said.

"Funereal?" said someone.

"But that's just because it's black," said someone else.

"It's sort of sexless," said a third person, and Piero nodded.

"Yes, it is, isn't it—a Mao jacket, really." He turned to the girl who'd brought it. "What were you trying to express?"

"Reclusive?" she said. "I was thinking, you know, the high neck, and how it's so loose it would kind of hide the person?"

Piero nodded. "Yes, I see, but have you perhaps been too literal? Let's move on."

Next was a slip hung over a bra, with the two stitched together so the lace trimming on the bra cups showed. The woman who'd made it already looked embarrassed.

"Sexy," someone said.

"Flirty," said someone else.

"My word was flirtatious," the woman said, looking hopefully at Piero.

"Yes, but it's the same problem, no? The garment doesn't *express* flirtatiousness, it relies instead on a kind of telegraphing. It says slip, bra, peekaboo, rather than through subtler means evoking the spirit of flirtatiousness in the way that, say, a little cotton sundress in a bright polka dot would. What does the word mean: not sex directly, but really more the opposite, the idea of sexiness, the promise. I think the point here is to evoke, not to translate."

On we went, past whimsical, melancholy, frantic. The one Piero seemed to like best was a skinny, horizontally striped navy-and-white T-shirt hung over matching vertically striped walking shorts. The guy who'd brought them in had also brought white knee socks and navy fisherman sandals, and I thought it was the first thing we'd seen that someone might actually wear.

"Lovely," Piero said. "Very playful. Was that your word, playful?"

The guy nodded. "I was thinking it was something a woman might put on for a fun day, just because she was in a good mood."

"Well done," Piero said. "That's just right." He looked around at everyone. "Do you see how the spirit of the word is expressed?"

Finally we came to mine. It had been sheer luck that I'd thought of something—sheer luck and a mirror, because last night, desperate to come up with a solution, I'd paced Kilroy's apartment over and over until I was stopped by my own reflection, the bathroom mirror showing me myself wearing my Adolfo-overtaken-by-the-Gap T-shirt, as Alice had put it.

Now it hung in Piero's classroom, braid-trimmed, a row of anchor-stamped brass buttons marching down the front. It was nearly the same red as the mock turtleneck Piero wore, a red that was just faintly tomatoey, as if the tiniest drop of orange had been added.

"This is great," someone said.

"Yeah, it's really clever."

"Witty," Piero said, turning to smile at me. "That was your word, right?"

I nodded.

"The nice thing about this project," he said, "is the way it juxta-poses two ideas—the basic T-shirt with the rather stuffy Adolfo suit. That's what much of wit is, really, the unexpected joining of opposing ideas. Well done, Carrie. I think we've learned something about mood today."

The class period was over and everyone began to scatter. I slid the T-shirt into my shoulder bag. I was halfway to the door when he called my name.

"I've been thinking about you," he said, standing at his desk at the front of the class, putting papers into a briefcase. "You're taking Draping also?"

I was surprised he knew. "And Patternmaking."

"And you already have your bachelor's?"

"From the University of Wisconsin."

He smiled. "What do you think so far, do you enjoy your work here? I think you might like to consider full-time, no? Working toward a degree?"

I was flattered but for some reason also suddenly unnerved, as if it wouldn't be my choice whether I went to college again or not. "I don't know—it's expensive, isn't it?"

"We have financial aid, of course," he said offhandedly. "Tell me, the T-shirt—have you thought of playing with the idea a little more, trying different versions, maybe?"

I bit my lip. "What do you mean, different versions?"

"Well, a T-shirt is in some ways a blank slate, no? A tabula rasa. You can sew on a fake pearl necklace and you have a play on an evening dress. I think a tuxedo shirt was done many years ago, but that's no reason not to try some other ideas now."

I considered. I'd worked on the red T-shirt as a lark; I'd have to think about alternatives.

"Play around a little," he said. "I'll be interested to see what you come up with. And think a little about what we've been talking about, yes? I think you are still young—it's not too late to pick a new career."

I thanked him and said goodbye. Out on the street, I wrapped my scarf around my head against the early-March wind. I usually took the subway to class, but I'd taken to walking home, something appealing about being out and among people at the end of the day, being part of the two-way stream of New Yorkers going home.

A new career. A career of fabric and silhouette, color, style, mood. What Simon had had in mind, but for real. As I walked I wondered: was it possible?

I thought of what Kilroy had said, long ago in McClanahan's: *See, there it is right there, the pernicious little idea that who you are should determine something as trivial as what you do for a living. Life's not like that. It's not that malleable. It's not that neat.*

But what if it was? What if it could be? I was someone for whom it was a thrill to browse among fabrics, to touch them, to play in my mind with color and shape. Why shouldn't these things move into the center of my life? Why shouldn't I move them there? I was walking down Seventh Avenue, cold and shadowy in the late afternoon, crowded with traffic and pedestrians, when all at once I stopped and laughed out loud. Up ahead of me in the intersection was the now-familiar sight of a guy wheeling a huge rack of clothes across traffic, and I thought how perfect it was that I'd been thinking what I'd been thinking exactly while walking through the garment district.

28

~

THE FOLLOWING WEEK, I headed out of Draping be-
hind tall, skinny Maté, who was the talker of the class, his lilting
Caribbean-accented English flowing around the edges of the brightly
lit room. He tended toward long, colorful sarongs topped by Oxford
shirts knotted at the waist, and today, preparing to leave, he'd wrapped
a capacious loose-weave brown shawl over the ensemble, leaving
nothing showing but his lean brown calves and his red suede clogs.
The first few class meetings he'd annoyed me, but today I'd found
myself admiring his extravagant sense of style, and now, walking
behind him, I realized that he reminded me of a model on a catwalk,
the way he strode along on his long legs and held the shawl close, the
angles of his body revealed with every move.

At the exit he held the door open an extra moment so I could pass
through, then stopped outside to wait for me. "Lime green," he said.
"I want women to wear lime green dresses with white embroidery
this summer. But drapey, not all stiff. Sort of Lilly Pulitzer meets
Badgely Mischka. With *very* thick-soled white sandals."

I smiled, wondering if I could have come up with such a sweeping
idea.

"I do," he said. "Don't you just look at all these wretched black coats and want to scream?"

It was lunchtime, and masses of people in black hurried by with their heads down, walking fast through the cold.

"Women should wear hats again," he went on. "Do I sound like Diana Vreeland? 'Pink is the navy blue of India!' " He waggled his fingers at me and then turned and headed off, his hips swaying as he made his way downtown.

I paused to wrap my scarf tighter. It was just a matter of thinking more broadly. Maybe *daring* to think more broadly. I turned, and there was Kilroy, leaning against a little blue car parked in a bus stop, looking at me. Surprised, I crossed the crowded sidewalk.

"Who was that?" he said, looking after Maté.

"A guy in my class. He thinks women should wear hats again."

"At least he cares about something."

"Ha-ha." I reached into my pockets for my gloves. "What are you doing here, anyway?"

"Do you also want to know why I'm leaning against this vehicle in such a proprietary manner?"

His back was against the passenger door of someone's car. He held up his hand, and a set of keys dangled from his forefinger.

"What's going on?"

"I rented it," he said. "For the weekend. We have to practice traveling together before France."

He'd never done anything like this before, and a wide smile pulled at my mouth. It was so romantic—so impulsive. He was smiling, too, a smile that seemed to acknowledge that he was acting out of character, and that I liked it, and that he liked my liking it.

"Where are we going?" I said.

"Montauk." He reached up and tucked my hair behind my ear. "Where women should wear warm clothes."

We drove to the brownstone and I ran in to pack a bag, then we took off, Kilroy speeding through the heavy traffic as if the little car were a marble rolling between bricks. We left the city through the Midtown Tunnel and made our way through Queens on the Long Island Expressway, the landscape gray and industrial, then gray and suburban, and finally gray and rural.

He was a button pusher. I waited to be sure, and it was true—we didn't hear a single song all the way through. Finally I reached over and stopped him as he was reaching for the radio again.

He gaped at me. "You *like* Cassiope?"

"Their second album was my first album."

"So much for France," he said with a shudder. "Cassiope is beyond the pale."

It became a game. We stopped for a late lunch, and I was appalled when he ordered clams: "No way I'm going to France with you."

I had trouble reading the map to get us to our motel: "I'm certainly not traveling in a foreign country with someone who can't read a map."

But in fact we were getting along well. Something about being in a car together, the hum of the road when we weren't talking, of our voices when we were. I'd been in bed with Kilroy, in restaurants, movie theaters, bars—but this was something new, something nice.

At dusk we parked on an empty stretch of road and walked down to the beach. The wind was sharp against our faces, the sand gray and swept with seaweed, the water dark. As we made our way along the shoreline, a bank of steel-colored clouds hovered at the horizon and grew. Kilroy's arms were tight across his chest to keep out the cold, and as I looked at him, his collar-length tangled hair and his pale, stubbly face, I felt happiness invade me like a kind of calm.

"Your first view of the ocean?" he said.

I shook my head. When I was four or five my mother'd taken me to visit a cousin of hers on the New Jersey shore—her cousin Brian, on whose shoulders I'd eaten a black cherry ice cream cone, only to think, years later, that the shoulders had been my father's. I could no longer remember sitting on Brian's shoulders, I could only remember remembering it, when I was nine or so and determined to resurrect what I could of John Bell. On and off for nearly a year, I fell asleep trying to retrieve my father from the void he'd left me for. It was a kind of boardless Ouija game, the fingertips of one hand meeting the fingertips of the other so that my hands formed a loose clamshell: a kind of prayerless prayer. Where are you, where are you? Finally, hearing me muttering to myself one night, my mother came into my room and asked if I'd called her, and I decided then and there to stop.

It was the next day that I tossed the pencil sharpener he'd left me into the Dumpster at school, with a nine-year-old's righteous vehemence.

Where was he, though? Where? Who had he been, and who had he become?

Kilroy touched my face. "Where'd you go?"

I shook my head. I'd told him the whole story—what more was there to say? "New Jersey," I said. "Where I first saw the ocean."

We checked into a little roadside motel, where Kilroy insisted on paying. Our room was the last in a line, creaking slightly in the wind. Brown-and-orange plaid curtains, a lumpy double bed. We took showers and then went out for dinner, to a drafty barn of a restaurant where we ate lobster with a view of the black beach, shadowy clouds obscuring and then revealing the dim half-moon.

Back in the motel room we stretched out on the bed. My legs were tired from the walk on the beach, and I closed my eyes, thinking I'd rest for a few minutes. I woke in the dark some time later and realized that Kilroy was easing off my shoes. At first I couldn't see him—I just felt his hands on my ankle, felt him peel my sock down over my foot. After a while there was wet warmth: his tongue flicking over my toes and between them, tickling almost to agony, kisses on the top of my foot, the sole, the heel. Gradually I made out his silhouette. I knew he knew I was awake, but I didn't speak. He moved up and unsnapped my jeans, then unzipped them. I stayed limp, didn't give him any help as he tugged them off. He slipped his palm into my underwear and slid a finger into me, then pulled it out and traced a wet circle around my belly button. I held my hands away from my sides, palms up, an exercise in anguished restraint. Our eyes met but we continued like this. Inert, I felt my sweater come off, then my bra. The room was cool. He sucked at my nipples, his head and chest covering my upper body with a light warmth. He moved away and I was instantly chilled, goosebumpy. The bedsprings squealed as he stood, and he stared at me through the dark while he undressed. I was very cold, but he lay next to me without pulling back the covers, and his cold hand spread itself out on my abdomen. Now it was harder not to move. I felt his erection against my leg, his hand moving up and down my belly. I was dying to touch him, but also dying not to, to continue this story of no feeling until the final moment when I burst, and proved it wrong.

.   .   .

WE WOKE LATE the next morning, heavy with sleep in the curtain-dark room. We dressed and got back into the rental car, then drove around the end of Long Island, through some of the charming small towns out there, empty in March though Kilroy said they made up for it in summer, when all of Manhattan arrived with their cell phones. In a poorly lit café with a little junk store at the rear, we finally had breakfast, dark, steaming mugs of coffee and huge, craggy pastries, a full half inch of oatmealy crumb baked onto their surfaces.

Afterward, we looked through the stuff on display in the back. Stained old quilts, tarnished copper pots, rough little pine side tables.

"I want a souvenir," I said, fingering a long-handled wood dipper.

Kilroy grinned. "I saw a saltwater taffy place down the street."

"A *real* souvenir," I said. "It's so nice being out here. Don't you sort of wish we could stay and hide out for a while?"

Hide out. I didn't like the sound of that, and I pretended to be absorbed by a chipped ceramic rooster. Why had I said "hide out"? "I mean," I said, "spend longer than just a weekend," but that wasn't right either: I'd miss Patternmaking if we didn't go back tomorrow, and I knew I didn't want to miss a class. What did I want? To be outside of life with Kilroy, and inside it by myself? I hoped not. I didn't want to want that.

I took his hand, then stretched it around me and placed it against my back. I reached for the other hand and drew it around my other side. We were inches apart now, embracing in an empty junk shop on Long Island. I lifted my face to kiss him, and he hesitated. He glanced up front, to where our waitress was standing looking out the café window onto the sidewalk. "I dare you," I said, and he turned back and pressed his lips to mine: once lightly and then again, for real.

GOING BACK TO the city the next afternoon, we talked a bit but mostly rode along silently, tired from a long walk on the beach that morning. My legs ached pleasantly, and my thoughts drifted from the vastness of the ocean to Kilroy's quiet presence near me to the things I'd do during the upcoming week.

The rental car place was on 17th Street, east of Third. We glanced around for a taxi before starting back toward his place, the city blocks stretching endlessly ahead of us now that we'd walked on sand. "One more block," he said with a rueful smile as we crossed Sixth, and then nothing more till we'd reached his building and he'd unlocked the outer door and pushed the button for the elevator. "Home, sweet home," he said, and then he smiled and kissed me on the jaw.

Upstairs, he dropped his shoulder bag in front of his apartment door and fished in his pocket for his keys. He unlocked the door and pushed it open, and there, lying on the hall floor, was a thick, cream-colored envelope.

"What's that?" I said.

He groaned softly, then bent and picked it up. On the back flap a flourish of initials eluded me, but on the front it was easy to read the single word written there: *Paul*.

"Fuck," he said under his breath. He shoved the envelope into his coat pocket and held the door open for me. I went into the bedroom and dropped my bag, then watched as he carried his in, unzipped it, and held it open over the bed, letting loose a free fall of dirty clothes. "Excuse me," he said, and he vanished into the bathroom, latching the door behind him.

Paul. It had to be from his parents.

I stared out the window at the graying light, people in twos and threes walking down the avenue. A taxi came to a stop at the opposite corner, and a man in an overcoat got out and then leaned in the front window to pay the fare.

The toilet flushed and Kilroy came out and stopped on the far side of the room, still wearing his coat. "Listen," he said. "I've got to, um, do an errand. Do you want to take a hot bath or—I don't know—go back to the brownstone?"

I pulled my lower teeth across the bottom of my upper lip, chapped from the windy weekend. "What errand?" I said. "Where are you going?"

He shook his head. "I've got to run uptown for something." He put his hands on his hips and looked at his shoes. "To see my parents, actually."

He looked dirty and tired, his hair a wind-blown mess, stubble sprouted from his cheeks. He just wanted to go, get whatever it was done with, but I couldn't stop myself: "Can I go with you?"

His eyes bugged out for a second. He recovered and said, "You don't want to do that, believe me."

"But I do." My palms were damp and I wiped them on my jeans. "I love you," I said. "I want to meet your parents even if—" I'd been about to say *even if you don't want me to* but I stopped myself "—even if you hate them."

"I don't hate them," he said. "It's just complicated." He licked his lips. "I'm glad you said that, though."

He meant "I love you." I'd said it in the dark, in bed, but this was the first time I'd said it when he could see my face. It made me feel a little seasick, having the words out there. Not because I didn't mean them but because they felt so frail.

"You know what?" he said. "Come. I actually think—" He stopped and shook his head ruefully, then skirted the bed and came to stand in front of me. He held out his hand and said, "Please. I'd like you to meet my parents."

We rode an A train to 42nd Street, then took the R to the Lexington Avenue line. They lived on 77th between Park and Madison, in an enormous house that was as wide as two brownstones put together, but made of a paler stone and fronted by two curving flights of steps that joined in front of a gleaming dark-wood door. A maid let us in.

I followed Kilroy through a living room full of antiques and lavish Persian rugs, into what I thought must be the library, a smaller, cozier room with dark green walls and several pieces of leather furniture. All the books seemed to be in sets, with gold tooling. On a lustrous mahogany table there was an enormous flower arrangement that must have taken hours to compose, each perfect out-of-season blossom in its place. There was a fire burning in the fireplace, a tray of decanters on a table. The whole thing made me think of *Masterpiece Theater*.

"Drink?" Kilroy said. He'd grown edgier on the subway, and now his voice was tight and uneven.

"Sure."

He put ice in heavy crystal glasses and poured from one of the decanters. I tasted mine, not sure I liked the strong, smooth smokiness of it.

We sat side by side on a deep couch. "Pleasant li'l place," he said drily. "Course I'd fancy sumpin' a bit nicer meself."

A small, compact man of about seventy appeared in the doorway, gray-haired and wearing a muted plaid sportcoat, and looking so much like Kilroy that I saw instantly how Kilroy would age, how his narrow mouth and intense eyes would come to be surrounded by lines, how his body would slacken at the waist. The man's smooth, unworried countenance, though: Kilroy would probably never have that.

At my side Kilroy stood up. "Dad."

The man came forward and offered Kilroy his hand. He was followed by an exquisite woman of about sixty-five, slender, elegant, dressed in what I knew was a weekend outfit, of brown-and-cream checked trousers and a brown cashmere sweater set. Her face was made up lightly, for day—for a day at home when your estranged son might stop by. She hadn't had a face-lift, and the softness at her chin and under her eyes contributed to her beauty—she was one of those women who would always be beautiful.

Kilroy stepped around the coffee table and kissed her pale pink cheek. "Morton Fraser, Barbara Fraser, this is Carrie Bell."

I stood up, and Mr. Fraser and I shook, then Mrs. Fraser offered me her slim, cool hand. "How lovely to meet you," she said, smiling and tipping her head to the side so that her soft, gray-gold hair brushed her shoulder. "It's not often that we get to meet any of Paul's"—she hesitated—"friends."

"So," Mr. Fraser said. "Glad you could stop by." He shot his wife a look, and she shook her head almost imperceptibly. I wondered what the note had said, some kind of summons. We all stood there without quite looking at each other until a man in a dark suit came in and poured drinks, Mrs. Fraser's mouth tightening a little when she saw we already had ours. I wished I weren't wearing jeans.

"How've you been?" Kilroy's father said to him. "It's been some time."

Kilroy nodded. "OK." One corner of his mouth rose into a cockeyed half smile. "Same old, same old." Then he glanced at me and added, quietly, "Well, almost."

Mrs. Fraser leaned forward, her hands clasped together. "Tell us what you do," she said to me. "Do you work or are you a student?"

"I'm a part-time student," I said. "I'm taking courses at Parsons."

"Is that right?" she said. "And what are you studying?"

"Fashion design."

"Right up your alley, Mom," Kilroy said, not unkindly.

His mother smiled. "Do you have *wonderful* fabrics to work with?"

"We pretty much just use muslin," I said. "At this level the emphasis is on learning how to fit and drape."

"I see," she said, nodding. "How interesting."

There was another long silence. Kilroy and I were together on the couch, his parents in separate leather chairs opposite us. Behind them, yet another servant walked past the open doorway, carrying a tall silver vase full of slightly spent roses.

"Well," Mr. Fraser said. "How did you, um—what did you do this weekend?"

Before he'd really stopped talking, Kilroy broke in to answer, his voice a half notch higher and louder than usual, as if he wanted to drown his father out. "Actually, Carrie and I went out to Montauk— rented a car and drove out Friday afternoon. She'd never been there. Traffic wasn't bad at all on the way out, though it got a little nasty coming back in this afternoon."

"And what did you think of Montauk?" Mr. Fraser asked me.

"It was great."

He smiled broadly. "It's one of the best places on earth. How was the weather?"

"Freezing and windy. The sky was so dramatic I kept kind of hoping it would rain."

He beamed. "One of my favorite things is to come inside after getting soaked in a storm on the beach."

"The consummate outdoorsman," Kilroy said, and the two of them chuckled a little.

Mrs. Fraser lifted her glass to her mouth, barely opening her lips enough to admit any of the drink. "Jane called yesterday," she said. She hesitated, and I wondered who Jane was. What was going on?

There was something in the atmosphere that the three of them were aware of, and I couldn't tell if it was just their discomfort with each other or something more.

"How is she?" Kilroy said.

"They're just back from diving off the Caymans. Mac came face to face with a shark."

"How ironic," Kilroy said, and his parents each suppressed a smile.

"She asked about you," Mr. Fraser said.

"I'm sure she did." Kilroy turned to me. "My older sister," he explained, and a look of faint surprise passed between his parents at his having to tell me.

"Lucia wants a pony," Mrs. Fraser went on. "Jane said she drew a picture of herself on horseback and left it on Jane and Mac's bed. She wrote, 'Lucia at age seven wanted to be an equestrienne.' " Mrs. Fraser smiled. " 'Equestrienne.' She got the gender right."

Mr. Fraser leaned forward. "She's quite the wit these days, Paul. Sweet, too, although boy, can you get her dander up. Then she's off to her room and there's no reaching her."

Kilroy snickered. "Must be genetic," he said, and his parents hesitated and then both smiled awkward smiles.

I'd barely touched my drink, but Kilroy's was nearly empty. He put it on the coffee table, carefully centering it on a coaster that was either made of malachite or painted to look as if it were made of malachite— it matched the green walls perfectly. He stood up and said to me, "We'd better go if we're going to make that reservation."

His mother looked up at him. "Reservation?" She glanced at me, a quick look that took in my jeans, my straggly hair. "Where are you going?"

"A place downtown."

"Paul thinks we never go below Fiftieth Street," she said to me, "but in fact one of our favorite places is in SoHo. Do you know Clos de la Violette?"

I shook my head.

"It's lovely," she said.

We were all still for a moment until, abruptly, Kilroy's father stood, too. "Well," he said. "Glad you could come by. Very nice."

Kilroy shrugged. "I'm a sucker for your Scotch."

His father brightened. "Really? Can I send a bottle home with you?" He turned to Mrs. Fraser. "Would you ring?"

"I was kidding," Kilroy said.

Out in the hall a clock chimed seven times, and after a moment Mr. Fraser shook Kilroy's hand again, and he and Mrs. Fraser walked us to the door. The entryway had a black-and-white marble floor and, running up the center, a staircase made of wood that had been stained a glossy black. I looked up to see what I could of the second floor, an open, yellow-walled space with two wide doorways leading deeper into the house.

Mrs. Fraser was waiting to say goodbye. She shook my hand, then put her palm on Kilroy's arm, her thin fingers against his tweedy coat. "Don't be such a stranger," she said lightly, and he flushed and looked down, then reached for the shiny brass doorknob.

29

~

KILROY WAS EDGY and remote that evening, not wanting to talk about the visit—not wanting to talk, period. In the middle of the night I woke to find his place in the bed empty. I crept out to the living room and found him asleep on the couch, huddled under his coat, the reading light on and his book lying near him on the floor. From the bedroom I got his pillow and wedged it between his head and the hard frame of the futon, then went back and lay awake for a long time. I rolled from side to side, wondering at what I'd seen and heard at his parents' house, how it added up to such a breach. They'd seemed so watchful of him, so careful. And their surprise that he'd never mentioned his sister to me. Jane. *They're just back from diving off the Caymans.* Jane and Mac and Lucia. I flipped onto my back. I hated to be awake in the middle of the night, fearful I'd be exhausted all the next day. *Morton Fraser, Barbara Fraser, this is Carrie Bell.* That house, sumptuous and full of servants. His mother had been so pretty. Her cool, slim hand in mine. I turned and turned again. I was still awake at dawn, shapes clarifying in the gathering light.

Then suddenly I woke to the sound of the front door clicking shut.

Eight thirty-three, according to the red numerals of Kilroy's bedside clock. He was on his way to work.

I was muzzy with exhaustion, thick-limbed and trembly. I burrowed back toward sleep, but something pulled me back: the fact that he'd never before left without saying goodbye. If I happened to sleep through his shower, he always came and sat on the bed, touched my shoulder and whispered a plan for later.

I thought of him on the futon in the middle of the night, just his head showing above the heavy wool of his coat. Then his parents again. The way they looked at each other, the way they looked at him. I kicked the blankets off but lay there for a while uncovered before I rubbed my face and sat up.

No note in the kitchen, no coffee in the coffeemaker. Well, he'd probably overslept, too. I wandered out to the living room and pushed his coat away so I could sit on the couch. Minutes after we'd gotten into bed together the night before I'd reached to touch his side, and I'd felt him flinch slightly, then deepen his breath so I'd think he was asleep. I thought of his mother's face, her soft, grayish blond hair. His father's smile. I pulled the coat close and felt in the pocket, half hoping he'd removed the note, but there it was, the stiff, smooth corner waiting for my fingertips. What a terrible thing to do. I pulled it out and looked at it, now seeing that the scrawly engraving on the back flap read BFL. Barbara Something Fraser. And *Paul* written on the front, in girlish, back-slanted printing.

I lifted the flap and pulled out a heavy card.

> *Darling, you must be thinking of the date as much as we are. Won't you come by and have a drink with us? It would mean so much to your father. We'll be home today and tomorrow.*

I slid the card back into the envelope and returned the envelope to Kilroy's coat pocket, arranging the coat haphazardly on the futon. The date on the card had been March 20th, Saturday's date: the note had waited a full day for Kilroy to find it. I wondered what *you must be thinking of the date as much as we are* meant, and why, rather than mail it, she'd come all the way down to Chelsea, maybe stood around until someone came out so she could enter the building and slide it under his door.

So he couldn't miss it, that was why. She'd probably called first: Friday evening, Saturday morning, Saturday noon.

I tried calling him from the brownstone after Patternmaking—at six, when he was usually home, and then at seven, and then, with mounting anxiety, at eight. No answer, and I couldn't leave a message because he didn't have an answering machine, of course. Was he there, letting it ring? I walked over to McClanahan's, the night dark and wet, a light rain misting my hair. The bar was noisy, Joe the bartender busy filling glasses, but Kilroy was nowhere in sight. At his apartment building I buzzed but got no answer, and I was afraid to use my key: I could use it when he wasn't there but not when he was, and I suspected he was. It was after nine when I returned to the brownstone, and I tried phoning one more time. By nine-thirty I was in bed, lying wide awake in the dark again. The house was quiet, and my room—*my* room—had a smell of old dust that was all but foreign to me.

STANDING AT KILROY'S door the next afternoon, I rapped once for good measure, then slid my key into the lock. It was before five, but I wanted to be there when he got home from work: so I wouldn't have another evening like last night, so I wouldn't have to find out how many days in a row he'd fail to answer my phone calls. Inside, a smell of burned toast hit me, and I was about to go into the kitchen when Kilroy appeared from the living room, looking bedraggled in sweatpants and a ragged white T-shirt. *Oh, it's you,* he didn't have to say: his expression said it for him.

"I'm sorry," I said. "I didn't expect—" I stopped and shook my head. "Did you skip work today?"

He lowered his head and moved it up and down without taking his eyes off the floor.

"I'm sorry," I said again. "I thought I'd wait here for you to get home. I was worried about you last night—are you OK?"

He let out a whoosh of breath, then looked up at me and smiled unconvincingly. "Sure."

"I can tell."

He scowled a little, then turned and made his way back to the living room. "Come on in," he said grudgingly, and then he flopped onto the futon, adjusting his position until his head was centered on the bed pillow I'd put there Sunday night. I wondered if he'd slept in the living room last night, too.

"What's going on?" I said.

He drew his knees up and crossed one leg over the other.

"Kilroy?"

"Do you mean 'wuz happenin'?' " he said with a jive accent. "Or 'what is wrong with you?' "

"Either," I said. "Both."

He didn't answer, and I sighed. There were several stacks of books in front of the bookcase, precarious towers of ten or twelve books each. The bookcase itself was partly empty now, two free shelves plus most of a third one, so I knew what he'd been doing: *When it's too full, I weed out whatever's lost its glitter for me.* When it was too full, or when he needed something to occupy his mind.

He reached for *Contemporaneity and Consequences,* the book he'd been reading since before Montauk—I had no idea what it was about. He opened it and raised it to his face.

"I smell burned toast," I said.

He lowered the book and stared at me. "Any other observations?"

I noticed his coat just then, in a heap on the floor behind the futon, and when he saw me looking at it, fear clawed at my stomach. Could he know I'd read the note? Was that what this was all about? But no, he couldn't, there was no way.

"Do you want me to leave?" I said.

"Whatever."

I turned away and moved down the hall and into the kitchen, where three or four plates of toast crumbs were crowded onto the counter, a dish of shapeless butter nearby. In the bedroom the blinds were drawn, and the bed was a mess, sheets wrinkled and twisted, pillows hugged into awkward shapes and abandoned. There was a half-empty coffee mug on the floor, another plate of toast crumbs. I skirted the foot of the bed to sit on my side. My photograph of the Parisian rooftop leaned against the back of the kitchen chair I used as a bedside table, and I picked it up, admiring in the half-light the perfect match between the gray paint of the frame and the gray roof of the building. I remembered the night he'd given it to me, how happy we'd been.

I heard his footsteps and turned to see him standing in the doorway, his book closed around his finger. "Want to get some dinner?" he said. "I could eat Chinese."

I put the picture down and buried my face in my hands—I didn't know whether to laugh or cry. *I could eat Chinese*—as if this were a normal night in the course of our relationship.

"What?" he said, coming around the bed to stand before me.

I looked up at him and shook my head. "How can you act like nothing's happened? You honestly want to go eat *Chinese* food?"

He held up both palms in protest. "Whoa, whoa—Italian would be fine, too."

I slammed my fist into the mattress. "Are you insane? Or am I, because there's something really wrong here and I don't even feel like we're on the same planet."

His expression darkened and he turned toward the window, slatted blinds covering the glass. I could see his face in quarter profile, his mouth working over his teeth. A smell of sweat drifted off him.

"What are you so upset about?" I said.

He lifted his hands away from his legs and then let them fall again. Still facing the window he said, "Nothing."

"Kilroy, this is *me*. You were upset Sunday night after we left your parents, and you still are, and I just feel *completely shut out*."

"I'm sorry," he said dully. Then he turned to face me. "All right?" he added, his voice tightening. "I'm sorry I subjected you to it."

"It was *fine*," I said. "They were perfectly nice—that's not at all what I mean, and you know it. I called you a million times last night, I came by. What's wrong?"

He exhaled hard and looked away. "It's just difficult for me to see them," he said. "I have problems with them. We just— Well, we're very different, that's all."

I shook my head. "No, it's not."

He stared at me for a moment and then turned around again, back to the window. After a while he separated the blinds with his thumb and forefinger and peered out. Dust motes swarmed in the bar of weak light that shone in. Watching him there, his back to me, I had a sudden sense of how it must be for his parents to have him living nearby—so close and yet so closed off.

"Kilroy?" I said.

He turned around. Against the blinds he looked pinned, trapped—like someone in a lineup.

"Why do you stay here?"

Color rose into his cheeks, and he looked away. "Do you mean why don't I take my obviously huge trust fund and buy a nice co-op on Central Park West?"

"No," I exclaimed. "God. I would never ask a question like that. I know I've said before that I figured your family had a lot of money, but what you do or don't do with it is none of my business."

"I try not to use it," he said evenly. "That's why. I'm not that much of an asshole."

I rolled my eyes. "You're not an asshole at all."

He smiled. "Of course I am."

"Kilroy." He looked so forlorn standing there, his sloppy T-shirt and his shaky smile. "You can't mean that."

"I'm not about to win any Mr. Congeniality awards," he said bitterly.

I got up and went to him, but when I got near he drew back, as if he were afraid I'd touch him. I stopped short, a sick, hot feeling coming over me. I wanted to touch him—I wanted him to want me to. "Mr. Congeniality would be a big, boring yawn," I said.

"Mike was Mr. Congeniality, wasn't he?"

"This has nothing to do with Mike."

"But he was, wasn't he? A nice guy?" A frown pulled at the corners of his mouth. "That's what I've always figured."

" 'A nice guy,' " I said. "That's what you say about someone you don't know. Mike was—Mike *is* a person. Sure, he's nice—how many people do you know who aren't nice?"

Kilroy shook his head. "Forget it," he said, scratching his bristly jaw. "Let's change the subject."

I sighed and looked away. To what? We weren't doing well with any of the subjects at hand. Maybe we just weren't doing well, period. My worries from the junk shop on Long Island came rushing back. Was it true that we didn't really work in the world, just in isolated, protected pockets of it? Mike and I had moved easily between our private and public lives: we were us at a party as much as in my apartment. Out of nowhere I remembered a beery frat blowout between the end of finals and graduation: we got separated for a while, and when I saw him again I was sitting on the steps up to the second floor talking to a girl from one of my classes. He was a little drunk, and he looked up at me and held out his arms in a way that I knew constituted an invitation to dance. He stood below us—tall, strong, hair curling in the humid party air, handsome in an impish, grown-up-boy way—and I felt a rush of pleasure at the fact that he was mine.

"What *did* you mean before?" Kilroy said. "When you asked why I stay here?"

I looked up. He was watching me curiously, and I wondered what he saw in me: a fetching small-town girl who'd been willing to break the heart of a nice guy.

"In New York," I said.

"Oh," he said, smiling a crooked smile, "that's an easy one. I like the traffic noise."

I sighed heavily and moved away from him, shaking my head. I sat on the bed again. On the floor I spotted a stray green sock I'd thought I'd lost, and I bent over for it, then picked a clump of dust off it and flicked it away.

Kilroy watched me from the window, his eyes narrowed, one forefinger laid along his jawline. He stared for so long that I started to feel nervous, wondering what would happen if he kept staring without speaking. How long would we stay like this? Apart, silent. My hands felt heavy in my lap.

At last he shifted and cleared his throat. "You know how you just got in your car and drove, that night in September? You just locked up your apartment and took out your garbage and drove? Well, sometimes it's just not possible to do that, or it's not going to solve anything. I don't see my parents much, and because of that it's hard when I do. And, to turn it around, because it's hard when I see them, I don't see them much. I'm sorry about last night—I should have answered the phone. I should have, but I didn't, and that's where we are now, and I don't really know what else to say about it. Either we go on or we don't. I can't be someone else, much as you might want me to be— much as *I* might want to be. So what I'd like to do is clean up and then go get something to eat." He gave me a pleading look. "OK? Please?"

I nodded. I was less hungry than tired, exhausted to the bone, but I understood that he couldn't say any more and that we had to leave the apartment for a while. I made the bed while he showered, and then, heading for the front door, we walked down the hall together, our sides jostling awkwardly.

30

~

DURING THE NEXT few weeks Kilroy was mostly his funny, sardonic self, but his overall demeanor had darkened, and the darkness was just under the surface. He complained about things he'd read in the newspaper, or ranted about something he'd seen on the street—two women, say, who stood blocking the sidewalk, shopping bags at their feet, never a thought for the people who had to step around them. Spring arrived with a cold, clear wind that whipped the sky blue and left behind it air that was softer and warmer than it had been in months. I was itching to go out walking, but Kilroy declined, instead spending whole weekend afternoons inside reading, the newly empty shelves of his bookcase gradually filling with thick histories and multivolume biographies. It grew hard to get his attention: he was on the couch one evening, reading a book about Gothic architecture, and I called his name four separate times without his hearing me. Finally I sat down and ran a finger up the bottom of his foot, and he startled so dramatically that he dropped the book and lifted his arms and legs in fright.

"Carrie, Jesus. What?"

"I said your name four times."

"Well, sorry—I was absorbed in my book."

It sounds as if he were snippy, but he wasn't, not really: he was remote, vague, but only for the exact amount of time that I could stand it. Just as I'd be on the verge of true frustration, he'd pull out of it, come stand behind me and rub my shoulders, suggest dinner, a movie, a game of pool at McClanahan's. It was uncanny how he knew my limits, as if I emitted something he could smell or faintly hear. We slept closer than ever, our legs entangled, our hands tucked around each other, but waking in the morning he was careful to reclaim himself, pull his arms away and roll onto his back before speaking to me or touching me again.

One early morning—very early, barely dawn—I got up to use the bathroom, and when I came back he was facing my side of the bed, eyes open. He reached for me, and I moved close and felt how hard he was against my leg, then between my thighs. He pulled me on top of him and onto him in something close to one fluid motion, and while we moved I pressed the side of my face against his, first seeking the abrasion of his stubble and then something more. I pushed my face hard against his and he pushed back, and we kept on like that until we were done and my face actually hurt.

Much later I woke to feel the sheets cool beside me. I rolled over, expecting an empty bed, but there he was, lying so far away that I had to reach to touch him. He was on his back, just staring up into space, and when he felt my hand on his arm he jumped a little, then reached up and tucked his hands behind his head, his elbows pointing at the wall behind us.

"Hi," I said.

"Hi."

I touched him again, on the side, but he didn't react—didn't look at me, roll over to face me, anything.

"What were you dreaming at five o'clock this morning?" I said.

"Nothing."

"Nothing, you don't remember? Or nothing, you're not going to say?"

He shrugged. "Nothing, I don't remember—I never remember my dreams."

"Never?"

"Only the most boring, banal ones. I had this recurring dream for about six years where I'd be walking along a road, walking and walking, and finally I'd arrive at this little store where I'd buy a pad of paper and a pen. After paying I'd walk to the door, then I'd suddenly turn around because I needed something else, and that's when I'd wake up." He looked over and smiled at me. "See, you're so bored you're not even paying attention."

"Yes, I am."

"No, you were definitely thinking of something else."

It was true: my mind had drifted off, but only to the way we'd been earlier and how he'd erased it. It was as if we'd sent emissaries to have sex, the two of them urgent and unacquainted—and one of them unwilling to report back. It made me think of my first time with him, the hesitation and the ecstatic falling into it. Then I found myself thinking of Mike, of our first time, at Picnic Point—the trees tall around us and the smell of the earth, the way the beach towel rucked up beneath me. Afterward he told me it had been very different from what he'd expected, but he couldn't say how. Having done it once, though, the state of not having done it yet dissolved—he said it didn't even feel the same to be aroused. Remembering that, I wondered: Did Mike ever have sexual dreams about me now? Was it possible to have a sexual dream if you couldn't have a sexual feeling? We hadn't talked in three months, but his ring was still on my finger. I thought of how he must look in bed, sleeping or not, in what used to be the den, his paralyzed body arrayed before him, and my mind made its reluctant way back to the first night in Montauk with Kilroy, when I'd lain motionless on the bed and let him make love to me as if I were unable to move a muscle. As if I'd become Mike.

ONE SATURDAY I convinced Kilroy to go for a walk. It was April now, and all of New York was out—the hip and the destitute, but also the people who'd been in hiding all winter: families with small children, the very old. It felt good to be out walking, the sun warming us and warming also the people we passed, so that they seemed slowed somehow, enlarged and happy. Kilroy, who usually strode along quickly and purposefully whether he had a purpose or not, moved today at more of an amble, and even stopped occasionally to tilt his face to the sun. As we made our way downtown I had an idea that we were walking toward ourselves, who we were together and who we could be.

At the corner of Sixth Avenue and Houston, he stopped to watch a bunch of guys playing basketball in a little chain-link park. I stopped, too. As we watched, one of the players—not particularly tall, but lean in his sweats, and fast—stole the ball and dribbled to the far side of the court, where he fired a long shot that hit the rim with a clank and then fell through the netless hoop.

"Nice," Kilroy exclaimed. He turned to me. "Imagine what that feels like. Having that power."

"Did you ever play any sports?"

He smiled. "Baseball. I wanted to be a baseball player when I grew up, seriously. I played second base five, six months a year from when I was seven until I got to high school. I had a good arm, but the main thing was I was fast. Not on my feet—I was fast enough like that, but I mean fast-reacting. I'd see a ball coming and I'd already be thinking about my tag or my throw. I was a solid hitter, too, nothing great, but I held up my end. What a game. I loved it."

"So why'd you stop?" I said. "What happened in high school?"

He shrugged. "You know. Things happen. I sort of lost interest."

"But you loved it."

He shrugged again.

Kilroy playing baseball was an entirely new thing to fit into the picture. It was surprisingly easy to see him as an intense little second baseman, skinny in those tiny white pants, a narrowing of concentration in his eyes. Eight, nine years old. Picturing him in high school was a lot harder. I wondered what he wasn't telling me about why he'd stopped. Was it like Mike and hockey, like Mike's decision our first year at the U not to go out? He would have made the team, but he would have been a supporter, not a star. Was that what had happened to Kilroy?

We headed across Houston, turned, and then turned again onto MacDougal, where we happened past the bookstore where the woman had stood behind me and said *the complacence of extreme beauty*. Squinting through the plate glass into the dark recesses of the store, I wondered who she was, where she was now. The connections among strangers in New York lay over the city like a faint grid, fragile as the strands of a spider's web.

We made our way to the Hudson, where we walked along the crowded riverfront walkway of Battery Park City. There were people zooming along on Rollerblades, people with dogs. Kilroy pointed out Ellis Island and the Statue of Liberty, as small in the distance as one of the replicas I'd seen for sale around the city. Color leached from the sky and the warmth of the day receded, but we kept going, through the chilly narrow canyons of Wall Street. I was surprised by the massive form of the Brooklyn Bridge suddenly looming overhead, and I stopped to marvel at the sheer enormity of it.

"We've never walked across it, have we?" Kilroy said.

I shook my head.

A big smile took shape on his face. "Ready for a thrill?"

I glanced at my watch. We'd been walking for three or four hours already.

"Come on," he said. "This can't wait."

A separate pedestrian walkway ran across the center of the bridge, above traffic level. Couples and families strolled along, a few lone businessmen heading back to Brooklyn after a Saturday at the office. The bridge itself was astonishing, the powerful stone towers, the four huge suspension cables, the dozens and dozens of smaller cables that seemed thin as thread as they soared upward and away.

"Pretty great, huh?" Kilroy said. "I can't believe I never brought you here before."

We had stopped, and I bent my neck back and looked up, granite and filigree against the fading, cloud-streaked blue. When I straightened out again Kilroy was watching me, his eyes crinkled against the lowering sun. The expression on his face was—there was no other word for it—soft. His cheeks were rounded, his mouth supple. I had an idea that what he felt was less about me than about himself, some sense of wonder that he was doing this, showing his places to a woman. Smiling, I reached up and touched him just below his eye, and he took hold of my hand and guided my fingertips over his face— down his cheek, around his mouth, and across his closed eyelids. He let go of my hand and looked at me for a moment, then took hold of my shoulders and pulled me close. Standing there with him, I felt the space between us collapse, the feeling of the last few weeks finally thinning and disappearing. Our heads together, I lifted my hand to his hair, tangled and bristly as I stroked it.

A little later we started walking again. In Brooklyn Heights we went to the Promenade and looked back at Manhattan, the downtown skyline sidelit by the setting sun. It was cold now, and we were both gloveless, shivering in light jackets. We found a bar, the Royal Ascot, and drank beers under a scarred dartboard while Frank Sinatra sang from an ancient jukebox. A pair of thick-bodied men in their forties stood near us holding pints of Guinness, foamy and black as espresso.

It was dark when we left. We found a subway station and went down to the platform. We stood there for a long time, until we'd been waiting for so long that we had to wonder just how long it had been. The platform filled steadily behind us. An indecipherable announcement flickered over the loudspeaker, and a groan went through the crowd. Fifteen more minutes went by, twenty. Finally I heard the train rumbling, still far off, and from behind people pressed against me. They were mostly dressed for Saturday night in the city, pushing forward with their perfume smells, their cold leather jackets. I reached for Kilroy's hand a moment too late and we were separated. The train came in with a roar, and before the doors had opened I was pushed to the side, my shoe nearly twisting off in the process. The car was crowded already, too full for everyone who wanted on. I stepped across the opening between the platform and the train and somehow got squeezed to a position between a seat edge and a tall man with sausage breath. I had no idea where Kilroy was. "Stand clear the doors," the conductor said, and the doors slid shut. Lurching a little, we took off and quickly gathered speed. I could see a side of head here, a shoulder there—not much more than that. Then there was a shift—someone squeezing into a new pocket of space—and suddenly there was Kilroy, ten feet away, his hand up for a pole. He was in profile, staring at the black window. I remembered a game I used to play, back in high school, when Mike and I were still new: I'd look at him from across a room—the cafeteria, or a class we had together, or even the lobby of a movie theater—and try to surprise myself into seeing him afresh. What about him? I'd wonder. What would he be like? I closed my eyes and shook my head a little. I thought that with the train noise and the people and the smells I might just be able to catch myself reacting to Kilroy as if he were a stranger. I thought that would tell me something. But when I opened my eyes he'd found me, and as I watched he smiled at me, then raised his hand and waved.

IT SEEMS TO me that we learn each other in stages: facts first, meanings later, like explorers who stumble on to bodies of water without knowing at first whether they've encountered fog-shrouded rivers or vast oceans. We press on until we know, but as we go something is lost: the new becomes old, and then taken for granted, and then forgotten. With Kilroy I wanted both to speed my way along and also to hold on to each separate moment of revelation.

That was what had gone wrong with Mike. I'd known everything about him but had failed to preserve the pleasure of discovery. Instead, I'd absorbed him. The landscape of his past, his mind: they were my landscapes, I'd traveled them so often. They were like Madison itself, the lakes pleasing and familiar, the Union terrace, the tree-lined neighborhoods where my friends lived. It was the same with Jamie. Jamie *was* my childhood to me: the plum tree in her parents' backyard, the ten-block walk from my mother's house, every Saturday afternoon at the mall. She was a certain smell, of mix cakes combined with Tide, that you got at the precise moment that you passed from the Fletchers' mud room into the kitchen if the door down to the basement happened to be open and Mrs. Fletcher had baked that day, as she nearly always had.

Our senior year of high school, Jamie and I talked and talked about whether or not we should room together at the U. We were in the Fletchers' kitchen picking at her mother's confetti cake, or we were whispering in the school library, or we were sitting at a hockey game watching Mike and Rooster sail across the ice while the crowd around us yelled. She wanted us to room together, and I saw the appeal—just move my life a mile away, Jamie in my room and Mike right there— but even then I felt there was something not quite right about it, something too easy. I thought our lives should change, that there should be a surprise ahead. Finally I said no, convinced it would be better to go into it like everyone else: if not without a safety net, then with less of one.

She had a hard time freshman year. Her courses were too difficult, and she had complaints about her roommate, a private-school girl from the North Shore of Chicago who Jamie claimed was a snob. The great dream of college was still outside her grasp—she was still herself, still Jamie. Late one November afternoon I returned to my dorm and found her lying in the corridor outside my room, actually lying on the grungy carpet, her backpack under her head like a pillow. Walking down the hall from the elevator, I thought she'd put herself in the position most likely to arouse my sympathy, although I wasn't being as cold-blooded as it sounds: it was more that I figured she needed me, was letting me know as best she could. When I got closer, though, and she didn't raise herself up on one elbow and look at me with red-rimmed eyes, I began to wonder. Was she hurt? Was she sick? I picked up my pace a little, and it turned out—it turned out she was *asleep.* Lying there at four o'clock in the afternoon, in a highly trafficked corridor of a busy undergraduate dorm, asleep. It gave me the strangest feeling, seeing her like that: honored and disturbed. I'd forgotten all about it until she called me in New York and asked me to come home.

It was a few days after my walk with Kilroy, and I was at the brownstone, fresh out of the shower and standing in my room getting dressed when Greg knocked on my door and told me I had a phone call. She wasn't crying at first—she said my name clearly—but then she started, a deep, terrible weeping. I said, "What? What is it?" but she cried on, and I thought it must be that she'd been dumped by Bill, the whole thing over before she'd ever gotten a chance to tell me about it.

But it had nothing to do with Bill. Her sister Lynn had been assaulted—in the parking lot of a bar on the far west side, beaten up by a man driving a Cutlass. She had a black eye, bruises by her mouth, *fingermarks on her neck.* The Alley, that was the name of the bar, a seedy place out by the restaurant where she worked. And Jamie's mother—Jamie's mother had flipped out. Jamie was hysterical, but that was the essence of it, and I didn't know what to say, because all I could think was that the Alley was the place I'd seen Lynn all tarted up. Standing out in front, her hair teased, her face so made up that she had to have been asking for something: trouble, excitement, rescue, *something*. I'd known it then, as surely as I'd been too self-absorbed to do more than note it and move on. Listening to Jamie cry, I remembered Lynn sitting next to me in my car, defiant and tipsy, her chubby legs and her big silver hoop earrings: *Don't tell Jamie,* she'd said, and I hadn't. I hadn't.

"Oh, Jamie," I said. "Oh, God."

"I'm scared," she sobbed. "I'm really scared."

"I know. I'm sorry—I'm so, so sorry."

I heard her blowing her nose, the sound of the tissue brushing against the phone.

"I need you," she said. "I know I haven't called you at all, and we've been, like, distant, but—" She started crying again. "I *need* you. Could you come? Could you come home?"

I'd been standing, the phone on the floor at my feet, and now I moved to the futon, pulling the phone after me like a recalcitrant little dog.

"Carrie?" she said.

"You mean now?"

"I was thinking tomorrow. Or this weekend?"

Tomorrow was Piero's class—one of his former students, now a knitwear designer for a major label, was coming to talk to us. *She's fabulous,* Piero had said. *She's* my *role model.* I didn't want to miss her visit, and beyond that I simply didn't have the money—a plane ticket on such short notice would cost a fortune. It was a bad time. That's what I said to Jamie: "It's a bad time for me right now. But I can talk—can't we just talk on the phone?"

There was a long silence. When she finally spoke, I knew I'd breached whatever remained of our friendship. Very coldly, with no trace of tears, she said, "I should have known. I don't know why I even asked. Someone who dumps her boyfriend right after he breaks his neck? Forget it, of course you wouldn't come." And then she hung up on me.

PART THREE

~

KILROY

WAS HERE

31

~

FROM THE PLANE I could see the end of winter coming. The snow at the edges of the fields looked tired and gray, and the farmland south of Madison was black with wet, cut into squares by county roads. I imagined I could smell the earth, the scent of it ripening day by day with the thaw.

I took a cab from the airport. The buildings I passed seemed squat, the streets wide open and empty. It was the middle of a Thursday afternoon, and after the morning spent flying and the previous night spent making arrangements to leave, I felt dazed. The quiet in the cab had a dreamy feel, just me and the driver sweeping across a barren landscape. I looked out the window and saw the turn to my apartment, but I didn't feel anything, not a bit of longing to see my old place.

My mother's house gazed blankly at the street. I dropped my bag in the front hall and went into the kitchen. The chairs were pushed close to the table, the salt and pepper centered perfectly. On the refrigerator, a magnet held her grocery list: rice, tomato paste, seventy-five-watt bulbs.

I opened the refrigerator and reached for a carton of orange juice.

I drank a glassful and put the glass in the sink, then changed my mind and washed it properly, setting it in the drainboard. My mother had a dishwasher but she used it rarely, only when she had company.

I went to the phone and dialed Jamie at her parents' house. I didn't have much hope that she'd speak to me, and she didn't: she hung up the moment she heard my voice, as she had six times now, four yesterday and two today. I called Kilroy.

"I was just thinking of you," he said.

"What a coincidence."

"Not really."

We both laughed, and I thought of how he'd kissed me that morning on Seventh Avenue, kissed me and said, *OK, go now.*

"So?" he said. "You're there?"

"Yep. Jamie just hung up on me again."

"Before or after you could say you were back?"

"Before."

"So what's plan B?"

"Go over there, I guess."

"Keep me posted."

"I will."

I hung up and left the kitchen. It would be a cold walk to the Fletchers', and I stood in the front hall and looked out the window, not wanting to leave. Ten minutes, I thought, five, and I turned and climbed the stairs, then wandered around my mother's second floor. Her bedroom caught the late-afternoon light, a bar of weak sunlight lying on her neatly made bed. I went over and sat down. The house was cold and I tucked my hands inside my sweater, then pulled them out at once, frozen by my own touch. I lay back on the bed. I'd been away less than a day but my body felt bereft of Kilroy, a jangle of untouched skin. I wanted his hands on me, his scratchy face against my bare shoulder. He hadn't understood my coming back. "Why not write her a long letter?" he'd said.

It was getting dark when I left my mother's, the early-evening dark of early spring, a high, cool dark coming down from the trees. An eerie silence. The Fletchers' house was ten blocks away, but I didn't pass a single person on the sidewalk. At one point a car drove by, its lights flashing over me for a moment, and when it was past I stopped walking and closed my eyes, overwhelmed by how still the evening was, how vast.

The house was completely dark; even the porch light was off. I used the brass pineapple knocker to knock, then rang the doorbell for good measure. No one was home. From my purse I withdrew a little pad of paper and scribbled Jamie a note. *I came home. Please call me at my mother's.*

When I got back my mother still wasn't there, and I went into the kitchen and put a pot of water on to boil. One of Kilroy's favorite things to make when there didn't seem to be anything at hand was spaghetti with olive oil and garlic, and I found a box of spaghetti in the pantry, even some fresh parsley in the crisper to sprinkle on top. When the water boiled I turned it to low, not wanting to cook the noodles until she'd arrived.

But she didn't. After a while I decided she was having dinner with a friend, and I cooked a single finger's worth of spaghetti and sat at the table, looking through the morning paper as I ate. Back in New York, Kilroy was reading in his living room, or maybe reading in bed. Or would he have gone to McClanahan's? I didn't like to think of him there, sitting alone at the bar while the place grew noisier and noisier.

My mother came in a little before ten, her hand going to her throat in the split second between seeing me and seeing it was me. "Oh, Jesus," she said. "Good Christ, you scared me."

"Sorry."

We hugged, and I smelled the moisturizer she'd been using since I was a child. She had her London Fog raincoat on, the belt knotted around her tiny waist. She set her briefcase down. "Is this because of Jamie?"

"You know?"

She gave me a tired smile. "I've been at the hospital since six."

It turned out Jamie had called her the previous day, even before she'd called me—called for advice, for help. My mother and I sat in the kitchen and she told me all about it, how Jamie'd phoned her from the hospital, how my mother'd cancelled the rest of her appointments so she could go. "I guess things have been difficult at the Fletchers' for a long time," my mother said. "Apparently Mrs. Fletcher's been taking Valium for a while, and when Lynn started waitressing last summer and coming home so late, she began having a drink or two to calm herself down while she waited." My mother shook her head.

"What?"

"It's a bad combination. That's—that's pretty well known. I think there are warnings on the Valium label."

I wondered what this had to do with what had happened to Lynn. Guiltily, I remembered Jamie's complaints about Lynn and her mother. I remembered the summer day when I ran into Jamie and Mrs. Fletcher: how vague Mrs. Fletcher seemed; and how, watching her drive away, Jamie asked if I thought she was *on* something. I'd thought she was kidding.

"Anyway," my mother continued, "when Lynn came home night before last and Mrs. Fletcher saw her, she broke down. Lynn was— well, she had a black eye, among other things, and she was hysterical, of course. Mr. Fletcher was out of town, and Mrs. Fletcher started with the Valium and the drinking, too much of both. Lynn didn't call Jamie home until yesterday morning, and by then Mrs. Fletcher was unconscious. Jamie had great presence of mind: she called an ambulance, found the meds—I'm not sure I would have guessed Jamie had it in her, but she did everything right. She called the police and they told her to get Lynn to the hospital, so the two of them drove over, about five minutes behind the ambulance. When I got there Mrs. Fletcher was in one room having her stomach pumped, and Lynn was being examined in another room, and Jamie was going back and forth between them."

I stared at my mother. Talking to Jamie, I hadn't understood the gravity of Mrs. Fletcher's situation. "Are you saying Mrs. Fletcher tried to kill herself?"

My mother frowned. "Whatever her intentions were, Jamie saved her life. The doctor I talked to said another hour or two and it might have been too late."

"Oh, my God," I said. "My God." I was horrified. I could hardly believe how cold I'd been to Jamie on the phone. *It's not a good time.* Jamie had been right to hang up on me, right to refuse to listen when I called back. "How is she now?"

"Mrs. Fletcher?"

"Jamie."

My mother shrugged. "As well as can be expected. Bill was there with her tonight."

I looked away, and my mother reached across the table and put her hand on mine. "Is it strange that life's gone on without you?"

I nodded. Strange but inevitable. My life had gone on, too. For a moment I wished Kilroy were with me taking it all in: so I wouldn't have to explain it to him, so he'd just know. How would I be able to convey what it felt like to sit across from my mother knowing she knew Jamie better now than I did?

"How's Mrs. Fletcher?" I asked her.

"They're watching her. I don't know what's going to happen." She bit her lip and sighed. She looked tired: she'd grown her hair out, and it made her face look smaller, more lined than I would have expected.

"What about Lynn? Do you know how she is?"

My mother frowned. "It's a long road back from something like this. I guess she's OK physically."

I nodded, nearly unable to ask my next question. "Was she raped?"

"Apparently not. I think you should hear about it from Jamie, though." My mother gave me a piercing look, and I wondered if she knew Jamie'd asked me to come home. Did she know I'd said no? She licked her lips, then stood and got a glass from a cabinet. She filled it at the sink and drank, her back still to me.

"I blew it when she called me," I said. "She asked me to come home and I said I couldn't."

My mother turned around, her face full of compassion now. She knew.

"I've tried her a million times since then. She won't speak to me. What can I do?"

My mother set her water glass on the table and then came around to my side. She gave me a pat on the shoulder. "I think you know."

THE NEXT MORNING, I put on a pair of the black pants I'd made in the fall and the velvet shirt I'd bought in January, and I set off for the Fletchers'.

There were no cars out front, only Mrs. Fletcher's station wagon at the end of the driveway. I tapped on the front door, then went around the back and tried the mud room. No one responded, but the door wasn't locked, and I pushed it open and quietly went in. Right away I saw Jamie's winter coat on a hook, and the sight of it galvanized me, sent me past the basement stairs and right into the kitchen, which smelled ever so slightly of—what was it?—cornbread.

It was after eleven—after twelve in New York. Kilroy was in Midtown this week, was probably at this very moment buying a hotdog from a street vendor. Before leaving my mother's I'd spoken with him briefly, nothing more to report than Mrs. Fletcher's situation; from his short silences I knew that he was frustrated, that what he really wanted to know was when I'd return.

I crept up the back stairs, then tiptoed to Jamie's old room. The door was all but closed, and I drummed my fingers against it softly, pushing it open at the same time.

She was in bed, asleep. Bunched in a fetal position, knees bent, arms held close to her body. Her wrists were so tightly flexed that her knuckles touched her chest, her chin the backs of her hands. She had scooted down below her pillow, and it lay above her head like a crazy stuffed hat.

I stepped in. Jamie's girlhood bedroom was as familiar as my own. There was twining ivy wallpaper, cream with dark green, accented by clusters of dark purple berries. She'd gotten it when we were about ten, and I was insane with envy: for the wallpaper, and for the gold-edged white furniture and the four-poster bed.

From downstairs I heard a noise, and I crossed the carpet to the window and saw Jamie's car parked out front, where I was certain it hadn't been five minutes ago. I made my way out of her room and down the front stairs to the dining room, where I found her middle sister, Mixie, sitting at the table with a cardboard cup of coffee in hand and a vaguely bored look on her face that didn't change a bit when she saw me.

"I barged in," I said.

She shrugged. She had always been pretty but was beautiful now, in a sulky, self-conscious way. She had a perfect, tanning-salon tan, and as we looked at one another she brushed a silky strand of hair away from her face. "Did she talk to you?"

"She's still asleep." I pulled out the chair opposite her and sat down. She'd spent last summer in California, which meant I hadn't seen her in almost a year. "How are you?"

"How do you think?" She took a sip of her coffee, and I wished I had one, too—something to hold.

I said, "I was really a jerk the other day but I'm here now. Do you think she'll talk to me?"

She shrugged. "I don't know. It's not just about the other day."

"What do you mean?"

"Lynn told us about running into you out at that bar last summer. She was sure you'd told Jamie. She was hurt Jamie didn't seem to care."

I heaved a big sigh. "She made me promise not to tell," I said lamely.

"Jamie thinks you should've anyway."

I turned and looked out the front window. A crow hopped across the sidewalk, then stopped to peck at something. A moment later, a light blue Oldsmobile went past, just like Mrs. Mayer's. Was I going to call Mike while I was here? How could I? How could I not?

Mixie reached for her purse and fished out a pack of cigarettes. She shook one up and lit it coolly, blowing the first smoke toward the ceiling. "So how's New York?" she said.

"Great."

"I have to say you look amazing. That shirt—I never knew you had it in you."

"I didn't."

We watched each other for a time, Mixie's eyes wide, curious, unrevealing. She turned away first. She curled a lock of hair around her finger and then reached for a section of newspaper lying at the far end of the table.

"So what happened?" I said.

"Happened?"

"To Lynn."

She let go of the newspaper and shook her head. "Uh-uh."

"Mixie."

She stared at a point somewhere over my left shoulder and took a long drag on her cigarette.

"Please?"

"Why should I tell you?"

I looked down at the table. Why indeed.

She blew out a stream of smoke. "She had a customer at one of her tables who kept flirting with her. He was alone and she figured, *Poor guy, must be lonely, I'll give him a little sugar with his dinner*. So she flirted a little, and he asked her out for a drink afterward, and he came on to her, and she freaked out, and he—" Abruptly Mixie broke off.

"He what?"

"He beat her up! He gave her a black eye! He hit her on the face and the arms, you should see the bruises on her arms from where he was holding her. And then he forced her into his car and made her suck him off."

I clamped my hands over my nose and mouth.

Mixie gave me a fierce look. "No one knows the last part except me and Jamie, so don't tell, OK? Not even your mom."

"I won't," I said, shaking my head. "I promise." I stared at her. "That's awful."

"Yeah."

We looked away from one another. *My fault*. That's what I was thinking: it was my fault. "I'm really sorry," I said.

From upstairs there came a sudden insistent chirping: Jamie's alarm clock.

"You should go," Mixie said. "I mean, whatever, you can stay, but she was up really late last night and I don't think . . ." Her voice trailed off and I stood. I watched her for a moment, sitting there with her cigarette, her golden forearms resting on the table. They weren't the forearms of someone in the middle of something like this. Her hair wasn't the hair of someone in the middle of something like this. The glow of trauma: it was as missing from her as it had been present in Jamie, even asleep. Somehow everything was resting on Jamie, a huge, terrible weight.

I walked back to my mother's. The only sound was the tap of my New York ankle boots against the sidewalk. The last time I'd seen Jamie had been a day or two before I'd left for New York: we got iced coffee to go and then walked over to Lake Mendota and sat together on a bench. What was about to happen between me and Mike sat between us, huge and unspeakable. She couldn't bear my not talking about it, and I couldn't bear her wanting me to. "I have to get going," I said after just four or five minutes, and when I held out my palm for her she grudgingly put hers on mine but wouldn't meet my eye.

At my mother's I called Kilroy. "Mixie?" he said. "What kind of name is that?"

32

~

IN THE AFTERNOON I walked to State Street. It was a long way, a route I'd rarely walked, and though I was used to walking for hours in New York, this tired me out—blocks and blocks of empty driveways, then the bleak, colorless stretch of Campus Drive.

I went to Cobra Copy first. Inside, a handful of students leaned against the counter while behind them the giant machines roared out copy after copy. As I'd expected Jamie wasn't there, but I got her schedule from a cashier, who told me she'd cancelled several shifts but was due back tomorrow.

Everyone looked dull on the street. It had warmed up a little, and coats were open, revealing tired jeans, ratty sweatshirts and dark plaid shirts. Hairstyles seemed arrived at by default, girls with their hair hanging by their faces, guys with wayward bangs and errant curls along the collarline. How funny that I'd ended up with the one man in New York who looked as if he could live in Madison. Actually, he did and he didn't: his hair and his clothes, yes, but he had a face that was pure New York, pointed and intent. And his walk was New York, head down, no eye contact, move, move.

Here, people strolled. I made my way past them up the street. I glanced in shop windows, but they held nothing to invite me—not after SoHo.

At a cart on the corner of Johnson I bought a bunch of daffodils and headed back to the Fletchers'. Jamie's car was in the driveway now, parked just behind her mother's wagon.

This time I went straight to the back. I knocked on the mud room door and then peered through the window, trying to see into the kitchen. I could hear a radio playing, the bright sounds of some pop song.

Jamie appeared. She stopped when she saw it was me, then came forward and opened the door.

"Jamie," I said.

She stood there staring, her blond hair tucked severely behind her ears, her face pale and tired-looking. She wore a plain black sweater with a U neck, and her collarbones appeared bony and fragile.

"Jamie," I said again. I held the flowers out, the yellow bright between us, then dropped them to my side when she didn't react. "I'm so sorry. About everything. I was horrible not to say I'd come right away."

Her face split in two, the top half flushed and teary while her mouth screwed into a knot and her chin tightened. I felt terrible looking at her, not just for the current situation but for all the months of being out of touch.

"Can I come in?" I said. "Can we talk?"

"No," she said, and she pushed the door closed and went back into the kitchen.

I started for my mother's. The daffodils were in a rubber band, and as I walked I pulled them loose and tossed them into the gutter one by one. I felt like Hansel and Gretel marking a pathway, the long line between where I should be and where I was.

THAT EVENING MY mother took me out to dinner. Without my saying so she seemed to understand what had gone on with Jamie, and we talked instead about New York and Parsons, the world of possibility I saw now in the world of clothes.

"Clothes are so closely aligned to who we are to ourselves," she said, and she went on to relate a story of how, as a teenager in the late sixties, she developed a covert obsession with lace-front hip-huggers—first any she came upon in fashion magazines and later an actual pair she saw on a Saturday trip into Madison. "I guess I thought they'd transform me," she said with a smile. "I never did buy them, though."

"Why not?"

"I lived in *Baraboo*, honey. And Dad would have had a heart attack." She paused and then rolled her eyes and laughed a little, since a heart attack was what her father eventually did have, a year before I was born. My grandmother had lived another five years, but I couldn't really remember her.

My mother took a sip of her wine. We were at the Good Evening—silly name, but it was the place we usually went together, down south of the Beltline in a residential neighborhood. It looked like what it sounded like—gingham curtains, matching ruffled gingham aprons for the waitresses—but the food was really good.

"Of course, then I met your father," she said. "He liked, how shall we put it, a modest look."

"No midriff showing?"

"No midriff showing, not too much leg, no bare shoulders. I was only too happy to oblige." She gave me a rueful smile. I thought of telling her about my afternoon at the New York Public Library, all those John Bells, but I didn't.

"Was he a prude?" I said.

"More of a controller. Everything was about imposing his will. When you were born—" She broke off talking and furrowed her brow. "Boy, I must be in my cups to be dredging up this old stuff."

"What?"

She shrugged. "Well, when you were born he tried to talk me out of breast-feeding. He said it would be hard to go out in public, which it was, but also that it would create—how did he put it?—an unnatural bond between us."

"Between you and me?"

She shook her head. "What a load of hooey. If I'd wanted to bottle-feed he would've had ten sound theories about how that would harm your development."

I forked up a bite of chicken potpie and chewed. "So did you?" I said.

"Breast-feed?" She twisted a wooden bangle around her wrist. "I tried for a while, but it didn't really work—you didn't gain fast enough and Dr. Carlson had me switch to formula." She touched her knife, ran her finger over the floral pattern on the handle. "I was just crushed," she added.

Her cheeks were pink, and she spoke in such a heartfelt voice that I felt a little embarrassed and looked away.

"Anyway," she said, "that's ancient history."

We finished dinner and shared a plate of homemade ginger snaps, then sipped coffee while nearby a large family party grew louder and louder. Grandparents, parents, grown kids, babies: there seemed to be four generations.

At last we left. Our coats were on pegs just inside the door, and we put them on and went outside. The night was enormous: bright with stars, full of an endless quiet. So unlike New York. We walked to my mother's car, our feet crunching on gravel. A grove of maples marked the end of the parking lot, but in the other direction fields ran to the horizon, and a crescent moon glowed halfway up the wall of the sky.

Driving home, we were silent. I felt my father hovering above us; and Mike, whom we'd barely touched on; and even Kilroy. At last my mother pulled into her driveway, igniting a sensor floodlight mounted to the garage. A spring wind had blown in during dinner, and my hair whipped around my face as I got out of the car. She waved in the direction of the next-door neighbor's kitchen window, then turned to me with her eyes wide. "Do you even know?" she said.

"What?"

"Rooster and Joan live next door—they're renting the Nilssons' house. The Nilssons moved to Arizona."

I turned and looked at the Nilssons' kitchen window, but whoever she'd waved at was gone. "Rooster Rooster? *My* Rooster?"

"The very same."

We went inside but I was antsy, couldn't sit for pacing, avoided the windows that faced the Nilssons' and then spent long moments in front of them, peering out. Finally I got my coat back on and went over, feeling strange about everything: being back in Madison and not having called Mike; the prospect of seeing Rooster; the notion that he was married in there, *married*.

He opened the door and his look told me he hadn't seen me when he'd waved at my mother. He was astonished. I thought of the telegram I'd sent in December—CAN'T MAKE IT AFTER ALL STOP SORRY STOP CONGRATULATIONS STOP—and I felt sick with remorse.

His red hair caught the hall light and shone like bright copper. He said, "This is weird in so many ways I can't even count them."

"I don't have enough fingers."

From the doorstep I looked past him into the living room. In the Nilssons' time it had been decked out in full Scandinavian regalia: lots of bleached pine furniture covered with heart and snowflake stencils, painted clogs displayed on the mantel. Now it was Laura Ashley: flowered couch, flowered armchair, flowered tablecloth covering a round table that held a flowered lamp with a flowered lampshade.

He followed my glance. "Joan's stuff," he said with a grin. "Remember my armchair?"

His armchair had been a blue-and-tan plaid La-Z-Boy that shook when you opened it.

"Didn't make the cut?" I said.

"Not even close. You have no idea."

He took a step back and I followed him into the kitchen, all bright and cheery, white with a lot of red accents. I noticed with amusement that there was a framed Matisse poster over the table. But was it "hard"?

There was an open can of diet cola on the counter, and he took a sip, then went to the refrigerator and got me one. "Cheers."

I hadn't had a diet cola since I'd left. I popped the top and took a drink, the taste dark and sweet and almost forgotten. "You look different somehow," I said, and it was true: he was trimmer for one thing, but it was more than that, there was something in the very way he stood and watched me. It was as if I'd stumbled upon his double, man where the Rooster I'd known was still boy, self-contained where my Rooster—and I'd never thought of this before—self-contained where my Rooster leaned over you, shadowed you somehow with his grievances and opinions.

He smiled and nodded, but didn't respond. "So you're back," he said after a while.

"Just for a few days."

"What's the occasion?"

I hesitated. Would he know? Was it OK to tell him? I said, "Jamie's family is having problems."

"Is Jamie OK?"

"I haven't really talked to her."

"Oh, you just got back this minute?"

"Yesterday afternoon, actually."

"O-kay," he drawled. He moved past me to sit at the table, setting his can down with a sharp tap. He wore a Polarfleece henley over cut-off sweatpants, and as he settled into the chair I was struck by his knees—by the matted red hair, the freckles, the bony definition.

He gave me a flat look. "Mike doesn't know."

I shook my head, but he was telling me, not asking. He looked away, took a sip of his cola.

"How is he?" I said after a while.

"Holding steady."

"Steady?"

"Good days and bad—you can imagine. I took him out for lunch today and he seemed pretty cheerful."

"You took him out for lunch?" For some reason it seemed odd to me, as if Rooster'd said they'd gone on a date. But of course Mike couldn't drive. "Where'd you go?"

"Brenda's. We go every Friday."

I was still standing, and I felt awkward suddenly, too exposed. I moved around the butcher-block island so it was between me and Rooster. On the counter by the sink there was a deep white bowl full of Delicious apples, obviously decorative.

Neither of us spoke. It wasn't that we were waiting each other out, but it got to feeling like that after a while.

"So where's Joan?" I said at last.

"Working."

"And how is she?"

"Great."

"Good," I said. I had a vision of Joan in her nurse's whites, standing over Mike's bed, turning to give me an encouraging look. It was hard to move her out of the hospital, to unpin her hair and put her into jeans, into this kitchen, where she'd wash a bag of apples, then buff each one before arranging them all in a bowl.

I cocked my head. "So marriage is good, huh?"

Rooster gave me a big smile, the kind of wide grin you try to control but can't. He slid his can from one hand to the other. "I can't speak for the whole institution, but I certainly like mine."

"I'm glad for you," I said. I really meant it. I wanted him to know that, almost said *I really mean it.* But why wouldn't I?

"Let's not talk about Mike," he said then. "OK? Were you wanting to do that? Because I really don't want to."

"OK," I said. "Fine. Agreed."

We chatted for five or ten minutes and then I left. My mother's house was silent. I went into the kitchen and found a piece of paper in a drawer, then set about writing to Jamie. I said I was sorry again, and that I'd missed her, and that I just wanted a chance to talk face-to-face. I found a spare key to my mother's car and drove through the late-night streets to the Fletchers' house. It was nearly midnight but the lights were all on, upstairs and down, and I wondered if any two of them were together or if each sister was upstairs in her own room while Mr. Fletcher was by himself in the den. My mother had told me that Mrs. Fletcher would be moved to a psychiatric hospital in the next day or two.

I knocked at the front door. After a moment Mr. Fletcher came and opened it, his hair a little grayer than when I'd last seen him, a little sparser. He wore a nubby brown cardigan over his white dress shirt.

"Carrie," he said. "What a surprise."

He had always been something of a cipher to me, and I couldn't tell if he was being cool or just himself. We stood looking at one another for a long moment, he in the entryway and I on the doorstep, until, almost simultaneously, we moved together for a stiff hug.

"Is Jamie here?"

"Well, she . . . she, uh—" He put his hand in his pocket, then took it out again. "I think she went to bed," he said. "She's kind of tired. We all are."

I ducked my head, sorry I'd made him lie. "I know," I said. "I'm so sorry."

He nodded.

I held out the note, folded in half with Jamie's name on it. "Could you give her this?"

"Sure," he said, taking it from me. He brightened a little, happy to have a task. "Consider it done."

JAMIE'S SHIFT STARTED at noon the next day. I waited until one, then borrowed my mother's car and drove over, parking where I'd always parked for work. I wondered if Viktor still worked at the library, how he and Ania were doing. It was extraordinary that they'd actually met Kilroy, that anyone in Madison had. Dinner at their house that night, when Kilroy and I'd met: it seemed expendable now, it was no longer part of us.

I locked my mother's car and headed to State Street, the morning's conversation with Kilroy on my mind. He'd been impatient, said he didn't understand my staying if Jamie wouldn't see me. When I said that I couldn't give up so easily, he got curt, said he had something on the stove, which I knew wasn't true.

The copy shop was quiet, not too busy on a Saturday afternoon halfway between midterm and the end of the semester. Jamie was behind the counter talking to one of the machine operators, a tall, gangly guy who'd worked there for years. Her face barely changed when she saw me. I waited until they were done talking, but before I could speak she turned and walked into the storeroom. From where I stood I saw her pick up the wall phone and punch in a number. I thought I could be patient, wait until she was done with the phone, until business brought her back out to the main room, but there was something in the way she stood—right hand at her waist, all her weight on one leg while the other was bent dancerlike at the knee—that collapsed my composure. It was so familiar, that stance, so Jamie. Affection and regret overcame me like a sudden fever, and I reached around to open the half-door that separated the employee area from the front of the store, then made my way to where she stood.

Her back was to me, but it took her only a moment to turn around.

She was still on the phone, and she scowled and turned sideways, then just as quickly turned back—as if she'd realized she should keep an eye on me.

"What are you doing?" she demanded when she'd hung up the phone.

"Nothing. I wanted to see you. I—Did you get my note?"

She stamped her foot. "Yes. And I *don't care*. This is my place of work—get out of here or I'll call security."

"Jamie," I said. "My God."

She brushed past me and left the storeroom. Out front, she spoke to the tall guy, glancing back at me while she talked. After a moment he came and stood in the doorway. "Listen," he said.

I shook my head, unable to speak for the tears all over my face. I made my way past him and then past Jamie, who looked the other way. Out on the street I leaned against a notice-studded kiosk and sobbed—hard, racking sobs that shook my shoulders and caused me to gulp and choke. People stared at me, whispering. Finally I got control of myself. I found some Kleenex in my purse and blew my nose, then swabbed at my face. Before I left I took a last look into the copy shop, and there she was, staring blankly out the window at me.

33

~

MY BEDROOM CLOSET smelled of cardboard. Boxes of my mother's papers, boxes of mine. Some newer cartons contained the things I'd asked my mother to clear out of my apartment before subletting it. By their weight I could tell which ones held books, and I pushed them aside and found the one full of clothes, then pulled it into the room.

I was home from the copy shop, exhausted and sad, too jumpy to sit still. I found a knife and cut open the box, curious at what I'd left behind. When I saw, my heart sank. What had I been expecting? A leather jacket I wouldn't recognize? A baby-rib pointelle cardigan? These were the things I *hadn't* packed, and I didn't want to be the person who'd bought them, let alone the person who still owned them. A Badgers sweatshirt, pleated wide-wale cords, a stack of cotton turtlenecks. I was dismayed. I closed the box and shoved it back into the closet, next to my old Kenmore sewing machine, the machine my Bernina had replaced. Sewing on the Kenmore—that was how I'd learned. Switching to the Bernina had been like getting out of a twenty-year-old pickup and sliding behind the wheel of a BMW.

The Kenmore outweighed the Bernina by a good ten pounds. I

lugged it to my desk and set it down with a heavy clunk. My mother was on the other side of the wall, in her office doing paperwork, and in a moment she appeared, a curious look on her face. She saw the machine and broke into a smile. "Look at that old jalopy."

"Pretty pathetic, isn't it?"

"Why'd we ever hang on to it?"

"Low blood sugar," I said. It was a Kilroy expression, his explanation for anything left undone, and I looked away, flushing a little.

"Are you OK?"

"Just tired."

"Jamie's pretty angry?"

I nodded.

She'd been standing in the doorway, and now she came in and looked over my shoulder at the machine. She wore a string of off-white beads over her work shirt, and I thought that must be the thing that separated her from other people living alone, that she would put on a necklace for a day when she probably wouldn't leave the house.

She said, "Does it help to know that she's probably putting a lot of her anger on you because it's too hard to put it on Lynn or her mother?"

I smiled halfheartedly. "Not really."

She put her hand on my shoulder and patted it. "I guess it wouldn't."

I faced the desk and rested my forehead on my hand. I heard her shift behind me, and I looked up and said, "I feel like if I could just think of the right thing to say we could get past it, and then I could go back to New York."

She cocked her head. "That's what you really want to do, isn't it?"

"Yes."

She had some new khakis she'd been meaning to get hemmed, and a little later I pinned them for her, then somehow managed to get the sewing machine working, finding an old needle in a basket in my closet, along with some thread and an empty bobbin. When I asked, it turned out she had some other alterations she needed done, so I sewed for a couple hours more, taking in the waist on a skirt, mending the torn lining of a blazer. It got dark, and I turned on my desk lamp and in the pool of light it threw worked until there was nothing more for me to do.

SUNDAY MORNING I walked over to the Fletchers'. Mrs. Fletcher was being transferred to a place called Wellhaven that day, a psychiatric hospital halfway to Janesville, and I stared at the empty house, wondering how she'd be moved: strapped to a gurney or vacant-eyed in the back of Mr. Fletcher's Lincoln Continental.

Maple trees with their smooth trunks. Sycamores with patchy bark, many-armed oak trees reaching for the sky. If New York was a city of noise, Madison was a city of trees. It was so early in spring that they were still leafless, but there was a feeling of new green about them, a feeling that in a week or so you'd start to see it, the tiniest pale hints.

I walked down the driveway to the backyard. Looking up at the beige house, I thought of a night when Jamie and I were fourteen and she snuck down and met me on the lawn, where I waited with a pair of contraband beers. Ten years later, I remembered it vividly: the feel of the damp grass as we sat leaning against the back fence; the way the house looked, outlined against the dark night. And how bold we felt, how reckless.

Back out front, I stood thinking for a moment, then set off again, covering another four or five blocks. I stopped in front of a brick house with a for-sale sign on the lawn. Next door was the house I'd always thought of as the baby house, although the baby was probably in third grade by now, and beyond that was the Mayers'.

From where I stood I could see the house's profile, plus the tail end of an unfamiliar white van in the driveway. It was nearly noon, and I tried to imagine what was going on inside. There was church, but Mr. and Mrs. Mayer didn't go every week, and the kids rarely went at all. Mrs. Mayer in the kitchen, that was easy. Mr. Mayer off playing golf, or maybe out in the garage fixing something. Julie away at Swarthmore. John Junior—well, he was probably still asleep. And Mike . . .

Where in the house would Mike be? What would he be doing? What did he do all day? All week? The president of the bank where he used to work had been a good visitor at the hospital, especially once Mike was in rehab. He made a big thing of assuring Mike that there'd be a job waiting for him when he was ready. Had Mike become ready? Had he gone back to the bank? I didn't think so, didn't see how he could have started working again without my knowing it. Wouldn't someone have told me, my mother? Then again, maybe not.

I stood in front of the brick house for a long time, a very long time for standing still on a square of residential sidewalk in Madison, Wisconsin. A well-groomed older man in a red windbreaker came out of the house across the street. He carried a spade, and after a curious look at me he set to turning the beds that ran alongside his lawn. The Colonel, that's what Mike used to call him. He'd always had a military look about him. Still did.

I turned and headed back. The air was damp and cool, but people had begun to come out for walks, stout and unfashionable people in their church clothes, young couples with babies in strollers. "Morning," they said as they passed me.

At my mother's I sat in the kitchen and drank a cup of coffee. After a while I went upstairs for my sketchbook from Piero's class. The things I'd stapled in there, the things I'd drawn: I couldn't quite retrieve my initial impulses. I got my colored pencils and tried to sketch something, but I couldn't find a way to start.

I went to the phone and dialed Kilroy's number. When he answered I told him about seeing Jamie at the copy shop yesterday, how she'd ordered me away. "At this point," I said, "I don't know why I'm even still here."

"I do."

"Why?"

"Because you're you."

His voice sounded strained, and I felt alarmed. "What do you mean?"

"Isn't it obvious? You can't leave because you're the person you are, and I can't want you to because that would be wanting you to be someone else when I want you to be you."

I want you to be you. I closed my eyes and imagined him into the room with me—his face, his stocking feet on my lap. I wanted his feet on my lap or my feet on his, his hand stroking the skin between the top of my sock and the hem of my jeans, his fingers sliding up my shin until the denim stopped them.

"Tell me about Madison," he said. "What does it look like, what's it like to be back there?"

"Dull," I said. "Dead."

"Is that what it's like or how you feel?"

"Both." I thought of my walk home from the Mayers' street. Without saying where I'd been, I told him about it, how friendly everyone was, good morning, good morning.

"Sounds surreal after New York," he said. "It's like you haven't been debriefed so you're having all this cognitive dissonance. You need to go through a decontamination process."

We talked a little about what I might do next, write a long letter to Jamie, go back to Cobra Copy. "I love you," I said just before we hung up, and there was a pause before he responded.

"As do I. Or I mean, As do I you." He paused again. "How's that for contorted?"

THE NEXT MORNING I drove my mother to work so I could use her car, then drove home again, wondering what to use it for. I wandered around the house, sitting for brief periods in the different rooms. I didn't want to go shopping, go back to State Street, go anywhere. I didn't want to stay where I was. I needed to reach Jamie, but how? I went out and got into the car, and I turned the engine on and then off and then on again before driving the familiar streets to Mike's house.

There were no cars out front, and I rang the doorbell nervously, wondering what I'd do if no one answered—if I'd come back again or not. How much did I want to see him, how much catch myself in the act of doing the right thing? I waited what felt like a long time, and then I heard a faint humming and a voice repeating the same two words over and over, though I couldn't make them out. Finally I opened the door, and there he was.

Sitting in his wheelchair, his knees angular inside loose khakis, his arms on the arms of the chair. His face was slightly pink, and suddenly I understood that he'd been yelling "Come in, come in" because he couldn't open the front door himself. His face was thinner than before, very pale and bristly at the upper lip with an unfamiliar mustache.

At the sight of me his eyes widened and then narrowed, and his lips pressed into a sidelong crimp. He opened his mouth to speak, then closed it again. A deep flush climbed from his neck to his forehead, and at last he said, "I guess this is what's called being speechless."

I took a step inside and hesitated awkwardly, then bent to kiss his cheek, not quite missing the edge of the mustache. "I could have called, but—" I broke off. "Is this too weird?"

He stared at me. "It's just that I've imagined this so many times . . ." He shook his head. "Never mind, that was stupid. Look, come in or something, let's not just stand here at the front door." He gave me a half smile. "Or sit, either."

He moved a lever that operated the wheelchair. It was motorized, unlike the one he'd had in rehab, at least the one I'd seen. He rolled backward and I closed the door, then followed him through the living room, where the furniture had been rearranged to open a pathway.

In the kitchen he stopped. "You caught me during my mid-morning lull. Breakfast has been accomplished, my eleven o'clock tepid tea break is yet to come, and I'm not on the computer at all today." He moved forward a last foot or two and came to rest at the table, which looked as it always had except that there were four chairs around it instead of five.

I pulled out a chair opposite him and sat down. "The computer?"

"I'm hooked up to the system at my dad's office. The exciting world of insurance. We've got a nice little racket going where I bang around on the computer here for ten or twelve hours a week, and they pay me fifteen dollars an hour, all so I won't feel completely useless."

"Mike."

"What?"

"Nothing. I'm sorry."

"You've already said that."

My face burned. The refrigerator began to hum, and I was relieved by just that tiny alteration in the way the room felt.

"Forget it," he said. "That was uncalled for. How are you—what brings you to Madison, the Athens of the Midwest?"

"I thought it was the Berkeley of the Midwest."

"We fell from the running when some guy in Ann Arbor started walking around naked."

We both laughed, harder than was really called for.

"I'd offer you something to drink," he said, "but you'd have to get it yourself."

"I don't mind that," I said. "Can I get you something?"

He directed me to a special glass with a built-in straw and said he'd have some water. I got myself some, too, and sat down again.

"So?" he said.

"Why am I here?"

He smiled. "Let's stick with why you're in Madison."

I took a deep breath. "Jamie. Lynn got hurt and I came home because of that."

"Hurt?"

I licked my lips. "Assaulted."

He'd been leaning over the glass, his mouth around the straw, and now he lifted his head again. "Lynn Fletcher was assaulted?"

I nodded.

"Is she OK?"

"As OK as can be expected."

"God, that's terrible." His arms slid forward a little, and I tried not to look at them—the boniness, the paddlelike flatness of his hands. "When did this happen?"

"Last week—Mrs. Fletcher's pretty shaken up."

"I can imagine." He bent for another sip of water. "So how long are you here for?"

"I'm not really sure."

He licked his lips, and I didn't know what to do, where to look. After a moment I stood and went to the window. A squirrel had paused halfway up the trunk of the tree outside, and I watched until it scrabbled upward again. I turned back. "Are you hungry at all? I'm starving, I never really ate breakfast."

"I'm fine," he said, "but help yourself. Mom's at the grocery store right now, but there should be a crumb or two in the usual places."

I wondered how long Mrs. Mayer had been gone, when she'd be back. I got an apple from the fridge and then went over to the pantry closet. Inside were row upon row of canned foods, packages of noodles and rice, economy-size boxes of dry cereal. Down at the bottom, several bags of chips were held closed by giant plastic clips. I bit into the apple and reached for some Fritos. "Corn chips?" I said.

"Salt's bad for me."

I ate a couple and put the bag back. The last time I'd been here, Julie had been smoking away, asking me whether I was still going to marry Mike. *Do you want to?*

I looked at him and found him watching me, less sharply than before but also less opaquely. His face had taken on the contours of emotion, the curve of his cheeks and the set of his chin speaking of loss. All at once I was very afraid.

He saw me looking and tightened up. "Come on," he said after a moment. "I'll show you my room."

I finished the apple and tossed the core, then followed him back through the living room. The fear abated, replaced by a sick relief that we were moving.

We came to the den. What had once been a small, dark room with plaid wallpaper was now light and airy and somehow seemed bigger, the walls white and decorated with framed pictures: a big photograph of sailboats on Lake Mendota; a poster of a painting I thought I should recognize but didn't, a blocky landscape with a mountain in the background.

"Cézanne," Mike said, seeing where I was looking. "Mom bought it."

"It's nice," I said. It was, too: edgy somehow despite the soft colors. Was Cézanne on Kilroy's good list?

"So what do you think of my new place?"

In his room upstairs, the walls had been hung with hockey posters, including a giant one of Wayne Gretzky. There'd been shelves of hockey trophies. Here hockey didn't exist. I recognized his old striped blanket, stretched over a hospital bed. His computer. And the picture of me that had sat on his bedside table, now on a big, swing-arm stand that he could see from the bed. I looked at my smiling face and then looked away. "Great," I said.

"Pretty different from my old room, isn't it?" he said with a smile. "I had to get out of that room one way or another."

There was a silence: we both knew how he should have gotten out of it.

"Hey, check this out," he said, and he wheeled toward a dark doorway I hadn't noticed. With the edge of his hand he pressed a panel, and light flooded into a huge, gleaming-tiled bathroom complete with shiny white fixtures for the handicapped. "Took a big bite out of the dining room," he said, "but what the hey."

"What the hey," I said. I couldn't think of another thing to say, so I said it again: "What the hey."

34

I WENT TO COBRA Copy first thing Tuesday morning, then Tuesday afternoon, then Wednesday, then Thursday. Jamie was there but she wouldn't see me. She fled the front room when I appeared the first few times but then got used to it and just looked past me, as if the space I occupied were completely empty. I felt manipulated but also heartbroken. When I approached her and said her name, she flinched but didn't react otherwise. She'd adopted a look of stone, and she was masterly at it, sliding it on and off at such perfectly calibrated moments that I began to think it was all a charade, that her refusal to speak to me had nothing to do with her feelings and everything to do with a simple decision she refused to reverse. Every now and then, though, maybe just twice that whole week, I saw it—a hot look around her eyes—and I knew she was suffering.

I decided to go back to New York. I dropped off a long note to Jamie, at her parents' house, where she was still staying. In it I apologized again, apologized more: for the last week and also for the last half year, the last *year,* for every moment since I'd begun to change. I even wrote that: *I know it must seem that I've changed a lot, since well before Mike's accident. I wish we could talk about it.*

We couldn't, though. That was the message she was giving me every day, the letter she wasn't writing back.

I'd charged an open-ended ticket, maxing out my credit card for the first time. Late Thursday I called to see if I could fly back the next day, but the earliest flight they had was at six a.m. Saturday. I booked it.

In my room I put the Kenmore away. I had my mother's car, and I drove to the grocery store and bought some chicken. Over dinner we talked about the possibility of her visiting New York in the summer, when her client load would be lighter. On the phone a month or so earlier I'd told her about finally getting a room in the brownstone, and now she said she'd like to see it, see New York, see my life there. And meet Kilroy? I wondered. I was sure she'd want to meet him, but would she *like* to meet him? Maybe the reason I hadn't mentioned him was that I didn't know how to describe him beyond the bare-bone eccentric facts. They weren't him any more than the information he'd withheld was. Sitting there opposite her, a thousand miles from New York, I felt a sense of *knowing* him, of knowing him deeply in all the important ways. I knew the exact smile he'd give me when he saw me in two days' time. I knew how his lips would feel on my eyelids, my cheeks, my mouth. How the hair on his chest would tickle my breasts, prickly and yet also somehow pleasant. Kilroy. I longed for him, couldn't stand that I had to wait two days to see him again.

My mother and I were cleaning up when the phone rang. It was Rooster, asking if I wanted to go to lunch with him and Mike the next day.

IN THE MORNING I saw him back his old red Honda from the Nilssons' driveway, but when he arrived at noon to pick me up he was driving a brand-new blue one, and as I got in I said, "What's going on here? Where's your car?"

"I traded it in," he said with a bored shrug. "We're going to need a four-door for the baby."

I felt my mouth fall open. "The baby?"

He grinned. "Hey, there's a lot you don't know."

We drove to the Mayers', where Mike was already waiting for us, at the top of a new ramp outside the back door. On Monday I'd left before Mrs. Mayer's return, and now I looked at the house, wondering if she could see us. I knew she was in there, because the white van I'd seen in the driveway Sunday was there again, and I'd learned from Rooster that she'd traded her Oldsmobile for it, a vehicle that could accommodate a wheelchair.

Rooster had his own set of keys. Mike wheeled down the ramp; Rooster lowered the van's lift and got him and the chair strapped in; and then we were off.

Brenda's was a greasy little hole-in-the-wall that I'd never really liked—it was the place Mike had gone with the guys. Brenda herself flipped the burgers, a round-faced woman in a flowered smock top and stretch pants. When we walked in, she waved and slapped four patties on the grill.

"Make it five today, Bren," Rooster called as he cleared space between the tightly packed tables so Mike could wheel his way to a clean one by the window.

"How do you know Carrie doesn't want two?" Mike said.

"One'll be fine," I said. "I may have to wear a bathing suit sometime in the next decade."

"Right," he said with a little snort. "Like that's your problem."

There was an awkward moment, none of us looking at each other, and then we all sat down. Or Rooster and I sat—Mike wheeled in. I wondered why I was there, whose idea it had been to invite me.

Rooster got up when the food was ready and brought it to the table. Mike ate more easily than I would have expected, with a clamping device Rooster helped strap to his forearm. When a little ketchup fell onto his lap Rooster clearly saw it and just as clearly ignored it. They had their ways.

We talked about Joan's pregnancy: morning sickness was a myth, Joan felt sick all day; Rooster had heard the baby's heartbeat just yesterday, and it was amazing. After a while the conversation turned to New York, and I told them about Parsons, how there might be a career in it for me some day.

"And it's something you like to do," Mike said.

"Yeah," Rooster said, "that makes a big difference."

There was a gloomy little silence. I glanced back and forth between them. "What?"

Mike frowned. "Nothing."

I looked at Rooster, who shrugged. "Nothing it is," I said.

Mike bent for a sip of his Coke. "It's that job I was telling you about. That computer job. I hate it."

I turned to Rooster again, hoping for some kind of clarification, but before I could say anything Mike was shouting at me, his face dark red. "What's your problem? Why are you looking at him? I'm the one talking, aren't I?"

"I'm so sorry," I exclaimed, horrified.

He stared at me for a long moment and then heaved a huge sigh. "No, I am," he said. "I am."

I felt tense and ashamed. There were photographs all over the restaurant walls, and I focused on them, years' and years' worth of football and hockey Badgers lined up in red and white uniforms. I'd heard somewhere along the line that Brenda had sent five sons through the U with not a little help from the athletic department.

"It's *boring*," Mike said.

I looked back, and his eyes were sad—the gray of a winter sky at dusk. "Boring?" I said.

"Incredibly. And it gives me a headache. And it's totally pointless. I mean, there's so much talk about being productive, leading an independent life. I'm a fucking quadriplegic."

Rooster reached over and gave Mike's shoulder a pat. "You're not a *fucking* quadriplegic," he said quietly.

Mike rolled his eyes and smiled a little. "Yeah, there's that, too."

AFTER WE DROPPED him off, Rooster and I got back into his new car and he drove me to my mother's, the two of us silent all the way. Out in front he put the car in park but left the engine running. I looked out the window. A giant root had pushed up the sidewalk in front of the house, and I remembered flying over the bump on roller skates, alone or with Jamie. There was that moment when you were airborne, the fear and the thrill indistinguishable.

Next to me Rooster shifted. I looked at him: he was staring out the window at some phantom spot on the road, hands tight around the steering wheel. After a while he reached down and cut the engine.

"I thought you didn't want to talk about him."

"I don't."

"Let's anyway."

He turned the key back far enough to get the radio. It was tuned to something terrible, and he hit the scanner button through half a dozen stations, watching intently as the numbers flashed by. Finally he turned the key back home. "It's what it looks like," he said. "Believe it or not, it was a lot worse." He paused, then said, "Listen, Carrie, I don't want to—"

"Please."

He pulled the keys from the ignition and dropped them in the change well behind the parking brake. "OK, here goes. My theory is that in the fall there were a lot of things happening. There was rehab and getting the halo off and being discharged from the hospital and the wedding—"

"And I was supposed to come home."

"—and you were supposed to come home, but you didn't, and then January came, and it was fucking cold, and Mikey—" Rooster broke off, shaking his head. He rested his forehead on the steering wheel for a moment, his shoulders rounded, upper arms straining against the fabric of his suitcoat. He looked up again. "Mike felt pretty hopeless, Carrie. Pretty stuck. Like, *Well, this is it. Welcome to life as a quad.* Harvey—did you hear about him, Mike's roommate from rehab?—he got very low around then, and Mike just didn't have much to feel up about. I mean, how much chess can a person play, how much TV can a person watch, how many books can a person read? And then there are all these little things you wouldn't think of, like in restaurants and stores and stuff people talk to the person who's with him instead of him. 'And what would he like to drink?' Can you believe that? That's why he said that thing to you today, about looking at me when he was the one talking. You get sensitive."

"That was so stupid," I said. "I feel awful about that."

Rooster gave me a funny look, and I laughed harshly: if I felt awful about *that* . . .

"Plus Stu basically bailed," he went on. "Even last summer, I don't know if you noticed, but he hardly ever visited, and when he did it was always with someone else. He'd talk to the other person more than to Mike."

I thought back. I hardly remembered Stu at the hospital, which I figured proved Rooster's point.

"After Mike moved home Stu went with us to Brenda's a few times, but he was incredibly fucking tense. Then once when we were both at the Mayers' Mike had a little accident with his leg bag, and that was the last we saw of Stu."

I sighed and shook my head.

"Anyway, Mike started talking about wanting to die."

"What?" I was confused. "You mean he—"

Rooster said, "I mean he wanted to die," and as I stared at him I felt a great sorrow invade me. It spread through me like a terrible drug, my heart pumping it to the farthest reaches of my fingers and toes. I buried my face in my hands. I kept thinking of Monday, the way Mike had looked for just a moment while the two of us were alone together—his pale face and his bristly mustache, and how his composure suddenly dropped away.

"He asked us for help," Rooster said. "He asked me, he asked his parents—he even asked Joan once. To help him kill himself."

I looked up at him. I wasn't tearful, I was past that: I was sick, blown apart. He held my glance for a moment and then looked away. I smelled the car, the newness of the upholstery and the carpeting. After a while I couldn't stand the feel of my own hands anymore, and I reached up and ran my fingers over the curve of the dash, cool and scaly to the touch.

"I guess I shouldn't have told you," Rooster said.

"No, you should've. I'm glad you did. Or not glad, but—Well, you know."

He looked at me again. He stared hard into my eyes, then he reached over and touched my leg, his fingers and the edge of his palm alighting on my thigh. Looking at them, his thick fingers chapped from the wind and covered with fine, reddish-gold hairs, I had a powerful urge to put my hand on top of his. I wanted to wrap my fingers around his, squeeze them tight. It was all I could do to stop myself.

His fingers felt heavy on my leg, and they rested there for a long time. Finally he pulled his hand back.

"Is it still going on?" I said. "Is that what happens on the bad days?"

He shook his head. "He seems to have gotten beyond it. I mean, who knows what he's thinking about alone in bed at night, but he stopped talking about it, and you know what? That's almost enough for me. Isn't that awful?"

"No."

"I think it's awful, but I can't help it." He sighed and looked out the window. "I'll tell you something else. Dave King helped a lot. A *lot*."

I thought back to the tape Mike had sent me. *I call him King Dave. He tells me what I should be worrying about and then I worry about it.* I remembered the night I'd talked to Dave King outside the hospital, how he'd wanted to tell me about quads and sex. It seemed a great failing now that I hadn't heard him out.

Rooster started the car. "Look, I've got to get back," he said. "I'm sorry I dumped this on you, OK? And don't tell Mike I told you."

"Why not?"

A wave of fear passed over his face, and he shook his head emphatically. "You can't. He wouldn't want you to know. He *doesn't* want you to know. I mean it, Carrie, you can't ever say anything."

"OK, fine," I said. "But why?"

" 'So if she does come back I'll know it's not just pity.' " He stared at me. "Get it?"

I didn't answer.

"His expectations are zero, Carrie. Zero. But his hopes? This is a guy who has a lot to hope for, and you're somewhere near the top of the list."

35

I CANCELED MY FLIGHT. I couldn't go back yet, not after what Rooster had told me. Kilroy wasn't happy, and his unhappiness made me unhappy, and when I told my mother that I was going to stay a while longer she searched my face hard, as if for an explanation.

"Do you really want to?" she said at last.

"Yes."

She'd cleared that afternoon's appointments and gone out to Wellhaven with Jamie. Mrs. Fletcher, she said, was in a private room overlooking a quiet terrace planted all along the edges with pink and white crocuses. When they arrived she was sitting motionless in an armchair near the window. My mother only stayed in the room for a few minutes, but Jamie told her afterward that eventually Mrs. Fletcher started talking, and what she talked about was some meat she'd defrosted. She told Jamie to look for it, a veal roast, and throw it away. She said she was worried she hadn't taught Jamie and her sisters all they needed to know to run a kitchen. Three days for chicken, four for beef. Don't let anyone cook that veal roast, she told Jamie. ("As if we would," Jamie'd said to my mother. "As if we weren't just nuking Stouffer's most nights.")

My mother told me this at the kitchen table over glasses of white wine. She said the conversation could be seen as a good sign, an indication that Mrs. Fletcher felt connected to her life.

"Does Jamie see it that way?"

My mother lifted her wineglass and took a sip. She set the glass down and twirled the stem back and forth between her thumb and forefinger. "Jamie can't quite get past the hospital," she said. "She thinks her mother being in the hospital spells out trouble, rather than that the hospital is addressing trouble that was already in her mother."

I nodded. "That reminds me of what you said to me."

She cocked her head. "When?"

"When I first called you from New York. I said leaving made me a bad person, and you said people aren't defined by what they do so much as they define what they do. It's like that." I fiddled with the saltshaker. It was also like what Kilroy had said: *Forty doesn't say what I am, I say what forty is.* I thought, *And I say it's solitary.* Then I shook my head hard, wanting to fling the idea away.

My mother was watching me. *Observing* me: the word came to me all at once. She stood up. "You remember a lot," she said. "You've always had a good memory."

I thought of my early childhood, when I'd tried and tried to remember my father. Maybe I never wanted to forget anything again. "I guess so," I said, and I watched her cross to the sink, where she poured the last bit of her wine out, then turned on the water and let it fill the empty glass.

I CALLED MIKE the next morning, and Mrs. Mayer answered. I said I guessed she'd heard I was back, and she said yes, she guessed she had. When Mike came on I told him I was going to be staying for a few more days and that I'd like to visit if I could.

They were all home when I got there—Mr. Mayer, Mrs. Mayer, John Junior. It was almost as if they'd hung around to get a glimpse of me, or it struck me that way about John, anyway, who wandered in and out of the kitchen four or five times for no good reason.

Mrs. Mayer was glacial. It was she who answered the door, and she held on tight, as if I might pry her away and try to force her into a hug.

She looked older and dowdier, nearly a year into Mike's tragedy: her hair badly permed, extra lines on her face. She wore a decade-old nylon sweatsuit in a bright jade green that cast a gray light on her skin. She didn't bother trying to be nice.

I stayed for about an hour. Mike and I talked about Rooster: about how happy he was, what a goon he would be as a father—Mr. Camcorder, Mr. Spoiler. He told me about Harvey, who'd developed some motor function in his left arm and was back in the hospital for more therapy. "He's a great guy," Mike said. "I learned a lot from him."

"About?"

"Just life," he said, and then he grinned broadly, the first really big smile I'd seen on him: it was familiar at the same time that it was strange, shadowed by the mustache. "Listen to me," he said. " 'Just life.' Yes, and he's a really caring individual." He rolled his eyes. "Never mind, you'll just have to meet him someday, I think you'd like each other."

"I'd like that," I said.

Mr. Mayer appeared, tall and broad-shouldered, his bald spot gleaming. From the doorway he looked at me, then he came in and circled the table to stand behind me, putting a hand on each of my shoulders. "Isn't she a sight for sore eyes?" he said to Mike, and then he ruffled my hair and bent down to put the side of his face against mine.

THE SILK I liked best was a sage green jacquard, small shadow leaves spilling across it. It came in mauve, too, but the green was more interesting, smoky and soft. Maybe it wasn't sage, maybe it was celadon. Or light olive. I loved the names of colors, the tiny distinctions between them. Cantaloupe, shrimp, salmon.

It was Monday morning and I was at Fabrications. I'd come just to look, half expecting to be disappointed after the place in New York, but the shop still had its old hold on me, the fabrics not just gorgeous but arranged to entice, exquisite pale earth tones mixed with whites and ivories to signal the coming of spring.

The bell over the door sounded, and a very tall woman came in carrying a Marshall Field's bag. She said hi to me, and I was confused for a moment, wondering if I knew her. But no, it was just Madison again, Madison friendliness. I was still suffering from cognitive dissonance. I looked at my watch. Back in New York, my Patternmaking class would start soon, and I was missing it again. Twice now.

"Could you help me?" the customer said to the saleswoman, a soft-bodied blond in an obviously homemade blue twill jumper with a lot of top-stitching. "I bought this dress and I'm not sure what to do about the fit."

The saleswoman showed her to the back room, and the woman came out a few minutes later wearing a red silk dress that just didn't fit her, never mind what the color did to her face. As I watched, the two of them talked, trying to come up with a plan for altering it.

"I think you'd have to take the sleeves off," the saleswoman said at one point. "Then you could take out the pleats and narrow it through here and get rid of that puffiness."

"Or I could just return it," the customer said.

"Or you could just return it."

The customer sighed. She looked at herself in the mirror, the same full-length mirror that had sold me on the washed silk for my nightgown and robe last summer. "I don't suppose you do any alterations," she said.

"Sorry," the saleswoman said, shaking her head. "I have a two-year-old at home."

The customer gave her reflection a last look. She had a long face, and she wore her shoulder-length brown hair pushed off her forehead with a wide hairband. She was turning toward the back room when I stepped forward and surprised myself by saying that I'd overheard her and that as it happened I was in the business of doing alterations myself.

"Are you really?" she said. "I desperately need this for Friday and I don't want to trust it to the tailor at the dry cleaner's."

The saleswoman said I could pin it right there, and we moved into a corner and got to work. I felt a little silly, but excited, too, because I knew just what to do.

The problem wasn't just the sleeves. The woman had narrow shoulders and wide hips, and the dress bowed at the neck and pulled across the belly—drag lines, in Parsons language. Using pins from a box I bought on the spot, I took in the bodice, adjusted the sleeves so they were less puffy and droopy, and shortened the skirt by about an inch.

"Look," I said, leading her back to the mirror. "Isn't that better? If you can kind of ignore the pins and squint a little, you'll get the idea. I can't do anything about the hips, but the rest."

"I don't have to squint," she said. "It's great, you're a miracle worker. And don't feel bad about the hips—I've tried and tried, and I can't do anything about them, either."

The work was easy to complete by Friday, and the Kenmore held up for me, although there were a few bad moments when the bobbin thread got tangled and oily. I charged sixty dollars, and the woman and I were both happy. Heading back to her car after picking up the dress, she turned and said, "Hey, could you make me a dress from scratch sometime?"

Standing there on my mother's front step, I knew the dress instantly— the neckline, the silhouette, the dusty blues and greens that would bring out her eyes and set off her hair. Just like that, in front of me, a whole dress. It was thrilling, and I shook my head regretfully. "Sorry," I said. "I'm just here visiting."

KILROY COOLED. HE went from a certain somewhat unhappy state of understanding to a more irritable state of wanting to know why I had to resolve everything at once, during a spur-of-the-moment trip that had gone on longer than planned. "You're getting sucked back in," he said. "You've got to see that you've done what you could. It took Jamie a long time to reach this point, it'll take her a long time to come back from it." I said I knew, I knew. I didn't mention that I'd stopped trying to see her. I didn't mention Mike.

I visited him every day. Just for a little while, a half hour, forty-five minutes. He liked going for walks around the neighborhood on week-day afternoons when the sidewalks were empty. It was sixty degrees out, sixty-five, and the tulips were opening, great stands of yellow and red.

Mrs. Mayer barely tolerated me. She tossed me sidelong glares, her arms crossed over her chest. When I knocked on the door she

opened it and then walked away, calling, "Mike, door." It was a pun-
ishment, and just: enduring it was a form of mortification, as in mortifying the flesh to cleanse the soul, except that I was mortifying the
soul to cleanse the soul. I survived it moment by moment.

On Saturday I showed up around one. Mr. and Mrs. Mayer were in
golf clothes, moving around the front of the house with clubs and
shoes and then going off to look for their gloves. She beckoned me to
the side.

"How long do you think you'll be staying today?"

"I don't know, why?"

She smoothed her skirt, a robin's-egg-blue A-line with a big lady-
bug appliquéd near the hem. "It's just John Junior has a softball game
and I hate to leave him home alone too long. It's our first time out this
spring—we only want to play nine holes." She looked at me, our eyes
truly meeting for the first time since my return. She gave me a faint,
neutral smile: no pressure.

"Sure," I said. "No problem."

She let out a heavy breath. "Oh, thanks. Thanks."

I joined Mike in the kitchen. When they were gone I got us each
some ice water and we went out to the deck. The yard was well
planted for spring, possibly more so than it had been the previous
year, even the grape hyacinths carefully controlled along one piece of
fence. I thought Mrs. Mayer must have spent many a fall day out
here, punishing her knees while Mike labored through rehab.

"So you're baby-sitting?"

"Mike."

"Mom's a little too protective. I can hardly get her to go to the grocery store."

A power mower started up a few houses away. I could almost picture the mower, how some man Mr. Mayer's age would have pushed
it out of his garage and given it a once-over, filled the tank with gas,
and then made a little wish before pulling the cord for the first time
since fall.

"I guess you don't hear too many of those in New York."

I smiled at him. "Not too many."

We sat together on the deck. A cardinal lit on the rail and we
watched it peck, then fly away. "Mike?" I said after a while.

"Carrie?"

"Can we be friends?"

He bent toward the redwood table for a sip of water, then straightened up and gazed into the middle distance. "I can't help loving you," he said, and his face slowly filled with color. "God, isn't that a line from some awful song?"

"I think so."

"Love songs are so stupid. I was thinking about this just the other day—Mom had some god-awful oldies station playing in the kitchen. I mean, when did anyone ever actually enjoy walking in the rain? It doesn't feel so fine."

We looked at one another. I remembered running with him through the rain, to the Student Union or to my dorm, his hand clasping mine as if he could actually make me go faster. How he looked with wet hair plastered to his head, strands stuck in clumps to his forehead as he searched for something to dry off with.

He motored away from the table, toward the rail, then turned to face me. "In answer to your question," he said, "I really don't know."

"I want to be," I said.

"You don't even live here anymore, Carrie."

I looked at my hands. How could I do both: live in New York and be Mike's friend? *Mike was Mr. Congeniality, wasn't he? A nice guy. That's what I've always figured.* How strange it had been to learn Kilroy was jealous. What would he think if I started calling Mike, writing to him? What would he think if he found out I'd been calling him and writing him and had never said so?

Mike sat across the deck from me in his wheelchair, the big black machine that both freed and imprisoned him. He wore a zippered gray sweatshirt over navy blue sweatpants, and the fabric lay on his body so that I could easily see the contours of his limbs, bony and spastic. There was pain, I'd learned, which seemed like a particularly cruel joke: no movement and no sensation, but the nerves were tricked out to keep on transmitting messages of hurt. There he was in his wheelchair. You could never take the chairness away from it.

36

~

ONDAY MORNING I sat at my mother's long, polished-wood dining room table. I'd always liked the dining room, its white walls and dark china cabinet and thick blue rug. It was the room where I'd sewn as a teenager, spreading my work out down the length of the table. I always put my machine at the end, just in front of a window that got the morning light.

I was in that spot, reading the newspaper, the sun slanting in over my right shoulder, when I began to feel uncomfortable. How can it be that your body knows when someone is behind you? There was no sound, not a change in shadow or light, but I felt in the middle of my back that I was about to flinch. I fought it for a while and then finally turned around, and there was Jamie, standing out on the sidewalk looking in.

I stood up. Clamped a hand over my mouth. Froze. By the time I had the front door open she was gone, and though I hurried out to the sidewalk and looked both ways, she had vanished.

I tried to settle at the table again, but I couldn't. I drove to the Fletchers' and knocked—no answer. I drove to Miffland for the first time since I'd been back, climbed the steps to her house, and knocked again: nothing. Leaving my mother's car, I walked over to State Street and went into Cobra Copy. No Jamie.

Still, she'd come to see me. Maybe just to *see* me, but she'd come. I tried phoning her later that day—at her parents' house, her place, Cobra Copy, Bill's—but I couldn't find her, and even as I was calling I understood how absurd it was to think I'd be able to track her down: that I'd still even know where to try.

Then, sitting there with the phone in my hand, it hit me: Wellhaven. At Wellhaven, visiting her mother. My mother had said Mrs. Fletcher liked having visitors. Jamie had probably driven down for the afternoon. Maybe she'd taken off immediately after standing in front of my mother's house; maybe her car had been idling at the curb while she looked. I imagined her alone in her little Geo, taking the interstate south toward Janesville. Sitting there at the wheel, her hair brushing her shoulders, the radio on loud. And a pit in her stomach, to think of where her mother was.

She was afraid of the world, Mrs. Fletcher. It was something I'd always known about her without ever articulating it. She wouldn't drive on the interstate. Hated having any of the girls go on sleepovers when they were kids—that was why the Fletchers' house was always sleepover central. When we were in high school she objected when Jamie stayed out past midnight, but in a tortured, pro forma way since Jamie was clearly going to win. Poor Mrs. Fletcher, sitting up all last summer, way past midnight, waiting for Lynn to get home. I thought of the day when I ran into her and Jamie, while I was having lunch with Ania. *Don't be such a stranger,* she said to me afterward.

Mrs. Fraser had said the same thing to Kilroy as we were leaving his parents' house. I remembered her thin hand on his coat, the way he looked down before reaching for the doorknob. Whom had he talked to, in the two and a half weeks I'd been gone. Anyone?

I wrote Jamie a note that evening, saying I'd seen her outside my mother's and hoped she'd want to talk soon, and that I was going to visit her mother unless I heard back that she didn't want me to.

I waited until Thursday and then drove down, on an afternoon of heavy gray clouds, the kind of afternoon when you have to hope for rain. The facility was low and modern, set far back in well-kept grounds. The lawn was plush as carpet.

At the desk I was told to limit my visit to half an hour. I sat on a bench and waited, the sharp smell of chemical cleansers reaching me from somewhere. I was wearing the nicest outfit I had, my black pants and velvet shirt. Again. Out of desperation I'd bought some underwear, and one day I'd even resorted to a dowdy flowered skirt from the box in my closet, but mostly I just rotated among the few things I'd brought with me, sicker and sicker of them.

Mrs. Fletcher appeared from a long corridor. Her hair was short and thin, but she was neatly dressed in her customary skirt and blouse, and on her feet were her customary made-for-comfort pumps. She tilted her cheek to the side, and I stepped forward to kiss her.

"Let's walk around," she said. "I'll show you the garden."

We went through the building and out a back door that led to a courtyard. From there a gravel path took us to a well-groomed rose garden.

"Aren't they lovely?" Mrs. Fletcher said. Like Mrs. Mayer, she had always been a dedicated gardener.

"Beautiful."

"My girls are tending the roses at home."

We continued on to a pair of wrought-iron chairs set at right angles under a tree. A uniformed attendant watched us from nearby.

"How are you feeling?" I said when we'd sat down. Her hands were tucked into the folds of her skirt.

"Oh, Carrie, you don't know your children until the family is challenged in this way. I can really rest easy knowing my girls are taking care of their dad, and he's taking care of them."

I looked into Mrs. Fletcher's face. I wondered what she meant by "this challenge," how she characterized it to herself.

"The other day Jamie was here in that new yellow shirt of hers, do you know the one I mean, dear?"

I said I didn't.

She pursed her lips. "I didn't say anything to her just then, but would you tell her to be sure not to wash it with darks? It's really important to separate out your yellows. Reds, too. I guess I should have told her myself."

She began to cough, and when she brought a hand out of the folds of her skirt to cover her mouth, I saw that it was raw and red, with nails bitten down to the quick.

"Sure," I said. "I'll tell her."

Clouds had been massing and darkening since my arrival, and now, suddenly, it began to pour. Without looking at me Mrs. Fletcher got to her feet. She started back toward the building, ignoring the path and instead walking slowly across the thick grass. I followed after her, holding myself back to her pace. In moments I was soaked.

At the courtyard she stopped briefly and looked up at the sky, then continued into the building. She waited just inside the door for me, then slipped out of her pumps, picked them up with one hand, and headed for the lobby.

Near the exit, she held out her free hand. "You're a dear to have come," she said. "I'm so glad Jamie's got such a good friend in you." She turned and walked away, and I watched until she was gone: her soaked hair, her mud-spattered hose, the water-darkened shoes dangling from her raw fingers.

Outside again, I hurried through the rain to my mother's car. I sat inside and listened to it drum against the roof and the windows. I sat perfectly still, as if I were trying to hear something the slightest movement would drown out. I heard cars driving through puddles, a distant crack of thunder, and then I found myself thinking of something Dr. Spelman had said during Mike's coma: that after a head injury, people sometimes seemed different.

That was Mrs. Fletcher. If you hadn't known her before, you might assume she was the same sweet, maternal lady she'd always been. Only her family and a few others, maybe not even my mother, would think what I thought: that I'd just visited some other sweet, maternal lady, an imperfect copy of a woman who seemed to be missing.

THE NEXT DAY was May 1st, and before heading out the door for the Mayers', I sat down and wrote Simon a check for the rent. I was down to a little over three hundred dollars, and I was going to have to get a job as soon as I got back to New York: temping, working at a library, something. I couldn't stand to think about how much money I'd wasted missing classes at Parsons—eleven as of today.

The rainstorm had cleared the sky, and most of the trees were leafed out now, the new leaves curled and pale green, a delicate pale green that reached in and fingered my heart, it was that painful and exquisite. When I stopped to deposit Simon's check in a mailbox, I peeled off my sweater and pushed up my shirt sleeves, pleased by the pressure of the cool air against my bare forearms.

Mrs. Mayer was waiting outside the house for me, her handbag looped over her wrist. I'd called and asked if she would show me how to use the van so I could take Mike out sometime, and though I'd meant the lift she handed me the keys and said she wanted to see me drive first.

I got in and she climbed in next to me. The gearshift rose up from the floor like a stiff plant. I'd never been behind the wheel of anything so high before, and I jerked out of the driveway a little roughly before heading up the street. At my side she was silent, gazing out her window at the familiar sights. We drove around town for a while, then she said I should go down to the Beltline.

"What were you thinking you might need the van for?"

I glanced over at her. Her perm had loosened, and it hung in waves around her face. She was staring straight ahead, both hands clamped on her purse.

"To go for lunch," I said. "Or just out."

She opened her purse, then snapped it closed again. "How long are you staying?"

I thought of Jamie, standing outside my mother's house on Monday. Of Mike. "I'm not sure. Maybe another week." I pictured Kilroy lying on his couch, his arms crossed over his chest, and I sighed.

Mrs. Mayer opened her purse again and pulled out a lipstick. She lowered the visor, flipped open the mirror, and rolled color over her lips, a light coral. She recapped the lipstick with a smart click. "Mr. Mayer and I have been parents for a long time, and it's strange, the things that bother you and the things that don't. I'll tell you this only once. We both feel that you're not reliable. We're both reluctant to have you back in Michael's life."

My face burned. I stared at the road, the steady movement of the car ahead of me.

"Shall we turn around here?" she said. "You're doing very well—I never knew you were such a careful driver."

I signaled to get off the Beltline. I stopped for a light and then drove back through town. "OK," she said once we were back in the driveway. "I'll show you the lift now."

37

~

"**Y**OU'RE NOT COMING back," Kilroy said, "are you?"

"I am."

"You're not. You just don't know it yet."

We were on the phone again, the day after my van lesson. I was in my mother's kitchen, looking through the window at the edge of Rooster and Joan's deck, where there was a row of clay pots planted with irises, tight sheaves of green spears. My mother had gone to have lunch with a friend.

Kilroy coughed, and I turned from the window. I wanted to go back, but not yet. I wanted to be with him, but I wanted to be friends with Mike: to *be there for him*.

If Kilroy were with me, I knew there'd be no question. He'd look at me and his face would say he knew me, and that would be that. He'd reach out a hand, veins raised and snaky, and that would be that. *Kilroy.* Of course I was going back.

"OK, when?" he said. "I want a date."

Something heavy tumbled through me. Silence fell along the line.

"Sorry," he said.

"No, I am."

He laughed sharply.

"What?"

"That's your great dodge, isn't it?" He elevated his voice to mimic me: " 'I'm sorry.' "

My heart thudded, reminding me of something: the sound of my own footfalls as I walked down a quiet Madison street in my New York boots. Thud, thud, thud. Sorry, sorry, sorry. True, true, true.

"Just say," I said. I twisted the phone cord around my finger, then slid it off. "I mean, I'm not saying this, but what if I did want to stay here? There are temp agencies here; you could come here."

"No, I couldn't."

"Why not?"

"Because I live in New York," he said in a tight, controlled voice. "I want to live in New York."

"More than you want to be with me?"

"Is that an ultimatum?"

"Didn't you just give me one?"

We talked a little longer, to no good effect. Afterward I climbed the stairs and lay on my bed. I felt dizzy. I thought of his hands on my arms, how they were just the right size for my arms, to smooth my arms. How they felt on my stomach, especially when they were cold, that exquisite chill. His hands on my legs. His hands on my breasts. I put my own hands on my breasts and they felt soft and flabby, they felt like nothing. Like pockets of flesh. How extraordinary, I thought, that someone could touch you and make you into something.

I TOOK MIKE out to lunch. Sandwiches one day, pizza another. In the van he was quiet, but once we were settled and eating, he grew animated. It was good to leave the Mayers' house, their neighborhood. Sitting opposite me in a restaurant on Monroe Street one day, he looked across his pork chop, which he'd earlier asked me to cut into pieces for him, and said, "Mike Mayer eats his lunch with gusto."

I smiled. "Mike Mayer does?"

"Yes, he does."

We talked and ate, and the place emptied out until at last it was just us and two women in tennis clothes. We sat in the lacy sunlight filtering through the branches of a tree just outside the window. From the kitchen we could hear voices and the sound of plates clattering. Near the back, our waiter sat in a booth and ate a sandwich.

I told Mike the story of me and Jamie, going back to seeing Lynn at the Alley that night in August, and how I'd never told her about it.

"Boy," he said when I was done. "Whew."

"I know."

"I wouldn't have predicted this, but Jamie's kept it completely to herself. Wouldn't you have thought she'd at least hint? She and Bill came over the other night, and when I said something about your visit she made it seem like everything between you was OK."

My visit.

"I guess she feels it's private," I said.

"It is," he said. "But still." He leaned over for a sip of water. "So what's going on between you now?"

"Nothing at this point. When I first got back I'd go stand in Cobra Copy and look at her, and she'd ignore me. That happened five or six times. Half of me just wanted to yell, you know, 'Should I do a cartwheel now? Just tell me what to do and I'll do it.' "

Mike smiled. "And the other half?"

I looked down at my paper placemat and traced its scalloped edge with my forefinger. "The other half felt she was justified."

"But you know that's crazy now, right?" he said. "I mean, yeah, maybe you should have told her about Lynn, but there's no way it's your fault."

"Something is." I stared at him for a moment, then couldn't stand it any longer and looked away.

"Carrie," he said. "Jesus. Shit happens."

"I guess."

We were silent. He sat there in his nice plaid shirt, which I was sure his mother had ironed. Things seemed tense between him and his mother. As we left the house earlier she called, "When do you think you'll be back?" and I heard him growl faintly.

We split a cookie and then left the restaurant and headed toward the van. The afternoon sun felt good on my face, something clean about it, about the air. The sidewalk was empty and I glanced in at shop windows as we went by. In one, a linen slip dress hung from a rack, and I paused. At my side Mike stopped, too. It was a nice grayed purple, some tiny crochet work along the straps.

"That'd look good on you," he said.

I looked down at him, and when our eyes met a worried look came over his face. "Should I not have said that?"

"No, it's fine."

"Are you sure?"

I nodded.

A jet sounded high above us. I looked up at the line of white it trailed. I watched it loosen and fade, soon to be absorbed by the deep blue of the sky.

Mike pressed the lever on his wheelchair, and we started off again. "Here we go," he said. "Mike Mayer takes Monroe Street."

KILROY AND I talked. Twice a day, every two days, it didn't matter. Being together required being together, and our conversations became grave and lugubrious. "I love you" was an idea that demanded physical proximity. Back in the fall, telling him about my life in Madison had been like handing him object after precious object to hold for safekeeping. Now I told him about seeing Mike, and it was like taking those objects back, one by one.

He didn't have much to report. One evening he told me about a mangy dog he'd seen wandering through a road construction site just off West Street, eleven o'clock at night. Three-legged, the dog was. Shuffling along. Then suddenly it keeled over, dead.

I asked if he'd been going to McClanahan's and he said, "Of course I have."

I felt split in half. When I was with Mike, I thought of Kilroy. When I was on the phone with Kilroy, I thought of Mike.

His hard time was late afternoon. He was tired by then, and his neck hurt, and he had to spend time in bed, lying on his side to avoid pressure sores from being in the wheelchair for too long. He could transfer himself with a board—incredibly slowly, incrementally, burdening his shoulders as he inched along—but on harder days he let his mother move him. If I happened to be there I watched while she planted her legs and went to work, silent with concentration, her face full of strain.

Late one afternoon he and I sat in his room together, right around the time he usually lay down. I knew he was exhausted: I'd taken him out to lunch and then to the mall for some new shirts. His face was pale under the bit of sun he'd gotten along his cheekbones.

"Tired?" I said.

"What gives you that idea?" He smiled, and I thought of what a sweet smile he had, easy and wide and full of good humor. At lunch earlier he'd been full of smiles, telling me a long story about a joke he and Harvey had played on one of the orderlies, a guy who had somehow earned the nickname of Bags.

"Can I transfer you?" I said. I'd been meaning to ask, though I hadn't decided on today. "I think I know how."

"It's not about thinking," he said. "Believe me."

"What isn't?"

I turned and there was Mrs. Mayer, looking in on us. She did that a lot: poked her head in to ask if he needed anything, stopped in to remind him to have a drink of water. It was like the old days, when she'd invent excuses to make sure we weren't having sex.

"Transferring me," Mike said. "Carrie offered to do it."

"She can't possibly," Mrs. Mayer exclaimed. "That's out of the question." She faced me with her mouth pressed into a thin line. "It's quite complicated. If you lose him for a second—"

"She wouldn't *lose* me," he said, rolling his eyes. "Obviously she'd be careful."

"People have to be trained," she said. "It's a question of training."

"Then train her," he snapped. "Or better yet, why don't you both just get out of here and I'll do it myself?"

Mrs. Mayer clasped her hands and brought them to her chest. She held them together in front of her flowered blouse as if she were cupping a tiny, wounded animal. "Oh, Mike," she said. "Oh, sweetheart." Her eyes were wide, and I thought she would cry. I couldn't look at him, but I felt him off to my side, sitting in his chair, rage massed in his useless body.

Then it was over. Mrs. Mayer came into the room and said, "All right, let's train her. Carrie, this is the best workout, you'll see."

It was harder than it looked. It took more strength than I would have guessed I had—I couldn't fathom how she did it. I stood in front of the wheelchair and wiggled my hands under his arms and around his back, where I locked them together. Bent close, I felt his ear against my face, smelled his soap and shaving cream and the musky, intimate scent of his body. I pulled him up, bit by strained bit, until we were both more or less upright. The burden of his body was enormous. I knew I had to swivel him around, but I was terrified to move, terrified he'd knock me over—my arms were shaking. Finally I just did it, swung us around until the bed was behind him, a dance of dead weight. I lowered him, and behind me Mrs. Mayer sighed extravagantly. I stood there panting, then let his upper body down, our eyes meeting as his head touched the pillow. At last I raised his legs and smoothed out the fabric of his pants so he wouldn't be lying on any creases.

"Well," Mrs. Mayer said from behind me. "Well." She clapped her hands together as if dusting them off. "Be sure there's plenty of support under his head."

Mike and I looked at each other. After a charged moment we both laughed. "Thanks," he said.

"You're quite welcome."

HE HAD OUTPATIENT physical therapy three times a week. I took him one day and watched from a chair by the window while an older woman with a squat, muscular body put his limbs through a series of movements. Mike lay on a mat, his arms and legs circling and bending and extending, front, side, front, side. I stood up and looked out the window. Lake Mendota was a mosaic of blue behind a stand of far trees. I hadn't really seen the lake since I'd been back, not up close, not standing still. Now, seeing bits of it from far away, I longed to be near enough to feel the wind, to see the way the sky broke up in the surface of the water, rippled and blue-black. Out of my view but nearby was Picnic Point, and I thought of the long walk out, how you felt the lake near you as you went, the water lapping just beyond the trees.

When Mike was done we went to see Harvey, in a room down the hall from Mike's old one. Heading along the familiar corridor, I felt tremulous and reluctant, and I stayed a pace or two behind Mike so he wouldn't be able to see my face.

Harvey was in the far bed, a dark-haired man with a steel-gray beard, full and untended like a mountaineer's. He had bright eyes and a quick smile, and he greeted me by name before Mike could introduce us. "So you finally brought her, huh?"

"It was her idea," Mike joked. "I didn't care if you guys ever met."

I sat on a vinyl-padded chair against the wall and listened to them talk. Occasionally I stole glances at the man in the other bed, a thick tube attached to his throat. He wore a halo, couldn't have turned to look at me if he'd wanted to.

A woman about my mother's age came in. She was tall and athletic-looking, dressed in jeans and old running shoes, her hair in a careless ponytail. She did a double take at the sight of me, then bent to kiss Harvey's cheek and then Mike's. "Hello to you," she said, "and to you, too. And is this Carrie?"

"It is," Mike said. There was an awkward moment, and then he added, "Carrie, this is Maggie, Harvey's wife."

Maggie gave me a cold little smile. "Well," she said. "Greetings."

She pulled a spare chair over and sat down near Harvey, sighing in a loud, doesn't-this-feel-good way, as if to say that she for one was perfectly comfortable here. "Chow's coming, hon," she said. "Want me to lock the door?"

"Don't stop there—why not a small nuclear bomb on the kitchen?"

She smiled and reached into a bag she'd brought with her, withdrawing a Pyrex dish covered with foil. "Do stir-fried veggies and rice sound good?"

Harvey gave her a look of mock outrage. "No milkshake?"

Maggie turned to Mike. "Is that gratitude? Doesn't this guy owe me some gratitude?"

Mike gave me an uneasy glance. I could see he wished she hadn't come in—that he liked her but didn't trust her. I wondered how he'd talked about me with her, if perhaps she was the person he'd complained to: another woman, stalwart. "Yeah, Harv," Mike said. "Don't you know a good thing when you've got it?"

Harvey laughed. "Stir-fried veggies and rice sound lovely," he said. "Perfectly lovely."

Maggie peeled the foil off the dish and set it on Harvey's swing-arm table. She got a fork from the bag, speared a piece of zucchini, and held it to Harvey's mouth. "We're watching the dairy and citrus these days," she said to Mike. "UTI prevention."

Mike looked at me apologetically. "Urinary tract infection," he said.

"Oh, sorry," Maggie said. "I assumed you'd know." She forked some rice and offered it to Harvey. His injury was higher up than Mike's, I remembered. No bicep, so he couldn't feed himself.

Half an hour later we left, heading to the elevator and then riding down in silence. Outside, I paused in a little plaza in front of the entrance so I could feel in my purse for the van keys. The parking lot was crowded, but we were right up front, in a handicapped spot.

"It wasn't just you," Mike said.

I turned and he was looking right at me, his gray eyes squinting against the sun. "I was sort of hoping it was."

"People are more comfortable when other people conform to their standards. It validates their lives, kind of." He gave me a sheepish look. "Thank you, Dave King," he added.

I helped him into the van and climbed behind the steering wheel, but I didn't start up. I was thinking that I'd like to pinch a handful of Maggie's nose between my fingers and twist hard. That I'd like to tell Mrs. Mayer to get over herself. *Here I am,* I wanted to say. *I'm here now, OK?* Outside the van was a sea of cars, then a university, a lake, a city—a flat, flat stretch of land that was fertile and endless. What if I never walked across 14th Street again, with its bodega smells and crowds of men to step around? What if I never woke to the sound of half a dozen sirens again, screaming down Seventh Avenue? What if I never wandered through SoHo again, imagining this skirt that jacket those shoes right onto me, transforming me into someone unimaginable?

What if I never saw Kilroy again?

I turned and looked at Mike. He stared vacantly out the window, tired from physical therapy, from the exhaustion of wondering what was going on with me, when I was going back. Inside his polo shirt his shoulders were knobby and angular. The muscles he could still use were overtaxed, stringy. He looked up. "What?" he said. "What are you thinking?"

"That nothing I do will be enough now." My face flamed, and I looked away. A row of birds sat on the arm of a streetlight, uneven black bumps like buttons along the shoulder of a dress.

"It won't be," he said.

I turned to see what he looked like, pissed off or fed up or what, but his expression was bland: bland as cream, bland as milk, bland as Wisconsin.

38

~

WATER SPLASHED INTO the pan I was washing, a skillet in which I'd sautéed zucchini and onion to serve with the lamb chops I'd broiled. I added a ribbon of dishwashing liquid and ran a yellow-and-red scrubber over the cooking surface. My mother had already loaded our plates into the dishwasher, which I'd convinced her to start using, and now she moved around the kitchen behind me, putting our placemats away and wiping the table. Evenings in the kitchen together, talking or not—there was something provisional about them, something awkward.

The phone rang, and she stepped to the wall to answer it.

"Carrie," she said, holding the receiver out. There was a question on her face, and my pulse sped up. Could it be Kilroy? I called him, not the other way around. Using my calling card, so the charges wouldn't end up on my mother's phone bill. Drying my hands, I felt a wave of guilt over not having told her about him. Why shouldn't I tell my mother about Kilroy?

I took the receiver from her and said hello.

"Listen, missy, you've been MIA too long—I need an explanation."

It was Simon, and I relaxed. I turned so I could mouth, "It's Simon," to my mother, but she'd tactfully left the room.

"So?" he said. "I'm all ears. What gives?"

I told him about things—how Jamie wouldn't forgive me and how I'd started spending time with Mike and how I couldn't leave.

"Yet," he said. "You forgot to say yet."

"I'm not sure."

There was a long silence, and then, "Carrie, are you for real?"

"I don't know what I'm for."

"God."

I stretched the phone cord over to the table and sat down. Simon and the brownstone and the room that was finally mine: I still wanted to paint. I wanted to get a rug, a lamp. I wanted a life in New York. I wanted to be with Kilroy.

"I can just picture it," Simon said. "I'll see you once a year when I go home to Madison to visit. You'll start frosting your hair and one day I'll realize you've been shopping at the Lands' End outlet store."

"That's so mean."

"Then promise you'll come back."

I touched my cheek, my fingertips surprisingly cool. I couldn't think of what to say.

"Carrie as in carry," he said. "I was right that fateful day in James Madison Park, except I guess it's not a canoe you'll be carrying."

"Simon," I said. "That's not how it is."

"Then how is it?"

I stood up and walked across the kitchen to the window. It was dusk, the sky a thick violet. I could see a lighted upstairs window in Rooster and Joan's house. When I ran into her out front she always made a point of saying more than just hello. *I have some extra nasturtium seeds, I wanted your opinion on this maternity dress, would you like to come in for some lemonade?* A friend if I wanted her to be one.

"Let's change the subject," I said to Simon. "Tell me something funny."

"That's a tall order."

"You're a tall guy."

He was silent for a moment. "OK, here's something. Remember Benjamin, my ex? He's madly in love with a dancer."

"Oh, Simon. That's hard."

"A blond dancer. A blond dancer from *Denmark*. I'm like, if this is what you wanted all along what the fuck were you ever doing with me?"

"It's not necessarily what he wanted all along. Maybe he really doesn't know so he's trying out some extremes."

"That's nice of you," he said. There was a pause, and then he added, "I really miss you."

I didn't respond, and he cried, "Do you think I don't mean it? I *really miss* you. You're a big part of my life."

I'd hardly thought of him since leaving, and I felt terrible. What was wrong with me? What kind of friend was I? "I'm sorry," I said, and then I thought *sorry, sorry, sorry,* and felt worse still.

There was an awkward silence, and he said, "It's not just me, you know—Lane was saying just yesterday that she wished you'd come back."

"How is she?"

"Not so good," he said. "Ever since Miss Wolf died she—"

"Miss Wolf died?" I said. "Oh my God, when?"

"You didn't know? It must have been right after you left because it was a while ago, maybe a month." He paused. "She had a heart attack. Three days in the hospital and that was it."

"How awful," I said. "Lane must be really upset. Was she with her when it happened?"

"She'd just left. She got home and there was a message on the machine from a nurse."

I shook my head. I remembered how worried Lane had been when Miss Wolf had a cold. How she'd walked up the steps to the Plaza just behind Miss Wolf, her hands up and ready to help if Miss Wolf stumbled. "Is she there?" I said. "Can I talk to her?"

"After you promise to come back."

"Simon."

"All right," he said, "but we *will* talk about this again. Hang on."

The phone settled onto something hard, and as I stood there waiting I heard my mother moving around upstairs. Footsteps crossing her bedroom, the faint creak of her closet door. In a minute the water would go on in her bathroom. I was overcome suddenly by the knowledge that she made these same sounds whether anyone was present to hear them or not.

Lane came on the line, her voice faint and a little dull. She told me about Miss Wolf's death, how for three days she'd sat there waiting for Miss Wolf to pull through. *I know,* I wanted to say, but of course I didn't. I knew about waiting for Mike to pull through, but there was no telling how different it had been for Lane, a daughter or grand-daughter figure, sitting there alone.

She was at loose ends, trying to decide on a next move. "Come visit me," I said, and to my surprise she agreed to, the following week.

THE NEXT AFTERNOON I learned that Mike had quit his com-puter job. He was tired of pretending it was more than just a way to feel useful. "I'm not useful," he said, "and gathering data about fucking life expectancy rates isn't going to change that, or how I feel about it."

We were in the van together, on the way home from another visit to Harvey. We passed a car wash where Mike had worked one summer in high school, a line of blue and yellow pennants flapping in the breeze. I'd had a job just around the corner, at a drugstore that had since closed down, and I remembered walking over after work and watching while he drove people's cars out of the chute and then dried them, both hands spinning blue rags.

I looked over at him, strapped into his wheelchair. His eyes drooped at the outside corners. Even his mustache drooped today, rimming the unhappy arc of his mouth.

"How'd your dad react?" I said.

"He was disappointed. Well, maybe not disappointed. He just—"

"Wants you to be happy?"

"I think he'd settle for a little less than that."

We rode along in silence. It was a clear, green day, the shade trees knitting together for the summer ahead. Lilacs were in bloom, lush purple and satiny green, their thick, heady scent everywhere.

He said, "Mom, on the other hand, was all for it. 'Why should you spend your time on something you hate when you don't need the money, dear?' She'd be perfectly content to have me be like that Tom guy."

"Mike, she wouldn't." Tom was Harvey's roommate, a C3 who'd never breathe without a ventilator.

"You know what I mean."

I knew: Mrs. Mayer wanted Mike to count on her no matter what. She didn't always see how hard it was that he had to.

"He's a head on a pillow," Mike blurted. "If that were me I'd rather be dead."

I braked and turned to face him. "Mike."

"I would." He looked at me defiantly, and my first impulse was to look away, brush it off, bury it. *You didn't say that.* But he had.

"Will you—" I hesitated. "Will you tell me more?" Immediately I felt my face fill with heat. *Tell me:* Kilroy's phrase. What would Mike say? How would I react? I was nervous but forced myself to wait, to not fill the silence with words, and after a while he sighed and began to speak.

"I read somewhere that after something like this you spend your life either looking for a reason or looking for a cure. But you know what? There isn't a reason and there isn't a cure. *There just isn't.* I went to this church thing a few times and it was crazy, it was like all these people were just dying to have me decide that God had a plan for me. Why would that make a difference? I think I stopped really believing in God around the same time I stopped believing in Santa Claus, and if breaking my neck was supposed to help me start believing again, why on earth would that be a comforting idea? If you had half a brain it would make you really pissed off instead." He shook his head. "Dave King says maybe the hardest challenge is having to live with suicidal thoughts, having to accept them as part of the whole damn package." He stared at me. "Are you going to take me home or not?"

I took my foot off the brake and drove the rest of the way to the Mayers'. At the driveway I eased up the bump and stopped in front of the garage. I cut the engine. My heart was pounding. I said, "Do you have suicidal thoughts a lot?"

He looked at me and looked away. "I did. I mean, I still do, but not as much."

"That must be—" I searched for what to say. "That must be hard."

He sighed. "It's exhausting. It's like, you have these pictures in your mind, and you're pulled toward them at the same time that you're trying like hell to stay away from them."

"Mike," I said softly. "God."

He looked away. After a while he said, "I'm ready to go in now," and I climbed down from the van and went around to the other side, then stood waiting while the lift lowered him. I walked up the ramp behind him, his wheelchair humming. At the top we stopped. "Want to sit out here for a while?" I said. "Would you like something to drink?"

"No, thanks."

Neither of us spoke. I leaned against the railing. Mrs. Mayer was in the kitchen, her shape as she moved around just visible through the clean windows.

"Mike Mayer has a morose spell," he said, glancing at me and smiling a little. "He sits in his wheelchair and contemplates the back lawn."

~

39

ON THE PHONE the night before Lane was due, I walked her through my dresser and closet, telling her what I wanted—this shirt, that skirt, those pants. When she asked if Kilroy knew I was getting her to bring me so much of my stuff, I said he didn't. The fact was, he didn't even know she was coming. I hadn't talked to him in a week, nothing to say until it was clear what I was going to do. Seeing Lane at the airport the next day, a tiny shoulder bag of her stuff and a giant duffel of mine, what I was going to do suddenly seemed obvious, and I thought: *OK, then.* Eight months earlier I'd left Madison abruptly, on the spur of a moment, though one that had been coming for a long time. Now, these past weeks, I'd been swinging back and forth between staying here and going back—swinging without even thinking about it all that much because thinking couldn't really help me choose as well as seeing could: my clothing, here. My life, here. Was this it?

Lane and I grinned at each other, awkward for a moment and then hugging hard. She wore a pair of chinos and a plain white T-shirt, like a little boy going to summer camp.

"It's so good to see you!"

I bent over and hefted the duffel, then slung the long strap over my shoulder. I started toward the parking lot, but she didn't follow.

"Carrie."

I turned back.

"I have to tell you something."

"What?"

She put two fingers to her mouth and blew against them. "Miss Wolf left me her letters." She moved her hand away and I could see that she was biting the inside of her lower lip. "I haven't told anyone in New York yet."

I put the duffel bag down. "What do you mean, left you her letters?"

"To edit," she said. "Into a book. The letters she got from people and copies of lots that she sent."

Now I understood, and I understood the enormity of it. Simon had told me once that Miss Wolf had been a central figure in society—in several societies. What was his line? She knew everyone from Lionel Trilling to Grace Kelly.

"Are you going to do it?" I asked Lane.

She shook her head slowly. "I haven't decided. It's tempting, and if I don't they're supposed to be burned. But it's not fair to put that decision on to me!" she cried. "It's up to me to decide how she's thought of from now on! If I don't do it, she's Monique Wolf, remember her, that writer from whenever it was. If I do she could end up being the flavor of the month or the year and people would have a completely different perspective on her. She could end up a hot literary topic."

"I see what you mean," I said. "You could, too."

Lane's pale face filled with color, and she looked down. "I know." With the toe of her black Converse sneaker she traced a series of short lines, one after another. "You know what?" she said, looking up. "I'm not sure I want to go that deeply into her life. I'm not sure I want to get to know her that well."

"You knew her really well."

"I knew what I knew. Do I want that to change?" Suddenly tears streamed from her eyes, thin trails running down her cheeks. She stretched the neck of her T-shirt up to blot her face dry. "Isn't this stupid?" she sobbed. "I can't stop crying."

"It's not stupid, it's normal."

"I'm a wreck," she said. "Your mother'll think I'm a real nutcase."

I shook my head and put my arm around her, her shoulder bony under my hand. "No she won't," I said. "And if she does, then you'll just seem very familiar."

IN FACT, MY mother took to Lane right away. We lingered over dinner for nearly two hours that night, easily quadrupling my mother's and my average. My mother seemed *interested* in Lane, as if she wanted to figure something out: maybe me.

Lane thought she was wonderful. "She's so low-key you don't really think much is going on at first, and then boom, she comes up with these incredibly smart responses to things." She was talking about something my mother had said about Miss Wolf's death: that the writer in Lane had to mourn the loss of the writer in Miss Wolf just as much as the companion had to mourn the employer. "And the lesbian has to mourn the lesbian," Lane said, and my mother cast me a curious glance.

Later, she went upstairs, while Lane and I stayed in the kitchen and made tea. Lane asked about Kilroy, and I told her about how our long-distance phone conversations had become impossible, about how torn I'd been feeling. And then more: about meeting his parents back in March, and the pall that seeing them had cast over him.

"It's not even like he doesn't like them," I said. "It's like he can't."

"You know," Lane said, "I didn't want to tell you this before, but remember how Maura felt like she recognized him from somewhere?"

I remembered Thanksgiving, Maura's curious glances. I nodded.

"She realized why. His name is Fraser, right? One of the big honchos on Wall Street—and I mean *big* honchos—is a man named Morton Fraser. Is that his father's name?"

Indeed it was. I thought of how we'd gone to the Empire State Building late on Thanksgiving night, and how, turning to look toward

Wall Street, he'd asked, not quite casually, *What does Maura do?* As if, I understood now, he feared she'd made—or would make—the connection. But why did he care?

I told Lane about the note I'd read, *You must be thinking of the date as much as we are.* "What could it be?" I said. "The anniversary of something awful, I figure."

She stared at me. "Why don't you just ask him?"

I laced my fingers together, twisted my engagement ring around and then back. I'd caught Mike staring at it a few days earlier; when he saw that I'd noticed, he quickly looked away.

"I can't," I said.

"According to whose rules?"

"His."

"Why do you play by his rules?"

I thought of the night at McClanahan's when I asked about other women. The day at MOMA when I asked who I reminded him of. So many other times. "You know," I said, "I didn't entirely. It's more like there were rules and I broke them and it didn't matter."

Lane looked at me carefully. "You're using the past tense."

I remembered the moment earlier in the day, at the airport, when I saw my duffel bag. Then I thought of Kilroy alone in New York—his slight frame disappearing around a corner, seen by no one—and my insides lurched. I was *still* swinging back and forth, though I imagined a moment would come when the swinging would change: no longer a movement between choices, but a movement into memory and regret, and back out again.

WE SLEPT LATE the next morning, Lane on my bedroom floor in a sleeping bag that hadn't been used in at least ten years. The contents of the duffel were in piles on my desk, and after my shower I peeled pants and a shirt off the top and put them on, thrilled to have something new to wear.

At lunchtime I took her to meet Mike. I was nervous, although I wasn't sure which of them I hoped would impress the other. Actually, it wasn't that: I was nervous over whether there was a single me I could be in the presence of them both.

We borrowed the van and drove to James Madison Park. Lake Mendota glittered in the sun, aquamarine with foamy white peaks on the little wavelets. Sailboats raced along in a light wind. The lake at last, the great blue spill of it. I breathed in deeply, as if I could breathe in the lake, the entire blue sky.

We sat at a picnic table and ate sandwiches I'd made, the same table I'd stood on with Jamie to watch Paddle 'n' Portage nearly a year ago.

"This is so beautiful," Lane said.

"Madison at its best," Mike said. "This exact moment in May."

Lane smiled. " 'Life, London, this moment of June.' "

"Huh?" he said with a grin.

"Virginia Woolf. Miss Wolf loved her."

She'd told him a little about Miss Wolf earlier, and he nodded. "Well, that makes sense," he said after a while. "Woolf and Wolf."

I was afraid she'd laugh at him—or worse, not—but she smiled and said, "That's what I always think."

We ate our sandwiches. I'd brought a thermos of iced tea and Mike's special cup, and from his place at the end of the table he leaned over and drank. A guy with blond dreadlocks walked past and gave us the peace sign, and Mike and Lane exchanged an amused look.

"So you grew up in Connecticut?" he said. "Were you a sailing type of girl—summers at the marina and all that?"

Lane shook her head. "My corner of Connecticut is pretty land-locked. Besides which, I've always really hated that crap. When I was ten my mother decided I should try to come out of my shell, so she sent me to this sailing camp in Maine where I spent the entire two weeks hiding in my bunk reading Hardy Boys books."

Mike smiled. "Not Nancy Drew?"

"Nancy made me ill. Or maybe it was her roadster."

We all laughed. I bit into a carrot stick and chewed happily, the sun hard on my back and the lake in front of me, a feeling of peace at hand.

"Why were you in a shell?" Mike said.

Lane set her sandwich down. "Probably because my father had died a few years earlier."

"Oh, I'm sorry," he said. He hesitated a moment and then looked at me. "You know, I always used to sort of hope your father would come back so I'd be able to stand up for you and tell him off."

I was surprised. "You did?"

" 'Fraid so," he said with a self-conscious smile.

Lane leaned forward. "Why did you think Carrie wouldn't be able to stand up for herself?"

He didn't respond at first, and for a moment I feared she'd offended him. But then he shrugged and said, "That wasn't an issue. Standing up for her was what I felt I'd been born to do."

It was hard for me to swallow, and I took a long drink of my iced tea. I'd always known this, but for so long it had discomfitted me. Why? Why did it feel so different now, so good? I wanted to stand up for him, too, to be there for him—every cliché in the book was what I wanted. There was only one way, though: to be there, period.

LANE LEFT TWO days later, the empty duffel folded into her shoulder bag. We were both a little teary when we hugged goodbye, and as I watched her plane back away from the gate I wondered when I'd ever see her again.

I'd only gotten about halfway through putting away the clothes she'd brought me, and when I got back from the airport I continued, meeting each garment with a sense of reunion, as if it had been years since I'd seen it, and it was an old, good friend.

One thing I hadn't asked for was the green velvet dress. It was hanging in my closet in the brownstone, and though I knew Lane or Simon would send it to me anytime, I found myself wondering if I even wanted it anymore. I recalled the December day I went to Bergdorf's, the eerie quiet as I moved from expensive dress to expensive dress, from dream to dream, imagining myself as someone who would wear such things. Maybe that was it: I'd made a dress for a life that wasn't right for me. As I put my clothes away, I thought I might just leave the dress where it was, a talisman for some future occupant of the brownstone as she forged a life for herself in New York.

I *had* asked for my silk nightgown and robe, and here they were. After all those months in my bottom drawer, plus the journey in

Lane's duffel, they were crumpled and sad-looking, and I set up my mother's ironing board and ironed them carefully, the hot, dry scent putting me firmly back in my old apartment. I remembered so clearly how trapped I'd felt then, but I remembered it from the outside: the feeling but not how it felt, not exactly. Was it something I could penetrate? The question scared me, and I thought the answer must be yes.

I finished ironing and hung the nightgown on one hanger and the robe on another. I put my arm between them and moved it back and forth, the feel of the fabric as exquisite as I remembered. There would come a day when I would wear them, I was sure of it—a day when I wouldn't worry about the reaction I'd get. I would wear them happily, proudly. At that future point, would I remember this moment? Would I look back and think: *That was when I knew I was home?*

My oldest jeans were at the bottom of the pile. Folded tight, they felt funny, a little stiff, and when I shook them out a thin blue thing fell onto the floor. I bent to pick it up. *Parapraxis and Eurydice. Poems by Lane Driscoll.* It was Lane's book—her chapbook. She'd never said a word about having brought it. She'd bought wine for my mother, and flowers at a stand one afternoon, but this she'd left behind for me to find once she was gone. I flipped it open and saw that there was something written on the title page, an inscription. *For Carrie,* it said. *Always my friend.*

40

A T THE TOP of the Mayers' basement stairs I hesitated. I could hear the dryer pounding, smell detergent and heated cotton. Mike was in his room resting, and I started down, wishing there was something to knock on. This was Mrs. Mayer's domain.

She was standing at a long table, a huge basket of laundry at her feet. In front of her everything was in neat stacks, socks sorted, shirts folded just so. It was warm and steamy.

"Excuse me," I said.

She looked up and frowned a little. "Oh, hi."

I continued down the stairs until I'd reached the concrete floor. "Can I talk to you? About next weekend?"

She pursed her lips. Memorial Day was nearly upon us—Memorial Day itself, the first anniversary of Mike's accident, but also Memorial Day weekend, which she and Mr. Mayer traditionally spent up in Door County, at an annual conference put on by his office. It had been from Door County that they'd been summoned to the hospital last year, pulled off the golf course and flown down in a twin engine that belonged to one of the other VPs. I was in the emergency room waiting area when they arrived, Mr. Mayer running in ahead of her, holding his glasses to his face so they wouldn't slip off.

"What about it?" she said. She reached into the basket, laid a pair of plaid boxers on the table, and folded them into a neat square. "It's already decided—I'm not going."

"I know," I said. "But Mike really wants you to."

She frowned. "You don't have to tell me what Mike wants. I know John Junior will be here, but that's not enough. Things can happen."

"Like what?" I'd asked Mike what was holding her back, and he'd said, "The fact that I might drop my rattle, waah, waah."

"Well, autonomic dysreflexia," she snapped. "You probably don't know about this, but there are a number of things—even just his bladder or bowel getting too full—that can send his blood pressure through the roof really fast. People can die if they don't get the right treatment *immediately*." She reached into the basket again, this time picking up a striped dress shirt of Mr. Mayer's, which she sprayed with a mister and then rolled into a ball and set aside.

"Are there symptoms?" I said. "Of the blood pressure rising?"

She had another pair of boxers in her hand, and she sighed and set them down. "What are you getting at, Carrie?"

"I'd like to stay for the weekend so you can go. I'll come on Friday and stay till you get back Tuesday morning. You can tell me everything I need to know. I'll be responsible."

Her mouth tightened.

"I want to do it," I said. "You can hate me for the rest of your life, but that doesn't change the fact that I'm here now, I'm back, and I want to be part of Mike's life. And I'm going to be."

"Carrie Bell," she said. "Well, well." She smiled a little. "Mr. Mayer does want me to go."

"Then go," I said. "Don't you want to? Spend a weekend away, go antiquing? Have a martini on Saturday night? You always loved going."

She patted her hair and looked down for a moment, her hand at her chin. "John Junior can do the catheter," she said.

I WENT OVER on the Friday afternoon. I baked a meatloaf Mrs. Mayer had left and put out a salad that was already in the bowl and needed only to be dressed. John had a friend over, and the four of us ate in the kitchen, the little countertop TV tuned to a baseball game on ESPN. John was already deep in training for his senior-year hockey season, and he had three helpings of meatloaf and at least a quart of milk.

"That's rude," his friend said when John found a container of cottage cheese in the refrigerator and spooned a large mound onto his plate.

"He's growing," Mike said, and he gave me a big grin from across the table.

After dinner John and his friend went out. I cleaned up and then joined Mike in the living room. "What'll we do?" he said. "Rent a video? I'm wiped, but you could go get one."

I opened my mouth to protest that I didn't want to leave him, and he gave me a look. "Just go."

I drove as fast as I could, grabbed something I couldn't have said the title of two minutes later, and hurried back. It wasn't until I'd parked that I could get myself to slow down. I didn't want to be like Mrs. Mayer.

Saturday morning after breakfast we sat in the kitchen waiting for the doorbell. Mike's attendant was due to arrive at nine, to help him shower and go to the bathroom—"administer his BP," as Mrs. Mayer said, his bowel program. It involved rubber gloves, lubricating jelly—Mike wouldn't let anyone in his family do it.

I sat on the deck while they were busy. Finally he wheeled outside, his hair still wet, a sheepish smile on his lips. "Remember when BP stood for Beautiful People?" he said. "The times, they have changed."

We got into the van and drove over to the State Capitol. The Farmers' Market at the end of May: there were tender lettuces, spears of rhubarb, tiny carrots and potatoes. We joined the crowd circling the stands. I bought some potted herbs and a jar of honey for my mother. A farmwife with worn-out fingers sold us a massive bear claw, and I tore off little bits and fed them to Mike, then licked the almondy crumbs from my fingertips. Green apples, big purple bulbs of garlic. It was still too early for sour cherries.

Back at home Mike was exhausted. A simple excursion could do him in. He took a nap while I worked on dinner, chicken stew with dumplings from Mrs. Mayer's recipe box. We ate early and then went for a walk. The sky was hazy, colorless. We passed people working in their gardens. They might not actually know each other, but they understood who each other was. Turning back toward the Mayers', we came upon a man playing catch with a little girl. On his back there was a baby in a backpack who laughed a toothless little laugh every time he caught the ball.

When we got back we could hear the shower running upstairs, John's voice hitting the high notes of the Sears jingle from TV. He came downstairs a little later with his hair blown dry.

"Hot date?" I said. He looked so much like Mike at seventeen, rangy but broad-shouldered, the same thin face.

"Yeah, where are you going?" Mike said.

John grinned.

"I think John might be a lady-killer," Mike told me.

"It's all in the Z," John said. He meant the 280 Z, the car Mr. Mayer had handed down to Mike. John drove it now.

"Don't sell yourself short," Mike said. "That cologne you're wearing counts, too."

I suppressed a smile. John smelled a little like a drugstore.

"Hey, that's my personal musk," John said.

Mike rolled back a few feet. "The hell it is."

Sunday we went over to Rooster and Joan's. She called him Doug, which no one had called him in all the years I'd known him. "Doug, hon, would you put some Doritos in a bowl and bring them out?" Rooster liked it: being called Doug, being called hon, putting Doritos in a bowl. Before we left he led us into the second bedroom and showed us a little wooden cradle he'd already made, painted white with a bunny decal at one end.

MONDAY WAS MEMORIAL DAY. We hadn't made plans, and I woke early, impelled to come up with some activity—shopping, a park, a movie, something to get us past the middle of the day.

Mike had other ideas. After his attendant left he rolled into the kitchen where I was cleaning up and said, casually as you please, that he wanted to drive up to Clausen's Reservoir.

He watched me nonchalantly, waiting for my response. My heart pounded. How could he go and not come back a little more broken? How could I? He sat there in his chair, face still pink from his shower, his mustache newly trimmed. He'd been waiting for this, I understood. For a long time.

There was a lot of traffic. We drove past farms and small clusters of houses, interchanges where narrow roads ran to rural towns. There was a holiday countdown on the radio, but with a new spin. "Out of Order," it was called, with the songs played out of order. "How dumb is that?" Mike said.

The parking lot at the reservoir was crowded. Lots of jeeps and motorcycles—fool's wheels, as Mike and Rooster had always said. I pulled into a handicapped spot and cut the engine. Out the window I looked at the hill that hid the water from view, grassy and choked with Queen Anne's lace. "What do you want to do?" I said. The path up the hill was narrow and rocky; it was not accessible.

"Get out at least."

I got down and went around to help him. All around us there were kids skateboarding, whole Rollerblading families, guys showing off their muscular, oiled bodies to girls wearing bathing suits you could carry in a Band-Aid box.

"Remember Mr. Fenrow?" I said. Fenrow had taught the one class we took together senior year of high school, Family Life.

"Yeah."

I reached into the van for his hat and settled it on his head so the brim shaded his face—he wasn't supposed to get sunburned. "Remember what he said to Mimi Baldwin that time?"

He wrinkled his nose. "I'm not sure."

"There was that camping trip he organized for seniors—come to think of it I don't think it ever happened our year. But in class one day when he was trying to get people to sign up she asked if we were supposed to bring bathing suits, and he said, 'That should be easy enough—two Band-Aids and a cork.'"

Mike snorted. "Guess *why* it never happened." He pushed the lever on his chair and began to move forward. "We'll get a pop," he said. "Then we can go."

The refreshment stand was at the far side of the parking lot. By the time we got there Mike was sweating; he looked unwell. Nearby, there were several picnic tables under corrugated plastic shelters, and I got him to go wait at one. I took my place in line and glanced back at him, thinking he looked impossibly vulnerable, spastic legs sprouting awkwardly from his loose shorts.

Two women came to stand behind me, and after a while I realized they were talking about him.

"He looks really hot," one of them said.

"Poor thing," said the other.

"It seems like he'd be a lot more comfortable if he'd stayed home."

I turned around and looked at them, women in their late thirties, in wide-strapped bathing suits topped by sarongs so their legs wouldn't show. I said, "Don't you mean *you'd* be more comfortable if he'd stayed home?"

They gave each other horrified looks.

"I'm so sorry," said the first one.

"Is he with you?" said the second.

"No, *I'm* with *him*."

I felt sweaty and irritable as I carried our sodas to the table. We drank them under the bright shade of the plastic shelter, neither of us saying much. When we were done Mike asked me to get some hot-dogs, and I stood in line again, thinking he didn't want the dogs so much as he wasn't ready to leave.

Finally we started back toward the van. When we arrived at the path over the hill, Mike stopped. He wheeled around so he could look at me.

"The helicopter landed right there," I said, pointing at the clear space where the road led into the parking lot. "You were still on the pier, where Rooster'd pulled you up."

I stared at the space, thinking back. It took twenty-eight minutes from the time the woman at the snack bar placed the call. The helicopter dropped from the sky with a huge racket, its blades ratcheting around and around. Standing there by Mike, I remembered how it had seemed to bounce as it landed. I remembered Rooster running to meet the paramedics, I remembered Jamie's hand in mine.

"What were you thinking?" Mike said.

"That it was my fault. That if I hadn't been mad at you I would have kept you from diving."

"Oh, Carrie," he said.

"Oh, Mike. Oh, everyone."

THAT EVENING WE watched TV. The house was dark but for a single lamp near where we sat, me on the living room couch and Mike just to my side. John was out again, and the Mayers weren't due back until morning. Mike fell asleep shortly after nine, his head slumped forward. When he woke a little later he was embarrassed.

One thing he couldn't do was get in and out of his clothes by himself—he could do the top but not the bottom. "Lower extremity dressing," as they said in occupational therapy. Actually he could, but it took about an hour.

We went into his room and I unbuttoned his shirt. He got it off and transferred onto his bed, where I eased the shorts down, rolling him from side to side to get them off.

"All set?" I said. He slept in his underwear, the catheter tube running down his leg to the collection bag.

"Yeah, I'm fine. I was wondering, though—" He hesitated. "Would you go put your pajamas on and come sit with me? Just—like a proper slumber party? For our last night?"

I went up to Julie's room, where I was staying. I'd brought a short, flowered nightgown—a giant T-shirt, really—and I got undressed and put it on.

I tapped lightly on the door as I went back into his room. I sat in the armchair near his bed. Outside, a car zoomed by, the sudden radio and then quiet. Teenagers, maybe even John.

"Remember cruising?" he said. "What was the point, anyway? Was it drinking?"

"It was its own point."

In the hall Mrs. Mayer's grandfather clock struck ten. I looked at Mike, lying there with the head of his bed elevated, his arms half-bent. He turned his head so he could see me. "If I asked you to do something would you do it?"

"What?"

He looked embarrassed. "I wish you'd take your nightgown off. I want to see something."

I felt unsteady for a moment, blood rushing to my face. I wanted to look away but didn't. He stared into my eyes. "Nothing you haven't seen before," I said, but he didn't smile.

"Please?"

I stood up. He watched soberly from the bed, a little furrow in his forehead. I reached for the hem of my nightgown. It wasn't cold, but my arms were covered with goosebumps, and I hesitated, not wanting to go on. At last I pulled the nightgown over my head and dropped it on the chair behind me.

I was in my underwear. I crossed my arms over my breasts and then let them fall again. My nipples puckered. I didn't know what to do with my hands, how to hold them—I clasped them together in front of me, then wiped them against my thighs to dry them. Mike stared—just stared, absolutely nothing visible on his face but the subtlest tightening of his chin.

"I feel a little weird," I said at last, and he sighed and looked away.

"It's OK," he said. "I'm sorry, you can get dressed again. I felt nothing. That's what I wanted to know, and I felt nothing."

I pulled the nightgown back over my head. Nothing. To have your sexual self frozen, locked away: it was almost easier to imagine my limbs without motion. Arousal was so involuntary. You couldn't force it on yourself, it just arrived—crept up or burst in. And then one day it didn't. I thought of nights in my apartment, Mike slipping between my thighs, the little moan he made when he came.

He was staring at the wall. After a while he lowered the head of his bed until he was flat on his back. "There," he said.

I went over to the side of the bed. He met my eyes with his, then looked away. It was a narrow bed, perhaps a little wider than a regulation twin. "Can I sit here for a minute?" I said.

"Yeah."

I sat down. The blanket scratched the backs of my legs, and I shifted my weight and pulled my nightgown further under me. The overhead was blazing. My back was to him, and I twisted partway around so that my thigh lay parallel to his body and I could look back and see his face. Across the room, the poster of Lake Mendota hung in its silvery frame. It had been photographed from somewhere near the Union, Picnic Point curving in from the left. I closed my eyes and tried to remember our little place there, the room made by trees where we'd first made love.

He coughed.

"Are you comfortable?" I said. "Should I go upstairs now?"

"No, stay," he said. "Stay with me a little longer."

I nodded. The night was so quiet I could hear the faint thum of a moth lighting on the window screen. "There," Mike said, and he lay there, and I sat.

41

~

MY MOTHER'S HOUSE was quiet, sliced into sections of dark and light by the afternoon sun. I'd turned down Mrs. Mayer's offer of a lift home, and I was sweating lightly from the walk, my shoulder sore from where the strap of my bag had pressed into it.

A large cardboard box sat under the oak desk where my mother kept mail and things. Tossing my bag toward the bottom of the stairs, I knelt by the box and saw my name in big Magic Marker letters. The return address was in a ballpoint scrawl, 188W18NYNY10019. All on one line, like code for something. Kilroy.

I got a knife from the kitchen and pulled the box out from under the desk. I cut it open, and there was my Bernina.

My Bernina, sent to me by Kilroy.

He'd packed it carefully, with foam blocks in the corners to hold it tight, not an inch of give for movement, breakage. There was no note, just the machine and, wrapped in bubble wrap and wedged in tightly, my photograph of the Parisian rooftops.

I sat next to the open box and put my face in my hands. It was terrible to think of him approaching the task, how he'd probably thought of it and then put it out of his mind and then thought of it again, hoping all the while that I'd come back before he could actually follow through. His expression as he bought the box, carried it home, cut the foam to size. In my imagination I reached for him and he turned away, his mind made up to *do* this thing.

I hauled the machine upstairs and set it on my desk. I found a rag and dusted the outside, then took off the free-arm cover and cleaned the feed-dogs and the underside of the stitch plate. I cleaned the hook race and oiled it, then sat down with a scrap of fabric and sewed a wavy burgundy line with the thread I'd used for Kilroy's corduroy shirt, still on the second pin where I'd left it. The machine ran beautifully.

My throat ached. I wanted to cry but didn't want to have the sound of crying in my voice when we talked. What was I going to say? It was past time for this conversation.

At five o'clock I went into my mother's bedroom to use the phone. It was six New York time, and he answered on the first ring.

I said, "I thought, I was going to, I would've . . ."

And he said, "I figured you'd want it."

Then neither of us spoke for hours, weeks. I held the phone loosely but my palm grew slick anyway, and I had to pass the receiver from hand to hand. "I feel terrible," I said at last.

"For whom?"

"Kilroy," I said. I hesitated a moment, then said, "For me, for you. For us."

"So you've destroyed me," he said.

"No."

"Maybe you have."

His voice was flat—flat on *So you've destroyed me* and flat on *Maybe you have.* My chest ached, as if I'd taken a huge breath but couldn't let it out.

"The thing is," he said, "you really don't know. You'll never know."

"Kilroy," I said. "Please don't do this."

"Do what?"

I was silent. I knew this was a front, that he was terribly hurt. But to say so would hurt him more. I said, "You know, I really meant it when I said you could come here."

"And I really meant it when I said I couldn't."

Another silence, and I felt myself move toward crying. I pulled back. It wouldn't be right to cry, it wouldn't be fair: it would suggest I thought I was feeling more than he was, when I knew I wasn't.

"It sort of reminds me of lemmings," he said.

"What?"

"The idea of my going to Madison."

I thought of lemmings, those little rodents that committed mass suicide in Norway or somewhere, running headlong off cliffs because all the other ones were. Madison as the edge of the world, because he liked the traffic noise in New York. Yet I knew why he really couldn't leave: the avenues of New York were his arteries, the streets his veins.

"Actually, it turns out lemmings aren't trying to die," he said. "Did you know this? They're blind or something, they just don't know what's up ahead."

I felt impatient—only Kilroy could turn a breakup conversation into a disquisition on suicidal rodents.

"I once knew someone who thought lemmings were people," he went on. "It was like he'd missed the part about them being two inches long or whatever and only tuned in on the big run off the cliff. 'That's terrible!' he said. 'Why doesn't someone try to stop them?' "

He laughed, and I joined in, a little halfheartedly. "Who was that?" I asked idly, not caring, certainly not expecting an answer.

"My brother."

"What?" I felt queasy. "I didn't know you had a brother." Dread gathered along the edges of my body, ready to invade.

"I don't anymore," he said. "My brother—he dead. That's from *Heart of Darkness,* you know: 'Mistah Kurtz—he dead.' You've read *Heart of Darkness,* haven't you?"

I lowered myself onto my mother's bed and began to tremble, sick with confusion, disbelief, rage. "Kilroy." I felt as if the bed were moving, and I put a hand out to steady myself. "You're telling me this now?"

"What a coincidence."

I dropped the receiver onto the bed. I picked it up again. "Kilroy, my God. When? How old was he? How old were you?"

"He was twenty-one, I was twenty-six. It happened fourteen years ago."

On March 20th. That weekend, meeting his parents—they'd wanted him to stop by because of the anniversary. Was that why we'd gone to Montauk? To avoid the cream-colored card with its sad, muted plea? *Won't you come by and have a drink with us? It would mean so much to your father.*

"He had leukemia," Kilroy said. "He'd had it on and off since he was ten."

I shook my head, as if he could see me, as if I could see him. How carefully he'd made sure I couldn't see him! "Your parents," I said. "That day we—"

He broke in sharply. "I don't want to talk about my parents."

I felt chastened. "Kilroy," I said after a while. "I'm so sorry to hear about this—I wish you'd told me before."

He snorted.

"What was his name?"

"What difference does it make?" he snapped. Then he softened: "You wouldn't believe me, anyway."

"What do you mean?"

"His name was Mike." He laughed. "Seriously. Isn't it all so crystal clear now? Isn't it just too perfect? Two people, each on the run from a tragedy named Mike. Cry or puke, take your pick."

I cried, sobbing and sobbing while he stayed silent on the other end of the line. I couldn't believe it—couldn't *believe* it. And yet, I'd known. Hadn't I? That something was missing? That in knowing him I hadn't really known him? There'd been hints of a larger truth, a terrible struggle. And hints of a missing person. That day at MOMA—he must have meant his brother. It must have been his brother who'd gone to Lane's school, whom he'd closed in on mentioning that night in the brownstone kitchen. Wanting to tell, and then not wanting to. Not wanting to. Oh, I couldn't bear it, all he'd hidden and all he'd shown me and all I'd failed to see.

"Carrie?" he said. "I'm going to hang up now."

"Don't," I cried. "Please, we need to talk more, I—"

"I am," he said. "Live well, OK?" And then there was the dial tone.

I collapsed onto my mother's bed and wept harder, my shoulders heaving. I thought of the December day when we walked through Gramercy Park, how he talked about wishing he lived in another century. And Thanksgiving night: *It might have been good to be an astronomer. Living in the middle of nowhere in an observatory on a hill.* Dreams of hardship. Of isolation. I walked him back in time, to when he was a boy named Paul. With a sister named Jane. A brother named Mike. Paul the family smart aleck, the wit. I'd seen it in his parents' faces, how things used to be. He was alone now, tonight, again, after thinking for a while that maybe, just maybe . . . *Same old, same old,* he'd said to his father, of his life. And then, looking at me, *Well, almost.*

I'd been *happy* with him. I'd loved him, I loved him still. My life with him rose up in my mind: Standing in his kitchen watching him cook. The beach at Montauk. Walking and walking through the city. Now that I knew about his brother, things could be different, better, closer. Couldn't they?

I could get on a plane and fly back tonight, to New York, the bustle and thrill of it, the noise, the smells. To *Kilroy.* I could use the key I still had to let myself into his apartment. If he was already asleep I'd undress quietly and get into bed with him. His warmth, the dryness of his skin, his bony shoulders. He'd feel me, smell my smell, and then gradually wake to my return. I imagined how we'd come together without speaking, our bodies at the forefront, making the first connection.

But Mike. Mike wheeling onto the deck after his shower Saturday morning, saying, *The times, they have changed.* He was rueful now: changed, like the times. *Mike Mayer has a morose spell.* He was rueful and deeper inside himself, looking out, looking in. Was a person an accumulation of past selves, or made new over and over again? I wanted to keep knowing him, to see where he went next. I wanted to keep seeing him, seeing his smile when he saw me; feeling mine when I saw him, pulling at the corners of my mouth. I thought of the September night I left Madison, heading through the darkness until I saw the sun rising over Lake Michigan, adrenaline keeping me going, adrenaline and coffee and despair. *Isn't it all so crystal clear now? Isn't it just too perfect? Two people, each on the run from a tragedy named Mike.* It was true: I'd turned Mike into a tragedy named Mike. And run from it—from him. I thought of yesterday at Clausen's Reservoir, how I'd known what he wanted to hear. About the helicopter. The wait. There was so much more for me to tell him, for him to tell me.

That phrase of Kilroy's again. Kilroy the listener, the questioner. With so much of himself he couldn't tell. *I don't want to talk about my parents.* Why not? Because they'd grieved and moved on, and he hadn't? I didn't know. It probably wasn't nearly that simple, but I couldn't have known and I couldn't know now, not if he didn't want to tell me. *I knew what I knew,* Lane had said of Miss Wolf. What I knew about Kilroy was what I'd always known, from the very beginning. That he didn't want to tell, *couldn't* tell. That he couldn't risk it.

I WENT OUT for a walk. The afternoon light hung late in the sky, and I walked fast, seeking the strain in my muscles, the faint searing in my lungs that would tell me I was moving. On the Fletchers' block someone was getting ready to barbecue: I smelled lighter fluid and burning briquets, the scent nostalgic and sustaining. I stopped and closed my eyes, and it seemed deeply significant that I could conjure what would come next, how the smell would veer in a few minutes to chicken, say, or lamb, or beef.

As I walked the smell got stronger. At the head of the Fletchers' driveway I understood *they* were barbecuing—Mr. Fletcher and some assortment of his daughters. Jamie, I knew from my mother, had more or less moved home. Just like me.

I made my way along the house, stopping at the low gate into the yard. It was empty, the grass mowed and edged, the plum tree thick with purple leaves. The roses grew in beds along the side fence, as well-tended as Mrs. Fletcher could want. On the brick patio, a black Weber grill threw smoke into the sky.

The screen door of the mud room swung out, and Bill appeared on the porch, a platter of meat in hand. He caught the door with his foot just as it was about to clap shut, then he came down the steps and stopped at the barbecue, all without noticing me. He set the platter on the picnic table. He glanced around, found a long-handled fork hanging from the handle of the grill, and used it to stir the coals. Then suddenly he looked over his shoulder.

"Jeez, sneak up on a person, why don't you." He hesitated, then came over to the fence. After a moment we hugged clumsily, the gate between us. I wondered if my face was still blotchy from crying. Kilroy was a thousand miles away, alone. Was he in his apartment, on the couch with a book? Or at McClanahan's, where he'd sit at the bar and drink a beer, entirely within himself? How could I have ever thought he confided in Joe?

"Fancy seeing you here," Bill said.

"It's called living dangerously," I said. "Steak for two?"

"About."

We stood there. The last time I'd seen Bill had been at the hospital, a week or so before I'd left. Bill in cargo shorts and Tevas; I wondered if he had Jamie hiking now. It was hard to fathom. Then again, it was hard to fathom them together at all. How would they look together, Jamie with her blond ponytail and skinny arms, Bill with his dark eyes and buck teeth? And that little silver stud in his earlobe. I tried to remember how he'd looked with Christine, and what I came up with was this: Nice. He'd looked nice.

"Well, I better go," I said. I looked away for a moment, pulled my lips into my mouth and let them loose again. "How is she?"

"OK. She's actually doing a lot better."

"Than?"

"Before."

I lifted a hand to wave. "I'm glad I saw you. Maybe I'll run into you again one of these days." I took a few steps away and then looked back and smiled. "It's so hard to think of you as Jamie's boyfriend."

"I felt that way too at first. You get used to it after a while."

I turned to go. I was past Mrs. Fletcher's station wagon when he called my name.

I looked back, and he motioned for me. "Try again," he said in a low voice when I was close. "OK? I can understand how you wouldn't want to, but—well, she misses you, I see it all the time."

"How?"

He rubbed his hand along his jaw. "Just in the way you see things in people you know well. Just in this little sadness when your name comes up."

I breathed in deeply. I waved again and made my way back out to the sidewalk. It was dusk now, and I walked back to my mother's,

where I sat at my desk. I vaguely remembered there being some stationery in the bottom drawer, and when I opened it I felt myself smile
at the sight: a box of Snoopy stationery Jamie'd given me for my birthday in third grade. I took a piece out and saw that there was only one
more left, and that someone had written on it.

> *Happy Birthday to you,*
> *Happy Birthday to you,*
> *You look like a monkey*
> *And you smell like one, too.*

> *I'm just kidding. Dear Carrie, happy birthday, your my best*
> *friend. Love and kisses from*

> *Jamie*

I set the page on my desk and uncapped a pen. I sat there thinking
for a long time, and then I wrote this, just under Jamie's loopy, third-
grade signature:

> *It's true, I smell like a monkey—even to myself. Can I tell you*
> *one last time how sorry I am? Apologetic, yes, but even more to*
> *the point just sorry for what you've gone through. I used to*
> *imagine us growing old together—or not growing old but being*
> *old, sitting on the porch of some nursing home in matching rock-*
> *ers and reminiscing about our teen years. Even once I was with*
> *Mike I never pictured anyone but the two of us, and I didn't pic-*
> *ture us sick, either, just wrinkled and white-haired and laughing*
> *about the time we tried to do our math homework by breaking*
> *potato chips into fractions and arranging them into equations on*
> *your bedroom floor.*
> *I'm back for real, and what I know is this: Carrie − Jamie =*
> *too much loss.*

I folded the page, put it in a Snoopy envelope, and walked back to
the Fletchers'. The barbecue smell was gone, and I put the letter in
the mailbox and walked home again in the sudden dark.

My mother was in the kitchen when I arrived. I told her a little about the weekend at the Mayers'—how tired Mike got, how the sheer business of living took so much out of him. Neither of us had eaten, and we made a big salad and carried our plates onto the back porch.

"You saw that box?" she said.

"It was my sewing machine."

"Did Lane send it?"

I speared a slice of cucumber and put it in my mouth. It was thin enough to fold with my tongue, and I did that, then poked at the seeds to dislodge them. "Someone else," I said, and my mother shook her head quickly.

"I'm not asking."

"You can."

She looked over at me. "Do you want me to?"

I studied her: her quiet, watchful face. "I guess I want you to want to—to want to know."

"Of course I want to know." She reached for her wine and drank a little, the stem of her glass catching a shard of light and glinting as she lowered it again.

"I had a boyfriend there."

"I thought you might have." Her fork scraped her plate, and she gathered some lettuce leaves into a small pile and put them in her mouth. We'd made an extravagant salad, a little of everything—asparagus, tiny steamed potatoes, green beans, baby carrots, chopped basil leaves from the plant I'd bought her at the Farmers' Market on Saturday.

I shifted. A mosquito whined in my ear, then disappeared. It was completely dark outside the circle of light cast by the dim porch fixture. "Did you have a feeling he was going to leave?" I said. "My father? Were there any hints, or did it just happen out of the blue?"

She set her plate onto the porch floor. She lifted her wineglass again but didn't drink—she held the rim against her bottom lip. "I thought he was going to explode," she said at last.

"You mean do something violent?"

"No, I mean I actually had a recurring image of his head literally exploding. Which was probably the closest I could come to wanting to kill him. So in answer to your question, I don't think I had a feeling he was going to leave, but it didn't happen out of the blue, either. He had a lot of momentum going." She tilted her glass and drank a little wine, then turned to me and smiled. "To quote one of my clients today, he was not a happy camper." She bent over, and for an instant I thought she was going to pick up her plate and go into the house. Instead, she set her glass down and sank more deeply into her chair, and something in me settled into place.

I put my glass down, too. "Were you horribly lonely?"

"Not really. More relieved. Hugely relieved, in fact, and of course really angry, too. I had you, though, and that's what mattered."

I looked at my hands. She'd had me, but only until she hadn't. I remembered all those dinners at the Mayers', all those weekend afternoons. Thanksgivings, when I took her with me. Christmases, when I wanted to go but didn't. I looked across the porch at her taut chin, the still-young contours of her face. Seven years older than Kilroy. She had something in common with him, the possibility of spending Christmas alone with nothing for company but a big book. And something else: a kind of stillness in the face of being left. She had friends, she had her work, but in some essential way the important thing had already happened to her. I was back, yes, but I didn't ever want to feel that way, that there was nothing new up ahead.

"Are you lonely now?"

She looked over at me, my mother in her burgundy linen work dress, glasses hanging from a cord around her neck. She shook her head. "Lonely is a funny thing," she said slowly. "It's almost like another person. After a while, it'll keep you company if you'll let it."

~

42

I SAT AT THE dining room table, the morning sun shining onto my sewing machine. It was a week since my conversation with Kilroy. I'd called the woman whose Marshall Field's dress I'd altered, and we'd met at Fabrications, where I'd steered her to a lovely cornflower blue silk. I'd drawn her away from the dowdy shape she wanted, instead resurrecting the vision I'd had weeks earlier, when she'd picked up the red silk dress I'd altered for her. A boatneck top over a flared skirt, just right for her narrow-shouldered height. I'd had her buy a couple of patterns, but I was using them more as a starting place than anything else. I had my experience at Parsons to help, although I also felt that I'd left it behind, a bright flag receding in the distance. Sitting in those classes, being encouraged by Piero: I remembered the excitement and knew I'd only scratched the surface. That day I stood with Maté on the busy sidewalk and listened to him pontificate: *I want women to wear lime green dresses with white embroidery this summer.* I wasn't going to have that after all.

But I had this: the perfect thing for one Midwestern woman. The skirt was six-gored with a trumpet-flare at the bottom, and I was working on the cutting line, completely absorbed by the question of how to shape it, when the doorbell rang at a little after eleven.

Jamie was on the doorstep. Blond hair hanging by her face, a pink tank top showing her pale shoulders. It would sound better to say we both burst into tears, that we fell into each other's arms right there, but in fact it was very awkward, the two of us with our arms folded across our chests, standing outside and then standing in the kitchen and finally sitting down, glasses of iced tea gripped in our trembly hands. We talked in the way of two people with something enormous and impossible to speak of: we talked about movies, the weather, a new CD she wondered if I'd heard. Gradually I relaxed. I realized we didn't have to say everything that morning. Or soon. Or ever.

She stayed for half an hour. Exactly, as if she'd decided in advance. Standing to leave, she asked if I'd like to come for dinner some night. "We take turns cooking," she said. "You can come on one of my nights, I'm the only one who ever cooks a green vegetable."

I said I'd like to. Walking to the front door, we passed the dining room. She glanced in at my work, and I told her what I was doing.

"Didn't I tell you you could make a ton of money sewing?" She smiled and tipped her head to the side. "Maybe I'll hire you next."

"What makes you think you can afford me?"

"Hey, I'm rich—I don't pay rent anymore."

I looked at her clear green eyes. I reached over and touched her arm, and she glanced away. I said, "Are you going to stay home for a while?"

She nodded.

"How is she?"

"She came home for a visit last weekend. Mixie and Lynn and I said it was like having this very polite houseguest."

"And your dad?"

She shrugged. "He didn't say much." She looked at me and then looked away and grasped her shoulders, her elbows coming together in front of her chest. "I shouldn't have blamed you," she whispered.

I shook my head. "It's—"

"I shouldn't have."

We reached the front door. I opened it, and we stood there looking at one another, the moment for putting our palms together suddenly upon us.

I held the doorknob. She kept hold of her shoulders. Out on the sidewalk, a tabby cat stopped to look at us, then trotted away.

"Your dad," I said. "Does he cook, too?"

She broke into a smile. "Are you kidding? You think we'd let him get away with that?" Her smile widened. "He's Mr. Taco King. He makes tacos every Sunday night."

AFTER JAMIE LEFT I called Mike and suggested lunch, then cleaned up the dining room and headed over. He was on the deck waiting, dressed in a short-sleeved blue-and-red plaid madras shirt, tennis hat firmly on his head.

We'd been eating a lot of ethnic food, or as ethnic as it got in Madison—enchiladas and pad thai. Today he suggested the Union terrace. We drove over and I found an easy parking place right on Langdon—graduation was over and summer school hadn't started yet. We went out to the lake and took the ramp up to the terrace. Mike waited at a shady table while I went inside for deli sandwiches, thinking that the deli sandwiches I'd gotten for us there must number in the hundreds. Back outside I sat next to him, both of us facing the lake.

We didn't talk much. It was one of those noontimes when all of Madison seemed to be on the lakefront, students and professors and secretaries and eccentrics, sitting or walking in the sun. The lake itself was a deep, deep azure, calm under a windless sky.

I put a straw in his iced tea and positioned it near the edge of the table so he could bend over for a drink. He'd asked for turkey and swiss but I'd forgotten to say no lettuce, and for a while he fed himself amid a shower of chopped iceberg until he asked me to give him bites instead.

He swallowed and looked over at me. "Dirk Nann called yesterday. He said they could use some help. He said I could start with twenty hours a week and then see."

Dirk Nann was his old boss at the bank, and I tried to contain my excitement. Mike could go on and on about the uselessness of trying to be useful, but I thought going back to the bank would be the best possible thing for him. "Are you going to?"

He made a face. "I thought I'd never go back there. It's so out there. Meet the public. But I realized the main thing I wouldn't be able to do is shake hands with people."

"Which doesn't matter."

He looked at me, something stirring way back behind his eyes. "It does matter. But it's not the end of the world."

He motioned for his sandwich, and I held it up so he could have another bite, cupping my hand underneath to catch what fell. His forearms rested on the armrests of the wheelchair, freckles showing between the hairs. I set the sandwich down and put my hand on his bare leg, just above the knee. "Can you feel that at all?"

He hesitated. "No, but I think I'd know it was there with my eyes closed." He closed his eyes. "Don't say anything," he whispered.

I didn't. I kept my hand where it was, curved over his leg, my diamond catching the light. I breathed in, breathed out again. I looked around while I waited for him to speak. I saw a pair of frat boys strutting by, a barefoot girl with a golden retriever, an elderly woman with a purple scarf around her neck, sitting on a bench in the sun. I thought of the weight of their lives, the long, hidden history each of them carried. That the frat boys were also sons, maybe brothers. That the girl might be from another continent. That the woman had thoughts about people no one on the terrace had ever seen, for reasons we couldn't imagine. I looked across the water, and there was Picnic Point, a finger of land pointing into the lake. I remembered Stu's story, of walking across the ice with Mike and Rooster, and I imagined Mike out there, wrapped in a down jacket, huge boots on his feet as he took step after dangerous step in the drifting chill of a December night.

"I'm not sure," he said at last, opening his eyes. "This'll sound sick, but sometimes I ask myself, Would you rather be blind? Would you rather be deaf?"

"And what do you answer?"

"Either, but not both."

I pulled my hand away, and at my side he took a deep breath and then sighed. "Can I ask you something?" he said.

"Of course."

He looked down and colored slightly, then looked up again and his eyes met mine. "Are you back to stay?"

"Yes," I said, but my throat felt funny, and it came out hoarse and scratchy, hardly even a word. "Yes," I said again.

He smiled a complicated, inward-looking smile: of warring emotions quieted, if only for the time being. He bent over for a sip of his drink, then straightened up again. "So you're what, going to fly back for your car?"

I turned and watched a gull perched on a low wall. It looked out at the water, its white neck curved like an S. "I sold it," I said.

He sucked in his cheek and nodded. "Oh. That makes sense. It must be hard to park in New York."

"I needed the money. You can't imagine how expensive it is to live there."

He scowled a little. "Yes, I can."

We sat there. A group of five professorial types arrived at the table next to us, each man bearded and serious-looking and each licking an ice cream cone, the pastel flavors of summer. Off to the side, the gull hopped twice and then soared away, wings stretching wide.

I felt Mike's eyes on me, and I wondered what he could see, if I had *Kilroy Was Here* written on me somewhere in a tiny, hurried scrawl. Of course I did. Just as Kilroy had *Carrie Was Here* on him, where it would stay whether he tried to rub it away or not. He was a map of messages, read by no one. I'd felt them with my fingertips, but they'd been hieroglyphic, indecipherable. I wondered how he felt about telling me about his brother. I hated to think he regretted it. Longing for him overwhelmed me, and my throat swelled. After a moment I busied myself with my sandwich: I leaned over the table for a big bite, and the harsh taste of the mustard pleased me. I chewed and chewed, then leaned back in my chair. My left hand was resting on the edge of the table, and Mike looked down at it: at my ring, his ring, our ring. Our eyes met. "Hock it if you want," he said.

"I would never." I twisted the ring around my finger, then took it off and put it on my right hand and held it out for him to see. "It's a friendship ring now."

"How'd that happen?"

"It just did. Presto change-o." I smiled at him. "The ring, it has changed."

"If you say so."

"I do," I said, and then I realized what I'd said—*I do*—and our eyes met again and we both laughed: awkwardly at first and then happily, chortling together over a joke only the two of us could fully appreciate.

A bit later we went back to the van. Instead of heading for the Mayers' I turned the other way and drove up past the observatory, then swooped down toward the hospital and past it. By the time I'd parked he had to know what I had in mind, but he didn't say anything. I cut the engine and helped him out.

The path was wide and smooth, and we moved side by side through deep shade and into spots dappled by sunlight. There were no other people around—no joggers, no picnickers, no kids playing hookey on one of the last school days of the year. How tall the trees were, making it an expedition by green tunnel, unseen water on both sides.

For a while Kilroy was there, too, walking a pace or two behind us. I wanted the anguish I felt to stay with me—knowing it would fade was the saddest thing in the world. I kept looking over my shoulder but saw only the path, running back the way we'd come, winding through the trees. Six weeks later I would get a postcard that I'd know only by inference came from him, blank but for my name and address. The photograph showed a sunny field of lavender in front of a row of silvery trees. "A hillside in Provence," it said on the back in three languages. And, in the ink ring that canceled the French stamp, the word "Var."

That was still ahead of me, though. Today, Mike and I moved along the path. The little clearing off to the left, where we'd lain on my beach towel—we passed it, neither of us commenting. It had been there long before we had.

A songbird trilled from high in a tree. A little later Mike looked up at me. "We never would have gotten married, would we?"

I reached over and pulled a glossy leaf from a bush we were passing. I ran my finger across the surface, then let it fall. "I don't know," I said. "It was beginning to seem like maybe not the best idea."

"I think I know why," he said. "It was like we already were married—we'd gone too far."

I nodded. We would say more about it later, both of us. For now I looked around, at the trees, at the sky high above. I breathed in the clean smell of pine. The path grew shadier and twisted to the right, then to the left again. We ascended a slight rise, and a blackbird beat its wings as it settled on a branch.

"Here we are," he said, and we entered the final, sun-filled clearing, the water pale blue and all around us, visible between the limbs of trees. He stopped moving and smiled up at me. "Well, what do you know," he said. "Mike Mayer returns to Picnic Point."

ALSO BY ANN PACKER

MENDOCINO AND OTHER STORIES

With humor, wisdom and tenderness, Ann Packer offers ten short stories about women and men who discover that life's greatest surprises may be found in that which is most familiar. In the title story, on the anniversary of their father's suicide a young woman discovers that her brother may have found a "reason for living" in the love of a good woman. In "Nerves," a young man realizes that the wife he is separated from no longer loves him but that it is his own life he misses, not her. In "Babies"—which was included in the prestigious O. Henry anthology series—a single woman in her mid-thirties finds that everyone, including her best friend at work, is pregnant, and that their joy can only be observed, not shared. In this well-crafted collection, Ann Packer exhibits an unerring eye for the moments in which lives may be transformed.

"[Packer's] writing is graceful and effortless, yet as controlled and purposeful as a nest-building bird."
—San Francisco Chronicle

Fiction/Short Stories/1-4000-3163-X